JIM FE

FIRST CIRCLE

CITY LIMITS
PUBLISHING

First published by City Limits Publishing 2021

First edition

ISBN: 978-1-955631-03-7

Editing by Kimberly Macasevich
Cover Art by Adon Henrik Dizon

DEDICATION

First Circle is dedicated to The Fenton Seven (our collective text handle). My wife, Beth, and children – including their spouses – provide the ongoing motivation, inspiration, and support to make creativity happen on a regular basis. We reinforce each other and make each other stronger – a veritable circle of strength within our family. They put up with my eccentricities and always look for the best in each other, including me. The journey we take would be far less fun and less satisfying without our own First Circle.

PROLOGUE

Lifeless. Cold. Dead. The body was clearly dead.

Michael W. Smith's "*This is Your Time*" played quietly in the background. The group gathered around the body to say goodbye one last time. Too soon. But perhaps this was part of a greater plan. One can only hope.

ONE

"Leave me alone," groused Bernice. "I just want to be alone."

The nurse quickly left the hospital room and hurried down the hall, grumbling about the audacity of the heavyset woman with the really bad hair in Room 512.

Bernice settled back into the pillows and adjusted the bed to a more fully upright position. She switched on the television and clicked mindlessly through the channels before settling on an Animal Planet show about cats—wondering how her own, at home alone, were faring. Her greasy gray hair, apparently self-cut, continued to stick out at every angle imaginable as she watched the episode.

"I've seen this one," she grunted. She reached toward the tray extended adjacent to the bed. She hauled a chocolate toward her pursed lips. Contentedly, she reached for one piece after another, chain-eating her way through the sampler box hidden beneath yesterday's newspaper. Her girth under the light top sheet suggested this was not the first box of chocolates Bernice had enjoyed.

The episode on habits of domestic felines ground to a close and was replaced by the habitats of African gorillas. Bernice flicked off the screen. The afternoon sun softened and faded beyond the window.

Bernice reached for the call button and pressed it, much harder and longer than necessary. When no one responded within fifteen seconds, she buzzed the nurse station again at regular intervals with a heavy thumb on the red button.

Footsteps were soon heard in the hall. "Yes, Mrs. Langdon. Do you need something?"

"I'm ready for my dinner. Where is it? I lie here and wait and wait . . . and there's still no dinner."

"Now, Mrs. Langdon, dinner should be here within thirty minutes. You know the routine. Now, what did you order this evening?" The thin nurse tried to pump life into her question as she hovered in the doorway.

"I do not need your condescending tone, young lady. I have half a mind to talk with your—"

Bernice was cut off by the PA system, "Code Blue. Stet. Room 507. Code Blue." With that, the nurse vanished and Bernice was left contemplating her dinner of "Clear Fluids Plus": Jell-O, chicken broth, mashed potatoes (a big step forward the doctor assured her), and pudding. Tea would wash the whole sorry mess down. How much longer would this agony of deprivation last? She was quite certain she was fine. Bernice returned to the television. Channel surfing filled the time.

"Professor Langdon?" A mop of black, untidy hair leaned into Room 512. "Is now an okay time to stop for a quick visit?"

Bernice's head jerked up. She had momentarily dozed off somewhere between an update on George W. Bush's presidency one year after 9/11 and the top ways to convert a garage into a spa. She pushed her oversized glasses back up the bridge of her nose. "What's that? Dinner. Yes, I'm more than ready. I was about to buzz the nurses to determine why the kitchen help here is so bloody incompetent. And then, finally, you arrive–"

"Professor, it's me, Bryan Brooks. I don't have your dinner. Can I get you something?" The twenty-something guy ambled further into the room, his backpack weighed down on his sinewy frame.

"Bryan. Yes, of course," stuttered Bernice as she ran a hand fruitlessly over her mop of bristly gray hair. "Come in, come in. I was just anticipating din–"

"It's okay. If now's not a good time, I'll stop back. I was just on my way back to the dorm and thought–"

"No time like the present. I'm pleased to see you. This is one helluva place to be. I appreciate your stopping by, though it certainly wasn't necessary . . . " As Bernice gathered momentum, Bryan knew his biggest issue would quickly become extricating himself in a reasonable timeframe. Tonight he hoped the interruption offered by dinner would provide cover for an escape.

"How's it going, Professor?"

"Harumph. I hate hospitals. I hate doctors too–even though I trained enough of them. I sure wish I'd had a chance to teach the group here a thing or two . . . They could use some remediation, this crowd. And a university hospital, no less!"

"They can't be that bad. The University Medical Center is probably the best in the state, if not the region. And, with you being professor emeritus, well–they must be putting their best foot forward. Yeah?"

Bernice grimaced, locked her fingers together, and windmilled her thumbs. "Bryan, I taught you plenty, but you have much to learn."

Bryan blushed and looked at the floor. "Jeez, I stop by to say hello, and you're raggin'."

"You're right. My apologies. I just don't know the outcome of the surgery yet," Bernice paused. "Goddamn labs and doctors. They cut me open forty-eight hours ago, and they have yet to share the results. What the hell is the matter with them?"

"No news is good news, right?" queried Bryan. "If it was bad, they'd be on it like there's no tomorrow . . . "

Bernice looked down. "I don't know," she whispered pensively. "I just don't know."

"Come on, Professor. You didn't always give us the results of our exams all that quickly." Bryan tried valiantly to jolly Bernice.

"A Gross Anatomy course is a far cry from cutting open a living human, probing their insides for 'diagnostic exploratory surgery' and sewing them up again without so much as a 'fare-thee-well.'"

"Well, I don't know . . . just seems to me that they'd want you to know if there was something going on . . . "

"I certainly hope so." Bernice paused, "What are you taking this fall? What's your courseload? Who do you have?" She shifted gears, leaving her medical diagnosis (or fears of what it might be) behind.

Forty-five minutes later, a knock on the door signaled the arrival of what would pass for the evening meal. Bryan successfully extracted himself with muffled apologies for leaving so quickly. The fall semester midterms were quickly approaching and he had plenty to do.

Bernice settled in for her official bland diet, highlighted this evening by the arrival of two-tone Jell-O: orange and green, mirroring the foliage transforming the small park outside the window of her room.

TWO

Rusty stirred restlessly in bed. Weak sunlight filtered through the semi-translucent shade. He pushed the sheet down off his shirtless chest as he stretched and turned, trying to bury his head deeper in the pillows to eke out another few minutes of sleep. Next to him, a dark head of hair lay similarly burrowed in the pillows.

At precisely 6:57 a.m., the alarm went off with an unmerciful blast of sound. Rusty reached across the body next to his and hit snooze. Brushing against the tanned skin of his bedmate, Rusty felt a surge of remembrance of last night. A warmth filled him as he lingered against the adjacent warm body–feeling it rise and fall with the slow, steady rhythm of sleep. He traced a finger down along the curve of the back. With a smile, he felt more blood surge.

When seven minutes passed, the alarm blasted again. He leaned over, letting his chest rub once more against slightly sweaty flesh. *'Enough,'* he thought.

He pulled upright and swung his legs over the side of the bed. *'God, my head hurts. How much did I drink?'* he thought wordlessly. As his muscled frame reached a standing position, the sheet fell from his body. He padded away not knowing a pair of eyes fluttered open just in time to watch the tan line of his lower back disappear into the bathroom. A small smile crept across his companion's face as the shower started.

Rusty let the Arctic blast wash over his head and back, allowing the water to drill out the pounding between his temples. At last, he turned to take the water face on; it hammered his chest unmercifully. Moments later he toweled off briskly, facing the mirror. The bathroom routines of teeth brushing, shaving, and putting some gel in his short, light brown hair occurred mindlessly.

Rusty slipped on faded jeans and an oversized Abercrombie shirt. 7:35 a.m. Not too bad. "Hey," he called out. "I've gotta get to work. Last night was fun. Can you let yourself out? No big rush. My roommates can show you where things are if you need anything. Maybe we'll connect again?" Rusty smiled toward the bed, but there was no time to dawdle. He had committed to be at the office by eight.

His head felt remarkably better already. *'Maybe I didn't have that much to drink last night. Who knows?'* He recalled meeting the whole gang from the office. What started as a quick drink with his best friend, Chip, after work resulted in staying out all evening. Quite late, Chip's housemates showed up.

One thing led to another and, unexpectedly, one of those roommates stayed the night. He smiled as he walked down the city streets. While paused at a traffic light, he caught his reflection in a mirrored window. *'I am hot,'* he thought smugly.

"Rusty, you're late," posed Sue the moment he walked through the door of the IT Lab. "We agreed you'd be here at seven thirty to process the test environment runs. We wanted a full hour before the rest of the staff arrived. I've gotten part of the diagnostic simulation up and running, but I need you–"

Rusty tuned Sue out as he processed his mistake. How had he screwed up? He could've sworn it was an eight o'clock commencement of the test. He swung into action, pulling out his earbuds, depositing the iPod at his cube, and booting up his computer. As the familiar sounds of the Windows operating environment filled his ears, Sue yammered on about where he needed to begin. Being far more familiar with the inner workings of the new knowledge management system than Sue, he engaged surgically–assessing Sue's initial progress and what was still needed. Before Sue finished venting, Rusty initiated the second round of simulation queries.

In parallel, Rusty processed the prior day's string of events. The pounding returned to his head. He really needed a cup of java to jumpstart his brain's circuitry. He again wondered how much and just what he had consumed last evening. He knew he still drank alcohol as if he were in college, an increasingly faded memory six years out.

Nearly every night was filled with barhopping, a different set of friends, and too much to drink. Fortunately, Rusty had never shown interest in the pervasive party drugs that many enjoyed with abandon, but alcohol was different. Beer, straight vodka, Jack & Coke, G&Ts, and "double-oh Sevens" were his libations of choice–though he made it a rule never to mix. Each evening was a specific drink.

"Rusty?" inquired Sue over the top of the cubicle, "How's it going?" Without giving him a chance to respond, she continued, "I can see that the first three sequential queries and data inputs have all been positive. You're running three in parallel . . . yes?" Rusty grimaced toward his screen. Why did his supervisor insist on questioning what she already knew?

His thoughts turned toward the weekend with its Friday night kickoff this evening. He hoped to connect with the gang from Support Ops. They always made for a fun time. It had been a while since he'd been out with them. Thoughts of having had too much alcohol from the prior evening faded as the morning progressed. Shortly before noon, Sue rematerialized in the opening to his cube. The last run of data and queries was underway, testing some of the more sophisticated and complex features of the new enterprise-wide system. All ran smoothly.

"We have a problem," Sue announced. "Stevens announced in his management meeting that Monday is our Go Live date for the new sales force optimization and management system. While not wholly unexpected, apparently he's feeling pressure from the Street and needs to demonstrate real progress on revenue management by the next quarter. Anything later than Monday, he believes, will give us insufficient data for Q4. Since this will also be year-end, he feels we must put our best foot forward."

"I see," muttered Rusty, his eyes still intent on the screen in front of him. *'Stevens, Ridgewell's CEO, is such an asshole,'* he reflected silently. This was really not his problem. He was not on the project; a different team was assigned to this year-long effort cutting over from an old, balky system to this new one. The technology was the least of their worries. He empathized with the pain they had encountered as they sought to change the sales force. The transformation necessary in how the rest of the company should operate was much more fundamental. Rusty didn't think the slightly accelerated schedule to Monday would be particularly problematic.

"Which brings me to you," continued Sue.

"How so?" questioned Rusty. "I don't follow. The knowledge management effort is not linked with the sales force optimization. Over time, I can see means of connecting the two, but–"

"Nothing to do with KM. We need you for test and diagnostic work. Run some simulated queries and data diags. We need to performance-test the system in every possible scenario."

"No way, right?" Rusty tried joking. "There's a whole team of people who are completely focused on the sales force system. They are better positioned to–"

"They would be, yes," agreed Sue. "But they are going to be completely consumed with several application innovations Stevens has added to what will be operational on Monday. They will be working the entire weekend. You, however, will only need to be here tonight and tomorrow."

"Ahh, come on, Sue. I have plans. I can't just bag out and be here. My project is going along just fine . . . I don't think . . . "

"Rusty, you're the man," smiled his boss coldly. "You know our operating environment better than anyone. You also have done so many performance tests; you could do this one in your sleep. We need you."

'Shee-it,' frowned Rusty, shaking his head. "I've got to make some calls. See if I can get out of what's already been booked."

"I know you'll find a way to make this work. We can always count on you."

Rusty turned back to his computer screen as Sue walked away. "I cannot believe this company. I have plans for my fucking weekend and they–once again–completely screw them up. Shee-it."

The test environment for the knowledge management system was coming to a successful close. Nearly finished with the current run of diagnostics, Rusty prepared to stop the application when he noticed a dull glow at the edge of his screen. A bluish-white light came from a layer under the top window on his desktop. He shut down the diagnostic application and closed the window. The bluish-white light remained, this time beneath the remaining open window—Outlook email. The light appeared primarily, and most intensely, at the bottom left corner, though Rusty watched with interest as the entire screen gradually became infused with a dullish light just under Outlook.

'What's going on?' Rusty wondered. *'Never seen this before. I just got a new desktop, so it can't be the monitor going already. Odd.'*

He minimized Outlook and returned to the standard Windows desktop with its myriad icons for various programs waiting for launch. The light continued burning, now below the desktop screen. The bottom left corner was growing to a blazing surreal white light just off screen. Rusty sat mesmerized. Minutes passed as the backlight grew in brilliance. *'Screwy machine. I'll just shut down and reboot,'* he decided. *'That'll kill it.'*

He opened the shutdown menu and toggled the appropriate buttons for a restart. The PC, however, would not shut down. *'It figures. This whole day could use a reboot,'* thought Rusty. *'I'll just restart the whole deal after some chow.'* The idea of lunch was preeminent, as he had not eaten since dinner. He pushed and held the button for a hard shutdown. The normal thirty seconds passed, yet the machine stayed on, the odd intense white light glowing eerily from deep inside the computer.

"What gives?" pondered Rusty aloud with growing exasperation. "I just want to stop the damn thing."

Finally, the machine kicked off. The hard drive whirred to a close, with one small lingering problem. The brilliant white light remained, cloaked just behind the now black screen of the monitor. "What the fuck is this?" hissed Rusty. He stabbed the monitor power button with more force than intended to ensure it was off, yet still the strong white light glowed.

Crawling under his desk, Rusty unplugged the monitor from the surge protector. The white light persistently remained. "Must be some electrical connection from the hard drive to the monitor. I've sure never seen this before." Rusty reached around the back of the computer tower and disconnected the monitor cable. The monitor was now a standalone, untethered piece of equipment with a mystical brilliant-beyond-white light radiating outward.

"Hey Rusty," Chip called across the cubicle wall. "You ready for lunch, or what? I thought you were going to grab me twenty minutes ago. Let's rock, man."

"Dude, you will not believe this. I can't get this light off my screen. I've been trying for more than twenty minutes to eradicate this bad boy, but it ain't going anywhere. Look at this."

Chip scrambled around the cubes and entered Rusty's. "Whoa, man. What's that all about?"

"I don't have a clue. I've completely unhooked the monitor—no power, no hard drive connection . . . and it's still glowing like some freak show. Creepy."

"Man, I don't know what to suggest. That's more than a little weird."

Sue wandered over with a diet soda in hand, in unexplained better spirits than earlier. "What are you two still doing here? It's gorgeous out. Thought you'd be grabbing a sandwich and catching some rays outside. What's that–" she stopped mid-question as she stared at the white light emanating from the edges of the blackened screen. The perimeter light incrementally widened and grew in intensity.

"No clue. I was closing down KM and somehow this got started. I can't turn it off."

"You just got a new machine, right?"

"Yeah. Three or four weeks ago. Can't be worn out . . . though I do work mighty hard," Rusty laughed nervously.

Sue edged out of the cube. "Go to lunch. Maybe while you're out it'll resolve itself. It can't do any harm. It's completely disconnected. Just go."

Rusty and Chip stared longer. Other than continuing its very slow progression from the edge, the light did nothing new. "Let's go grab some food. I don't want to leave it for long." The two guys left the office, descended the wide staircase, and exited the building to the plaza bathed in mid-October Indian summer sunshine.

Rusty returned after a quick lunch. He chose not to linger outside with the guys from the IT group, talking and catching some rejuvenating rays. Taking the internal steps two at a time, he nearly knocked down two secretaries smoking furtively in the stairwell.

"Fuck, what is this?!" he blasted to no one in particular. The white light had changed, but not in the way he had hoped. Words now glowed ominously across the middle of his screen:

ENGAGE PRODUCTIVELY. WORK WEEKEND.
FOREGO PARTY.

The machine remained unconnected to any other equipment or power source. *'Who did this? Some practical joker–maybe Sue. What party anyway? I don't know of any party; someone guessed wrong,'* he thought to himself.

Rusty touched the screen, tracing each of the emblazoned words. As he finished tracing "party," the words faded away and the screen went dark. "Finally," he muttered. He spent the next few minutes reconnecting power and cables. On rebooting, the familiar Windows operating system and desktop reemerged. "Good. I don't know what that was all about, but–"

Chip interrupted, "What's that? Talking to yourself again? I worry about you . . . " He laughed as he disappeared behind the cubicle wall. Moments later his voice punctuated the quiet.

"Hey, what happened with your computer? You back up and running? It just burn itself out or what?"

"Don't have a clue. I came back and some practical joker got the thing to spell out words."

"No way."

"Way, man."

"What'd it say?"

"'Engage productively. Work weekend. Forego party.' Whatever that means."

"Sounds like Sue. She wants you to work this weekend. Hey, where's the party? I'll go in your place," snickered Chip.

"No clue, but if there's a party, I'll be there," countered Rusty. "I'm gonna ask Sue what gives . . . "

Rusty wandered in the direction of Sue's office. As he approached, Sue hustled out with a sheaf of papers. "Am I glad to see you, Rusty! Just back from Bob. Is he on a rant or what?"

"You were with Bob?" Rusty quickly speculated what consequences an ad hoc encounter with the CIO would bring.

"Yeah, he called a quick discussion over sandwiches in his office. I got yanked in at the last moment. He's all riled up by the morning exec discussion. He wants to ensure all hands are on deck this weekend to be one hundred percent good to go on Monday. 'I'm glad I can count on you,' was how he ended our discussion."

"So, you weren't back at my cube since Chip and I saw you . . . " Rusty trailed off.

"I haven't had time to breathe since I saw you. I–" and Sue began another long discourse on what Bob wanted done this weekend, what needed to happen on Monday morning, and what metrics he would be watching to measure progress. Rusty tuned Sue out, lost in his own thoughts. He could not think of another soul who would have reason to go in his cube during lunch.

Sue wound to a close. "So, what about you? You know, you look a little pale. Are you feeling okay? How did that monitor issue shake out?" Rusty rallied and refocused.

"It's okay. Just like you said. Seemed like lunchtime brought the monitor back around. Maybe it just needed to cool off. About this weekend, I really hoped to get to the beach. One last time, you know, before the weather sucks. Is there any way I can sidestep this one?" Rusty thought fast with an extemporaneous injection of a beach trip.

"Rusty, Bob said it in his pithy, forceful way: 'I'm glad I can count on you.' What gives? You're always willing to do one for the team? Everything okay?"

"Yeah, I guess. I just hadn't planned to work this weekend. I really hoped to get a break; we've been doing twelve- and fourteen-hour days these last few months getting KM off the ground. I hoped to chill."

"You've been busting, no issue, but we need you." Sue turned more conciliatory.

"I see." Rusty walked away as Sue settled back down with the pile of papers at her desk. Given his star status in the IT group, Rusty had leverage, but he needed to walk a fine line. He slowly sauntered back to his cube.

There, emblazoned across his darkened screen the same words burned:

ENGAGE PRODUCTIVELY. WORK WEEKEND.
FOREGO PARTY.

'*What's going on?*' he thought as the phone rang. He noted the caller was a friend in Support Ops.

"Hey, Dawg. How ya doing?"

"Jay-eff," feigned Rusty in a long southern drawl, "You're my main man. What's happenin' in the world of Ops?"

"We was just thinkin' of you and your party animal antics, Bro. We want you to join us. Bring your lampshade, man. We is throwin' a big 'un . . . "

"Jay-eff, I am more than honored. What's goin' down?" Rusty countered in the drawl that he and Jeff reserved for one another. In person, this was accompanied by some playboxing and cuffing one another–like two exuberant dogs.

"Bro, we are congregatin' Saturday afternoon Harborside. We is gonna hang fast and loose at the Marina Grill . . . watching the pretty people, partying with the upper crust. Come and party with us, man."

Rusty looked back at the phone puzzled. "When did y'all decide to have a party, Bro?"

"Just moments ago, Dude. And you, the resident professional party animal, were the first good lookin' stud we chose to call to come join the festivities. What you say, Dawg?"

Rusty thought back on the odd message, 'Forego party.'

"I don't know, Bro. Seems like I may have to work this weekend. Not happy about it, but it's coming down and you know where shit flows . . . "

"All downhill," returned Jeff. "Well, you know where to find us. Leave the sweatshop, man."

Rusty laughed. "I'll keep it in mind, Bro. Thanks for the call. I'll see if I can find you."

They hung up. The words faded from his screen as the phone call ended. *'So much for the party. Work the weekend? Well, I suppose it could be worse. At least, I'm preserving brain cells,'* Rusty reflected as he hunkered down for the afternoon. Thoughts of a relaxed, brain-dead weekend faded as he focused on the task at hand.

THREE

Bernice woke with a start. She had dozed off watching the late-night news. Disappointed to miss Leno, she lay in bed listening to the quiet sounds of the hallway. She didn't know what time it was, but clearly it was late. The light over her bed had been extinguished while she slept.

'Wonder when they'll be back to check my vital signs?' she pondered. She contemplated when her doctor might share results from her surgery two and a half days prior. The outcome held the key to next steps. As if watching a news documentary, she reviewed the last several months since retiring from the university.

After thirty years teaching at the university, Associate Professor Bernice Langdon, Ph.D. in Anatomy and Physiology, remained bitter over never having been granted the title of full professor. She had no place for politics. She wouldn't play the games required to publish at the set pace and schedule, but she consistently received stellar reviews for her teaching. Her late husband had been the dean of the business school for more than twelve years. Grimacing in the dark, Bernice knew that this was probably key to her receiving tenure many years back.

Little did the university care about the loveless nature of her marriage. Bill Langdon was all about his career. She should've realized that when they first met. Then again, Bernice was similarly focused. Surprisingly, they had a child–Bill Junior. Like his father (and mother, Bernice could reluctantly admit), young Bill was success-driven and now a well-regarded lawyer in the city. Bernice rarely saw Bill these days, which was probably just as well. They maintained a cordial relationship. She tolerated his wife, Beverly, and their two offspring somewhat better.

Bill blamed Bernice for the unexpectedly explosive and deadly brain aneurysm that killed his father ten years earlier. Bernice had found her spouse stricken at home one early January afternoon when she returned from campus. Slumped over his desk in his study, his pale blue eyes gazed vacantly; a puddle of saliva soaked his papers, and the ink of his latest notes swirled in a growing pool. Bernice called 9-1-1 immediately, but her son believed she could've saved Bill Senior if she had been home earlier.

The ambulance rushed to the same hospital where Bernice now lay. Bernice abrasively questioned whether operating would yield any meaningful hope of recovery even as they wheeled her husband toward the OR, but he went straight into surgery anyway ("He is the dean of the business school, you know," she was told.) He never regained consciousness and was pronounced dead on the table. Later, when Bernice coolly reported the whole scenario, her son was angered that she had debated the surgery.

"Didn't you want to save him? Those few minutes you spent arguing might have been the difference, you know . . . "

Over the decade since, they had made their peace. Bernice's life was not all that much different: she lived in the same house, in the same bedroom. Bill's bedroom—a separate one for the seven years preceding his death—had been cleared out and converted into a TV room, mostly for the grandkids. Bernice did not watch much TV. Bill's office was left intact.

When Bernice retired in the spring, she bowed out gracefully. The biology department gave her a plant and hosted a modest reception in the greenhouse. The university president sent her a note of appreciation: an insincere form letter. Remarkably, the academic provost attended the greenhouse reception. A few students showed up; a number of biology professors did not. Bernice was okay with all of that. She was ready to move on, she convinced herself, though to what, she didn't know.

She spent the summer organizing her books, which had been shipped from the campus to the house. Bernice reclaimed Bill's study over the summer. Out went volumes of business texts and scores of popular management and leadership books from the seventies and eighties. In their place, she hoisted book after book of anatomy and physiology. She collected them all—from the most fundamental to the arcane.

While lifting books, Bernice first felt the odd pain in her abdomen. While not a sharp pain, when she stretched to put *Latest Findings of Human Endocrinology–2001* on the top shelf, she had to stop.

'I pulled something,' she thought as she came down off the little ladder that rolled along the shelves in the floor-to-ceiling library. She paused for a moment before lifting another tome (*Suffridge's Thyroid Compendium*) and stepped onto the ladder. As she reached up, the sensation in her rather stout midsection returned.

'Odd. Perhaps I should stop for the day.' Bernice stepped back down, pushed her glasses up tighter against her face and wandered to the kitchen. Her sweatshirt (a faded university logo stretched across her chest like a roadside billboard) was in need of a good washing . . . or, better yet, replacement. A flashing neon sign could not have sent a clearer signal of "frumpy and disheveled," should anyone have stopped to visit. Then again, no one was likely.

Bernice rested the remainder of that day and the next, as the following morning the uncomfortable abdominal sensation remained. "I must've strained something," she told Beverly later that day. "I don't remember doing it, but I'm sure it's nothing. How are the kids?" Bernice was not one to dwell on her health.

Over the remainder of that late August week, Bernice noted a few additional unusual twinges in her torso. Her appetite was quite light, though she wrote that off to the summer heat. "What can you expect at sixty-eight?"

she muttered to her male cat, Tigger, on more than one occasion. Spider, her female, was less of a confidante.

"So, Tigger, what are we going to do this fall?" questioned Bernice that week. "No classes, no students dropping by for help or just to chat. What should we do? Maybe we should just swing by the campus and take a walk. What do you say? Maybe we'll run into someone. We can always stop and see Albert." Albert was one of Bernice's favorite colleagues. He taught organic chemistry in the adjoining wing of Science Hall. A confirmed bachelor, Albert and Bernice spent hours dissecting the administration of the university and cackling viciously about colleagues across the schools. Many thought them an odd couple: he was ruggedly handsome, dressed well, and had multiple interests ranging from classical music, European art, and world travel to glassblowing and fine wines. Bernice had her cats, but a close friendship endured.

A week later, Albert convinced Bernice to see a doctor. "What's to lose? You find out why this little stitch in your side won't go away. He'll tell you to stop eating something you're not supposed to eat. You go on about your business."

"But it's just a pull. A stretch. It's nothing."

"You've been dealing with it for ten days, right? Why let it linger? Find out."

"I know my anatomy. Sure, I could stand to lose a few pounds, but, frankly, my appetite is off. Those pounds will melt away. As they go, the pain will stop."

Albert looked troubled. "Bernice, you've been grumbling about this discomfort for over a week. Now, you say you've also lost your appetite. Have a doctor check it out."

Bernice dismissed the idea. Deliciously, they moved on to discuss the new head of the physics department and why she had really landed the role. Most campus cognoscenti believed the appointment had more to do with her understanding of biology than physics.

A week later, when the sensations in her belly had not only not gone away but had intensified, Bernice finally took Albert's advice and called her internist. She received an appointment for the first week of September, on opening day of classes at the university.

"At least I won't be wondering how to spend that first day, will I?" Bernice confided in Tigger.

As September began, the dull achiness proved near constant. While Bernice tried not to imagine the parade of horrors it could be, her mind occasionally lapsed into some of the more gruesome calamities human physiology running amok might wreak. September 4 came and went. Dr. Elway was not especially alarmed, though he believed an abdominal CT scan would prove useful.

When the scan proved inconclusive, Dr. Elway sent Bernice for an ultrasound. "With all your female anatomy in there, we can't really detect the origin of the discomfort. Could be a few different possibilities . . . " Between the two tests, some suspicious shadows stood out. "They are just some extra me–that's all. Can't you fellows read an X-ray?" Bernice pushed back as she reviewed the output. "At worst, it's probably a cyst. Maybe one of those dermoid buggers. You know," she smiled wickedly, "Fingernails, hair, bone?"

Dr. Elway looked at the same reports. "You know, Bernice, I think we should go in. Figure out what we've got. You're right. It might just be a cyst–ovarian or otherwise. I doubt it's dermoid. It's probably full of liquid, as it doesn't appear to be a solid lesion. We can drain it. But, if it's not . . . look at this mass here," he pointed toward a darkened area on the X-ray. "I'm frankly just not certain we know."

"Harumph. It can't be an unknown. It's got to be something." Bernice turned more clinical. "I believe it's a cyst. It's unlikely to be ovarian as it sits higher than that. It's more likely a growth of some sort, though I imagine my extra fat cells are not helping diagnosis. Let's drain it and do some liposuction simultaneously," she smiled deviously. "Losing some weight couldn't hurt, now could it?"

The forty-something internist smiled back. "I suppose not. Let's get you scheduled for an exploratory laparoscopic procedure. I expect you'll be in and out. No more than an overnight deal."

Initially, Bernice was not ready to go under the knife–even a very small knife, even if the pain continued growing. She delayed scheduling the elective surgery for several weeks. "I'll just see if it goes away on its own," she rationalized with Tigger. "I have too much to do. The files need to be organized. I want to get to the beach. I want to see some of my students from last year."

However, the files and books stayed boxed in the study precisely where she had left them in mid-August. Now, like a lingering, unwanted houseguest, the abdominal pain settled in. Bernice didn't get to the beach in September. She read. She enjoyed her tea in the small backyard garden. She went for slow walks. She visited Albert. She sat in her sweats in the University Center–hoping to talk with former students who never seemed to pass her way. Bernice quietly took in the fall . . . slowly withdrawing as she focused increasingly on the discomfort growing inside.

On October 1, Bernice called Beverly. After the initial updates on school (Caitlyn was enjoying middle school at age fourteen, Brad was very active in soccer at twelve) and how busy Bill was in his practice, Bernice cleared her throat.

"Beverly, you may recall I had a little muscle strain during the summer."

"Yes, in fact, I do remember you mentioning it."

"I was moving some books from my campus office to Bill's old study."

"Since you'd said nothing recently, I assumed it went away."

"Well, actually not. It's gotten slightly worse over time."

"Mother, we're talking six or seven weeks. That's a long time to let that fester."

"Beverly, dear, I did not let things fester. I've been to see Elway."

"Your internist?"

"He didn't seem particularly alarmed, but did order a few tests. The scans showed a shadow or two."

"A shadow?" Anxiety entered Beverly's voice. "What do they think?"

"They don't know. Elway would like to do some exploratory work."

"They want to do surgery? Isn't that radical?"

"Well, full-on surgery would be. He's proposed laparoscopy—more or less, a little roto-rooter procedure." Bernice attempted to lighten the conversation.

"I suppose that makes sense. If they can't figure it out externally, that's minimally invasive. Bill had that done on his knee two years ago. He popped back quickly."

"That was arthroscopic, but, yes, the idea's similar." Bernice paused, "I think I'm going to have it done."

"You think? What's to consider? You need to determine the problem and get it fixed."

"Thank you for your counsel. I just wanted to let you know."

"When is this going to take place?"

"Well, I met with Elway back near the start of school, and—"

Beverly interrupted, "You've waited a month? Mother—"

"I don't need your mothering." Bernice snapped. "I appreciate your concern, but I am more than an amateur when it comes to human anatomy. I anticipated the problem would rectify itself. It has not. I now believe I shall have the procedure done."

Beverly, having dealt with Bernice for nearly twenty years, was not put off by her blunt abrasiveness. "What can I do? Shall I drive you to the university? I assume that's where you're getting this done . . . "

"Yes, at the Medical Center. I hope to get it scheduled in the next week or two."

Due to its elective nature, the procedure was scheduled for the third week of October. By then, the gradually growing pain woke Bernice at night: steady, throbbing, and occasionally sharp. Bernice no longer thought this was a cyst. Cysts were silent, generally benign growths. This intruder was becoming quite vocal in its residency. Something volatile grew within.

Beverly drove Bernice for the overnight procedure. Bill was in court that morning and sent his best wishes. Bernice insisted that Beverly need not stay during the procedure.

"I'll call when I'm awake. There's going to be nothing to report initially, I'm sure." Reluctantly, Beverly headed back to the endless chauffeuring duties of soccer games and after-school activities.

When Bernice awoke in recovery, the nurses were taking her vitals as monitors whirred and blipped in the background. She was sore—much more so than she had anticipated. *'Laparoscopy is not as painless as they make it sound,'* she thought in her semi-groggy state. *'I wonder what time it is.'*

As if responding, a nurse leaned in, "Mrs. Langdon? Are you awake? I thought so. It's already late afternoon. You were out like a light. You must've needed the sleep!" The R.N. smiled warmly as she took Bernice's pulse.

'Late afternoon.' Bernice's mind processed the information. She had been wheeled into the OR just before eleven. She couldn't imagine what would have taken so long. Anesthesia was administered for just the amount of time needed to do the procedure. *'Late afternoon? Perhaps I did need the sleep. I've not been sleeping very well these last few weeks . . . '* Bernice dozed back off.

Later, Bernice was wheeled to Room 512. She was vaguely aware of the shift.

"Bernice, it's Dr. Elway."

Bernice roused more fully. "Oh, Doc. Good of you to stop by. Thank you."

"You had a strong reaction to the anesthesia. We had to give you some anti-nausea meds. As a result, you were out much longer than expected. Your time in recovery was extended. You're okay, but you worried us."

Bernice felt dazed. She thought in slow motion. Dr. Elway remained out of focus, as did his words.

"Are you okay? You look pale."

"Yes, I'm fine," she said unconvincingly.

"Bernice, the procedure went differently than expected." Dr. Elway paused. "Your surgeon needed to perform a relatively small incision between the laparoscopic entry points."

'Why must he use such long words?' processed Bernice with slow-firing synapses. "Incision? How big?"

"No more than two to three inches." Dr. Elway held his fingers apart demonstrating. "They needed some space to extract the tumor after the initial, fresh, frozen specimen was taken."

"Specimen? Tumor?"

"Yes. As you know, they do preliminary biopsies real-time. While not conclusive, it proved sufficiently suspicious to suggest extracting the full growth—a small, exceptionally dense tumor—particularly surprising, given the characteristics we detected during the preliminary tests. While we think it likely benign, we are doing complete biopsies. Even tilting you on your head, they couldn't excise the tumor without a bigger incision."

Bernice rallied more with each piece of increasingly disturbing news. "Did they get it?"

"We don't know yet. You were having some trouble with the anesthesia; they didn't want to keep you under longer than necessary. We're running tests. We'll know shortly. Why don't you rest? I'll come see you in the morning. Drink clear fluids. No food tonight."

Bernice sagged as Dr. Elway quietly left the room. Her throat was parched. Food had no appeal, so she had no disagreement with his evening directives. Even with her expertise, she was deeply troubled by the alarming growth within her. Hopefully, as the doc suggested, it was all benign.

Beverly visited each day, surprised to see Bernice remaining incarcerated in the hospital bed. Bill and the kids had not stopped by; Bernice insisted. "No need. I'll be home in a day or two." Despite Beverly's concern, she abided by Bernice's wishes, sensing her husband would be relieved.

Sliding back to the present, Bernice lingered on the notion that she was now entering her fourth day in the hospital. Days two and three brought no news. Dr. Elway had suggested nothing except that lab tests were delayed; a second opinion was being sought. Her incision was healing nicely. She was progressing well, evolving back into her acerbic self. For now, Bernice's eyes grew heavy once more. The night remained dark beyond her window shade. Her last waking thought centered on her anxiously anticipated release from Room 512 with a clean bill of health.

FOUR

Skip knotted the Ferragamo tie and pulled it tight to the collar of his starched, custom-tailored white shirt. He pulled on the charcoal gray, pinstriped suit coat and took one last admiring look in the floor-to-ceiling mirror of the master bedroom. The gray beginning to show at his temples and throughout his dark hair lent an increasingly distinguished profile. He recalled his early days of practicing law when partners would say, "Skip, when you show a little gray, clients will take you more seriously. Intellect only gets you so far. They need to trust you. It'll come."

Now at the age of forty-nine, he was a partner in one of the most prestigious law firms in the city. He pulled a high six-figure income with an elegant house in the enclave community of Bedrock. Despite the humorous connection with the sixties cartoon, *The Flintstones*, Bedrock was anything but a Stone Age village. Bedrock boasted the best schools in the metropolitan area, the lowest crime rate, and the highest per capita income in the state. To live in Bedrock proper meant coming from "old money" or having achieved substantial success. Physicians, senior business executives, and partners in the professional services–management consulting, investment banking, and law–comprised the overwhelming majority of Bedrock residents.

Amy, his wife of nearly twenty years, played an adjunct faculty role in the English department at the university, typically teaching one class each fall. Occasionally, she would teach in the spring, but she didn't like the run-up to summer being spent in the classroom. She preferred spending a majority of weekends at their beach house on the Atlantic doing whichever redecorating project best caught her fancy.

Knowing that Amy drove the three boys to school on the way to campus, Skip enjoyed the peaceful quiet. On the way downstairs, he opened his Blackberry and reviewed his calendar. Personal digital assistants were both a godsend and a curse, Skip fully realized. The day was busy but not unbearably so. Several cases were heating up in their inevitable march toward the courtroom. He was lunching with a new client followed by a firmwide partner meeting.

As he reached the kitchen, he saw a yellow Post-it Amy had stuck on the coffeemaker, knowing he wouldn't miss it.

Hon–Don't forget. Connor's school play is at seven o'clock tonight. He'll be really disappointed if you're not there. Hugs, A.

Glad that she had taken the moment to jot him the reminder, he poured a cup of steaming coffee. While it cooled, he confirmed the play information in his Blackberry. The partner meeting would wind down by six o'clock; even a quick drink with some of them at Bernardi's would allow him to see the curtain rise. He had missed too many of Connor's events lately, which his middle son was minding.

Their boys, arriving in quick succession, were now fifteen, thirteen, and twelve. Connor was always looking to find his niche in life. He seemed to be settling into acting and theatre. While not Skip's first choice, he enjoyed seeing Connor find something he could call his own. He did not have Matt's natural athletic ability or John's musical gifts. Matt and John each had found their talents rather effortlessly.

Connor had taken more time to land. He was creative and remarkably imaginative. Why Amy and Skip had not considered acting earlier remained a mystery. They had certainly considered nearly every other possible hobby and sport. Skip looked forward to seeing Connor in the original comedy being presented by the middle school, "*The Devil is in the Details.*" Connor played a key supporting role: Humor. *'How appropriate,'* smiled Skip, upon first hearing the casting.

Taking his travel cup of coffee, he walked through the comfortably decorated downstairs. Pausing to sip in the foyer, he surveyed Amy's latest interior redesign. The formal living room had been transformed from its blue denim casual look to a more clubby environment with textured merlot hued walls and dark leather furniture. He always appreciated Amy's discerning eye for pulling a room together. *'And, if you're not going to spend the money, why make it?'* he chuckled inwardly at their running joke.

He stopped briefly in his study, grabbed his packed briefcase, and headed to the garage and his black Beemer. He had waited a long time for this car. The 5-series was everything he anticipated: lush interior, powerful engine, and great sound system. He slid in a Michael W. Smith CD, "*Worship,*" and headed downtown.

The morning passed quickly as Skip conferred with various colleagues on cases progressing toward trial. Shortly after eleven, an associate stepped into his office.

"Hey, do you have a minute?" inquired the lanky first year, whose name escaped Skip. "I've got the materials you requested for your lunch. The client's name is Arnold Baker, who's coming for an initial 'get acquainted.' He's the SVP of human resources over at Amalgamated Foods. I believe the issue he wants to discuss is a brewing class action suit Amalgamated fears, from a group of their employees. He was pretty hush-hush about it when I called to do background prep, as you suggested," he quickly added. "I've also got the most recent business stats on Amalgamated–annual report, recent 10-K, third quarter earnings report to the Street. I summarized in bullet points the key trends and issues they're facing. Beyond that–"

Skip interrupted, "This is great. You put some real effort into this. No doubt there will be more specific follow-up after the lunch, but this certainly gives me more than enough to start." Skip paused, "As you know, I've worked with other guys over there, but the updated info is good. Hey, one other thing: do we know anything in particular about Baker?"

"That's what I was about to say," effused the young lawyer. "I pulled a D&B on him and also went on the Amalgamated website to pull down his bio. It's right here." Skip earmarked the most relevant pages.

"Excellent. I'll give you the debrief when I get back. Let you know how things went and what we need to do next."

The young man smiled and exited. Before his heel finished shadowing the transom, Skip was on the phone with his executive assistant. Before he uttered a word, she spoke:

"Vince Weigand–first year. Graduated with highest honors from Harvard Law this past spring. He started three months ago. Anything else?" Penny's perky smile nearly burst through the speakerphone as she laughed.

"Am I that predictable?" grimaced Skip good naturedly.

"Yes, you are. While I've got you, the reservation is for twelve fifteen at Bernardi's. You can meet Mr. Baker there."

"Thanks, Penny. Vince. Vince Weigand." Skip repeated the name, more to himself than to Penny, but worked hard, committing it to memory. It would be nice to acknowledge Vince by name after lunch.

Arnold Baker was gaunt. He looked older than his fifty-eight years, at least as reported in the D&B information. His thin, mousy gray hair was disheveled and looked unwashed. He smoked a cigarette in the Bernardi's vestibule as Skip arrived. His clammy hands trembled slightly as he and Skip shook and exchanged business cards.

They adjourned to Skip's normal table in an alcove by a window overlooking the busy street. After the initial stilted introductions, Arnold Baker proved a man of few words. Skip's early attempts to jump-start the conversation were fruitless. *'I suppose he'll start when he's ready,'* thought Skip. The hostess handed them menus, which they perused in silence.

A waiter took their order and disappeared quietly into the recesses of the restaurant. The nervous executive drew another cigarette from a pack hidden in his suit.

"Mind?" inquired Arnold as he flicked open his lighter.

Skip actually did mind as they sat in a nonsmoking section of Bernardi's, but Amalgamated was one of the firm's larger clients at present. The old adage, "the customer is always right" came to mind as Skip shrugged in a quiet, noncommittal assent.

A busboy materialized from nowhere and subtly placed a small ashtray on the table near Arnold. He disappeared just as unnoticeably.

"Dirty habit, eh?" rasped Arnold. "I picked it up years ago, in the Army. I quit, but, recently, I, uh, have found it soothes me. Calms the nerves. Helps me deal with stress." He paused. "Want one?" he gestured with the pack.

"No, thanks. Never been a smoker. I'll hold off," smiled Skip, as the peculiar start to this new client engagement continued.

"I appreciate your making time to meet with me. I know you and your firm have been working with us for a number of years now. Tell me about you."

Skip gave the quick rundown on his career–summa at Yale undergrad, quick MBA, graduated with distinction from Columbia Law, a clerkship for a federal judge and now just hitting his twenty year anniversary with Dane & Caldwell. His corporate practice generally focused on employment law issues, though he still considered himself a generalist. He maintained a substantial roster of individual, generally wealthy clients with their personal legal needs, in addition to working with several of the larger corporations in town.

"Family?" Arnold inquired.

"Yes, married with three sons. All in that pre-teen and teenage adolescent stage. Always a challenge, eh?" Skip smiled again. "And you? Do you have children?"

Arnold ignored the question. "I'd like to talk about why I need–well, perhaps why Amalgamated–needs your help. Let me give you some history. We–"

Arnold was interrupted by the arrival of salads. The conversation stopped until the server had slid once again into the background. Each man took several forkfuls of salad chewing methodically. Skip watched Arnold curiously.

"Mind if I have another smoke?" Arnold raised the question rhetorically as he lit up another cigarette, pulling it from his jacket as if by magic.

"As I was saying, I'd like to give you some background. Amalgamated made an acquisition last year. We purchased a division of Mexicani–their processed food line. We got a good brand position in the growing Mexican food segment. We got a quality product–well, good quality for the price point–and we got a couple of manufacturing facilities. One in Mexico City. The other in San Antonio."

Arnold took a drag on his cigarette. Skip noticed his hand trembled less at the moment. The smoke from the cigarette drifted up into the air.

"Amalgamated's proposition was to expand distribution of the product line. We have great channels to push product. We have a strong marketing organization. We believed –and still do–that Mexicani could be a big winner. Naturally, we are keeping the brand name. People know it; it resonates."

Skip interjected, "Isn't that the one with the little Mexican dog in a serape and sombrero?"

Arnold took another long drag, "Yeah, that would be the one. Carlos Chi-Chi-Hua-Hua." His thin, yellowed teeth flickered with a smile.

He paused for yet another smoke infusion. Collecting his thoughts as he deeply inhaled another lungful, he finally exhaled and hoarsely continued. "We also got some labor problems. Turns out Mexicani had hired a whole bunch of illegals down in San Antonio. I don't know how they did it. They also treat the Mexican group—more or less—like slave labor. Pay 'em next to nothing, give 'em 'food benefits,' and work 'em twelve hour days (or more)."

Skip interrupted, "Food benefits?"

"Ah, you know. They give 'em free lunch every day—rejects from the production lines, mainly—and allow them to take more rejects home with them at the end of each day, if they wish. The food is okay, but the same half-dozen products or so only goes so far, you know?"

"I see." Skip scribbled a quick note to understand more deeply the Mexicani food line.

"I'm not particularly alarmed by the Mexico City issues. I can't lose sleep over them." Seeing Skip's skeptical reaction, Arnold continued quickly, "I'm as much of a humanitarian as anyone, but Mexico is a different economy, different laws and regulations. We've got more pressing issues in San Antonio. Once we've resolved them, I'll focus on making Mexico City right."

Skip nodded. *'A question of triage,'* he mentally noted. *'While not a choice I can condone, American business is pragmatic, if nothing else.'* Outwardly, Skip was more circumspect, "I understand."

Arnold plowed ahead as salads were cleared and lunches arrived. "There's been some unrest in the San Antonio plant. We've had some 'sickouts' where more than half of the workforce on a given shift called in ill. Production has been slowed consistently over the last month or so. There's also been a leak to the local press that Amalgamated makes a practice of hiring illegal aliens to work at sub-minimum wages to boost corporate profits on the backs of these workers."

"So, why not just let these staff go? Do it in a supportive fashion—don't just throw them on the street, but get the illegals off your payroll. Rehire legal workers."

"Easier said than done. You see, it turns out we are paying below minimum wage to these staff. We are also not paying taxes. In fact, the leak is based almost wholly on substantive facts. If we stop the production line, fire the workers, rehire and retrain, we, in fact, will not make a profit, unless we raise the prices . . . rather substantially in a very competitive market."

"And, as you said, the product is a good value at the current price. Raising prices calls into question the value proposition, which will siphon off sales, sending consumers to some other Mexican product line."

"You're quick. I like that. We need it. You do marketing work?" Baker appeared, momentarily, genuinely appreciative in having a fellow conspirator.

"More management focused but enough marketing to be dangerous." Skip smiled, though lost in thought trying to determine how to lay out the possible options for Amalgamated and help them get out of the current mess they had uncovered. It was curious how the due diligence done before the deal could've been so poorly executed as to land them in this apparently unwinnable position.

"What firm helped Amalgamated on the deal? I'll want to talk with them."

"We didn't use a firm, other than to execute the final agreements. No, we did it in-house. We have a small strategy group. They led the effort, under the direction of our COO. He got help from one of your partners."

"Oh?" Skip raised an eyebrow. "Who?"

"Well, Mr. Caldwell, of course," Arnold quietly rasped.

Skip exploded inside. *'And why's he not sitting here at the table with us?'* he wondered.

"I'd like to continue this conversation," Arnold broke into Skip's reflections. "But I must get back to the office," he looked at his watch. "I assume you can take care of the formalities here," waving a hand absently toward the restaurant surroundings. Skip nodded. "I'm hoping you can join me this evening for a few minutes at my office. I'd like to share some of the key documents."

"Tonight?" responded Skip.

"Yes, this evening works well. Can you make it?"

"I can make that work," responded Skip, swallowing hard.

"Let's say seven o'clock, shall we? The security guard will let you up if you say you're there for me."

Arnold arose and walked briskly toward the exit and out onto the street. Skip watched him head curbside to call a cab. As he watched, he recalled Connor's show.

"Ah, jeez. I can't believe it. Of all nights." He pulled out his Blackberry to confirm what he already knew, but before hitting the button to illuminate the PDA, he noted an odd discoloration along the edge of the screen. A light already shone—a very bright light hidden just behind the nearly black screen.

"That's odd. What's going on? Dying battery?"

As he watched, the frame of bluish-white light widened around the perimeter of the dark square screen. Thinking that flicking on the Blackberry would dispense with the surreal glow, Skip rolled the side scroll wheel and touched the light button. The screen lit up with his daily calendar, as he had last left it. The same appointments and meetings remained for the day—including Connor's show. The blindingly bright light along the sides remained. *'I actually didn't think this thing put out enough wattage to produce that bright of a light,'* mused Skip. He was intrigued, figuring some technological explanation would resolve the minor issue.

He keyed in the parallel information on the meeting with Baker. He would call Amy from his office and let her know he'd be late but would make the tail-end of the show.

At his office, Skip returned the Blackberry to its docking station to sync up with his computer. He didn't look at the screen as he got distracted by Penny handing him background reading before the afternoon partners' meeting.

He called and updated Vince on the meeting with Baker providing a download on Arnold ("seemed nervous, a lot on his mind, a chain-smoker, and a little awkward") and a top-line review of the emerging issues ("some buyer's remorse over the purchase of Mexicani. They are having some labor issues in their San Antonio plant. I'll learn more details tonight.") Skip decided not to share the sub-minimum wage issues just yet and certainly was not going to share the involvement of one of the law firm's founding partners in what appeared to be some bad, or at minimum, incomplete counsel on the acquisition.

"So, Vince, to move forward, we need to get some more inside info on the San Antonio plant. Can you do some searching? Determine what's available in the public record, see what's been in the news down in Texas, figure out what we can about the number of employees, type of backgrounds, etc. While we'll get some of this from inside Amalgamated, I'd like to do an objective review from the outside, if possible. Also, dig up the product line for Mexicani, pricing, and competition. Anything you can pull together on the economics of the Mexicani business unit would be useful." Skip paused and then concluded, "And let's just keep this effort between you and me for the moment, okay? Really appreciate all your work on this to date."

Vince frenetically took notes and nodded as Skip stopped. He seemed to understand and hightailed his way from Skip's office.

Skip turned to the pile of papers to review in the next hour. As he started to turn the top page, he looked over at his Blackberry, which had completed its quick synchronization. Seeing it reminded him of the funny issue with the backlit screen. He pushed his papers aside to grab it. Even before lifting it from the docking station, he could tell the problem remained.

The backlit perimeter glowed bright. It shimmered as if a fire were burning, white hot, on the other side of the screen, though the PDA remained cool to the touch. In addition to the burning frame, words now blazed in the middle of Skip's calendar. They shimmered and vibrated with the same bluish-white color:

BRO–DETAILS MATTERS
FAMILY 1ST
FOREGO MTG

"What is this?" whispered Skip to himself just as Penny stuck her head in the doorway.

"You talking to yourself again?"

"Hey, Pen, look at this. My Blackberry is acting up." As Penny came around the corner of the desk, the words faded. Just the burning white frame remained.

"What's up with the square, Boss?"

"That's not all, Pen. It's been doing that perimeter thing since lunch with Baker. Moments ago, words in the same color formed across the screen."

"You're seeing things. You been drinking at lunch?"

Skip laughed. "You would think so. Shoot. That Arnold Baker is one odd duck. Maybe he's got me seeing things. Maybe I just imagined the words."

"What did they say out of curiosity?"

"'Bro—Details matters. Family first. Forego meeting.' Didn't even get the grammar right. Should be 'Details matter.'"

"What meeting? You have so many. You have meetings on the mind."

"You know, you're probably right. I know subconsciously I'm thinking about a follow-up Baker wants this evening. It's a dead-on conflict with Connor's play. My brain's just on overload."

"Interesting," Penny responded unconvincingly. "I'll leave you to it."

Skip remembered he needed to call Amy. He would still see the play, just not all of it. Amy answered on the second ring.

"Hey, how ya doing?" inquired Skip.

"Oh, hi, Hon. Great day, so far. Class was really good this morning. This group of freshmen really gets it. They are so far ahead of where we were this time last year. How's your day?"

"Okay. Been busy. What else is new? Penny says, 'Hi.' "

"Right back at her."

"Hey, Hon, a conflict's come up."

"Uh-oh. What's that?"

As Skip began to tell about the odd lunch including Caldwell's unexpected involvement, his Blackberry's red light began blinking rapidly, indicating an incoming email. Skip automatically looked down at the screen.

BRO – DETAILS MATTERS
FAMILY 1ST
FOREGO MTG

Skip continued telling Amy about Amalgamated as he watched. The words flickered and convulsed like a campfire.

" . . . which brings me to the conflict. Baker wants to discuss the emerging situation and legal implications . . . " Skip paused and then continued, " . . . this evening."

"Connor will be crushed. Can't you do it some other time?"

"I'm worried about Caldwell's involvement. It sounds dicey for Amalgamated if the whole deal was predicated on crappy economic analysis based on paying illegal aliens sub-minimum wages."

"This is such a big deal to Connor. You've missed the last two shows. Granted, he only had bit parts, but this time, he's got a big, funny role. He can't wait to get your reaction. It really matters to him."

"I know. I hate when these conflicts come up."

"Skip, you have to put your foot down somewhere. The situation with Amalgamated didn't begin today. It won't be resolved tonight. Put your family first. Tell Baker. You always say, if you lay it out for a client, they're human–they typically understand."

"Yeah, I know," Skip agreed, though distracted by Amy's words. Family first. *'Odd coincidence,'* he thought.

Amy moved into her close. "Make your own decision. Just remember, the kids are only kids once. I hate to lay it on that thick, 'cause I know you know, but remind yourself. This play is really important to Connor. For him, *Details* matters."

Startled, Skip interrupted. "What did you say?"

"I just said the play really matters. He wants you there. Hey, I've got to go–there's someone at the door. Leave me a voicemail once you know what you're doing, okay? Love ya, Sweetie," and Amy was gone, leaving Skip holding the silent receiver.

The message on his Blackberry still burned somewhat ominously. While Amy had not verbalized the last directive of the glistening words, her expectation was just as explicit as if she had. Skip stood incredulous over the more than coincidental choice of her language.

Skip finally put the receiver down. *'Okay, I get the message though I can't fathom how it's gotten here. I wonder who Bro is.'* He picked up the phone once more and dialed Arnold Baker. He would go to Connor's play on time and postpone the meeting until tomorrow.

FIVE

Friday, at last. Bernice was awakened before seven o'clock by a nurse arriving to take vital signs. Breakfast materialized shortly thereafter. Dr. Elway had suggested trying soft foods if she felt up to them. As a result, she received two soft-boiled eggs, some buttered toast, and a cup of dreadfully weak tea. She slowly worked her way through most of the eggs and was pushing around the remainder with the toast when the physician strode grimly through the door.

"Bernice, good morning. How are you feeling?"

Not overanalyzing his serious demeanor, Bernice responded curtly, "First day in four that I'm having something to eat with a little substance. You tell me: how am I doing?"

Dr. Elway plowed forward. "How did you sleep? The nurses said you were restless . . . " The thought hung in midair.

"How would they know? They never–I repeat, never–check on me. Not once."

The physician waited expectantly.

Bernice scowled over the top of her glasses. "If you must know, I did have some stretches where I couldn't sleep. My incision remains sore and achy. My insides feel gelatinous; nothing feels stable. I'm hoping a little," she paused and waved her hand for dramatic effect, "breakfast will help."

"We have results."

"Yes? And the answer is–? Wait, I know. It doesn't look good. You believe it's–" but now Bernice stopped. Her attempt at sarcasm wasn't working. She caught herself, realizing the news might not be so good. She looked up at Dr. Elway.

"So, Doc. What's the verdict? Don't sugarcoat."

"Bernice, you have a rapidly metastasizing malignancy. The goal of the biopsies was to determine the type of cell structure and just how aggressive this might be. We believe you either have an adenocarcinoma of the colon or some form of pancreatic malignancy. The slides of your small, highly dense tumor proved so consistent, the lab thought they had erred. As you know, they sought a second opinion to ensure they were reaching an accurate diagnosis. Unfortunately, all the results are the same. Now that we know, we need to do more. I can now see that those suspicious shadows we first saw are highly likely from the same malignancy. I'm sorry to break this to you so early in the day."

Bernice's world shook. After the first phrase, she barely heard anything more that Dr. Elway said. No wonder the dull, aching pain in her abdomen had not gone away. She questioned why she had delayed taking action; in hindsight, believing this to be a muscle strain was preposterous. Emotions and recriminations raced through her head. While most mornings required a prolonged wake-up period, this Friday, Bernice was fully wired by seven thirty.

"Cancer," Bernice rasped out in a whisper. She sagged. "So Doc, what's the prognosis? What's the suggested protocol?"

"I'd like to bring in one of the surgical oncologists later today to review the results and discuss a game plan with you, and, I suppose, your son," he raised this more as a question than a statement. "I'm thinking Barbara Gerhart would be ideal. She will have a point of view on the course of action."

"So, you have no opinion on what's next?" Bernice was angry. Her face reddened, "You come in with a cancer diagnosis, and you have no plan?"

Dr. Elway tried valiantly to hide his frustration. "Of course, Bernice. I have several thoughts. More extensive surgery is likely required to remove all of the tumors. Based on the metastatic state of the biopsy and the shadows on the X-rays, several more malignancies appear highly probable in your abdomen. We will need more detailed diagnostics to pinpoint precise positioning. As you well know, different locations lead to varying treatment protocols and resulting prognoses."

Bernice reacted slowly, like a simmering pot of water nearing a boil. "I hear you, but I want to know more, and I want to know it now. It's been three solid days since the exploratory work was completed. I was prepared to go home and convalesce this weekend. Now, my plans are shot to hell and all you can say is 'unclear next steps.'" Her volume reached a crescendo by the end of her outburst.

And then, Bernice's sapphire-blue eyes welled up. First one tear and then another and another slid down her plump cheeks. Dr. Elway reached over and touched her shoulder. "Dr. Gerhart is very good. I believe you will respect her and engage quickly. Should we call your son to ensure he can be with you when you meet with her this afternoon?"

"No, I do not want him here. I will handle this. Thank you." Bernice regained her composure and dabbed the moisture from her face. "I will inform them later today."

"If that's what you want, of course. I've seen others gain real strength and benefit from having family near them as they plan significant medical procedures—"

"Not my family." Bernice shifted gears, "So, surgery is likely. Then, what is the most probable course of action: Radiation? Chemo? I assume the latter . . . " The words once again faded into the weak morning light streaming through the window.

"While not certain, of course, I anticipate chemo as a plausible regimen postsurgery. With an aggressive malignancy such as this appears to be, we can't be certain where all secondary sites might be. A comprehensive chemo regimen should stop it while it's less well developed elsewhere—"

Bernice interrupted, "I understand the principles of chemotherapy. My concern is over which organs are truly involved. It seems from the early evidence that the colon and pancreas may be compromised. I am wondering whether the liver is also involved. The prognosis heads south more quickly if that's the case."

"Let's not get ahead of ourselves. While seemingly fast-moving, I am hopeful the cancer has been caught and held. Let's learn what Dr. Gerhart would suggest and go from there. I will try to join you for the consultation. For now, unless there are further questions, I'll be on my way. I did want to get to you early—despite the news. We can fight this, Bernice. We really can, and we'll win."

"Thanks for the pep talk, Doc. I'm more interested in the plan than the cheerleading," Bernice nodded to Dr. Elway as he left. With his departure, she found that her appetite, what little had existed, had also exited the room. She lay in bed imagining the thousands of malignant cells doing battle inside her body and felt wholly powerless to do anything about it. Her eyes closed and she slumped down further in the bed, as she suddenly felt both very tired and every one of her sixty-eight years.

In the late morning, Beverly stopped for her daily visit.

"Mother, you're looking better today. How are you feeling?"

"Well, I'm not dead yet," grumped Bernice. She pressed Power on the TV remote.

"Have you gotten any news? When are you going home?"

"Don't know when I'll be out of here. Elway did stop this morning . . . "

"And?" queried Beverly.

"The tumor was malignant."

"Oh, Mother. Have you called Bill yet?"

"No, I've not called Bill. He's not even been in to see me. Why would I call him?" snarled Bernice.

"You know he's been asking about you. He's in the middle of a trial. It's been difficult for him to break away. He would've, you know, but you insisted there was no need . . . "

"Harumph," muttered Bernice.

"What did Dr. Elway suggest? What's next?"

"They need more data. Always the case. Not willing to make a call or give you a straight answer."

"Will he be back?"

"I don't know, and frankly, I don't give a damn. He did mention something about a Dr. Gerhart stopping by."

"Who's that? Does he have a specialty?"

"She," Bernice put biting emphasis on 'she,' "is a surgical oncologist and gets her jollies from looking at diseased stomachs, intestines, and colons . . . "

"When will she be in?" Beverly ignored Bernice's condescension and attempts at black humor.

"Elway said sometime this afternoon. I don't know when."

"I'd like to be here."

"There's no need. Go home."

"Stop it. I resent your telling me to leave. Malignancies are not to be–"

Beverly did not finish. "You can use the word cancer. I've studied the human body for decades. The word is not a death sentence," Bernice paused, "at least not yet."

Beverly exhaled with exasperation. "We need to take care of this," the forty-year-old woman steeled herself and continued, "cancer aggressively. No fooling around. I will see if Bill can join us."

"Don't trouble him too much, dear," said Bernice, dripping with sarcasm. "I wouldn't want to create a client issue."

"I will be back right after lunch. I really think someone else should be with you for the meeting with Dr. Gerhart. I'd like to hear what she has to say."

"Have it your way. I won't throw you from the room. There's just no need to hear the travails of an old woman in her fight with a metastatic tumor."

"It's metastasized?" Beverly's eyes widened.

"Yes. Elway believes it's aggressive." Bernice was relieved to share. "He thinks I need more surgery. I can't tell you how blessed that makes me feel."

Beverly gravely shook her head. "I will certainly be here this afternoon."

"I'm feeling a bit peaked. I think I'll rest," Bernice interjected, ready to end the conversation. Beverly took the not-so-subtle hint. "Of course. I'll see you later."

Attempting to slide deeper under the thin bed covers, Bernice closed her eyes once more as her daughter-in-law headed out the door. Once Beverly was gone, Bernice reopened her eyes, adjusted her glasses, and began channel surfing. She did so with little energy or interest in what was airing. The monotones of all news, all the time, served as a backdrop to her reflections on the battle raging inside.

Barbara Gerhart's visit was purposeful and professional. The fifty-something, blonde-haired ("No way that's a color found in nature" was Bernice's immediate reaction) oncologist was all business. She had reviewed Bernice's charts, spoken with Dr. Elway, and pulled the lab work. Beverly joined the meeting, entering the room just after Dr. Gerhart had walked through the door. Bill was not in attendance. ("He'll stop by this evening, but he hoped you wouldn't be upset if he bowed out now–not knowing exactly when the doctor might arrive," whispered Beverly to Bernice.) After brief introductions, Dr. Gerhart spoke.

"Mrs. Langdon, the tumor is aggressive, as I believe you know. Based on the biopsy, your adenocarcinoma–be it colon or pancreas–shows signs of a rare form of metastasis. On reviewing the CT scan and ultrasound readings from nearly a month ago, it appears even then that the tumor was spreading from the wall of your colon into the pancreas and spleen. It's unclear whether the liver has been compromised or not. I would anticipate, given the strain of malignancy your body is fighting, that it has likely invaded the small intestine as well. I would like to order another CT scan, to update the extent of the spread. Given the size of the tumor extracted compared with its image on the month-old film, we can gauge the pace of growth."

Dr. Gerhart paused for breath, giving Beverly and Bernice time to digest her words.

"So, the next step is more pictures?" questioned Beverly. Bernice lay in the bed looking more and more drained as the conversation progressed. She rolled her eyes at Beverly's question.

"Yes, we need to assess more fully the extent of the metastasis. From there, we can determine the best course of action."

"Am I going to die?" injected Bernice. She said it with as much loud, negative energy as she could muster.

"Mrs. Langdon, we're going to do everything we can to stop the spread of the cancer and remove the malignancies. I expect we'll be doing surgery and then an aggressive course of chemotherapy. From there–"

Bernice interrupted with continued newfound energy, "But, after all of that, am I going to die? We could save ourselves the hassle–"

"Oh, for God's sake, Mother, stop. The doctor is trying to outline a plan." Beverly looked at the physician expectantly. "What is the prognosis?"

"We don't know. We need to see more. I am concerned with the apparent spread to so many other organs before detection . . . " she trailed off. "But that doesn't necessarily indicate it's not wholly removable. High density tumors–such as the first excision–can yield more success in complete removal from subsequent sites. If other tumors you have are similarly structured, the chances for efficacious treatment are high and your prognosis strengthens. Loosely structured tumors can be a heckuva lot more difficult to treat."

"But with your patient experiences to date, Dr. Gerhart, what is the likely outcome of this particular cancer?" Beverly persistently pushed.

"I've had approximately ten similar patients over the years. Most arrived in my care earlier in the cancer's progression than where we appear to be." She quickly added, "However, tumor density can be key. Many prior patients had more permeable, loosely structured tissue types. As I said, you have a rare form. That may prove advantageous."

Beverly was not wholly satisfied with what they knew or didn't know, but realized that the doctor wasn't sure. In the current medical environment, Dr. Gerhart had already ventured more supposition than prudent given the limited number of current, high-resolution scans.

Dr. Gerhart closed the file. "I would like to send you to Radiology and Diagnostic Imaging today. Let's find out more of what we're dealing with. If Dr. Elway concurs, I will recommend discharging you immediately. Spend the weekend at home. It's always more comfortable there. We can talk on Monday with more details and results in hand."

The blonde doctor turned to leave. "Mrs. Langdon," she looked directly at Bernice. "I know of your background in the biology department here at the university. Several of my interns and residents speak highly of the early influence you had on their careers. While this is a difficult time to meet–I wish the circumstances were obviously better, I will do all that I can to help you beat this cancer. I look forward to seeing you Monday. Call my office for a specific time." She handed a card to Beverly.

Bernice had become quiet. "Hey, Doc," she called as the physician reached the door. "Thanks." Dr. Gerhart gave a small smile and left.

Beverly spoke first, "I liked her. She seems to know what she's talking about. While not able to give us all the answers, she cares. She tried to tell you as much as she could at this stage."

Bernice responded, "I suppose she'll do. I wonder which of my students she's had."

Beverly smiled, "I'm sure we can find out. Now, that's good news that you may get out of here today. Would you like to come to our house for the weekend? I don't want you being by yourself–"

"I will be perfectly fine at home, thank you. I would like to sleep in my own bed." No debate was possible on where Bernice would spend the weekend.

"Well, I will bring dinners over so you don't need to cook. Perhaps Bill and I could eat with you tomorrow evening."

"Thank you, but let's see how I'm feeling."

Remarkably, the Medical Center was able to accommodate Bernice late that afternoon. With minimal fuss, she was rolled to and from Radiology in a wheelchair. "I really can walk on my own, dear," she spouted at the candy striper. "Hospital procedure, ma'am. I'll get in trouble if you're not in the chair." The perky teenager smiled back at Bernice. Always one to care about students, Bernice's heart warmed sufficiently to allow the ride . . . and she didn't protest on the return trip.

Around five o'clock, Dr. Elway appeared. "I gather you've met with Dr. Gerhart. Did you like her?"

"What's there to like? She's a cancer doctor. Not someone you want to see too often," responded Bernice curtly.

"We agree that you can go home today–right now if you wish. I have taken the liberty of letting your daughter-in-law know of your discharge. I do hope that wasn't overstepping . . . but I figured you would want to depart as soon as possible. I expect she'll be here–"

As he finished his sentence, Beverly stepped into Room 512 for the third time that day.

"Well, hello, Beverly. Good to see you," smiled Dr. Elway. "I was just telling your mother-in-law that she could go home. Well, very good. I'll just be on my way. I'll stay in touch, of course. Do take it easy this weekend. Do you have an appointment with Dr. Gerhart yet?"

Bernice started shaking her head, but Beverly nodded, "Yes, Mother is scheduled for two o'clock on Monday."

As Bernice grimaced at the thought of more doctors, Dr. Elway concluded, "Excellent. Now, don't overdo it this weekend. Your incision is looking fine. No real restrictions on food or liquid intake–just eat what you feel like eating. I wouldn't go too exotic!" He smiled, "Nor would I drink an excessive amount of alcohol."

"And here I was, ready to hit a frat party . . . " Bernice's humor fell flat.

With the doctor's departure, Beverly helped Bernice get ready, and they left for home shortly thereafter. The weekend was quiet. Bernice enjoyed the beautiful autumn weather in her backyard garden, watching the gold and red leaves begin their initial descent from the trees and dozing with Tigger and Spider. Two quick drop-ins from Beverly were–generally–welcomed. The food she brought was far too much for Bernice's sparse appetite. Even a visit with Bill and Beverly on Saturday evening was mildly enjoyable. They sat in the back garden in the gathering chill with a bottle of red wine. Bernice was less cantankerous than usual, but her quiet was welcome to her guests.

SIX

Carol Kneffler had watched Bernice and Beverly leave the fifth floor Friday afternoon. The heavyset woman had not looked well as she was wheeled toward the elevator. Carol had listened to several of her colleagues talk about the rather irascible "Mrs. Langdon," but she had not dealt with her. She was assigned to Five-East and Room 512 was on West.

A caring twelve-year veteran of nursing, Carol moved her tight, sturdy frame toward the central nurses' station on Five. She wore the requisite white pants and "comfortable nurses' shoes." Her mosaic pastel top contrasted nicely with both her whites and her dark tan, Filipino skin and long black hair, currently knotted up. Carol smiled warmly at her colleagues.

"So, the old battle ax is gone?" Her laugh was joined by the others. "I was just thinking to myself: is she ever going to leave? They weren't doing anything with her. What's up with that?"

The nursing supervisor, Annette, turned toward the other three nurses, "She'll be back. They're doing tests. She's got some fast-growing cancer. We haven't seen the last of her!"

"Just my luck. She'll be on East when she returns. Mark my words, a bookend to the Old Man from the Sea in 523. When's she due back? I'll take my iron pills," Carol chuckled. "She's going to be a story, that one."

Carol was known for her endless storytelling and one-liners. She could spin even the most tragic situation into one full of humor and zany comebacks. Her take on life—whether developed in early childhood on the other side of the globe or in years as a parent—was distinctly unique. She found comedy in the most unlikely places.

"So, Carol. What's up for the weekend?" inquired Dan, a clean-cut young nurse. Now on the fifth floor for three months, he was just beginning to fit in with the fast-talking, tightly knit group of thirty- and forty-something women who staffed the floor. As the first man to join the Fifth Floor Sorority, he remained a novelty.

"I am busy. Have I told you what Kelly is up to? She is out of control. She is not ten yet, and I'm dealing with a teenager. She wants butt shorts for cheerleading. Butt shorts. Can you believe it?"

Dan smiled sheepishly.

"I told her: you are not wearing butt shorts. I do not want to see 'Princess' or 'Cheers' or 'Football' or 'My Butt' plastered across your posterior. And I don't care if all the other girls are wearing them. You are not."

"What's the matter with them?" Dan pushed back.

"Well, you wear a pair. Let's see what you think when everyone's looking at your buns. I bet you come back saying, "Well kiss my—but no, I won't go there." Carol laughed. Dan couldn't help but smile broadly.

"I don't know that butt shorts would do much for me attracting women," smiled Dan.

Carol whistled, "I don't know, Danny Boy. Long hairy legs, some skimpy satin shorts with a personalized billboard 'Boy Toy': you'd be shooting fish in a barrel."

"Maybe we'll get you a pair . . . " Dan trailed off impishly.

"Yeah, and what will that say: 'Two-fer'? 'Jumbo-licious'?" The group around the central desk howled. Though grinning, Annette redirected the group. "Enough, already. You've got patients to deal with. Dinners are on the floor. Let's do a round of check-ins, shall we?"

Carol, Dan, and the others trooped off in the direction of their assigned rooms.

"Mrs. Worley, how are you this evening?" Carol sang out as she entered the first room on the hallway. "Are you enjoying dinner?"

Mrs. Worley didn't say anything, apparently engrossed in the evening news. She silently spooned more of a colorless oatmeal-like mush toward her mouth, occasionally hitting the target.

"Come on now, I know you know I'm here. I can't believe that dinner is more engaging than a big hello for me, your favorite nurse." The elderly lady continued to mechanically shovel gruel with no reaction to the spark plug of energy breezing through her room.

"Well, I suppose that gourmet dinner and those captivating stories of murder and mayhem are too much competition. I'll stop back with your pills in an hour. You know where the call button is, right?"

Mrs. Worley continued to gaze unblinkingly at the small television screen as Carol left. She noted the visit and shoved the Alzheimer's patient file back in the holder outside the door. The patient was to be released tomorrow after one more night in the hospital following her recent fall. Despite multiple attempts, Carol had been unable to break through in conversations with her. The other bed in the room, mercifully, was empty.

In her next room, the 'Old Man from the Sea' was sitting in his chair, yelling answers at *Jeopardy*, which blared at full volume. "Good evening, Mr. O'Henry. I see you're enjoying the game. You winning?"

"Shhhh," shushed the bald gentleman, straining to hear. "Who is Michelangelo?" he shouted at Alex Trebek, who failed to acknowledge him.

"I need to take your pulse and blood pressure," said Carol. "We also need to do a blood sugar stick. This should only take a moment."

As Carol hooked up the blood pressure cuff, Mr. O'Henry nervously twitched in his chair trying to see around her and follow the gameshow's progression. "Now, Mr. O, don't move so much–you'll raise your reading!" kidded Carol. Simultaneously, she put her hand on his wrist to count out his pulse.

"Looking good. Pulse 69, blood pressure 106 over 70. Give me your finger. Let's just get a little stick." Moments later she reported, "120, Mr. O–that's real good. It's come down nicely since yesterday. I think you're on the mend."

"I guess you're anxious to return to your boat?" suggested Carol. "I'll bet living on the water at the harbor is relaxing, though I'd think the winter would be a tough time to be at sea." She paused, "Do you stay on land during the worst weather?"

Mr. O'Henry looked up at Carol, as a commercial interrupted the game. "Course not," he muttered. "The sea is my life. I regret the day I sold my fishing equipment. Damn son of mine. Make me give up my livelihood. Just because of a little stroke. People go on and live . . . "

"Mr. O'Henry, I'd say you've done mighty well this side of that stroke. If I didn't know better, I wouldn't know. How long ago was that?"

"Damn near five years. Damnedest thing."

"Do you visit your son during the winter? Perhaps at the holidays? I mean, with the types of storms we get around here, it would be prudent to–"

But *Jeopardy* had returned. "What is the Yucatan Peninsula?" he yelled as Carol moved behind the curtain to the other bed.

"Can't you make him quiet down? I just want to sleep." The newest patient on the floor had arrived from surgery earlier in the afternoon. While not life threatening, the man in his sixties was clearly in pain and worn out from the day. He groaned as he shifted and grimaced with discomfort. "Please."

"I'll see what I can do," whispered Carol. "These rooms are small and it's hard to share them sometimes, I realize. How's the pain?"

"I can handle it. I don't really want to take anything. Painkillers make me ill–"

"There, there. No worries. I just want to ensure you are getting what you need. Let me take some readings and get you back to resting." Carol moved efficiently through the routine numbers, noting them in his file at the base of the bed. "Now, here's the call button–if you need anything. I'll check back later. If you need something to sleep, your doctor said you can have it. Just let me know."

The man had already dozed off as Carol finished talking. As a result, she didn't see the need to say anything to Mr. O'Henry as he ran the category in Double *Jeopardy*. Instead, she stepped out of the room and headed farther down the hall.

Carol finished her rounds uneventfully. Her generally elderly population was quieting down for the evening. With staff cutbacks at the hospital, she continued to be frustrated with the limited time she had to engage with her patients. It felt more like an assembly line than a care-giving facility. Eight or more patients at any one time were just too many.

Her colleagues shared the frustration. None of them had sufficient time to truly nurse their patients. Rather, they all ran against a stopwatch, trying to get rounds done, seeing to the various "urgent" requests by their patients, and coddling the arrogant potpourri of physicians, residents, and interns.

Carol maintained a spunky, good-humored attitude about the whole affair but kept a watchful eye on job openings in the nursing profession. Unbeknownst to her colleagues, she was contemplating a switch to home care nursing. She believed it might provide more opportunity to develop deeper, more caring relationships with her patients, but the money was not as good nor were the benefits. With two kids at home, she and her husband, Jay—a local government manager, were on a tight budget. Each dollar proved precious. Recently, Carol had spoken with an acquaintance who was with HomeHealth and heard all the benefits of jobs with the entrepreneurial organization, but she remained unsure.

Back at the nurses' station, Carol reengaged with her colleagues over a cup of decaffeinated tea.

"—and then, Kevin says, 'But Mom, I like picking my nose.' And I say, 'And what do you like about picking your nose? Is it the variety of colors you can retrieve? Does the consistency vary from day to day? Tell me about your technique.' And Kevin goes into great detail on the engineering behind extracting boogers from his nose. Well, you know me, I ask, 'Just what do you do with them when you've got them?' His quick reply? 'I put them in my pocket.' Well, I say, 'Kevin, you should share them. Surely, if you're going to go to the trouble of collecting them, you should put them in positions where others might find them . . . under tabletops is a good example. Now that would be good.' Well, Kevin, he just rolls his big brown eyes and says in a great elongated fashion, 'Mah -ommm.'"

The nurses rolled with laughter as Carol concluded. "You are always into something. How these kids will turn out is beyond me!" laughed Annette. "I couldn't have that conversation with my son."

"But, you know, it's so easy. You meet them on their level. You make them laugh. They see how silly they're being, and they move on. Really." Carol loved parenting though she never felt like she had enough time. She was always working, maintaining the house, or playing soccer mom and chauffeur to her own two, plus others in the neighborhood who viewed the Kneffler minivan as public transportation.

The group gradually dispersed to fill out paperwork and see to occasional calls from patients as the evening shift rolled toward ten o'clock. After seeing

Mr. O'Henry's roommate, Carol realized her most recent cup of tea had cooled. In the pantry, she placed the cup in the microwave for a quick warm-up.

On taking it out, she was astonished to see an odd glow around the edge of the dark tea, where it met the side of the cup. The light flickered and shimmered with a brilliance one might see if the sun reflected off a piece of metal. She watched, fascinated as the edge of her tea glowed.

'What's this?' she thought. *'Could the microwave overheat a liquid and cause this? Perhaps there's something in the composition of the cup that's creating some sort of reaction . . . '*

As she watched, the glowing liquid circumference widened, undisturbed by her efforts to slosh around the hot tea. The band of light simply sloshed around with the liquid. "Well, this is very odd. I'm gonna have to share this," she said aloud, while heading back to the nurses station. There she found Dan.

"Hey, would you look at this?" Carol called out as she held her cup.

Dan looked over, then stood and moved toward her. "What's up?"

"No clue, Danny-O. Maybe something from a different planet? What do you think?" Carol quizzically handed him the teacup; he looked at it skeptically.

"Whoa, how'd you do that? Pretty cool." He swirled the liquid around with the same effect as Carol.

"Dan-Man, it came out of the microwave glowing."

"It's a little freaky; maybe you left it in too long," responded Dan.

"I think it's a message from the great beyond. It's telling me to expect a ring, yes, a ring of light . . . maybe a diamond anniversary ring from my husband. What do you think?"

"I think you have an overeager imagination. That's what I think."

Annette returned to the station. "What are you two staring at?"

"Look at Carol's cup. She's doing magic tricks."

Annette looked into the glowing cup. The edge of silvery-white light was now holding constant in width. "Well, look at that. What's that all about?"

"Beats me. I want a simple cup of tea. I leave it here on the desk while I see 523. It cools down, I warm it up in that old microwave, and–voila–I have a halo. Maybe that's it. It's telling me I'm an angel. All my patients think so." Carol laughed.

"Perhaps we should call Maintenance to check it out. The microwave's not that old, but I've never seen a reaction like this one. I'm not sure I'd drink it," warned Annette. "Get a new cup."

"Oh, I'm always one for adventure. I was just going to down the whole thing. Maybe I'll get superpowers. Didn't something like that happen to

Spiderman?"

"Just what we need: Supernurse. I don't think I'd drink it, Carol."

"Perhaps you're right. I'll leave it here on the desk and see what else it does," concluded Carol.

The shift wound down over the hour before eleven. The corridor was quiet. Carol checked her mysterious teacup periodically but no change transpired. The glowing perimeter remained, but—somewhat disappointedly—no further chemical reaction occurred. Just before the shift ended, Carol carried the cooled teacup to the pantry to dump its contents.

After emptying the cold tea down the drain, Carol turned the cup over to rinse it out. She gasped. In the bottom of the cup were sodden tea leaves. They emitted a distinct glow, with the same bluish-white coloring that still encircled the edge of her cup even now, with the liquid gone. More oddly, however, minute specks of the leaves were arranged specifically.

HH GOOD FAM 1ST
TAKE JOB

'That's a heckuva message to fit in the bottom of a cup,' she paused thinking. "HH is obvious. What else could it be? HomeHealth sure knows how to market . . . " Carol's voice faded. The tea leaves continued to glow as Carol processed this turn of events.

"Now, wait a minute. I use tea bags. I pulled the bag out and discarded it hours ago; there was nothing unusual about the bag: not one tear, no gaps, nothing. It makes no sense that there are tea leaves at the bottom of my cup. Particularly, tea leaves that glow." She paused, "Of course, having a message spelled out by the tea leaves—well, what else would one expect?" She stopped again. Carol knew instinctively that she couldn't share the message—as much as she wanted. No one knew she was thinking about a different job. "Bummer, I guess the cup is just for me," Carol murmured. "I'll talk about it with Jay when I get home."

Carol shoved the unrinsed cup in her bag and returned to the nurses' station to hand off her patients to the next shift.

"Hey, what happened with the teacup?" inquired Dan.

"Nothing. Nothing at all. I just dumped it and—ahhhh—rinsed it out. I'm, uhhh, going to take it home to put it through my dishwasher. Odd, huh?"

"You bet. Well, I'm gonna bolt. I'm dead tired," smiled Dan, pulling on a light jacket to wear into the cool evening. "I'll see you next week?" he raised rhetorically, since they always worked the same shift Thursday and Friday evenings.

"Yeah, sure," Carol replied distractedly. "Have a nice weekend."

With minimal further conversation—highly unusual for Carol—she wrapped up and headed for the elevators. Thirty minutes later at home, Carol shook Jay.

"Wake up. I need to show you something."

Barely alert, Jay rolled over on his back. "Ahh, Carol, right now? Can't it wait? I was sound asleep . . . "

"No, Pud–it can't. Something really odd. I need you to see it." She shook his shoulder again as he attempted vainly to burrow deeper. "Come on. Wake up."

Carol turned the bedside lamp up a notch as Jay squinted. Having come right to the bedroom, Carol still had on her burgundy windbreaker. Jay sat up. His hair–what little there was–was a mess from being asleep; his t-shirt ("Government officials do it slow") was rumpled and barely covered his growing middle-age spread; his boxers remained covered by the sheet. He reached for his glasses.

"Okay, what can't wait 'til morning?" He rubbed his eyes as Carol pulled the mug from her bag.

"Look at this."

"It's a very nice cup. I like it. Now, can I go back to sleep?"

"Stay with me. You won't believe this. I'm not sure what to make of it." Carol launched into the story of the glowing teacup and later, the glowing alphabetic leaves. Jay became increasingly alert as Carol progressed. " . . . so, let me show you the bottom of the cup."

She tilted the cup in his direction. Soggy brown tea leaf sediment had settled at the bottom. The leaves were not glowing and were most certainly not arranged in letters. "Sweetie, it's nearly midnight. Maybe you dreamed the leaves were telling you something. They're not."

Carol studied the cup. "But they were. Just moments ago. I even checked them one more time in the kitchen as I came in. Clear as day. They glowed faintly and spelled out a message."

Jay leaned back against the headboard. "And what did they say, again?"

"'HH good. Fam first. Take job.' I don't think I'll forget that for a long time. It's not everyday your teacup talks to you. What do you think it means, Pud?"

"If you really buy that there were words," Jay stopped. "Well, sounds self-explanatory. Quit the university and go to HomeHealth. Maybe that's what you really want to do. Then again, maybe you imagined the words. Perhaps–"

Carol interrupted. "No, I saw them. Dan and Annette saw the glowing edge. Sure, they didn't see the words, but they saw the shimmering metallic light. They would vouch for that. I couldn't very well show them the message, now could I?"

"Babe, I believe you." Jay stroked Carol's back, "Of course, you couldn't show them. Regardless, the words aren't there now. I suggest you get a good night's sleep, and we can talk about it more in the morning."

"You think?" Carol's face scrunched up in thought.

"Yeah, I do. I'm gonna get some shut-eye. Come join me." Jay gave Carol a kiss, laid his glasses on the end table, slid back into the warmth of the bed, pulled the covers up over his shoulder, and closed his eyes.

"Jay," Carol still sat on the side of the bed. "Jay."

"What?" groaned her husband keeping his eyes closed.

"I think the message is real. I needed something to push me to make a decision. This may be a sign."

"Could be," grunted Jay.

"Pud, I've not been spending enough quality time with the kids, or with you. I want to put family first. Maybe HomeHealth will enable me to do that. What do you think?"

"I'm tired, Carol. I coach Kevin's soccer team tomorrow morning in their eight o'clock game. I want to go to sleep."

"I know, I know, but this is so exciting. I am excited."

"I'm glad, I really am."

"Pud, you don't sound excited."

"Carol, I'm beat. Please, can we talk about this more in the morning?"

"I guess, but I think I know the answer. I could start at HomeHealth in two weeks or so. Give my notice on Monday and start well before Thanksgiving. What do you say?"

Jay didn't respond, his breathing having transitioned to the rhythm and resonance of someone in deep sleep.

Carol smiled, turning off the light and heading toward the master bathroom. With little doubt, they would talk about this more tomorrow, but the conversation would focus on how to make the transition work–not whether. She'd received clear guidance and the nudge she needed. Better yet, she was excited about the new path. *'Wow, all from a little teacup,'* she thought as she slid under the covers. *'I'll have to watch my teacups more closely from now on.'* With that, she closed her eyes.

SEVEN

Bernice shifted uncomfortably in the front seat as she fastened the seat belt. Her incision was healing, but the shoulder strap came down across it. The grazing strap was an irritant, and the car hadn't moved. Beverly backed out onto the quiet street.

"You have more color this morning," bubbled Beverly as they got underway. "Did you sleep better?"

"Yes," clipped Bernice. She was in no mood to talk. She couldn't fathom why Beverly insisted on going to lunch before the doctor's appointment. The retiree would have been far happier staying at home, in her kitchen with the cats, sipping some chicken noodle soup before facing the visit with Dr. Gerhart.

"Mother," Beverly insisted on Sunday evening. "You really should get out. You've been holed up in the house all weekend. Monday's supposed to be glorious. Let's go for a drive and then stop at Isaacson's for a sandwich before the doctor."

"Don't want to," mumbled Bernice. "I've no appetite, and I have no interest in sitting in a damn car riding around in traffic."

Beverly relented and dropped the notion of a morning drive. Bernice acquiesced to a stop at Isaacson's, her favorite New York-style deli, before the doctor. Though she still anticipated no appetite, the strength eluded her to fight off Beverly's efforts any further. As a result, they now joined a long line of cars waiting to enter Interstate 82 heading downtown.

"The kids have such a busy week. I really don't know how they are growing up so fast. Let me tell you . . . " And off Beverly went with a long monologue regarding the two kids and their sports, school, and extracurricular activities. Bernice closed her eyes as both conversation and traffic dragged.

" . . . and I was just saying to Bill, I don't know if I'll have time to get their costumes done for Halloween. Heavens, I just don't know . . . " Beverly paused expectantly and looked over at her mother-in-law. "Are you awake?"

"Yes," Bernice curtly responded. "I'm just resting my eyes. The sun is awfully bright," she emitted from behind her large, dark sunglasses. Her mouth barely moved as she gritted her teeth to get the words out slowly and deliberately.

"So, what do you think?"

"What do I think about what?" replied Bernice.

"About the kids' costumes? Should I make them or buy–"

"I don't know, and right now, I really don't give a damn. Let me know what you decide," groused Bernice.

Beverly averted her eyes and pressed the accelerator a little too hard, causing the automobile to lurch forward.

"My God, what are you doing?" yelped Bernice.

"Sorry," Beverly sheepishly swallowed. Beverly brushed a tear off her left cheek unceremoniously. She missed her own mother so badly. Bernice did not notice as she sank deeper in her seat. Moments later, Beverly braked sharply to avoid the SUV directly in front of them.

"For God's sake, slow down. I may be sick at this rate," Bernice injected bitingly. "I really am not feeling well."

Beverly kept her eyes on the road and reached over to turn on the radio. She tuned in the country music station WEIO and moderated the volume. "What is this twangy nonsense? Can't you find some real music?" snarled Bernice.

"You find a station," expelled Beverly with some exasperation.

"I don't know how the damn thing works. Find something better." Bernice paused as a tune by Dolly Parton began. "Here we go. The blonde bimbo with the big–"

Beverly savagely punched the power button. The silence in the car was deafening. The two women rode in silence for the remainder of the twenty-minute trip to Isaacson's. The quiet continued as they studied the menus.

"I'm starved," stated Beverly. "Breakfast seems so long ago. I ate just after seven o'clock with Bill and the kids."

"I don't have much of an appetite," asserted Bernice from behind her sunglasses.

"You know, you might want to change glasses. Those must make it so dark."

Bernice grimaced but removed her oversized shades and replaced them with equally disproportionate clear spectacles.

"Still not hungry," she continued.

"But you always enjoy the overstuffed Joey Bishop–with roast beef, baby Swiss, and horseradish. Why don't you order it? If you can't finish it, we'll wrap it up to go. I think I'll have the antipasto salad. I always like the hot rolls that come with it, right from the oven. Don't you?" Beverly's attempts at conversation proved fruitless. Bernice remained stuck, deep in her own world.

When lunch arrived, an overflowing roast beef extravaganza was placed in front of Bernice.

"I've put together a list of questions for Dr. Gerhart. I thought we might want to go in prepared. It seems like so often they give you so much information in these appointments that–later–you have questions you wished you had asked. I remember–"

Bernice cut her off, "Sure, that sounds fine."

"Did you have any questions you want included?" Beverly reached in her bag and brought out a pen and the page of questions she had scrawled in her very neat cursive writing.

"No. I'm sure your list is complete. Can we go now?"

"It's only 12:45. We are going to be early if we leave now. You know how these doctors always run late." Beverly gave a small laugh, the first of the outing with Bernice.

" . . . and, you've barely touched your Joey Bishop. It looks so good."

"Here, then, you have it," gestured Bernice pushing her plate toward her daughter-in-law. "I can't eat anymore."

"Are you sure? You've taken barely three bites," persisted Beverly.

"I don't wish it. I feel nauseous and don't need you to foist more food on me. Please stop."

"Well, we'll just have it wrapped to go. Maybe you'll want it–"

"I won't wish any later. It tastes like cardboard. If you want it for Bill or the kids, be my guest." Bernice exchanged glasses once more. With her dark shades in place, she pulled her sweater around her shoulders more fully. "Did they turn up the air conditioning? They could hang sides of beef in here."

Beverly quizzically looked at her mother-in-law with concern. "You're chilled? I actually don't think it feels too bad."

"Well, I'm frigid. And, I'm not offering an editorial on my late husband's bedroom abilities. I'm ready to go."

Beverly paid the bill, left a generous tip, and followed the older woman. They continued the trip to the Medical Center complex. With some difficulty, they found Dr. Gerhart's office and parked themselves in the not-too-comfortable waiting room chairs, joining a dozen other ill patients and their companions. Judging from the faces, all represented varying stages in respective journeys toward death. Gray coloring and obvious pain–from severe to more modest–provided the common thread.

"Well, this is depressing," said Bernice far too loudly. "Do I look this bad?"

"Mother, let's not disturb the others," Beverly stage whispered and smiled congenially, spinning her head smoothly toward the room.

"Well, do I look this bad or not? This looks like God's waiting room. Do you think any of them will make it?"

"Please," said Beverly emphatically. "The room is looking at us." The younger woman's whispers became pointed and embarrassed.

Bernice's blue eyes widened intensely as she erupted in a tight-lipped hiss, "Well, I'll be goddamned if I'm going to go through some long drawn out march to death's door. This damn well better be good news."

"Well, I think we need to be prepared . . . " Beverly trailed off, unsure how to complete her thought.

"What? Be prepared to look like these—" Bernice waved toward the room, "patients of Dr. Gerhart's?"

"Let's wait and see what the doctor has to say. We don't know yet."

At two thirty, Bernice was called back. Beverly accompanied her to the little, windowless examining room.

"I never understand this whole process. Out there in the waiting room, at least you have something to look at, some magazines to read. Back here, you never know how long you'll be waiting, and all they provide is some obscure medical literature. See, look here." Beverly picked up *Maintaining a Vital Pancreas.* "Just what either of us might want: a vital pancreas!" She shook her head.

Bernice showed no interest. She settled into the marginally less comfortable chair than her seat in the waiting room. She closed her eyes, attempting to ignore her surroundings. With no conversational success, Beverly browsed through the pancreas pamphlet and moved to a booklet on postsurgical care for endoscopic and abdominal surgeries. She absorbed nothing, as the clock inched forward.

Just before three o'clock, the door opened, and a nurse requested they follow her to a bigger corner space with two windows letting in crisp autumn sunshine. Dr. Gerhart turned from her computer screen and smiled as they entered the room.

"Oh, Mrs. Langdon—so nice to see you again. I'm glad you brought your daughter with you."

"Daughter-in-law," muttered Bernice.

"Yes, of course. I'm Barbara Gerhart. I don't believe I caught your name the other day." She extended her hand.

"Beverly Langdon," she reciprocated, relieved at the prospect of someone else helping to conduct a conversation; the last four hours with Bernice had been draining.

"Mrs. Langdon," Dr. Gerhart turned back to Bernice. "As we suspected last week, we have some work to do. With a more detailed biopsy, your cancer is as aggressive as we anticipated. I'd like to tell you differently, but that's not the case. You have a rapidly metastasizing malignancy, which I believe is adenocarcinoma, initiating in the colon. The scans we took on Friday afternoon confirm the extent of its spread. While, as you know, CT scans only provide a certain amount of information, they can–"

"How bad do I have it, Doc?" Bernice cut to the chase.

"Your case is considered a Stage Three malignancy. Are you familiar with the stages we use?"

"Yes," responded Bernice. "Stage Four is near death. Stage Three is broadly distributed, but still feasibly treatable, if aggressive, tailored approaches are used."

The surgeon smiled thinly. "Well, I'm not sure I'd use the same definition with my Stage Four patients. While the prognosis does deteriorate for Fours, hope still exists. Stage Three does require aggressive treatment. As we discussed Friday, I recommend surgery: remove the multiple, visible tumors. We should then pursue a full regimen of chemotherapy. I expect that to run over the course of four to six months, on a weekly basis."

Bernice shrank in her chair, her color draining. "Six months?" she murmured. "Oh, God, six months . . ." She visibly sagged.

Dr. Gerhart paused. "We'll want a detailed plan of attack from one of our pharma oncologists. Potentially, you'll get by with a little less time on chemo–or perhaps less frequently." The physician's brow furrowed, "But your tumor is aggressive and I suspect you'll be following a comprehensive regimen."

Beverly was rendered speechless as she fought to absorb the news. She anticipated the surgery and a brief run of chemo, but six months was overwhelming. Having watched her mother and uncle go through chemo years earlier, she had a visceral sense of the devastation the treatment was likely to wreak. Admittedly, Beverly did not always relish spending time with her ever-complaining, irritable mother-in-law, but this was not something she wished on her; this was a tough verdict.

Dr. Gerhart watched the women and broke into their reflections. "I know you must have questions. Let me take them one at a time."

Glad for the prompt, Beverly pulled out her list and began ticking them off one by one. Bernice remained stunned and appeared to only occasionally follow the dialogue. They covered all the expected topics: prognosis ("with treatment as outlined, success in the fifty to sixty percent range with patients in remission or apparently cured, five years after surgery"), potential complications, likely postsurgical recovery time and convalescence protocol, as well as side effects of chemo.

Dr. Gerhart quietly closed the file, "Well, I suggest getting underway as soon as we can. I know this is a lot to absorb." The physician stared directly at Bernice's somewhat glazed eyes. "But our chances for higher rates of success rise exponentially the sooner we get in there, eliminate the tumors, and start chemo. I have time later this week, if it works for you and provided–of course–you are ready to move forward."

Beverly leaned forward, "What about a second opinion? This is an extensive set of procedures. As we understand it, the next six months could really be challenging."

"Of course, I would want to know the same if it were my parent. In fact–"

Bernice interrupted. "I don't need another opinion. Dr. Elway recommended you, and your diagnosis and treatment plan align with what I anticipated. I see no reason to wait, provided we're going to do anything."

"Mother, of course, we're going to do something. We need to get this taken care of and get you back to enjoying your retirement!"

"It is my body, and I will choose the approach we take," struck back Bernice. "I am not resigned to a living hell for six months if it turns out to be a prolonged death sentence. Might as well just get it over with sooner!"

"Mrs. Langdon, I see your prospects as good. Of course, we'd all like ninety-plus percent probabilities, but we can give you a pretty good shot."

"I'm not convinced," responded Bernice.

"What I mean: you have every chance to be on the high side of the probabilities. While of course there are no guarantees, I am optimistic."

"If this was your mother or father, is this the course of action you'd be taking?" inquired Beverly.

"Yes, without a doubt. Of course, I wouldn't do the surgery myself on a relative, but this is my area of expertise. I do between one hundred and one hundred-fifty similar abdominal surgeries–largely for malignancies and benign tumor growths–annually. I will, of course, collaborate closely with another oncologist on your chemotherapy plan."

Bernice looked at the floor. Her eyes had grown heavy once more. She just wanted to go home and go to bed.

"I've heard enough. I would like to think about this."

"Of course, Mrs. Langdon. I would encourage moving quickly. Let's get on this and take care of it. Don't let it get any further ahead of us than it already has. Mrs. Langdon," Dr. Gerhart looked at Beverly, "you will discuss this more fully with your husband and his mother?" she nodded hopefully.

"No doubt, we will discuss this tonight," Beverly took charge.

"Should you have any questions, leave me a voicemail if you can't get me directly."

A burning tightness gripped Beverly's throat as she glanced at the woman slumped in the adjacent seat. What would the days ahead hold for her husband's mother? "We'll try to let you know tomorrow, after we talk with Bill." She touched Bernice's hand. "If we're going to beat this, we need to move quickly."

"Yes, I agree. Good day, Mrs. Langdon."

Surgery was scheduled for Friday morning. There was little debate on

Monday evening. Bill insisted on pursuing an aggressive treatment plan. Beverly tried valiantly but with little luck to elicit Bernice's point of view, but the older woman had withdrawn. She appeared resigned to the surgery, though wavered in her appetite for "up to six months" of chemo. After an additional consultation with Dr. Elway on Tuesday, the family concluded they should schedule the surgery.

Friday dawned gray and foreboding, matching Bernice's mood. The only modest benefit of her current predicament was evident when she dressed for the trip back to the hospital. Her typically snug, navy wool slacks hung loosely around her waist.

"Helluva way to diet," she smiled grimly at the reflection in the wall mirror.

Surgery under Dr. Gerhart's sure hand proceeded smoothly. The tumor count rose from the expected six to eight, as two smaller growths were discovered–one on the anterior side of the small intestine, the other on the diaphragm wall tucked above the stomach. The skilled surgeon successfully removed all the growths and closed up, with the help of a resident who had studied under Professor Langdon eight years earlier. Unbeknownst to Bernice who was heavily anesthetized, the upbeat twangy country tunes of Kenny Chesney and Tim McGraw filled the OR throughout the four hours she was under the knife.

EIGHT

Roger Gallo was fourteen and a freshman at Whittaker High School. Having just completed another growth spurt, Roger stood five foot ten. His short blond hair framed his tanned face. Broad shoulders and a newly emerging chest sat atop a lanky frame. He was considered a pretty good-looking guy by the girls. While quiet, Roger had a ready smile for his friends and an occasional still-shy smile for the girls.

Football defined October in a big way for Roger. He played on the freshman team at Whittaker and also liked going with his dad to the university games on Saturday afternoons. Seeing a top-notch game with more than forty thousand fans was really exciting. Sometimes his dad would let him bring along a buddy or two, usually from Roger's team at school.

Keeping his commitment as a paperboy was tough during the football season. Each afternoon, Roger squeezed in delivery of *The Ledger* to seventy-five houses in his development. He liked the paper route most of the year and really didn't want to quit, as it provided great spending money. He also enjoyed riding his bike through the neighborhood.

Friday afternoon was crisp and clear. Roger had a day off from football practice, as they had just won a game on Thursday. They had won big–despite Roger missing a pass toward the end of the second quarter. He was bummed, as was the quarterback, but his coach had told him to buck up and "forget about it." While easier said than done, that was yesterday, and now the weekend stretched magnificently in front of him–no homework and no responsibilities, and his painfully intrusive little sister Emily would be away at their grandmother's. His dad had to work this weekend, but had said that Roger and Jesse, his best pal, could go to the university football game on Saturday if he could get tickets.

Roger folded newspapers on the front porch. Mid-autumn sunlight filtered through the lingering red and orange leaves in the front yard of the rambling white colonial. Norman Rockwell could not have painted a more classic fall scene in New England.

"Roger, you still here?" called out his mom.

"Yeah, I'm on the porch doing papers."

His mother's face appeared at the screen door. "Want some apple cider before you head out?"

Before answering, his mother came out with a frosted mug. "Want me to ride along with you today? I've got time."

Roger shrugged. Inwardly, he grimaced, though he tried to maintain an even expression. He'd learned that explicit eye-rolling was immediately met with an escalation in tension with his mom. His dad seemed more even-keeled, but even he would occasionally react strongly to some immaterial shift in Roger's countenance.

"Doesn't seem like you're too excited about the idea . . . " his mother's sing-songy voice was more grating than usual. *'Please don't spoil a perfect afternoon,'* thought Roger.

"I don't know. I was thinking I might swing by Jesse's. Maybe see if he wanted to do the route with me and then bike over to Dunkin' Donuts. Maybe I could pick up something for you?" Roger tried to navigate his way to a successful outcome that would not include a mother-son neighborhood tour.

"That's a thought. I could use some decaf. Would you be willing to pick up a pound–ground, of course, but not too fine? Tell them our machine is a little sensitive. If they go too fine, it . . . "

Roger stopped listening as Mrs. Gallo detailed Mr. Coffee's eccentricities. Whether Jesse was available was unimportant, as his goal was achieved.

Just then Emily yelled, interrupting the coffee-grinding specifications. "Hey, Mom? Where's the paint brush?"

"It is right where you left it. I saw it earlier." Mrs. Gallo turned from the doorway and disappeared.

"Thanks for the cider . . . " called out Roger, smiling as he finished the last set of papers. After retrieving money for coffee, Roger put the heavy bag of Friday papers on his back and mounted his bike. Deliveries started with the adjacent neighbor. Midway through his route, he stopped at Jesse's house.

Knocking on the open screen door, he called out, "Hey, anybody home?" Mrs. Stauffer came to the door and smiled. "Hi, Roger. Jesse's at soccer. Can I get you a drink?"

"No, thanks, Mrs. Stauffer. I'm good. Tell Jesse I stopped by. Here's your paper."

"Personal delivery. Why, thank you. What are you up to this weekend? Did I hear Jesse say you guys might go to the game?"

"Yes, ma'am. My dad is gonna try to get us tickets."

"Well, I know Jesse would love to go. You let us know, okay?"

Roger rode back down the driveway and took off in the direction of the descending sun. Several streets later, toward the end of his route, he came to the Langdon brick house on Fox Den. He never really liked the old lady who lived there. She used to teach at the university. He vaguely recalled biology being the subject. Roger had little use for biology, other than when they did dissections. Cutting something up that was all squishy and gross was cool. He liked waving entrails at the girls who, predictably, would scream or shrink rapidly away. No doubt, they thought he was cool to pick this stuff up with his bare hands.

Professor Langdon's residence was dark. All the curtains were drawn. Thinking back, Roger couldn't remember the last time he'd seen her. Many times, Roger could count on the professor to meet him at the door with an outstretched hand. She was never mean about it, but she always seemed to be anxiously awaiting the paper's arrival. It was like she had nothing else to do.

He considered it odd that he hadn't seen her in a while. He parked his bike, opened the gate in the wrought iron fence, and walked up the brick path to the front door. When had he seen her last? His mind did a fast rewind over the last couple of months and stopped.

"Wow," he said aloud. "Mid-August since I've seen the old lady? Really?" He frowned.

The house stood silently in front of him. His bag had gotten lighter over the last thirty minutes, and he sat down on the front step.

'I hope the old battle ax is okay. What if she's in there dead or something?' His adolescent mind went over some of the more horrible things that could've befallen Professor Langdon inside her manicured home. What was it she had said to him last time? He recalled the interaction well.

"Hello, Professor Langdon," Roger had called out as he rode up. She was sitting in the small alcoved area at the side of the house. It was sunny and hot, though the little brick patio was shaded by several expansive trees.

"Hello," Bernice responded. "How's the paper route today?"

"It's okay. Kinda hot actually." Roger perspired profusely as he stepped off his bike. His yellow muscle shirt clung to his sweaty frame. Even his feet felt hot inside his Nikes.

"You look warm. Would you like something cold to drink?" The professor gave him what passed for a slight smile.

"Well, I guess so; that would be great."

"Tell you what. I'm not feeling quite myself today. Why don't you just go in through the side door here? There are some big cups on the counter. Pour yourself some iced tea."

Roger handed over *The Ledger* and put down his paper bag. Following her instructions, he entered the kitchen. While not one to notice inattentive housekeeping, even Roger was surprised. The inside of the house was not as immaculate as the outside. The professor must not be feeling up for cleaning, he surmised. He tried to get ice from the dispenser in the door, but nothing came out. He gave up. Looking in the refrigerator he found the pitcher of iced tea and poured some. Putting it away, he paused.

"Hey, Professor Langdon? Do you want some?" He called out through the screen door.

"Why, yes, that would taste good."

He poured another cup and carried both to the door. As he opened it, Bernice curtly interjected, "and don't let the goddamn cat out of the house, you hear me?"

Taken aback as no cat was obvious, Roger responded, "Yeah, sure."

Handing Bernice the cup of cold tea, Roger stood awkwardly sipping his own.

"Sit with me," commanded the grumpy old lady.

"I've still got papers," stammered Roger but wound up perched on a chair opposite the frumpy woman at the glass-covered patio table; she didn't seem to want excuses for standing.

"So what's a strappin' young man like you up to this summer?" inquired Bernice. "I hope using your time wisely."

"Yes, Professor." Roger looked down at the ground between his Nikes. He felt awkward and a little embarrassed. He sipped more tea.

"I've been organizing this summer. Getting my library together." Bernice stared at Roger through her large glasses.

"Yes, ma'am. Sounds like a good thing to . . . "

"Not much of a conversationalist?"

Roger stared intently at the ground. The crack in the brick nearest his left foot was particularly intriguing.

"You have a nice tan," tried Bernice. "Go to the beach?"

"We went there a month or so ago. Went to the Cape. I also like swimming at the pool," Roger volunteered.

"Where on the Cape?"

"Chatham. My grandparents rent a house there. It was fun."

The conversation halted once more.

"I've not been feeling well today," Bernice looked a bit more drawn as she uttered the words to Roger. Unbeknownst to him, he was one of the first people to learn that the professor wasn't feeling well that summer. Not being one to share, Bernice had needed to say the words aloud.

"I'm sorry. Can I get you anything?"

"No, you already have. Thank you."

"I better be going now." Roger gulped down the remainder of his iced tea. "Sure I can't get you anything else?" he awkwardly stuttered, as he stood and looked at the heavyset, gray-tinged lady.

"No. I'm just going to sit here and rest a moment longer. Then it's on to the paper and back to organizing." Bernice feigned more energy than she felt in the late-afternoon warmth.

Roger had left; then looking back over his shoulder, he had seen the professor's chin droop softly onto her collarbone.

Now in late October, Roger pondered, *'She really didn't look that good. Maybe she did die . . . What if her body's in there and no one's discovered it?'*

He jumped up. Not wanting to be the one to find her body, Roger headed back toward the street but stopped in his tracks. *'Nah, couldn't be. Someone's been getting her papers. Maybe she's sitting on the patio like last time. I'll just check it out.'* He headed across the lawn toward the secluded sitting area.

The patio bricks were shaded and cool. After quickly looking around and seeing no one, he pivoted to return to his bike. As he spun on his Nikes, he noticed a section of brick that stood out. The patio corner closest to the house had distinctive coloring. Granted, the brick was in the shadiest section, but it was more than that.

Roger was intrigued; sufficiently curious, he walked over to look more closely. The weathered, red brick on first appearance looked just like the other hand-hewn pavers that covered the side patio.

'What caught my eye?' Roger thought. And then, he saw. The mortar around the brick had a glow to it: oddly translucent, yet brighter and more distinct in the thin crack between brick and mortar. It was as if something burned under the brick and sent luminous rays up wherever they could be released. As Roger watched, the mortar edge shimmered, flickered, and appeared to brighten. Its intensity rose quickly, though it moved back and forth from bright white to gold to orange and red.

'That is too odd. Cool, but odd. Wonder what's causing it?'

Roger reached down to touch, but both brick and mortar were cool. He looked around the patio. Only the shady section nearest the house shimmered and burned with this backlight dancing intensely. A circular section of illuminated bricks grew as Roger watched. *'What the heck?'* thought Roger, as he stood perplexed, his newspapers and bag long forgotten on the lawn. He continued staring as the circle of light expanded.

The circle stopped growing at five feet in diameter. Roger stood just outside the circumference, wondering what would happen next or whether the light would just disappear. The circle of outlined bricks continued glowing.

'What if I dug up some bricks? There must be something going on behind them . . . ' Roger knelt down and tugged the edge of a brick fruitlessly. He whacked the side of his head, *'You idiot: they're not gonna come up. They're cemented in place.'*

As he sat back on his haunches, his butt landing on the ground, he noted that the sparkling outlines blinked–as if some unseen hand was throwing a toggle switch, turning some on and others off. The twinkling of the brick outlines was a real mystery; it reminded him of the omnipresent white lights that decorated the town at Christmas. He watched, mesmerized by the quivering flame-colored outlines blinking on and off.

As he watched, trancelike, he started to realize that some of the outlines stayed off, and others blinked less and less frequently. As the minutes passed, some of the outlines didn't turn off at all. Like watching the lights in a small town wink off at night as various townspeople headed to bed, some outlines burned out and others stayed on like sentries guarding the town. It was only after nearly fifteen minutes of watching the light show, that realization dawned. The highlighted brick outlines looked suspiciously like block letters. When Roger stood and leaned up against the house, he confirmed his suspicion: each illuminated line contributed to letters, which miraculously spelled out words—all within the glowing circle's edge.

CHOOSE LIFE
GO DANCE
COFFEE NOT FREE

"What's that all about? That is one odd friggin' set of words. I don't get it." Roger looked around. He wondered if anyone else had seen the words, but the house and the street remained quiet. The words flickered and burned as the afternoon sun waned. Roger wondered if his eyes deceived him. He rubbed them hard and looked. The odd phrase continued to shimmer on the ground among the weather-worn red bricks.

"Hey, Roger. Wassup?" shouted Jesse good-naturedly from his bike in front of the Langdons'. "What are you doin' back there?" Roger broke from his reverie and focused on Jesse.

"Bro, you gotta see this! Come over here," Roger shouted back.

Jesse leaned his bike on the fence and leapt across.

Roger grinned as he watched Jesse land on the grassy side of the wrought iron, "Better watch the equipment, Bud. You—"

Jesse interrupted with a laugh, "Not to worry, Dawg. I'm cool . . . and very clear of the fence. What are you doin' prowling around the Langdon place?"

"You won't believe this. You gotta see this."

The guys walked across the grass toward the patio. "You sure it's okay for me to be here? I don't want any hassle from the old lady. She's mean."

"She's okay. I don't think she's around . . . hasn't been. You gotta check this out."

"What are you so jazzed about?"

The boys entered the patio and the blazing circle was still boldly apparent.

"Whoa. Would you look at that? What's that all about?" Jesse strode quickly across the bricks. "That is just the coolest. How'd you do that?"

"I didn't do it. It just sorta happened while I was standing here watching."

"Boy, that's cool. You should take a picture. I've never seen anything like—"

Roger interrupted, "I'm really glad you can see it. I thought I was going nuts. Look at it from this side." The boys walked to the house-side of the circle, all the time watching the glowing circle. As they rounded the circle, Jesse shouted out:

"Wow! Words. This is wicked cool. Maybe it's some sci-fi thing." Standing still, Jesse sorted out the letters. "What the—? What's that all about? Weird words. Think it's some saying? Maybe Old Lady Langdon had it put in."

"No friggin' way. Why would you write that? What kind of saying is: 'Choose Life. Go Dance. Coffee Not Free'? That's one whacked-out thing to write."

"Yeah, I don't get it. So what are you gonna do about it?"

"Beats me. I guess just leave. I gotta finish my papers. Wanna ride along?"

The boys finished the last couple of papers and then pedaled the extra mile to Dunkin' Donuts for a snack. "The Dunk" was a popular local high school hangout on the edge of town. Inside a throng of locals congregated; the Dunk was hopping.

The guys each bought a doughnut and moved to a table. They were joined by a couple of other freshman guys. They were horsing around when a group of ninth grade girls walked through the doors. The girls looked over and broke into big smiles.

"Hey, Roger, I think she's got it baaa-d for you," razzed Jordan. "I think she wants you." Wearing her tight jeans and blue and pink striped polo shirt, Melissa Hillcoat looked over and smiled again, letting her long blonde hair fall just so.

"I can read 'em like a book," added Bobby. "She's sweet on you."

Roger blushed under his tan. The blood rushed to his head. "Guys, cut it out," he snapped. "Be cool."

"You just might be a little sweet on her too," leered Jordan.

Roger shoved Jordan's shoulder causing him to bounce into the window on the side of their booth. "I don't want to hear it. What about you and Lindsey? Seems you've got a little something for her . . . "

"No way, man. She's history. Absolute zero interest but back to the main event: you and Missy . . . "

"Hey, look she's checking you out again," Bobby added. Sure enough, Melissa looked their way. She then leaned over and whispered to her girlfriends. With resolution in her step, she strode over.

"Hey, guys. What are you up to?" she beamed her all-American smile, after three years of braces.

The guys stammered staccato replies.

"Hey, I wondered, Roger, if you, uh, might have a moment to–uh," Melissa paused expectantly. Roger wavered between excitement and embarrassment over receiving her megawatt attention.

"He certainly has time for you, Melissa," Jordan nudged Roger in the side.

"Of course, anything you want to tell Roger, you can share with us too . . . " smirked Bobby.

Melissa frowned, "Hey, if now's not a good time, I'll just–"

"Forget these idiots," interrupted Roger as he stood. "I was just about to leave."

"Leave? You just got here, man. What are you talking about?" Bobby persisted.

"Let him have his moment of glory," suggested Jesse. "He'll be back soon enough. Hope she lets him down easy."

Outside, Melissa plunged headlong into a rapid-fire, nerve-induced invitation:

"Well, I was just wondering . . . well, there's this thing going on at Whittaker in a couple of weeks. It's kinda like a Homecoming, and I was thinking . . . well, they're having music, and a band, and–I think there's going to be some dancing. Well, I don't really care about the dancing, but I was wondering and sorta hoping that maybe you and I could, uhh, go together to this, uh, dance-like thing . . . " Melissa trailed off. Catching her breath, she looked at the ground and then Roger's Nikes.

Early on, Roger figured out where Melissa was headed, which allowed him to think. Dancing was really not his thing. He downright hated dancing, but Melissa was cute and maybe they wouldn't have to dance much. In his heart, he recognized that these things always went the same way: girls love to dance. He just couldn't, even if Melissa's megavolt smile made him feel like jelly. As Melissa paused, the ensuing awkward quiet forced Roger to remember the bricks.

CHOOSE LIFE
GO DANCE
COFFEE NOT FREE

"That's really odd," he erupted unexpectedly aloud.

"Oh, I see. I didn't know if you'd want to or not–" Melissa replied apologetically.

Roger looked up, "Oh, no, not that you asked is really odd. No, I'm sorry," Roger stuttered. "I was just thinking of–no, it's not important."

Silence reigned once more.

"Well, if you want to think about it . . . " Melissa's smile disappeared.

"Choose Life. Go Dance" resonated. *'What a wild coincidence,'* he thought this time determinedly in silence. *"'Go Dance' indeed,"* he reflected. Oddly, it fit.

"Okay, I'll do it," he said with more conviction than he felt. "I'd like that."

"Really?" a very surprised Melissa smiled a big grin. "That's great. Well, we can talk through the details. Call me, okay?"

"Yeah sure, I'll do that," Roger smiled shyly back.

"Oh, here comes my gang, I've gotta go. This is gonna be great. Well, I'll see you," and Melissa was swallowed up by the passing group of girls and disappeared down the sidewalk, leaving a dazed and confused Roger.

"What was that all about, Bud?" queried Jesse on Roger's return to the table. The entire scene, of course, had been avidly watched by the guys. Only because Jesse had bodily held Jordan's arms had the guys refrained from pounding on the window–to what would have been their delight and Roger's complete mortification.

"Nothing. Homework thing," stammered Roger.

"Yeah, right. You don't want to tell your best friends what's going on . . . she's sweet on you. I can just tell," Jordan never let girl issues fade.

Shortly afterward, Roger rose. He and Jesse headed for the door. "Later, Buds" they both said to Bobby and Jordan who had decided to do homework while sitting at the table. Outside, the boys mounted their bikes and headed for the street when Roger stopped abruptly.

"Hey, wait a minute. I told my mom I'd buy her some decaf."

Jesse halted. "I'll wait out here. You don't need to lock your bike again."

"Thanks." Roger headed back toward the doors.

"Hey, Rog–just remember: 'Coffee Not Free" ya know!" Jesse's laughter was joined by Roger's as he went inside.

"Yeah, nothing's free. No free lunch, my dad always says," he mused.

At the counter, Roger ordered the pound of decaf coffee–finely ground, but not too fine. As the guy handed over the pound of coffee, Roger gave him a ten dollar bill. Moments later, the cashier handed back the change.

"Fifty-nine cents makes eight dollars, two ones makes ten, and another ten makes twenty. Thanks so much, and hopefully we'll see you again real soon!" The clerk turned away to wait on the next customer. Roger stood there perplexed. It happened so quickly. Suddenly, he stood with the coffee and with more money than he held at the start of the transaction.

He walked outside with the bag of coffee and $12.59 in change. "You won't believe this," he started with Jesse. "I just got the coffee for free."

"Get off it. No way."

"Way. Really. I gave the guy a ten dollar bill and he gave me the coffee and more than twelve dollars back."

"You are one lucky guy. Real lucky."

"I'm not sure. Wait a minute. That's too coincidental. Did you put him up to that?"

"No way. How could I? I didn't know you were gonna go back and get coffee. Why would he let you out of the store without paying?"

"I've gotta give the money back. It's not right."

"Hey, his mistake. Your win. I'd go with it," countered Jesse.

"No, I can't," replied Roger. "The message on the bricks. 'Coffee Not Free,' you know."

"Hogwash. Purely coincidental. I'd call the extra ten bucks a lucky break."

"Okay, well then how do you explain this and also getting asked out to a dance, all within an hour of reading the bricks?"

"Whoa, wait a minute. You got asked out to a dance?" Jesse stopped quizzically. "So, that's what Melissa wanted."

"Okay, so it's what she wanted. Big deal. I'm going to a dance, but–"

"But nothing; you hate dances. So do I. You gotta dress like a dweeb and hang out. You can't be serious . . . "

"Well, I am. I thought about the brick notes. 'Go Dance'–remember? Hey, I figured I should go. Now the bricks are saying, 'Coffee Not Free.' It's too odd. I have to give the money back. It's the right thing to do."

"You are one sick puppy. Maybe you're love-sick, but you go do what you gotta do."

Before Jesse even finished his statement, Roger was back inside, explaining the mistake and returning the extra ten dollar bill–much to the relief and surprise of the cashier.

On the ride home, they discussed the bricks again.

"Okay, so Rog–the bricks told you what to do about the dance and the coffee, but what's 'Choose Life'? What's that all about?"

"You got me. Maybe it was meant for someone else. Maybe the bricks send messages to whoever is standing there."

"Hey, Man. I was standing there too. I didn't get any message. Just you."

"Yeah, well, I got there first. I don't know what 'Choose Life' means."

"Sounds more ominous. They sound, well, kinda everyday like, ya know?"

"Yeah, makes me kinda nervous. Hey, I've got an idea. Let's stop by again and see if the words are still there . . . or maybe there'll be something different."

The guys pedaled to the Langdon house, which they found still desolate and quiet. Several lights showed, but they were probably timer-activated rather than suggesting life behind the window shades.

The freshmen crept to the side patio. Being past five, it was nearly pitch black, save a sliver of light from a neighbor's spotlight that shone through the shrubs lining the property's perimeter.

Roger whispered, "Look, the circle is glowing."

"Yeah," replied Jesse. "But where are the words?" As he finished, the bricks suddenly illuminated.

CHOOSE LIFE
GO DANCE
COFFEE NOT FREE

"Well, look at that. It's still there," murmured Roger. The words shone out quite brightly, though as the boys watched, the phrases began to change. 'Go Dance' flickered and faded to black. Then, 'Coffee Not Free' twinkled brightly and sputtered out. The circle remained—a blaze of quiet fire. Inside it, 'Choose Life' glowed ominously with unearthly luminescence.

"What the—" started Jesse.

Roger nodded his head, "It knows."

"What do you mean, it knows?" whispered Jesse.

"I followed its instructions. It's like a checklist."

"Buddy, you're warped. How could it know?"

"No clue. It's haunted, but it knows. And the last direction is still there. I need to remember it."

"Choose Life? Well, hopefully, that's not exactly a hard one to recall."

"I sure hope not."

Adrenaline and nerves kicked in as both guys sprinted back to the front of the house where they climbed on their bikes and whisked off into the gathering darkness.

NINE

The weekend passed mercifully through a haze of leftover anesthesia and painkillers. Beverly dutifully stayed at Bernice's side. Bill showed up each day as well, working around playing kid chauffeur. Caitlyn and Brad came to see their grandmother on Sunday afternoon. The visit was short, and Bernice remembered little of it.

Monday morning dawned crisp and clear. While generally past peak foliage colors, Bernice could see some bright reds and oranges from across the campus. She awakened more alert than she'd been since Friday before surgery. Her abdomen hurt but was bearable. She lay in bed wondering what the prognosis was now that surgery was completed.

Nurses came and went from Room 518 monitoring her stats and the status of the morphine pump. Bill had insisted on a private room and, for that, Bernice was thankful. She had not shared her gratitude; she figured Bill knew.

"I believe we can take you off that pump today, Mrs. Langdon," chirped one cheery nurse as she moved about the room. "I suspect the medication may be worse than the pain," she chuckled as she opened the drapes and tilted the blinds.

"I think not. Have you had this surgery before?" grunted Bernice.

"No, but I have had three C-sections. The incision is similar; in fact, one of them was an emergency C-section so my incision, like yours, is vertical. That one hurt like a bugger. So, I have some sense of what you might be feeling."

Bernice was taken aback. Bernice detested cerebral practitioners who believed that reading about the efficacy of certain approaches, therapies, and drugs was equivalent to actually experiencing them. Whenever some group of interns or residents came through following an attending physician, she became a specimen under the microscope. *'Someone should teach bedside manner,'* she thought.

Bernice turned on the TV. All the news was dreadful and depressing; war with Afghanistan, growing tensions with Iraq, murders, and crime filled the airwaves. She channel-surfed and looked for entertainment. She finally settled for the Weather Channel—a rather benign haven.

She picked at breakfast—a bland array of liquids and semi-solids that Dr. Gerhart suggested. She had no appetite and nothing much appealed to her palate, save the supply of ice chips she perpetually asked nurses and visitors to bring her.

"Goddamn hospital. I hate the place," she groused as the hours stretched endlessly ahead. She suspected Dr. Gerhart would stop by this morning. She hoped to have a clear head to hear the implications and next steps. The thought was barely articulated when the blonde physician strode into the room.

"Good morning, Doc," replied Bernice. "I was hoping you'd be through. So what's the plan?"

"Well good morning to you too!" The physician smiled, "Not one to mince words, are you? Just get right to the point." She paused. "I looked in on you throughout the weekend. You were heavily sedated. I thought it best to delay a conversation until now. How are you feeling?"

"Well, I'm not ready for the forty-yard dash, but I'll do. The incision is sore. My insides are a jumbled mess. Everything feels abused."

"To be expected. You had major surgery." The surgeon pushed up her wire-rimmed progressive lenses. "I want to discuss a proposal for moving forward." She looked at Bernice expectantly, but the professor merely stared back.

"Go on," Bernice put up a brave front, though her face paled.

"We removed eight malignancies throughout your abdominal cavity. The good news: they were each relatively well-contained. Like the first biopsy, the tumors were exceptionally dense. The bad news: there were quite a few. While we took all we could see, I am concerned about further metastasis. This cancer is aggressive. The tumors appear to move quickly and are recurring at secondary sites with great speed."

Bernice nodded gravely. "I see," she said. "I'd say the suspense is killing me, but I think there's something else doing the job." Bernice tried for humor, but fell flat. The doctor looked over the top of her glasses which were sliding down again.

She grimaced mildly. "I've consulted with Doctors Elway and Esch."

Bernice interrupted, "Sounds like a law firm. Who's Esch?"

"Dr. Esch is a noted oncologist dealing with a host of cancers, primarily those which present initially in the abdominal cavity. He is a distinguished expert in the metastasis of aggressive malignancies, with a focus on adenocarcinomas. Many times, his patients have had cases that presented initially with ambiguous origins."

"But I thought this originated in the colon?"

"Perhaps. While difficult to pinpoint with certainty, in reality it doesn't change the plan."

"Not at all?" Bernice paused, confused.

"Your case fits Dr. Esch's area of study quite well. He has written several papers on the treatment of said cancers and specializes in the various chemotherapies available to . . . "

"Doc, I appreciate his academic credentials, but does he cure people?"

"Oh my, yes. He's been highly successful with a host of patients. While all cancers have an assessed mortality, Dr. Esch has been well above the norms with his "cocktail" approach to cancer treatment. His five-year survival rate and his time to initial remission are well–I mean well–above average. While quite promising, all patients have unique progressions, and you can't base decisions and expectations wholly on track records. In fact–"

Bernice interrupted again. "Save the legal fine print. I get it. No guarantees, but he's the best the university has?"

"Without a doubt. He would like to meet you and, most likely, take you on as a patient."

"Has anyone really told him what to expect?" queried Bernice slyly.

Dr. Gerhart grinned, "I've let him in on your style–shall we say? I think you'll find him to your liking. He's direct and bold. He is, how shall we say this? He's not a bullshitter."

Later that afternoon, a white-coated physician who looked to be in his early thirties appeared. Of medium height with a runner's build and ash blond hair, Dr. Esch knocked as he entered.

"Professor Langdon?" his eyes twinkled. "Are you *the* Professor Langdon?"

Bernice looked up through her spectacles. "That would be me. What's this? Visiting day for the interns? I've already had my vitals taken within the hour. If you'd like to get me a cup of coffee, I would be quite delighted."

The doctor laughed. "Jeremy Esch, at your service. I hear you're recovering from surgery. I'm here to help you with your sit-ups. Nothing like them to help mend the abs."

Bernice couldn't help but chuckle. "Okay, you found me. Where'd you go to undergrad?"

"Oh, just some little school in Pennsylvania, but I've been out of there twenty-five years."

"A child prodigy? What's this: Doogie Howser?" Bernice laughed again over her glasses. "My stomach hurts. Stop. Be a doctor. Stop with the comedy."

Jeremy let out a belly laugh. "I can tell we're gonna get along just fine, Professor. Do you prefer Professor? Or Mrs. Langdon?"

"I come to whatever. I'm not picky. At my age, it doesn't pay to be picky."

"Dr. Gerhart suggested we connect. I've reviewed your files both pre- and post surgeries. You have a very interesting case."

"I only go for interesting. I've waited this long to get something, and I certainly wanted to get it good."

"That you have gotten." Dr. Esch became more serious. "You do have one aggressive bugger of a malignancy. It appears that Dr. G got all visible evidence in the most recent round–even some that was effectively hidden in the CT scans and ultrasounds. But with this type of metastasizing adenocarcinoma, you can never be too certain." He looked at Bernice more carefully, assessing how she was following him, and inquiring with his eyes if she had questions. She did not, so he proceeded.

"Professor, I believe–"

Bernice interrupted. "You know, Doc, if we're going to work together for some time–which I sense we are–you should call me Bernice."

"If that's okay with you . . . " Dr. Esch paused awkwardly. "Well, Bernice, I believe a new and more novel approach to chemo is appropriate. While many surgeons and advising oncologists would recommend a singular approach with one of the leading-edge cancer fighters, I prefer a multiplicity of pharma . . . .some call it a "cocktail" approach to fighting the Big C."

"Yes, Dr. Gerhart referenced your work with cocktail drug therapy. I've certainly read of the efficacy of such approaches on AIDS and similar auto-immune disorders; I'm less up to date on its use and results with more standard cancers . . . " Bernice trailed off.

"Say no more. My research–recently funded by a grant from NIH–has shown preferential rates of both remission and apparent long-term cessation of metastasis through an analog approach to what is used in HIV-positive patients. I have to tell you it's still clearly in an investigative stage, but I'm finding this well-controlled and monitored "cocktail" of sorts leads to quite impressive returns. While nothing is certain, I believe . . . "

"Save the legal mumbo jumbo. Tell me the difference in remission rates for single-drug versus multiple-drug regimens."

With that, Jeremy Esch got down to business and went through the details of the different approaches being embraced by the medical community. He also shared his story of early interest in multiple-drug approaches (fueled by several friends of his gay brother who had contracted AIDS in the eighties) and his recent studies on the subject.

During their meeting, Dr. Esch scribbled a number of hard-to-read charts and factoids on his clipboard to share with Bernice. She engaged energetically, as she once did with her university colleagues; her old color and persistence in getting to truth showed. Toward the end of their discussion, Beverly arrived outside the door. Though concerned when she first arrived, she quietly observed her mother-in-law and this new physician going at it in a congenial, yet highly dynamic manner.

When Dr. Esch paused, Beverly entered. "Hello, Mother."

"Beverly, this is my oncologist, Dr. Jeremy Esch. This is my son's wife,

Beverly Langdon."

"We were just wrapping up," said the doctor. "In fact," he looked at his watch, "I really must run. Do you have questions, Bernice?"

Beverly's head shot up hearing her mother-in-law's name. A quizzical look passed over her face quickly, which Bernice noticed.

"What? You've never heard my first name?" Beverly shrugged, as Bernice looked back to the physician. "No, I don't. It sounds like 'cocktails' are the way to go, though I've always had a penchant for wine." She paused, allowing Dr. Esch to smile. "I'm convinced. When do we get underway?"

"We'll get you signed up for the trials of this approach. We can start quickly, though I'd like you to regain your strength post surgery before the first round. While chemo tends to be cumulative–as I'm sure you know," Bernice nodded sagely in response as Dr. Esch continued. "That initial dose can really knock you back. I want to be as certain as possible that you're ready to do battle."

"Oh, I'll be ready to fight. Some suggest I'm feisty."

"You? Really? I had no idea," smirked Dr. Esch.

Beverly interjected, "Have you already gone over the side effects, frequency of treatments . . . "

Bernice grimaced, but Dr. Esch answered. "I believe we've covered all that ground, but I'd be happy to email you information if you wish. I believe we should start on Monday –a week from today–with the first round. We do it right here at the Medical Center." The women nodded in return.

"Good. Monday it is. Call my office. Arrange a time. I suggest late morning. Don't eat too big a breakfast. Keep it light. You might become nauseous. Then again, you may not. It affects people in different ways. Expect to be with us for several hours, though perhaps somewhat longer on the first day, while they set up your file. Have someone come with you, Bernice."

With that, Dr. Esch and Beverly exchanged email addresses, and he was off.

Bernice closed her eyes once the doctor departed. Remaining focused, keeping her energy high, and engaging as she did proved exhausting. She was drained.

"I liked him even though my visit with him was short. I take it you liked him too?"

"Yes, he's a good man and realistic. His sense of humor should make this whole thing bearable."

"His results are good? I gather they're experimental."

"Beverly, nothing's guaranteed. But at this point, nothing could be guaranteed."

“I’ll arrange an appointment?”

“Yes, that would be grand.”

“You look tired. Shall I let you rest?”

Bernice nodded and lifted off her glasses.

“I’ll stop back this evening. Bill wants to visit as well. Perhaps after dinner, we can stop with the kids. I was thinking . . . ” But Bernice never heard what Beverly thought as she dropped off to sleep. The visit proved more draining and unnerving than she had realized. Her sleep was dreamless and deep.

Beverly left quietly, leaving a voicemail for Bill. “Most engaged I’ve seen your mother since the initial diagnosis and first surgery. She really connected with the oncologist. I hope she stays just as upbeat and energetic. Chemo starts Monday.”

TEN

Late October sunshine streamed through the stained glass windows of Bedrock Hills Presbyterian Church. The three Altar Guild ladies worked at a measured pace positioning the newly dry-cleaned vestments. They chatted quietly as the organist practiced the Sunday prelude on the majestic pipe organ. After getting the green tapestries hung, the ladies turned to the communion settings.

"Do you think the trays need polish?" inquired Doris. "They look dull from a distance, but my eyesight is not what it used to be." Janet, another petite gray-haired matriarch of the church, surveyed the stacked silver servers.

"They look okay. If you believe they could use a once-over, I can run a cloth over them."

"Peg, what do you think?"

Peg scanned the silver tower as Janet brought it toward the altar. "I don't see any fingerprints. Then again, better safe than sorry! You know how Lois Jennings can be!" They all laughed. Lois was a loudly opinionated member of the congregation.

Janet walked back to the adjoining supply room. She brought back polish and soft cloths. "I'll do them. No problem at all."

As Janet worked, Peg and Doris retrieved the black and white alphanumerics and began placing them on the board above the lectern to identify the week's hymns.

"So, I was wondering how your daughter-in-law was doing? I've been praying for her."

Doris paused at the hymn board and looked over at Janet. "She's coming along well. No doubt prayer has really helped. Her incisions are healing. The doctors say she needs to watch what she eats in the short-term–nothing spicy, nothing too unusual–but with Brooke, she's not likely to do that! Jake has been so helpful."

Janet nodded, "I'm so pleased to hear. I've been so concerned."

"How are the children?" questioned Peg.

"Doing fine. You know how kids are. They barely acknowledge she was in the hospital. It was nearly outpatient surgery, you know." The other two shook their heads. "It is mind-boggling how quickly they move you out. Brooke was home in less than forty-eight hours!"

"When I had my Caesarean, my heavens, I was in the hospital more than a week. Her surgery must have been similar to remove that ovarian cyst," Janet suggested.

"The world has certainly changed."

"True enough," concluded Doris.

Janet finished polishing. "Better?" She stated it as a question, but didn't sound like she planned to do more.

"Yes, very nice. Lois should have nothing to criticize on Sunday," commented Doris.

Janet stepped back and looked at their collective work. The sanctuary sparkled in the crisp fall sunlight. The silver communion pieces added sparkling elegance. Having stopped practice, the organist was packing up. The church exuded a quiet, comfortable presence. *'This truly is God's House,'* thought Janet.

Peg and Doris came up beside her. "Penny for your thoughts?" smiled Doris.

Janet responded thoughtfully, "It really is beautiful, isn't it? I always feel more centered when I leave, whether on Sunday or a day like today. God is in this place."

"He most certainly is," agreed Doris. Looking down at her watch, she continued, "I've got to be on my way. I'm supposed to be over at Brooke and Jake's within the hour. Peg, I'll give you a lift?"

Peg accepted. "Janet, are you staying?"

"Yes, I have some work in the office. After stepping down from church council, Dr. Andrews asked if I would keep an eye on the books. It's a wonderful day to walk home."

With warm assurances that the three would see each other on Sunday, Peg and Doris left. Janet stepped slowly around the now empty sanctuary. The sixty-five-year-old retired executive secretary offered up silent prayers. She was thankful for so much–good health, her family, her friends, and her deepening relationship with God. She finished her quiet words with the Lord, reverently left the sanctuary, and headed to the church office.

After a few quick words with Verna, the secretary, she collected the ledgers and the bag of receipts from the past Sunday's offering plate. She also picked up the inbound checks and deposit tickets from the mail. Janet moved to the staff workroom. She liked this room with its small window overlooking the front doors of the church and the expansive lawn. The border of stained glass yielded warmth in the room as the sun hit it and cascaded onto the desk.

Before starting on the books, Janet looked over the upcoming Sunday bulletin. This week's sermon was entitled, "Living the Unstuffed Life."

'What an interesting theme,' she thought. *'It certainly is appropriate in*

today's overstructured world, with overpacked agendas and time-constrained schedules. Steve should hear this one. He works too hard and doesn't have enough time for his family,' she sighed. A warm smile crossed her countenance as she thought of her oldest son. Even with far less time from Steve than she would choose, his young family was thriving.

She scanned the bulletin, noting the many activities as Bedrock Hills marched through mid-autumn. Her eyes paused on the list of parishioners who were ill or convalescing. She made a mental note to visit Hilda Baumgartner. After being widowed and seeing the kids move away, she had moved to a retirement community. After nearly twenty years, her health had recently been declining. Seeing Hilda's name, Janet wondered if she had taken a downward turn.

Below Hilda's name:

Bernice Langdon – recuperating from surgery at University Medical Center.

Bernice was not a church regular, but Janet–knowing nearly everyone associated with the church–could identify Dr. Langdon. The former professor was fighting cancer. Bad news moved through the church at lightning speed. As her perusal continued, Janet fleetingly considered visiting Bernice.

Janet finished the bulletin and turned to the books. An hour later, she removed her bifocals and rubbed her eyes. She grimaced, "It just can't be. I've gone over the numbers at least four times. The receipts don't match the deposit ticket for the bank. Where am I off? Odd. This is the fourth week that the numbers don't align. I must be missing something. The receipts show almost $250 more than the bank deposit . . . " She trailed off. "I know I jotted that down last week. Let me see where I put it." She rummaged through her purse until she found her small address book.

"I knew I'd written it down." For the last three weeks, Janet had noted three discrepancies–each entered in her rounded handwriting. The first week had been less than $25, then just over $50, and then last week almost $150. Including the current deposit shortfall, the month's total neared $500. *'My goodness,'* thought Janet. *'I can't be making that many mistakes. There is something wrong here. Would going back further turn up more?'*

"Verna?" Janet stuck her head out of the workroom. The secretary looked up. "Do you keep the tallies for the weekly church offering?"

"Of course. They're filed right here. Why?"

"I just want to take a look and compare them with the ledger, that's all," Janet suggested innocently.

"Something wrong?"

"I don't believe so. Just a periodic look I like to take for auditing our processes."

Verna seemed satisfied. She handed over the bulky files for the calendar year. "My goodness, that is a lot of paper!" Janet laughed, and Verna smiled back. *'Good,'* thought Janet. *'Verna will, hopefully, not be spreading rumors about my curiosity. I need a little time to see if I can find my mistake.'*

"You know, perhaps I could just borrow these overnight? I don't want to get started and have paperwork spread out all over when it's time for you to leave."

Verna looked relieved. "Thank you. I was worried I wouldn't get out of here on time if you were in the middle of a project. I need to leave promptly this afternoon, perhaps even a little early," she smiled conspiratorially. "My mother-in-law is coming this evening, and I'm just not ready."

"Of course. Let me collect my things, and I'll be on my way." Moments later as Janet departed, Verna surveyed the bulging bag with curiosity, but not being numbers-oriented, she ruminated no further on the accounting books.

The walk home felt longer with the heavy bag, but Janet took her time. When she reached home, Walt was just unlocking the side door. "Hello, Hon," she called out. Walt, a late-sixties contemporary of Janet's, turned and smiled easily. His tanned face was in sharp contrast to his full head of silver white hair and sharp blue eyes.

"What do you have there?" he inquired.

"Just some paperwork from the church."

"You and your projects," Walt smiled. "I suppose you'll be up half the night with this one?" He gave Janet a quick peck on the lips.

Janet chuckled. "I sure hope not." With her soulmate and personal bedrock now beside her, the money issue seemed less dire. "I'm just doing some detective work."

The couple grabbed a quick bite to eat, comparing their mornings. For the afternoon, Walt planned to work on one of his birdhouses in his basement workshop. Janet mentioned visiting Hilda later in the day. Visiting Bernice Langdon was forgotten.

With lunch finished, Walt headed downstairs. Janet moved to the dining room and unpacked the files. *'I'll work on this for an hour,'* she thought. The grandfather clock in the foyer struck two o'clock. She smiled, *'That sets a clear deadline. I'll just listen for three.'*

Walt came back upstairs periodically throughout the afternoon. Each time, he looked in on Janet who was buried in paper. Beyond getting her an iced tea when he got his own, Janet needed nothing.

As the sun cast lengthening shadows across the dining room, Janet finally closed the ledger book and put the last of the files back. The clock chimed the half hour. *'Running a little late,'* she thought absently. Walt stuck his head in the dining room, "So, what are we thinking for dinner?"

"I suppose I'll pick something up on my way home from Hilda's. I really should get over there."

"You're still going? It's after five thirty. She's probably at dinner."

"Five thirty? It can't be. I just wanted to spend—" Janet studied her watch. "Oh my, I can't believe it's so late. I guess we do need to think about dinner. I'm sorry."

"I could tell you were deep into it, but I am famished. Let's just go out."

"I didn't mean to make us go out. I can pull something from the freezer. It'll just take a few minutes. Really . . . "

"Get a coat. We'll do something light at Isaacson's. I can almost taste their sandwiches."

Janet acquiesced, and they drove to the deli. Over sandwiches and decaf coffee, they talked about the kids, Walt's morning golf game, Peg and Doris at church, and university football. After ordering dessert to share, Walt focused more seriously.

"So, what's this big project? You work on it all afternoon, and then not one word over dinner?"

Janet looked back at her husband of forty-five years. "Well, I just thought I was making a mistake. I figured there had to be something I was missing . . . "

"Whoa, whoa, whoa." Walt held up both hands, palms facing Janet. "I'm not tracking. What mistake? Start at the beginning."

Janet launched into the deepening mystery of the missing money and her afternoon quest to discover her error. Starting in mid-March, discrepancies began occurring. Initially, the errors were modest and infrequent: twenty or twenty-five dollars every two or three weeks. From mid-May onward, the mistakes became weekly. Other than two weeks in August when church receipts precisely matched bank deposits, every week was in error, with amounts ranging between $25 and $75. Recently, the errors escalated significantly. Alarmingly, all of the errors were in one direction: church receipts always exceeded bank deposits. As best Janet could calculate, roughly $1200 was missing.

Walt listened carefully. "Hmmmm," he responded periodically. No apparent holes existed; the story was compelling.

"Do you think it's possible one of the pastors is doing a special outreach or community service effort of some kind . . . maybe supporting someone that he wants kept quiet? Perhaps someone who doesn't want to be identified as needing charity? It's probably something like that." Walt paused.

Janet looked skeptical. "I'd like to believe that, but the church can keep things very quiet. You don't want any appearance of impropriety. Having been on Council for six years, I sure know that."

Walt persisted. "I'll bet Dr. Andrews or one of the Associates is aware. It's not that much money at the end of the day. I don't think you should worry about it." He smiled. "I know it bothers your sense of detail and closure. You like things—how do they say it?—buttoned up."

Janet smiled, "You think so?" She paused. "You're likely right. This is probably a wild goose chase. My overeager imagination got away from me. Too many detective spy-thrillers." She laughed.

After a comfortably quiet evening, Walt headed to bed early as he planned to attend a men's breakfast meeting in the morning. Janet stayed up to watch a news magazine program and then the late news at eleven o'clock.

Around 11:45, Janet woke with a start. She had dozed off and missed Jay Leno's monologue. He was now doing a man-on-the-street segment, Jaywalking. At first, Janet did not notice the bright border on the edge of her screen, but as she became more fully awake, she couldn't avoid noting the growing light.

'What is that?' she wondered. *'Is the TV conking out? It's less than two years old.'* The perimeter exuded an odd bluish-white light, surreal in its strengthening brilliance. Staring at the screen, Janet thought something might be burning in the back of the TV. The light shimmered and danced as its intensity grew. Walking to the set, she felt a slight, normal vibration with the sound, but otherwise, it was cool. The perimeter widened until it was roughly a two-inch strip.

Janet considered waking Walt, but she hesitated. *'It's not on fire. It must be a malfunction of some sort. He can't do anything about it this evening. I'll just tell him in the morning. It should go away if I turn it off.'*

Back on the sofa, Janet touched the remote, and the picture disappeared. The blazing perimeter did not. She touched the remote again and back came Jay Leno, now with a heavily tattooed blue-haired young man. The intense white-lit edge remained.

Again, Janet turned off the set. The illumination stayed constant. She decided the best course of action was to deal with the issue in the morning. Behind the TV, she grappled with many cables and cords until she found the right one. It, too, felt cool, but she determinedly pulled it from the wall.

The perimeter flickered, faded momentarily, and then burst back to its full brilliance. The darkened screen fluttered like a black flag in a breeze. The white-light fire behind made the faux flag wave.

'This is rather fascinating,' thought Janet. *'Maybe I should rouse Walt just to see it. How could it still be lit when it's unplugged? Maybe I got the wrong cable; it's a real jungle back there.'* Janet returned to her hands and knees searching, cable by cable. Believing she had pulled the right one, she now disconnected all of the wires and cables from the wall, disrupting the stereo components, the grandkids' video game, and what had to be the TV. For safe measure, she also unplugged the lamp. The room was now dark, save the continuing light from the shimmering screen's perimeter, as well as some light coming from the kitchen.

However, when she looked up at the screen, words beamed. The words appeared burnt into the center of the screen. They matched the light on the edge. They danced like bright light from an arc welder's torch hitting a pool of diamonds.

COLLEAGUE   C BERNICE AP $
TELL ANDREWS   SOON

Janet stood quietly. She watched the words, wondering if they would change or disappear. The words kept shimmering in the darkness. *'What could this be?'* she wondered. *'Perhaps I should write this down. I really should wake Walt.'* The worries over the church money washed over her again. Something was not right at the church. She felt an odd sense about it despite Walt's reassurances. Her mind raced in a jumbled fashion; her pulse accelerated.

Janet grabbed the notepad next to the phone. In the dark, she quickly scribbled down the message. *'Where's it coming from? It's so specific.'* Janet rubbed her eyes and cleaned her glasses with the ever-present cloth in her pocket.

COLLEAGUE   C BERNICE AP $
TELL ANDREWS   SOON

Janet's mind raced through possible interpretations. *'Who is this 'colleague'?'* she wondered. *'And Bernice: From church, perhaps? AP $? The dollar sign seems straightforward. It must stand for money. But AP?'* Accounts Payable was her first thought, but she couldn't place that. The kids' Advanced Placement tests years earlier bore no apparent relevance. *'Tell Andrews and Soon seem to be the most straightforward,'* she reflected. *'Though how soon?'*

Her thoughts toppled over one another in their race to be articulated and clear in her mind. "Perhaps Walt will make sense of it," she spoke aloud as she turned to move from the room. As she did, the light dimmed. The perimeter faded. The words were not as bright as just moments ago. When she turned back to the TV, the light brightened again. *'How very odd,'* thought Janet. *'It's for me, I imagine.'* She turned to walk to the kitchen. *'Perhaps a glass of water will help me wake up and think more clearly,'* though Janet felt decidedly quite awake. As she walked toward the adjoining room, the study faded to black. The shimmering, burning light disappeared.

Returning with her glass of water, the screen stayed dark. No more burning lights. She turned on a different light to brighten the room. With some light, Janet reconnected the TV, and the set returned to life. Jay now interviewed a young actress starring in a hit TV series. The border on Janet's TV was normal. No words burned across the screen. *'What a dream!'* she thought, but her neat penmanship on the pad suggested otherwise. All the other cords were unplugged. *'If it was a dream, it was mighty real,'* she grimaced.

She stared at her neat loops moving across the pad.

COLLEAGUE   C BERNICE AP $
TELL ANDREWS   SOON

"I'll have to figure this out in the morning," she whispered aloud.

Walt was gone by the time Janet arose the next morning. Next to the coffeemaker she found a note.

Hon, I was out like a log last night.
Coffee's all set.
See you around 11 or so.
Happy Halloween.
Love, W.

"Oh my, Halloween. I'm glad I already have candy on hand. I've got so much to do today."

After settling down with the prior evening's *Ledger*, her coffee, and a buttered bagel, she turned on the small TV in the kitchen. The *Today* show zipped merrily through its second hour as she scanned the paper, without really reading. Janet barely saw the words nor listened to Katie and Matt. She thought about the burning message. Janet retrieved the tablet with her notes and returned to the kitchen.

'What a mystery,' she thought yet again. *'Even with sleep, I can't decipher this. Colleague. Bernice. AP Money. All of them are so cryptic. The money must have something to do with church. Maybe if I pull the files, I'll see something I missed.'*

With her coffee cup in hand, Janet took the notepad and returned to the dining room. Katie and Matt continued unnoticed in the kitchen. At the table, Janet pulled the tote bag toward her and unloaded it again. She opened the ledger book to the most recent weeks. As she did, the bulletin for Sunday fell to the floor. "I don't remember taking that," she muttered. "I thought I gave it back to Verna. No harm, I'm sure."

She placed it on the table. An hour later, nothing materialized to resolve the mystery. *'So much for that needle in a haystack,'* she thought. *'Tell Andrews is straightforward, but tell him what? Tell him about the money discrepancy, I suppose, but then what?'*

She smiled and recalled this week's sermon title, "Living the Unstuffed Life." *'I could sure use that now,'* she thought. *'Perhaps if I unstuffed my mind a little, I could figure this out; then again, perhaps I dreamed the whole thing.'* She kept returning to whether this was real or imaginary. As her eyes drifted across the bulletin again, she saw it.

Bernice Langdon

"That confirms it!" she nearly shouted. "Good Lord, you pointed explicitly. I might have forgotten. I wanted to visit Bernice, and you aren't letting me forget. 'C Bernice.' How obvious! My goodness. I wonder if anything else will jump out of here. Could it?" Her gaze passed across the bulletin once more, but nothing stood out.

'Well, I will go see Bernice Langdon. Perhaps the rest will be more apparent afterward. Maybe visiting Bernice will be what I share with Dr.

Andrews.' On her way to the hospital, Janet stopped at the church to drop off the files.

"All finished?" Verna queried.

"I believe so. I was wondering. Verna, do you recall if any of the staff were on vacation during August? It struck me that the staff never seem to take vacation, and I was curious."

"They do seem to work all the time, don't they?" agreed Verna. "Well, let's see. In late June, Reverend Andrews took that tour group on a trip to Greece. In early July, Barb was out–with Sunday School on break, she figured it made sense to get away. In late July, Pastor Scott was at the beach. And in mid-August, Pastor Bob and Rita went to New England, I believe. I remember, because Simon Lipton filled in for Rita on the organ. He is remarkably good for someone so young, don't you think?"

Janet was riveted. "Yes, Simon is quite good," she agreed distractedly. "Well, I just wondered. I guess they are out more than I thought. I'll best be on my way."

In the car, Janet regrouped. The money discrepancies stopped for two weeks in August. While potentially a coincidence, Pastor Bob–make that Associate Pastor Bob–and his wife Rita, the organist, were out for two weeks. Janet wondered if it happened to be the critical two weeks. Janet hated to think ill of either Bob or Rita, but what if they were doing something inappropriate? Perhaps the money was tied to an "AP" after all. Perhaps this was what she needed to tell Reverend Andrews. She would pray on all of this. Maybe there would be another sign.

ELEVEN

While Bernice entertained a visitor from the church, Dr. Gerhart joined them in Room 518 and unexpectedly signed the hospital release papers. Bernice's recovery continued to progress smoothly, the incision was less inflamed, her appetite grew, and she had successfully produced a sizable bowel movement. ("Like a toddler getting praised for taking a dump. I hope the color was to everyone's liking," Bernice fussed.)

As Janet Walker excused herself, Beverly arrived and helped pack the few belongings scattered about the room. Bernice suffered through her last institutional lunch, with its requisite neon yellow Jell-O complementing the olive green canned peas and artificial mashed potatoes. By midafternoon on a chilly Halloween, the Langdons were in the car headed west after navigating the hospital corridors ("I don't need any damn ride in a wheelchair," Bernice insisted, but was overruled by a cheery Filipino nurse wearing a pointy witch's hat whose Jack-o-lantern nametag glowed, "CAROL." Unacknowledged, the wheelchair ride was welcomed).

Beverly, Bill, and the kids visited throughout the weekend. Bernice kept a strict regimen of sleep, TV, light meals, and naps. Periodically, she allowed one of the cats to join her on the bed or sofa. They could not join her on the lounge chair–as that required sitting on her lap. After one early disastrous attempt ("Damn that hurts," squawked Bernice when the cat landed on her incision. "Get off now, ya damn feline,"), the cats and Bernice reached a truce. They could rest next to her, but not on her. (Bernice subsequently apologized to the offender. She knew she had hurt Tigger's feelings with her uncharacteristic yelling.)

The days were growing shorter and cooler with November's arrival. Bernice chatted with Caitlyn and Brad on the brick patio Saturday afternoon. The sun provided some warmth as she sipped some tea. Beverly cleaned in the house while the grandkids caught up with BeBe–a name derived in Caitlyn's toddlerhood. ("I will not be called Grandmom or Grandma or Nana. I find them distasteful. I am not yet sixty years old. I will not embrace a name more suited to an octogenarian with silver-blue thinning hair. Find something else." Caitlyn chose Bee-Bee, which subsequently was shortened to BeBe. Bernice found it to her liking.)

Despite direction from Beverly to keep their visit smooth and congenial, Brad and Caitlyn started bickering nearly as soon as the threesome got outside. Bernice had limited tolerance for this in the best of times. After two sharp admonishments, conversation of any kind ground to a halt.

The weekend closed with a gloomy Sunday (though the flowers from

Bedrock Hills Presbyterian were a nice touch). "Must've been a slow day for illnesses at the church if I'm the designated recipient," grumbled Bernice on the phone with Beverly. "That same woman dropped them off."

"Just a quick stop on my way home from church," Janet had professed. "My husband is waiting, and I just wanted to say hi. Can I get you anything? I must go to the store anyway and . . . "

"No, but thank you," interrupted Bernice. "My daughter-in-law loves to shop."

"You've been through the wringer, I imagine! How are you feeling?" continued Janet. Bernice, still in her ratty blue and turquoise-striped robe, blocked the door.

"Could be better. Could be worse."

"I suppose." Janet lingered. "I'll just be going then. Perhaps I'll stop in later this week?"

"Up to you."

"Do let me know if I can bring anything." The conversation paused awkwardly. "Well, Walt must be wondering what's taking so long." Walt was clearly evident in the car, though he was reading and paid no attention to the conversation. As Janet turned, Bernice closed the door and took the flowers to the kitchen. She reflected briefly on this alien terrain. She was unaccustomed to kindness from people she barely knew. Accepting favors and support from others was difficult.

"These people from the church must think I'm gonna be pushing up daisies soon. They are probably looking for a piece of the Langdon estate," she scowled. While she and Bill had saved, no massive estate awaited. "And I'm not about to lie down and die," she muttered to Tigger and Spider.

With rain overnight, Monday dawned gray and overcast. Bernice's good humor from the initial visit with Dr. Esch steadily declined. Monday's sunrise made the reality of chemo palpable. She awoke in foul spirits.

She watched *Good Morning America*, but a segment on breast cancer and its correlation with ovarian cancer and aggressive metastasis proved disconcerting. She turned from Diane Sawyer to Katie Couric who reported (again) on colon cancer for *Today*.

"What is it with these shows? Must the whole world revolve around cancer?" Bernice turned off the TV disgustedly. She turned on some classical music and sipped her tea. She was told to have only a light breakfast. ("Yes, Beverly. I heard the doctor. I can follow directions," retorted Bernice Sunday when reminded.) As a result, Bernice fixed an English muffin lightly buttered. Halfway through the first side, she stopped. Her appetite nonexistent, she tossed the remainder in the garbage. Carrying her tea to the kitchen nook, she looked outside unseeing. Her mind spun through the possibilities of chemo, the ravages it could wreak, and the what-ifs. All revolved around one question. *'What if we do all this and I die anyway?'* she pondered. Her mind spiraled downward through a parade of end-of-life horrors. The commencement of rain pounding on the window broke her concentration. She arose slowly.

"Spider, I am not looking forward to this at all."

Showered, she dressed in another pair of drab sweatpants complemented with a zippered bright red university sweatshirt. She debated wardrobe choices on Sunday. ("This will be easier to get on and off," suggested Beverly and surprisingly, Bernice acquiesced, though not in the moment. "What? You think I can't dress myself?") Prepared, Bernice had another cup of tea. She finished half before the doorbell rang and the door opened.

Beverly shook rain from her sleeve as she entered. "Sorry to barge right in, but I thought you wouldn't mind . . . " Beverly trailed off uncertainly as Bernice looked her way. "How are you feeling?"

"Well, I'm not dead yet," she clipped.

Beverly frowned. "I see you're wearing the new sweatshirt. The color looks good. I like–"

"Enough. I'm not up for small talk. Can we just go and get this over with?"

Beverly's short-lived smile evaporated. "I'll just get a few things together . . . "

"What could you possibly need to get together? I'm ready. Let's go."

"I realize this is stressful. I thought I'd get a couple of your CDs for the car. I thought . . . "

"Suit yourself. I'll get my coat."

The two women drove in silence with Hayden and Mozart as musical companions. Bernice kept her eyes closed. Periodically, Beverly dabbed at hers, which remained rather full. She recalled similar car rides with her own mother all too well.

Dr. Esch was out of town giving a presentation. Not having him present was a bad omen. In his absence, Bernice was poked, prodded, weighed, and assessed in endless measure. With each new reading, she became more anxious, grumpier, and increasingly caustic.

Through gritted teeth, Bernice snarled at the staff, "I do not appreciate being treated like a side of beef, you know."

Beverly attempted to smooth the waters left in Bernice's wake. "She's somewhat nervous about this procedure . . . She doesn't mean what she says . . . Please don't take it personally . . . She's just getting over surgery, you know."

The staff in the chemo unit bustled about with purpose. The professor was one of many anxious patients. She soon assumed a semi-reclined position to receive the prescribed intravenous infusion.

"Dr. Langdon?" A technician inquired sweetly. "The potassium may make this burn a little when it first begins. I just want you to be prepared."

Bernice's eyes pierced those of the petite woman settling in next to her. "I will persevere," she hissed back.

"A little pinch to insert the needle," Bernice grimaced as the needle penetrated her arm. "There now, hopefully that wasn't too bad."

"Must you give a running commentary?" snarled Bernice.

"I like telling you what to expect. That's all," the technician responded politely and smoothly. Having experienced all types of patients, she was not fazed by this particular sixty-something gray-haired lump of a woman.

"Now I want you to relax as much as you can," breathed Hiroko, her badge indicated. "Now, I'm opening the feed. This will take some time, as Dr. Esch prescribed a slow pace for your first round. Depending on your tolerance, we may adjust the infusion rate in the coming weeks. Now remember, this will likely burn–"

"I heard you the first time." Bernice closed her eyes in anticipation. Despite trying to force thoughts of serenity and tranquility, the idea of poison entering her veins proved pervasive. Nothing else could squeeze into her brain, dominated by a sense of helplessness.

"Shit, that hurts like hell," yelped Bernice as the drip began. "Oh my God!"

Beverly stuck her head through the curtain separating Bernice and Hiroko from the rest of the hallway. "Are you okay back here?"

"No, goddamnit, I am not okay. Oh, my God," Bernice groaned. Tears leaked from both eyes as she dealt with the onslaught of burning chemicals. "I don't think I can take this. When will it stop?"

"Dr. Langdon, give it another moment or two. The burn should dissipate shortly. I understand it hurts. I'm so sorry."

Bernice gritted her teeth and scrunched her eyes tightly shut. Tears rolled down her cheeks. After another minute, she gasped, "Shit. This hurts so much more than I expected."

Hiroko looked up at Beverly–whose head still stuck through the drapes to the hall. "Would you like to come in? It's a little tight, but in a moment I can give you my chair. The drip should take about two hours. I believe Dr. Langdon will begin feeling less uncomfortable in just another minute or two."

"Mother of God, this is brutal. Are you sure this is normal? This is lasting so long . . . "

"People have different reactions to Dr. Esch's treatment approach. The cocktail is quite caustic. I've seen other patients sustain this burning sensation for a similar timeframe."

"Mother, is there anything I can do? Perhaps a cold cloth? Ice chips?"

"No ice chips, ma'am. We need to get her reaction stabilized. A cold cloth is fine. The nurses' station can direct you."

Beverly, after dabbing away Bernice's tears, hustled out. By the time she returned with a wash rag in hand, Bernice was quiet. A few tears still sparkled on her cheeks, but the flow had slowed.

"Are you feeling at all better?"

Bernice kept her eyes closed but nodded almost imperceptibly.

"Dr. Langdon, are you doing okay? About ten minutes have passed. How are you feeling?"

Bernice nodded again. "It's better. I can handle this." A long pause followed. "But it's not without pain, even now. I still feel it."

"That's unusual—not unheard of, but atypical. I'll note this in your record. Dr. Esch will want to know and may adjust your dosage or the pace of transfusion. If you can handle it today, I would like to continue. You are likely having a mild reaction at the point of entry—"

"Mild, my ass," groaned the professor.

"I understand it hurts, but I'm not seeing physical signs of extreme allergic reaction."

Bernice said nothing. She appeared to be in a trancelike state of meditation. Her breathing became slow and rhythmic. Her eyes stayed closed. Hiroko whispered to Beverly that she would be right outside. The monitors continued to relay vital data remotely.

Beverly browsed through an old *People* magazine left in the cubicle. Her brain absorbed little, but it provided a diversion. After visiting the curtained area every fifteen or twenty minutes, Hiroko returned for the last time. "Dr. Langdon?" she inquired. "Your chemo is done for today. Let me unhook you, and you'll be good to go."

Bernice opened her eyes, looking drained and gray. "Good to go is a matter of opinion," she grumbled.

"Well, I'm sure you're glad that's done."

Bernice said nothing, settling into the passenger seat for the ride. At home, Bernice headed upstairs. "I'm going to lie down. I'm exhausted," she muttered as they entered the dark house. Without a word, she ascended the staircase with heavy feet.

Beverly called home, spoke with Caitlyn, and indicated she was with BeBe. She suggested Caitlyn heat up leftover pizza for dinner. She called Bill, left a voicemail, and encouraged him to get home as soon as possible. She poured a cup of ice water and one of ice chips before heading upstairs. Bernice moaned softly in bed.

"I don't feel well at all," she groaned. "I'm feeling dreadfully nauseous. Could you get me something in case I get sick? Oh, Lord."

Beverly hurriedly collected an empty trashcan from the bathroom and put it beside Bernice's bed. "Do you think eating a little something–perhaps crackers–would settle your stomach?"

"Oh, God, I can't think about putting something down my–" Bernice retched badly. She sat up and dry heaved before putting her head back on the pillow. Beverly stood perplexed. "Should I call the hospital and see what they suggest?"

Bernice sank deeper in the pillows, moaning softly.

"Mother, what can I do?"

But Bernice had fallen asleep. Thankful, Beverly left the water and ice chips by the bed and returned downstairs. Within the hour, she heard Bernice coughing and zipped back.

Bernice was pale. "I'm still feeling ill. I also have a headache."

Beverly put the back of her hand to Bernice's forehead. "I believe you have a slight temperature. I think I should call the Center and see what they advise."

"It's poison. No surprise it's causing a reaction."

"But perhaps we can find ways to make you more comfortable. I've brought you–"

Beverly was interrupted as another round of dry heaves racked Bernice. Tears flowed once more. After several endless minutes, Bernice sank into the comfort of her bed. "Oh Lord, this is shitty. I don't know if . . . "

Another round of wrenching coughs and spasms rippled through Bernice. She kept her head in the trash can. Her body shaking, Beverly brought a cold washcloth to press against her forehead.

"God, that's cold," yelped Bernice.

"It should feel good. Keep it on. It will help your fever."

Until ten o'clock, Bernice wrestled with severe nausea. While fortunate not to actually get sick, at times, she thought vomiting would be preferred. Beverly stayed with her, only excusing herself briefly to talk with Bill, say goodnight to the kids, and consume a yogurt she found–remarkably–in Bernice's refrigerator. She had little appetite, but forced it down.

Just after ten, Bernice used the bathroom and then got back under her covers.

"Feed the cats, would you?" she directed. She promptly fell asleep. Beverly wasn't quite sure whether to stay or to go, but decided she should probably stay. What if Bernice needed help during the night? She called Bill at home and apprised him. He seemed curiously distant and preoccupied. Beverly breathed deeply, attempting to center herself and avoid getting annoyed. She shouldn't be surprised that even now–in the throes of a battle for his mom's life–Bill's work took priority.

Beverly found an old robe of Bernice's that—while big—would suffice. She also discovered the necessary items—albeit dated—to remove her modest makeup and clean her face. She took a long hot shower in the guest bathroom, enjoying the warmth pounding on the outside of her body. The steamy shower water camouflaged artfully the tears coursing down her cheeks. Her tears fell for many things—her mother-in-law's cancer, her relationship with Bernice, her own mother's agonizing death, and her relationship with Bill. The tears fell long, hot, and steady.

After drying with a dense white Egyptian cotton bath towel—a luxury in which Bernice indulged, Beverly slipped under the covers of the guest room bed. Sleep came much later after reviewing a movie-like run of the day's events. This was going to be a long road with Bernice. She tensed at the thought of the next chemo, just two weeks away. The night passed quietly into Tuesday. Bernice and Beverly each slept long, dark sleeps.

TWELVE

Beverly stayed with Bernice until Friday. Caitlyn and Brad would take the school bus to Bernice's neighborhood each afternoon and quietly do their homework, and Bill would pick them up to go home. Beverly tried not to be bothered by no one apparently minding her absence, but nagging internal doubts grew.

On Thursday afternoon while Bernice snoozed, Beverly reflected on her life. *'When did I become so unhappy?'* she wondered. Her mother's untimely passing had been the only meaningful dip in an otherwise apparently perfect path: she married the love of her life and had the two kids–both healthy, strong students, well-adjusted, and good-looking. They owned a nice home. She was involved in many school and neighborhood activities. She worried that she was perhaps overextended. Was that what started the downward slide?

'No. The issue is Bill,' Beverly sadly resolved after trying to sidestep the conclusion for more than an hour. She had diligently avoided this unwanted thought for several months. Bernice's illness reinforced the problem. Despite having attempted to fill a void over the years, her tenacious efforts to build a mother-daughter relationship were rarely reciprocated and met with limited receptivity. Now, Bill was just not engaged. "This is his mother, for goodness sake. Where is he? Why am I doing all the work?" She voiced. By default, Beverly had become the primary caregiver. Bill barely even visited.

"Loveless" characterized their recent months together. If she was honest, she'd have to admit that Bill's growing distance preceded his mother's illness. Even lovemaking was perfunctory these days. They still "made a little whoopee"–so named since their early marriage, but relegated without fail to Thursdays after the kids were in bed and just before the start of *David Letterman*. "When did we get so boring?" murmured Beverly.

"It takes two to tango," she said as Tigger settled on her lap. "It's not just Bill, but it sure seems like he's absent anymore. Even recently, he runs late consistently, has unexpected business dinners, goes on more frequent client trips, he . . . " She paused. "Listen to me, Tigger. That has all the markings of something else." She hesitated. "Could Bill really be having an affair?"

The clarity of that realization slowly dawned. While no specific event triggered the notion, Beverly recognized that subconsciously this thought had been present for some time. Her speculation caused Beverly's eyes to tear up as she considered the implications of Bill having a relationship with someone else.

"It's probably just an overactive imagination," she murmured, "combined with sleep deprivation." Vocalizing her thoughts with the cat, however, forced consideration of the possibility and the consequences.

'Could it really be?' Beverly's mind raced. *'I work out all the time. I play tennis. Maybe I don't always take care of myself; it just seems silly to wear make-up consistently. I've gotten overstretched at school. Maybe I'm not paying enough attention to him. But I want to do something meaningful; I don't want to be just another soccer mom. Maybe that's what I've become . . . and perhaps that's unattractive.'*

"But no," she asserted forcefully as she paced. "These are important responsibilities: giving the kids security, having their parents participate in their activities, and being there to talk (even though they have told me not to talk to them in front of their friends!)."

'Bill's career is taking off. He's closing in on senior partner at the firm.' She rationalized, *'He's probably just busy and trying to get promoted. All this worry over what's probably nothing.'* Her inner thoughts turned vocal, "I am making a mountain out of a molehill."

"Mountain out of what molehill?" inquired Bernice entering the kitchen.

"You startled me," blushed Beverly deeply.

Bernice watched Beverly's color shift and deepen. "I could use a cup of tea and perhaps a bite to eat," she noted archly.

"That's good news. You must be feeling a little better."

"For the moment. I called and called but figured you must've gone out."

"I'm sorry. I must've gotten carried away in my thoughts."

"Creating mountains, no doubt." Bernice spit out with a nasty tone.

Beverly was taken aback. "I'm sorry. There's just been a lot on my mind."

"You're telling me. Now just step aside, while I make myself some tea and a bagel."

"I can do that. Sit down. Rest."

"Goddamn rest. That's all I've been doing. I'm pleased to have a little energy to get down the stairs. Let me make my own bagel, please," she hissed out the last word venomously.

"You can be so difficult," snapped Beverly.

"You're no picnic either," retorted Bernice.

Dissolving in tears, Beverly ran outside where she sat on the little patio, shivering in the pale midmorning sun. Bernice paid no attention.

When Beverly returned, the smell of burnt bagel greeted her. Bernice was not evident. Stepping across the kitchen, Beverly ran into Bernice who was sprawled on the floor leaning against the kitchen island.

"Mother! What happened?"

Bernice was pale and breathed shallowly.

"Nothing. I felt a little lightheaded. I decided to sit."

"Can I get you some water? Perhaps a cold cloth?"

"You weren't here."

Beverly's mouth tightened. Turning away, she filled a glass with cool water. She ignored the charred bagel peeking above the toaster. She handed Bernice the drink.

"I don't like sink water."

Beverly retrieved a bottle of water and rejoined Bernice. "Let me help you up," suggested Beverly after Bernice had consumed most of the water. "Do you want to sit here in the kitchen or . . . ?" She trailed off, hoping Bernice would volunteer a location.

Bernice closed her eyes. "I am going back to bed," she announced. "Help me up."

With some deep grunts, the two women got up from the floor. Bernice reluctantly leaned on Beverly as the two shuffled to the front of the house. After a short pause and a labored ascent, Bernice was back in bed.

"I believe I'll nap," she muttered, closed her eyes, and became silent. Beverly stood awkwardly at the foot of the bed. When Bernice's breathing became regular, she quietly returned downstairs. She discarded the burnt bagel and put the kettle on for more tea.

Spider joined her at the table. "So, Little Spider. You miss your mama," she purred. "She overdid it. She should've called down for some breakfast. That's the first she's ventured downstairs and it was too much. I doubt she'll sleep too long. Maybe then, you can go visit."

With a cup of steaming tea, Beverly decided to pull together her to-do list. She began a grocery list and then paused. *'Perhaps, I could make a decent meal here, have Bill and the kids join me, and serve Bernice all in one shot. Excellent idea!'*

Hoping it might begin to rebuild the bridge to Bill, she assessed Bernice's sparse refrigerator and pantry shelves. With renewed energy, Beverly worked through a menu of family favorites, identifying the necessary ingredients when the phone rang.

"Hello," she answered.

"Hey, Bev, it's me." Bill's baritone voice resonated. "I wanted to see if the kids could stay over at Mom's tonight. I've got an issue that's come up. We need to go to the client late this afternoon, a working dinner tonight, and then an all-day session tomorrow. I know it's last minute, but . . . " Bill trailed off.

Beverly reacted sharply, "Shoot, Bill, I was hoping . . . "

"It's okay isn't it? I don't mean to push, but I've got someone standing outside my door."

Beverly's annoyance rose. "Would you like to know how your mother's doing?" she caustically inserted.

"Sure, how's Mom?"

"She overdid it this morning and landed on the kitchen floor. She's back in bed."

"Oh, that's too bad. Is she okay?" Bill paused.

"I think she'll be fine, but–"

"About tonight, what do you think?"

"I think we need to talk is what I think. We've not talked all week, and now you just drop this little surprise."

"Bev, you know how things are. I'd like to talk, but now's not the time. How 'bout over the weekend? I'm really sorry, but I've got to get going. Milbank just showed up."

Beverly knew Milbank could advocate Bill's advancement to senior partner. Much as she wanted to push immediately, she knew better.

"We'll see you tomorrow night? How about dinner at your mom's?"

"Sure, that makes sense. I'll call you tomorrow with a better sense of timing. Say hi to Mom."

Bill was gone before Beverly could say goodbye. She sat with the silent phone still pressed to her ear. The whirring duotones signaling "phone off hook" broke her reverie, and she returned the cordless handset to its cradle.

"That's just the issue," she said to no one. "The kids and I are way in the back seat . . . barely even in the same car. More like coach, while Bill rides in first class." She regrouped. "Maybe tonight, we'll do pizza. Then the kids can sit with BeBe while I grocery shop."

As Beverly developed her lists, she kept returning to Bill. With nothing to go on, she couldn't fathom how she could initiate a discussion on her worries. They barely talked currently. Suggesting a fall from faithfulness would be incendiary with the possibility that her imagination was merely overactive. *'He's just busy. All marriages go through phases of heightened intimacy and less intense periods. We're obviously in the latter,'* she concluded.

Picking up the ringing phone once more, Beverly heard the animated tones of Albert, Bernice's colleague. After a medical update, Beverly agreed to a visit. It just might lift Bernice's spirits. No one had stopped by since her first chemotherapy. Beverly smiled: just as she thought no one could maintain a relationship with Bernice, Albert proved her wrong.

For the third time, the phone's ring shrilly filled the air. Simultaneously, the doorbell chimed. Beverly answered and carried the handset with her to the front door. Opening it, she motioned to the gray-haired lady on the front step to come in. She mouthed, "Hold on just a moment."

Into the phone she brightly said, "I'm sorry, the phone rang just as someone came to the door. Can I help you?" As the caller started speaking, Bernice yelled down.

"Can anyone get a little sleep around here? What in God's name is all the noise?"

"Hold on, I'll be right with you." Back to the phone, "I'm sorry; I didn't catch your name."

A hearty laugh greeted her. "This is Jeremy Esch. Have I caught you at a bad time?"

"Dr. Esch, I'm sorry. I was just–"

"Say no more. I can hear our patient. How's she doing?"

As Beverly responded, she motioned the woman she now recognized as Janet Walker to the study off the front hall. Janet smiled and quietly took a seat.

"Who's on the phone?" yelled Bernice from her bedroom. "And could you get me some water? Bottled," she commanded.

Beverly rolled her eyes but continued to update the physician.

"Do you hear me?"

"Just a moment, Dr. Esch. I must talk with Mother. She just woke up and–"

"Let me talk to her. I know she had a tough go of it on Monday."

Beverly entered Bernice's room and extended the phone. "It's for you. It's–"

Bernice cut her off. "Where's my water?" She glared at Beverly and then stared at the phone, "I don't wish to talk to anyone. Tell them I am indisposed."

"But–"

"No buts. Not one damn person. You hear?"

The doctor yelled from the phone. "Bernice, it's me, Jeremy. Pick up."

Bernice, hearing the doctor's voice, reluctantly reached for the handset.

"Hello," she growled.

"Bernice, I hear you had one hell of a time here on Monday. I'm just sorry I wasn't here for the fireworks. How ya feelin'?"

"Never better. I was thinking of running a marathon."

"I'm so glad to hear. Nearly all of my patients run marathons after their second round of treatment. You are well ahead of schedule. Well done."

"I was always in the accelerated program," remarked Bernice. As conversation continued, her expression softened and she occasionally smiled, and when Jeremy got serious, she listened. Beverly shook her head over the change.

"Janet, I apologize for keeping you waiting," she stated, entering the study.

"No problem whatsoever. I won't stay. I was driving by and thought I'd stop by and see how Bernice was doing . . . "

"Oh, she's a pistol."

"Is she up for visitors?"

"I suspect not, but I can check. She's on the phone right now with her doctor."

"I did a little baking and hoped these might be suitable." The church lady had clearly been busy; the aroma of warm chocolate chip cookies wafted in Beverly's direction as she accepted a plate piled high.

"How is Bernice? I understand the surgery was extensive."

"The operation went well. She's healing smoothly. She just started chemotherapy, with the first round on Monday. It was hard."

"It can be brutal. I remember . . . " Janet launched into a long, detailed story of a childhood friend who battled ovarian cancer three times, finally succumbing to the disease after eight years. "It was a long, hard struggle, but her times of remission were quite good. But listen to me. Blathering on about someone you don't know."

Beverly smiled. The woman exuded sincerity and warmth. "That's quite all right. I hope my mother-in-law's battle is at least as successful as your friend's."

Bernice called down, "I'm off the phone!"

"Mother, Janet Walker stopped by. Could she stick her head in to say hello?"

Bernice grimaced, despite the lovely conversation with Dr. Esch. "If she must, I will say hello."

Janet gave a hesitant frown. "Perhaps now's not a good time. I can just go," she whispered.

Perplexed, Beverly responded, "It's up to you. She's right at the top of the stairs. Perhaps you could just–literally–say hello."

"If you think so." Janet moved reluctantly toward the stairs. "I won't stay."

Janet knocked softly on the slightly ajar door. Beverly joined her, and they entered the room together.

"Bernice, it's so good to see you. I was in the neighborhood and just wanted to see how you were doing. Beverly tells me you've had a rough week."

Bernice glared at Beverly. "I'm doing better today, thank you," Bernice uttered each word with precise diction. "I appreciate your stopping by."

Janet smiled at Bernice. "My women's group has been praying for you. I spoke with Reverend Andrews this morning, and he hopes to see you this weekend. I suppose he hasn't been here yet?"

"No, not yet," a thin-lipped Bernice replied.

"Janet brought you some warm chocolate chip cookies. They smell heavenly. I can bring them up if you—"

"I'm not hungry. In fact, I'm feeling a bit peaked. Perhaps a little shut-eye will help."

"Well, I don't want to overstay. I just wanted to say hello. If there's anything I or the other ladies at church can do, please don't hesitate to let us know." Janet practically raced through her goodbyes.

Beverly showed Janet out. "I'm sorry about Mother's demeanor. She's just not herself."

"Don't fret. She's not feeling well. I'll stop back." Janet stepped through the front door and retreated down the path to her car.

"Certainly wouldn't surprise me not to see her visit again. I don't know that I would," she murmured to Spider who slinked toward the front door as Beverly closed it.

"Is she gone?"

"Yes, she's left."

"Good. I need something to eat."

"What would you like? A bagel? An egg? A little toast?"

"I don't care. Surprise me," Bernice's voice dripped with sarcasm.

Tears built up in Beverly's eyes once more. *'I am just a mess,'* she thought as she toasted a bagel. She made a cup of tea as well and carried the tray upstairs. "Here, perhaps a little something in you will make you feel better."

Bernice stared at the television.

"What did Dr. Esch have to say?"

"Nothing." Bernice glanced at Beverly who stood stone-faced. "Really. He said my reactions are in the 'to be expected' category. We will see how the next round of chemo goes. That's it." Bernice returned to the television.

"Well, if you don't need anything, I'll just be back downstairs." With no further word, Beverly quietly exited.

Beverly returned to her to-do list. She continued feeling edgy, her emotions at the surface. *'I can't drink any more tea. I've had too much. Maybe some water.'* She walked to the sink and filled a glass. While looking out the window, she noted Bernice's CD player attached to the underside of the cabinets. For a recent Christmas, she and Bill had given the mini-audio player to Bernice. A stack of CDs sat on the countertop.

'Music would be nice,' thought Beverly. She scanned the titles and picked some piano music. As she inserted the CD and pushed Play, she noticed an odd discoloration on the little screen that showed what track played and the elapsed time. On the right side of the pale green screen with its dark gray letters, a shimmering bright white sliver of light grew.

Piano music filled the room as the light blossomed in width and intensity. *'I wonder what that is. A malfunction?'*

Intrigued, she stood and watched the light as she sipped her ice water. The narrow strip of light worked its way around the edge of the little CD screen. Eventually, the light made a bright, glittery frame to the CD monitor, which currently showed: "CD TK 1 3:05." The light flickered, like a little flame in the back of the monitor. *'It's rather pretty, but so odd,'* reflected Beverly. *'What could it be?'*

She decided to turn off the player. "I don't want to burn the house down. Just what we'd need!" She smiled bitterly. With the unit powered down, the dark gray letters faded from the pale green screen, but the brilliant bluish-white light remained. Unplugging the unit had no effect: the effervescent, white miniature picture frame stayed brilliantly lit.

"Very odd." Beverly looked down at Tigger who purred and shuffled back and forth between her legs. As she watched the CD unit, from the right edge letters emerged. They ran across much like a news flash ticker tape at the bottom of a television screen. The usual dark gray letters now moved across the mini-monitor–disappearing into the glittery white light on the left side. The band of letters seemed to repeat, though it took some time to determine what they said:

MRS L NO JOB CONFRONT BILL

Beverly rocked on her feet. *'What sort of malfunction is this?'* she thought. She pushed multiple buttons on the CD unit, but the same message kept scrolling. *'Am I just imagining this?'* pondered Beverly. *'I know I was upset, but this is rather extraordinary.'*

Hoping her head would clear, she took her glass of ice water to the nook and sat for several minutes looking out over the backyard. Her curiosity unsatisfied, she returned to the CD player. The same message moved at a consistent pace. The white border blazed brightly.

'I don't understand this, but it seems so specific. Could it be reminders that Mother programmed?' Beverly speculated. *'I don't see it. It could be, but if it was, she would've entered Dr. L!'* Beverly laughed.

'So it appears to be me. 'Confront Bill' is certainly timely. But what's 'No

Job'? It's all so vague and may not even be real.' She kept looping through the same thoughts.

"Are you going to collect my dishes or not?!" Bernice interrupted from upstairs.

"Coming," Beverly tore herself from the CD player and trudged up the stairs. The wear of the week showed.

"You didn't eat half your bagel. Should I–"

"I wasn't hungry. Get me more tea."

Beverly ignored the command, "Mother?"

Bernice turned her eyes from the TV but said nothing.

"I'm going for some groceries this evening. Is there anything you need?"

"No."

"By the way, have you had any trouble with that little CD player Bill and I gave you? You know, the one that hangs–"

"I know which one you mean. No issues. Why? Did you break it?"

"No, I don't think so," Beverly stammered.

"You don't think so?" repeated Bernice incredulously.

"No," stated Beverly more emphatically. "Words continue showing up on the screen even when it's unplugged. I'll investigate further . . . "

"I like that CD player. Don't you go messing it up," snarled Bernice.

"Of course not." Beverly left with the tray and a promise to return with more tea. ("And make it decaf!" hollered Bernice as Beverly descended the stairs.)

The running ticker tape remained when Beverly reentered the kitchen.

MRS L NO JOB CONFRONT BILL

As Beverly fixed the tea, she pondered the meaning. The screen kept twinkling its tailored message, burning it deep into her consciousness. *'Maybe I'm just projecting my worries. I will talk to Bill this weekend. I really must, even if it's uncomfortable and leads to some unpleasantness.'*

She carried the tea upstairs to Bernice who took it wordlessly.

"Mother, I'll be out for a while. I'll have my cellphone on. I just want to collect a few things for the kids–they're going to stay here this evening."

Bernice stared at the screen and the midday news.

At home, Beverly showered, enjoying the pounding of the warm water. She stayed in the heavenly heat and humidity for twenty minutes. Decadent, she knew, but worth every moment! Sitting at the vanity wrapped in a long robe with her hair in a towel, she did her nails and applied light make-up.

She listened through several voicemails from neighbors and relatives asking about Bernice. The seventh message yielded a new voice.

"This is Max Diamond with the Diamond Ed Group. I'm looking for Beverly Langdon. We are an educational consulting group. We work with secondary schools on a variety of issues—including educational curriculum development, cost containment, and extracurricular programs. At Bedrock Middle School, I hear you've served on a series of committees with the principal and the guidance counselors. You've had a big impact. I'd like to meet you and tell you about an opportunity with Diamond Ed. Give me a call."

Beverly was stunned, not having received calls like this in years. This was just the ticket to break out of her blues. Perhaps a job, even a temporary or part-time position, would be perfect. In years past, she and Bill had talked about her returning to work when the kids were in school full time. Though Brad and Caitlyn had been full time for quite a while, a running list of projects always delayed consideration of rejoining the workforce. Perhaps now the position was coming to her.

Her mind raced for the thousandth time since dawn, thinking of new possibilities. While money was no issue, commanding a salary might reassert her credibility and worth with Bill. With both working, perhaps they would draw closer. No longer would Bill only hear about the mundane details of a suburban housewife's life. Smiling, she hummed a tuneless song as she threw clothes for the kids in an overnight bag. Back in the car, the mysterious message absorbed her thoughts:

MRS L   NO JOB CONFRONT BILL

'*What a coincidence,*' thought Beverly. *'I see this message and then I get a call regarding a possible job. What are the probabilities of that? Could it be all about me and not about Bill's job whatsoever? Though maybe it means I won't get the job after all,'* she reflected. *'I probably shouldn't get my hopes up.'*

Even so, Beverly's spirits rose. Just being considered as someone who was having impact and could possibly lend her hand elsewhere was invigorating and reassuring.

The rest of the day passed quietly. The kids joined Beverly for homework and pizza. Beverly sprang for gooey CinnaSticks, knowing the kids were not thrilled about spending the night at their grandmother's, away from their video games and internet connection. Caitlyn and Brad spent a few "quality minutes" with their somber grandmother, who barely spoke.

"She seems lost in her own world," cited Caitlyn.

Brad was more direct, "Is she gonna die or what?"

Beverly indicated that BeBe was worn out from the first treatment. She needed rest and didn't feel much like talking. They all should say an extra prayer for BeBe's quick return to health. As Beverly sank into the guest room bed later, her mind returned to the intriguing communiqué. She made one last personal commitment to "confront Bill" over the weekend and decided to explore the Diamond Ed position. Her eyes closed as she contemplated, "Beverly Langdon, Project Manager, Diamond Ed Group."

THIRTEEN

Beverly went home Friday evening. Bernice appeared stable. When Beverly mentioned leaving, Bernice responded with, "Suit yourself. I'll survive." Beverly tried not to take it personally. "Put yourself in her shoes," she repeated as a personal mantra. "Though I do think I'd be a tad more appreciative."

The house was quiet on Friday evening. With no caregiver present, Bernice visited the first floor—her first expedition since the dizzy spell. She muttered to the cats and filled their bowls, scattering dry cat food onto the tile unnoticed. Spider and Tigger stayed close as Bernice trudged around the kitchen. Her ratty, stained robe dragged on the floor, hanging loosely off her body. Her greasy gray hair matted down stuck up in random places. Her glasses ("bug eyes," Brad called them) were smudged and perched precariously on the bridge of her nose.

Bernice reached down and stroked one of the cats absently. "What to eat?" she muttered. "I wonder if Beverly got any groceries." She opened the refrigerator. Some leftover pizza was wrapped on the shelf. Random odds and ends greeted her but clearly no cornucopia of groceries. "Figures," she grumbled. "I finally have an appetite and there's nothing."

Bernice pulled some frozen yogurt from the freezer. Sitting at the table, she slowly ate directly from the box. She enjoyed each successive spoonful less and less until she finally stopped. Quite a bit remained. *'Guess I don't have much of a taste for this,'* she thought. Leaving the box on the table for a moment, she decided a glass of wine might be enjoyable.

With more effort than planned, Bernice uncorked a California red. She poured a hearty glass and settled back in the kitchen nook. Tigger jumped up beside her. He stuck his nose in the frozen yogurt container. After sniffing, Tigger put out a tentative tongue to taste the melting substance. "No," Bernice muttered. "Don't put your nose in there." She pushed Tigger away and then reached for her wine glass. Bernice sipped the red wine, closed her eyes, and felt the warmth of the wine gradually move from her tongue to her throat to deeper in her body. Keeping her eyes shut, she took another small sip. Tigger moved back and inconspicuously put his nose and tongue back into the cold box. Both enjoyed their respective treats as the clock in the hallway continued its long, rhythmic march through the evening.

Bernice slept well. At eleven o'clock on Saturday morning, she awoke to the phone.

"Hello," she grumbled on the fifth ring.

"Good morning. Did I wake you?"

"No, I was out back doing calisthenics. What do you think?"

"I'm sorry. Perhaps I should call back."

"I'm awake now. What is it?"

"I just wanted to check on you." Silence hung heavily. Bernice closed her eyes again. "I wondered if you needed anything. We have to run some errands, and I might stop by later with the kids . . . "

"Stop. You're making my head hurt. If you must drop by, I expect I'll be here."

"Did you sleep well?"

"I did until the phone woke me up."

Bernice was exasperating. "Mother–" Beverly started, but stopped. "Okay, then. I'm sorry to have woken you. We'll probably see you later."

Bernice took a deep breath, summoning up as much sarcasm as possible, "Have a nice day," she sneered through the phone.

"Maybe I'll have Bill check on you later." The connection clicked. Bernice placed the phone on its bedside cradle.

After a trip to the bathroom (*'God, I look like shit,'* she thought when looking in the mirror), she slowly headed for the stairs. Her head hurt. *'Jesus, just what I need: a headache on top of the rest of this shit.'*

In the kitchen, she surveyed the remains of last evening's party. The frozen yogurt container remained on the kitchen table. The remainder of the contents–what the cats hadn't consumed–had spilled out onto the table and one of the chairs and dripped into a now sticky puddle on the tile. The wine bottle with some residual red liquid still sat on the table. *'I drank all of that?'* thought Bernice with surprise. *'No wonder my head hurts. Shit.'*

She moved around the kitchen, pulverizing scattered cat food into a gritty substance, soon to be tracked throughout the house.

"I could use a cup of coffee. Wake me up," she said as Spider joined her, rubbing against her leg. "Did you help with the ice cream last night?" inquired Bernice. Spider purred. "I thought so."

The doorbell rang. *'Who in God's name could that be?'* thought Bernice. *'I'm barely up and there are visitors.'* She considered ignoring it when it rang again. *'It's probably Beverly and the kids. And I look a wreck.'* She started to the door. She looked out the side window next to it, just in time to see the back of her paperboy walking down the path to his bike.

She opened the door just a little and called out. Roger looked back startled. His eyes grew as he took in Professor Langdon's appearance as she swung the door open more fully. She appeared to have slept in her garments for weeks. Professor Langdon's appearance typically was intimidating. Now, she was dirty and intimidating.

"Well, are you just going to stand there?"

"I was collecting for the newspaper. I can come back later. I was trying to–"

"Have you been delivering the paper? I've not seen it."

"Yes, every day. It's always gone the next day when I come back." The fourteen-year-old paused. "Do you think someone's stealing it?"

"I've seen no paper in the last week." Bernice stared down at Roger.

Roger paused, "I wonder where your papers are going. I swear I've been leaving them."

"Maybe my daughter-in-law has picked them up. She's been visiting, you know."

"Maybe that's it. You should just ask her. Maybe–"

Bernice cut him off, "Perhaps I will. Now, what do I owe you?"

Roger handed her the neatly printed bill. "Come inside; I'll find money."

"That's okay. I'll wait here. It's okay."

"I insist. Come in."

Roger entered the dark front hall. Bernice closed the door. The whole house felt gloomy; it also smelled. A cat crept out from under a bench in the hallway leading toward the kitchen. It slunk over and sniffed at Roger's jeans and sneakers. He shuffled his feet, shifting his weight from one foot to the other. Bernice glided into the study. With no luck there, she went to the kitchen.

"Do you want a drink?" she hollered.

"No, but thank you, Professor Langdon." Roger was eager to move on. This unexpected visit was not part of the day's plan. The university was playing an archrival this afternoon. His dad had scored tickets for the two of them. Kickoff was at four thirty and he wanted to be done collecting, so they could go early. His sister had agreed to deliver afternoon papers.

Bernice returned triumphantly with a handful of bills and coins. "I had to raid the cookie jar." She handed Roger the money. "Here you go. I put in a little extra for you."

Roger smiled, showing his full set of white teeth and his dimple. "Thank you, Professor. I really appreciate it."

"Nice teeth. Braces?"

"No. I was lucky. My dad says I have good genes."

"Killer smile. Have a girlfriend?"

"Well, uhhhh," Roger stammered. "I go out now and then. Sure."

"I certainly hope so. Well, you best be on your way."

"Are you okay, Professor? I heard you were sick."

Bernice stood quite still, raising her eyebrows. "You heard that?"

"Yes, ma'am."

"Well, that's true, but between you and me, I think I'm over the worst of it."

"Well, that's cool. Hope you get well soon." Privately, Roger wished the professor looked better real soon. "I guess I'll head out." The conversation remained strangely stilted. "I'm going to the game this afternoon. Actually, me and my dad."

"My dad and I," corrected Bernice.

"Yeah, yeah. I get corrected all the time." Roger opened the door. "My sister'll deliver your paper this afternoon. Feel better."

Down the steps and walkway in a flash, Roger was back on his bike with a modest little wave before Bernice shut the door. She watched the teenager bike to a neighbor's. *'He's growing up. He's bigger than the last time I saw him.'* Spider came back to her feet. *'He's a nice kid.'* Oddly, Bernice felt a stronger bond with Roger Gallo than with either of her grandchildren. *'Why is that?'* she wondered.

* * *

Chemo did not improve. A rhythm emerged, not unlike the first round. The chemo cocktail burned brutally each session, as it started. Dr. Esch had chosen to slow the drip, attempting to alleviate the burn, but it made no meaningful difference. The infusion time grew to just over three hours. Following the biweekly Monday afternoon sessions, the rest of the week blurred. Blindingly painful headaches punctuated waves of dry heaving and severe nausea. The worst of the headaches, mercifully, lasted no longer than an hour, but accentuated the agony of chemotherapy.

The second week of each cycle was generally better. By the "off Monday," Bernice felt less nauseous and avoided the headaches, other than new ones imposed by her now nightly ritual of several glasses of red wine. "How bad could it be?" she challenged Beverly who questioned the growing number of bottles in the recycling bin. "The doctor didn't say no, did he?" sneered Bernice. "I will damn well drink myself to death if I want to. It can't be any worse than the chemo." Beverly merely shuddered.

Bernice handled the chemo independently. Beverly drove her to and from treatments, but Bernice insisted she could be home alone. It seemed reasonable, as there wasn't much she needed or much help anyone could give during the worst of the posttreatment cycle.

Thanksgiving passed in a blur though fortunately in the "off week" of a cycle; Beverly invited Bernice for the traditional feast, but the professor declined. "I'll do nothing but retch and dry heave throughout–not a pretty scene for you, not especially motivating for me. Thank you, but no thanks." Instead, she enjoyed a full bottle of cabernet–"It's the holiday; let's celebrate," she cackled to Spider and Tigger–and a plate of crackers.

By the middle of December, Bernice noticed more hair clogging the drain at the end of her weekly shower. She felt the remaining tufts of hair clinging in odd places across her scalp. *'Gonna be a looker today,'* she grimly thought. In the fogged mirror, the remaining gray hair clung to her scalp like lichen on the side of a rocky mountain: some places dense, other places scraggly.

She considered shaving off the rest, but couldn't work up the energy. Shivering in the cold of the house, she pushed up the thermostat. She threw some more cat food in the direction of the bowls. Little landed where targeted. The rest joined the growing detritus in the corner near the bowls. Spider and Tigger did not seem to care where the food was. Nor, apparently, did Bernice.

The biweekly cycle grew old. Each Sunday preceding a treatment, Bernice became increasingly apprehensive. Subtly, the recovery period lengthened. She knew, intellectually, that the benefits of chemotherapy were delivered cumulatively, but the notion that each round got tougher was increasingly depressing. "Before long, it will just be one long cycle," she admitted reluctantly.

Monday, December 16 dawned bright and clear. A dusting of snow had fallen overnight. While not completely covering the grass, it gave a cold, clean look to the neighborhood. Bernice's treatment went off as expected. The burn was long and hard, the nausea severe, and the accompanying dry heaves and occasional vomiting wrenching ("Oh joy, a new addition," gasped Bernice at one point). The splitting headaches rolled in like waves on the shore–hitting every two hours or so and lasting for better than an hour. Bernice could barely sleep, but she stayed in bed with the curtains drawn for the recovery period. By Friday afternoon, when Beverly visited, she was still in bed, still in the depths of her "recovery." Concerned, Beverly suggested she stay with Bernice who rallied sufficiently to adamantly say, "No. There's nothing you can do. Get me water. Throw the cats some food. Go."

On Sunday, Beverly and Bill stopped by. Bernice remained in bed. The lingering tufts of hair had now joined a very furry pillowcase. "Mother, let me change the sheets. You'll feel better in clean linens. Maybe a shower too?" Beverly valiantly tried encouraging Bernice to no avail. She stubbornly stayed in bed. The nausea and headaches remained well into the new week.

Christmas came and went. Bernice remained in bed. She existed largely on crackers, which Beverly insisted be placed on the bedside table. Unopened Christmas cards sat atop her bureau, as did a poinsettia delivered by Janet from the church. "I'll stay but a moment. Bedrock Hills wanted you to have this," she said on the day after Christmas. Fortunately, Beverly was present to accept. Bernice did not budge from the bed.

"I'm concerned about your mother," Beverly shared with Bill that same day. "She's not popping back from this most recent round. She's due for another session on Monday and it's Thursday already."

"Don't you think the doctors know what they're doing? This is cumulative, right?"

"I'm just concerned. It seems like the cycle is deteriorating. She doesn't get out of bed. She's not eating. She looks awful."

"What do you think we should do?"

"Bill, what do *you* think?"

"I'm not a doctor. I'm just going with the plan."

Beverly sat silently, looking at her husband of more than fifteen years. *'What was going through his head?'* she wondered. *'The afternoon* Ledger *holds his attention more than his mother's condition.'*

"We should hire a visiting nurse–someone who could look in and help her through this stretch. Someone who knows what they're doing. Maybe your mom would be receptive."

Bill gave a loud harrumph without looking up. "I doubt it. She wants to sulk in her own misery."

"She feels awful." Beverly surprisingly played defense. "She can't help how she's feeling, but maybe someone–without a relationship–could challenge her more, take her on without the history."

"What are you talking about?"

Beverly stared at Bill. "You're kidding, right? Your mother and I don't precisely see eye to eye. I suspect she was the same with her students–always keeping them off balance. The cancer has only exacerbated that. I've tried, but I don't know how to help her. Maybe someone else would be better."

"Maybe. Why don't you look into it? See what the options are."

"Can't you make some calls? Maybe your firm's benefits group would know–"

"Bev, I don't know who would have the right info. I can do that, but it will be after the holidays–no one's around right now. If you want to wait that long . . . "

"Never mind. I'll see what I can find."

Beverly spent the evening online doing research on home health care. She kept returning to one group, HomeHealth. Their ad was big and bold in the Yellow Pages. Their information online was comprehensive. They appeared professional, caring, and competent. Local medical professionals gave them glowing reviews; local citizens had voted them 'Number One' in *The Ledger's* "Annual Best List."

On Friday morning, Beverly spoke with the executive director at HomeHealth who asked a long series of questions regarding Bernice's condition and care to date. Beverly sensed the woman was not pleased with the lack of in-home care currently provided. Beverly tried explaining why no one was with Bernice, but the director kept harping on the notion that no one was present to ensure Bernice had support if a crisis arose and–as importantly–to promote getting her consistently out of bed. "Her health will decline if she stays in a dark room, feeling sorry for herself, watching TV."

The director gave Beverly a password to visit the HomeHealth website and complete the appropriate forms. Bernice's doctor also needed to evaluate patient needs. After the call, Beverly completed the appropriate form within the hour and spoke with Dr. Elway's answering service to request his input.

Bernice rallied over the weekend. She rang in the holidays with a bottle of wine and two slices of toast. "One good thing about this," she explained to Spider. "I must be losing some weight, eh?" She cackled meanly at the thought. "One helluva diet." She took her bottle of red and wheat toast into the study and sat in the recliner to watch TV. While nothing was particularly riveting, she viewed a passing array of criminal investigations and detective series.

Sunday morning found Bernice still reclined in the lounger, sleeping fitfully. An empty wine bottle lay on the floor. Some toast crumbs remained on the plate resting on the end table. Her glasses had slid down her nose. The bulky Sunday morning newspaper lay on her front walk, under several inches of overnight snow. Beverly would retrieve it later in the day.

FOURTEEN

On Monday morning, Beverly went back online to HomeHealth. Having finalized the application, she hit SEND. In a follow-up call to the executive director, she indicated that Dr. Elway would not be completing his form until after New Year's. The director firmly stated that service could begin only with the doctor's input.

Thinking extemporaneously, Beverly suggested Dr. Esch. With agreement that his perspective would be satisfactory, Beverly hung up and quickly dialed the oncologist. Managing Bernice's care was becoming a full-time job, even when not sitting at her house. Surprisingly, the physician was available. Delighted to hear from Beverly, he inquired about his irascible patient's status.

Beverly apprised him of the precipitous deterioration. Bernice's physical and mental condition increasingly concerned her. While always abrupt and harsh, Bernice was now disengaged and withdrawn. When she did speak, she was more caustic than usual. "Plus," Beverly added, "she's drinking quite a bit of red wine."

"Well, at least she has good taste," the doctor's voice twinkled over the phone. "I'm a red wine guy myself." Beverly was surprised and silent. "More seriously," the physician continued, "a glass or two of wine shouldn't hurt. I'm surprised she has a stomach for it; most patients have no interest in alcohol during treatment. With a history of social drinking, she's probably able to handle a bit. She's tough."

"In more ways than one," agreed Beverly.

"Given chemo's stress on the liver, I'd suggest she stick with no more than two or three glasses of wine at any time. Alcohol is likely to hit her harder, given the liver's status. If she enjoys it, I'd say let it be."

"Easier said than done, I'm afraid." Beverly paused. "Doctor, I've been exploring the notion of a home health aide or perhaps a nurse. Given how long the recovery from each treatment requires, I think a professional may be helpful."

"I agree. Too many times having a family member involved in day-to-day care is fraught with difficulties. I don't know if you've—"

"Say no more! 'Fraught with difficulties' is a kind way of describing the last couple of months!"

Dr. Esch laughed. "I'm not surprised. She's feisty. Glad I didn't have her for class!" He added, "I would certainly support getting some assistance for her. Probably doesn't need to be twenty-four seven, but daily help would be good."

With his agreement to complete the necessary form, Beverly concluded, "I don't know that my mother-in-law will be happy about this."

"Tell you what," Dr. Esch responded. "When Bernice is in later today, I'll talk with her about HomeHealth. They've got some great staff. Perhaps I can cajole her into giving them a try."

"Fabulous. She'd take it better from you. Would you?"

Whether Bernice's discomfort later that day played a role or not, she reluctantly agreed to Dr. Esch's suggestion of getting someone to visit "periodically" at home to "help out." HomeHealth rapidly confirmed that someone could swing by that evening. Beverly would be there for introductions.

Now buried deep in her bed, the reactions from this round of chemo racked Bernice. She yearned desperately for elusive sleep, but she moved from rounds of vomiting to deep, lingering shudders as waves of nausea swept across. Her head pounded consistently; no let-up appeared imminent. In the midst of her misery, a series of insistent knocks on the front door broke through.

"My God, I can't believe someone is here. Go away," groaned Bernice. "Just let me die."

Having forgotten that Beverly was in the house, she assumed the visitor at the front door had left. However, the nurse stood patiently debating whether to ring the doorbell or to knock again. Just as her finger descended to press the button, she heard the deadbolt move. The door opened to reveal Beverly Langdon.

"Good afternoon. My name is Carol Kneffler, and I'm with HomeHealth," she chirped. She smiled broadly toward the fatigued woman. "Have we met?"

Beverly swung the door open. She took Carol's coat and suggested they chat for a moment before going upstairs to meet Bernice. In the background, Bernice erupted again with a round of dry heaves.

"Let me check her and we'll sit," suggested Beverly.

"Oh my, no. That's what I'm here for. Let's go together."

At the doorway to the bedroom, the two women stopped. "I don't know if I should say this, but Bernice can be difficult and demanding. I hope you won't take it personally if she's nasty."

Carol smiled and gave Beverly a long, slow wink. "We'll see just how tough she is. I used to work at the University Medical Center. I know a thing or two about tough patients. Though having two tweeners is probably teaching me a whole lot more. I could tell you stories—"

Carol stopped abruptly as Bernice yelled, "Who's there?"

"Let's go see our patient, shall we?" suggested Carol. They entered the darkened room.

"It's me, Beverly."

"As if I didn't know?" said the lump beneath the covers. "I am awfully hot. Pull down the covers. Not too much, mind you."

Beverly gently pulled the comforter partially down, revealing the bald gray skull of her mother-in-law. Her face was drawn in clear discomfort. She looked at Beverly with deep, unfocused eyes. "Who's with you?" She breathed raggedly as she rasped out the query.

"This is Carol, with HomeHealth. Remember Dr. Esch suggested we have someone come to help during the hardest part of your recovery? Carol just got here."

"Mrs. Langdon? Hi, I'm Carol," the nurse brightly enunciated.

"It's Dr. Langdon," came the curt response.

"Of course, Dr. Langdon." Carol winked at Beverly. "I take it you're not feeling too tippy top."

"I see they sent a bright one. Just what I need."

"Mother," reprimanded Beverly.

"Did you bring something to take away the pain? Perhaps a gun?"

"No guns today, Dr. Langdon. I only stock a few, and they're at the office. I'm afraid we'll just have to persevere with more conventional means. Let me see if there's any fever." Carol leaned in with an ear-sensor thermometer. "You've got a mild fever, which is not unusual given the chemo regimen. Let's get a couple of Extra Strength Tylenol in you. They won't hurt the chemo and may help with the fever." She paused. "What else hurts?"

Bernice started to answer but suddenly reached for the spit-up container. While nothing emerged, several minutes passed as she struggled to overcome the rippling spasms shaking her. Carol reached over and stroked her back. "There, there," she murmured.

"My head is killing me: deep, throbbing pain. I'm seeing starbursts of light, migraine-like. This is the worst it's been." Bernice closed her eyes.

"Headaches with ocular side effects are not uncommon, unfortunately, Dr. Langdon. The Tylenol should help with the pain but may not do much on the fireworks. I wish I could be more optimistic." Carol handed Bernice the pills from her large medical bag as well as the cup of lukewarm water that sat on the nightstand. "Here, let's see if you can get these down."

Bernice took the pills in one gulp. She immediately began retching. Carol injected, "Now I'm betting on you. I believe you can keep those pills down. I'd say the odds look good."

The odds on the pills staying down looked anything but promising to Beverly who watched the scene unfold as if in a movie. With each gut-wrenching gurgle, the pills appeared destined for daylight, but, surprisingly, Bernice held them down.

Bernice lay back down on her pillows and closed her eyes. She looked more drained; the final remnants of color had departed, giving her the pallor of a corpse. Within moments, Bernice's breathing became regular. The elusive sleep had found her, at least briefly.

Carol pointed to the door. She and Beverly silently made their way to the kitchen.

"Is this a normal week?"

"Pretty typical. Each week gets worse," responded Beverly. "I don't know what to do. She is so difficult to help." Beverly's eyes welled up. "I'm so glad you're here."

"There, there, not to worry. The cavalry has arrived. She's gonna be a pussycat. And look at that, she has pussycats. Here, kitty." Spider came over, while Tigger stayed near his food and surveyed carefully.

"Is this normal from your perspective? I mean her reaction?"

"Chemo is a frontal assault. It's poison." Carol paused. "You know that wart removal stuff you use on your hand or your foot? Think how carefully you put that stuff on. When you don't get it on precisely enough, the skin around the wart looks like it's been through war; it gets all ulcerated and blistery. It can look downright burned. And that's the medicine! Many times the wart keeps thriving and you've got all this ugly, abused skin all around it." Carol looked at Beverly thoughtfully.

"Chemo is kinda like that. It goes after the wart, but it ravages a heckuva lot of good stuff on the way. And, there's no way they can target chemo as well as you can direct the wart drops. Hence, your mother is looking worse for the wear and you can't even be sure the cancer isn't like that big ol' wart—still looking vibrant and big, while the rest of her shrivels up and looks worse. The docs won't know for a while. They just hope and pray."

Beverly nodded. "I suppose. It's just really hard."

"I know," Carol extended a hand toward Beverly's shoulder and rubbed. "It's okay to be scared. You're in the middle of a war zone."

Beverly's eyes filled once more. "God, I am always on edge."

"Just let it out. I've been there. I'm here to help Dr. Langdon, but I'm also here to support you guys. The more I can do, I will."

"You're a godsend."

As the digital clock over the oven shifted to six o'clock , the doorbell rang. *'Who could that be?'* wondered Beverly as she exited. Carol stayed behind.

Holding a casserole dish, Janet stood on the other side of the front door. The pungent aroma of hot food rose as Beverly warmly greeted her.

"I just had some extra and thought Bernice or your lovely family could enjoy it. Walt and I will never eat all of this."

"You are so kind. You didn't need to. I wish Mother was up for you."

"How is she?" Janet paused, looking carefully at the young woman and nodding, "Chemo can be so hard."

"So right you are. She's just back from her most recent round. She has had a pretty tough time of it those first few days. She just got off to sleep."

"Not to worry, I only wanted to drop this off. It's still warm, but if you want to stick it in the refrigerator and heat it up later you can. I'd suggest freezing it–you can, you know–but put it in a different container. Sorry to cause you that trouble. I should've thought . . . "

"No need to apologize. I think we'll eat some right away. I'll certainly return your dish."

"No hurry. Enjoy."

As the ladies talked, Bernice started coughing upstairs. Carol materialized from the kitchen, heading toward the stairs.

"Janet, this is Carol. She will be working with us during Mother's recovery each chemo cycle."

Carol and Janet exchanged hellos, but the Filipino woman quickly excused herself and headed upstairs. Janet left shortly thereafter–"must get home to Walt; he won't eat dinner without me!"–and Beverly took care of the casserole.

When Carol returned to the kitchen, she and Beverly reviewed necessary details, including providing house keys. Carol planned to stay each day until Bernice appeared asleep for the night in the critical days post chemo. Each morning, for the remainder of the week, she would stop by, and, depending on progress, might also make afternoon visits.

"I don't have a particularly full plate right now," she assured Beverly. "I can put in a little extra time." She paused, "Since I got here, I've been trying to connect the dots. I remember Dr. Langdon. She was on my floor during my last weeks at the Medical Center. While not my patient, I remember the nurses talking about her."

"I bet they had stories!" Beverly looked more closely. "Did you wheel us out after Mother's last surgery? That would've been Halloween."

"Black witch's hat?"

Beverly smiled.

"We drew lots at the nurses' station. I lost. I was told it was meant to be. One nurse said, 'The witch for the bi-' Oh, but maybe I'm being too bold."

Beverly laughed her first real laugh of the day. "No, not at all. Welcome to the Langdons. I sense you're going to fit in real well."

FIFTEEN

Beverly, Bill, and the kids stayed at Bernice's house for New Year's Eve. The kids hibernated in their grandfather's former bedroom. Beverly acquiesced and allowed them to bring the GameCube to supplement regular TV. "You must keep the volume down. You're just down the hall from BeBe."

Carol was off for the evening, after Beverly proved persuasive in their debate. "We will be there. Spend time with your family." Even so, Carol stopped by for most of the morning. She took Bernice's vitals, cleaned up used tissues and vomit-laced buckets, and insisted they change the sheets—despite Bernice's vigorous protests.

"You know, Dr. Langdon. You'd feel better if you got cleaned up. Maybe a bath?"

Here Bernice drew the line. She sat unhappily for the sheet exchange but refused to undress and bathe. "Forget it," she hissed. Carol found the compromise acceptable.

Bernice returned to bed as quickly as possible and restlessly tossed and turned, trying to quell the raging internal tempest. Her failure fueled a downward spiral in her spirits.

"Oh, Dr. Langdon," sang out Carol shortly after noon. "I think you may want a little snack. What can I get you?"

Through the continuing fog of nausea and headache, Bernice could only groan. "I know. The sound of food does not inspire, but I think something in your stomach may help."

Bernice groaned again, but Carol did not hear as she had vanished. Moments later she brought Ensure and some buttered wheat toast. The inviting smell eked its way into Bernice's consciousness. "Well, perhaps I could try something. It can't be much worse," she shuddered.

She reached for the toast and bit off a tiny piece. As she slowly chewed, she surveyed the glass of brown liquid. "What the hell is that? More poison?"

Carol laughed. "Would I do that to you? It's vitamin-fortified ambrosia, nectar of the gods—well, at least those who are women of a certain age."

"Just what I need," muttered Bernice.

"It's Ensure and a fine vintage I must add. Taken from my own private collection—I've chosen a lovely chocolate."

"No such doddering old folks' drink for me."

"Surely you know the desirable impact of rebalancing lost electrolytes and nutrients? This is standard operating procedure for a light appetite. No real magic. Give it a try."

Bernice shrugged her shoulders and ignored the concoction. "Light appetite? Hardly. I'll not."

"Suit yourself, but I'll leave it. You may want to try some over the afternoon. It's not bad."

Bernice took another bite of toast and sank back into her pillows.

"I'll be on my way. I believe you're set for the moment. Beverly will be over later. I'll see you tomorrow." Bernice continued chewing with her eyes closed, concentrating on getting the small morsel to stay down. "Okay, I'm off. Happy New Year."

Upon arriving, Beverly checked on her napping in-law. A half-eaten slice of toast and a small glass with some chocolate milk residue sat at the bedside. She was pleased to see Bernice had tried to eat.

Bill joined his wife. Their whispered concerns woke Bernice. "So, you're here?" she looked at her son. "You've come to watch me die?" She peered in his direction.

"Happy New Year to you too. You know, Mom, I don't want to hear that kind of talk. It's New Year's Eve; we thought we'd spend it with you. I hear you've got a great new nurse."

"She's a peach all right," quipped Bernice. She looked out from deeply sunken eyes. "Give me my glasses."

Beverly handed them over. After positioning them, Bernice stared more intently at Bill. "I want to put my affairs in order. I also want to ensure my living will is up to date. This living hell cannot–will not–sustain." The words were spoken with cold conviction, the most resolute words Bernice had spoken in some time. "Will you get that done? And quickly?"

Bill looked at his mother. "Your affairs are in fine shape. After Dad's aneurysm–"

"You can say the word death. He died. I'm gonna die too. I want a complete update. You hear me?"

"The doctors believe you are pursuing a good course of treatment. Sometimes the medicine hurts more than the disease. You're in a particularly grueling period of–"

"No more. This is pure living hell. I want to know things are prepared."

Bill shrugged. "I'll look into it. I'll need to get a colleague to do it, of course. Perceived conflict if I prepare them myself."

"Use your father's firm. They did the originals." Bernice removed her glasses. "I need to rest. Even a conversation is goddamn exhausting." She closed her eyes, effectively ending the discussion.

Bill and Beverly descended to the kitchen. "What was that all about?" Bill queried.

"She feels awful. She'll get through it. She just needs reassurance that her paperwork is together."

"You think?"

"You know her better than I. But, yes, I think that's it. It's a surprisingly thoughtful thing to do."

Bill stared back. "I'll look into it after the holiday. Dad's lawyer was with Dane & Caldwell. I'll see if he's still there. He may have retired."

"How about opening a bottle of wine? I'll put out some munchies before dinner."

Arranging snacks, Beverly smiled; she and Bill were doing better. The early-November conversation had been hard. She wasn't able to voice her speculation about an affair, but she had shared much of the tension she had been feeling. Bill took it seriously. He acknowledged that he was swamped with work, his client load was heavier than ever, and the race to senior partner was all-consuming and proving to be a high-stakes affair. Beverly's tears had probably opened him up more quickly, but they had a good heart-to-heart that Saturday night.

Their lovemaking had been sweeter, more tender and thoughtful than it had been in months. Beverly smiled at the thought as she wrapped little cocktail hot dogs for the oven. "Confront Bill" had been solid guidance, whatever the odd message's origin. She looked up at the CD player. The mini-screen was dark: no messages and no surreal lights this evening. Life didn't change overnight, but things were definitely better. She and Bill were becoming partners again. Her doubts on his faithfulness had evaporated.

The job was a different story. The Diamond Ed opportunity on the surface proved interesting, but Max Diamond reminded her of a smarmy used car salesman, though with better attire. They met for lunch just before Thanksgiving. He talked incessantly; she barely spoke. She felt like she was being sold on something that would prove less satisfying than promised. As lunch ended, she told him she'd consider the opportunity and get back to him. Shortly thereafter, she politely, but firmly declined. Max tried valiantly to persuade her differently, but she had made up her mind. Fortunately, the kids' arrival home from school allowed her to end the call. *'No Job,'* she thought and smiled again. The CD player should give advice more often.

As the little wieners baked, she and Bill clinked wine glasses. "Cheers," they said simultaneously. "To a better 2003!" They sipped and shared a quick kiss before calling the kids down for pre-dinner snacks.

SIXTEEN

In Harborside, Rusty's New Year's Eve rocked. He connected with a host of guys from work at the Marina Grill for dinner including Chip and Jeff ("Jay-eff, you Dawg"). They got a big window table, which became quickly loaded with munchies and innumerable Jack & Cokes, draft beers, and Marina Mud. By tradition, each round of Mud–a mix of vodka, rum, coffee liqueur, and Kentucky Bourbon concocted by Marina bartenders– was quaffed simultaneously.

By nine, the table of ten was in rare form. Their raucous behavior did not, however, distinguish them at the Grill. The whole establishment rocked, as Rusty held court at the table's far end.

"Another round on me," Chip yelled.

"It's my turn," countered Rusty.

"It don't matter to me. We're all just gonna split the bill anyway," contributed another twenty-something. "Let's just get another. Yo, Deb–" Their embattled waitress returned. Her face conveyed the unending demands of a New Year's Eve.

"Boys, what can I get you?"

"Another round."

"No, let's do shots."

"Yeah, shots. That's good."

"We want shots. Tequila."

"B-52s."

"Let's not mix. Iced vodka."

"You wimp. Tequila rules."

"You only live once."

"Boys, I need to know what I'm getting."

Rusty took command. "Sounds like tequila. Ten tequila shots, and can you bring lemons? Also, another round of what everyone's drinking." He turned back to the table, "More food, guys?"

Deb had already disappeared. "We'll get food when she comes back."

Out of the chaotic energy of the Marina, Deb reappeared with the shots and a tray filled with ten more libations. As quickly, she crafted a food order from conflicting suggestions and vanished.

"To 2003!" shouted Jeff.

"Yeah, 2003!" echoed each colleague as he downed a tequila shot, sucked a lemon wedge, and licked salt from the skin between his thumb and index finger.

"Whooo, baby. That burned," gasped Rusty, reaching for his Jack & Coke. "Good, but f'ing hot."

Chip gave a friendly pat on the shoulder. "Hang in there, Buddy. The evening's young." Rusty laughed. Table conversation refocused on where to go next.

Just after eleven, the guys left the Marina Grill. Spirits were high, speech was slurred, and talk was loose. They headed along the harbor front to The Railroad, another establishment serving the twenty-something crowd that dominated apartments in Harborside and the adjoining University Sector.

The Railroad was hopping. Dance music throbbed. The overall lighting was dim, but strobe lights and moving spots kept the crowd frenetic and occasionally blinded individual clientele. The guys joined the tightly packed humanity, working their way to a bar. Chip and Rusty agreed to alternate buying drinks. Rusty bought two drafts first. With beer in hand, they retreated to a table overlooking the dance floor. Most of the others in their group found their way over, but some peeled off to connect with other friends.

"Happenin' tonight," shouted Rusty.

"Never seen it so jammed," responded Chip. "Kinda tough to hear."

"We'll just have to drink then," laughed Rusty. They clinked glasses and watched the gyrating crowd.

With the clock approaching midnight and the TV monitors around the room turned to Dick Clark's countdown from New York, The Railroad erupted in cheers as the ball dropped. Strobe lights swirled and ricocheted off the walls. Jeff, Chip, and Rusty raised their glasses in a toast. They clapped each other on the back and agreed 2003 was going to be great.

"Here's to a banner year for Ridgewell. Let's hope this first full year being public, we make boatloads of moola," shouted Chip.

"Here's to Ridgewell. And its next millionaires!" added Rusty enthusiastically. The trio drained their glasses.

"Another round?" queried Chip.

"Sure, you're up," grinned Rusty. "Go get 'em."

Chip headed toward the bar. Jeff and Rusty watched his progress, but he rapidly merged into the craziness of post midnight festivities. They continued watching, enjoying their respective buzzes, pointing out who was hot (and not), and deciding which dancers were hooking up for the evening. With beers, Chip rejoined the talent audit committee.

Shortly, Jeff wandered off to join his Support Ops colleagues. He was followed by Chip who headed to the dance floor ("There's this woman I've got to meet"), leaving Rusty alone with his beer. With a healthy buzz, his eyes closed, his body swayed with the music with increasing rhythm and motion. Deep into the music, he moved more energetically with each new tune, drinking absently from his beer.

Feeling increasingly warm, he opened his eyes to find one of the minispots illuminating his solo gyrations on the stage-like second level above the dance floor. He realized a number of people now watched and applauded when they saw him looking back. He widened his mouth in a big grin and kept right on dancing, letting his torso and hips accentuate the motion of his hand like that of a cowboy swinging a lasso before roping a calf. As the song ended, the growing audience clapped and catcalled loudly. Rusty took a small bow, doffing an imaginary cowboy hat to the crowd.

The spot turned to someone else as Rusty drained his beer. He collected another draft at the bar and decided, despite the cold, to go outside for some air. He stepped out on the small deck overlooking the river. The breeze was chilly, but the side of the building yielded protection as Rusty sipped his beer.

"Quite a performance."

Rusty looked up. A medium built guy of about his age joined him.

"Yeah, I suppose. Just feeling the music," smiled Rusty.

"Hot in there . . . "

"I suppose." Rusty continued sipping his beer.

"Dan," said the young guy extending a hand.

"Rusty."

"How ya doin'?"

"Feelin' fine. Been an excellent evening."

"Hung out with some buds, but they took off. Wasn't ready to head home."

"Sounds like me. Sorta tough to stay together. It's packed."

"You're telling me." Dan gulped his beer as they looked out over the river. "You know, I don't want you to take this wrong, but when I said it was hot, I didn't actually mean the temperature."

"Really?" Rusty glanced sideways, as he added a long drawl.

"Yeah, really."

"Interesting. Very interesting." Rusty turned and looked more closely at Dan in the weak lighting. He had dark hair, was about Rusty's height, and was dressed in tight jeans and an open-necked shirt. A thin chain with a gold cross hung around his neck.

"Damn nice to meet you. I'm about done with my drink. Can I get you something?"

"That would hit the spot."

Dan held the door. As Rusty passed, he ensured his hips and his arm grazed the fleetest of touches, yet he felt an electric surge. The sharp intake of breath assured him that Dan not only noticed but leaned in just a little.

The guys retreated with new beers to a table toward the back of The Railroad. They traded vitals, without sharing too much: jobs, where they grew up, where they lived (both in the University Sector), and their interests. Both liked music: Rusty sang in the Metropolitan Men's Choir, Dan played in a little jam-band, doing light rock and Christian contemporary. As they talked, their knees inadvertently rubbed against one another periodically.

As the clock inched its way toward two, they agreed to share a cab; their apartments were not that far apart. The ten-minute cab ride jostled them together in the backseat.

As the cab entered the University Sector, Rusty upped the ante, "So where to?"

Dan remained quiet.

"Perhaps a nightcap?"

"I'm not—well, it's just kinda late."

"Oh come on. What's a little nightcap?"

"I don't know . . . "

"I don't bite, promise." Rusty gave his trademark big white-toothed grin.

"Well, okay. I could stop by. It looks like we're not that far from my place anyway."

"Surprised we haven't run into each other before," nodded Rusty.

Rusty gave the final directions to the driver who sat stoically. After the two young men exited the cab in front of Rusty's building, the driver stomped hard on the gas as he accelerated.

Rusty and Dan didn't have much of a nightcap. By three thirty, the two young men breathed steadily and rhythmically in Rusty's bed.

* * *

Choir practice on Thursday night went great. Rusty loved singing with the Metropolitan group. The 43-voice group was performing in a suburban church on Friday evening. Rusty looked forward to getting out of the city periodically, and any chance to sing with a choir brought back fond memories of his college days.

The New Year was off to a banner start, building off the outstanding performance review he received at Ridgewell for 2002. While he resented the sales force optimization effort in October, his involvement that weekend (he worked his butt off) was a turning point. The CIO was duly impressed with how far the team got and touted it so strongly that the CEO established a new stretch goal for the IT team to achieve before year-end. He wanted to close the year strong and give the Street something to talk about.

Rusty was pulled from the final stretch of the knowledge management effort ("Sue, how can you? This is my soul, my lifeblood . . . " "Rusty, you're right, but this hurry-up sales force effort is, frankly, more important. KM will wait. Ridgewell needs you.") He worked every weekend from late October until Christmas, with the exception of Thanksgiving, but the project was a huge success, especially his workstream. He got word on December 23 that he would receive a bonus almost equaling his salary ("Equal, do you believe?" he relayed to Chip). A possible promotion awaited.

He grinned, thinking back. The odd message from October popped to mind. *'Strange, for sure, but shee-it, that message nailed it. I not only engaged productively, I got everyone else to do so. I missed a bunch of parties and I sure as hell worked one heckuva lot of weekends, but it was worth it!'*

2003 was going to be great, and now a concert was icing on the cake.

On Friday night, members of the Metropolitan Men's Choir made their individual ways to the Bedrock Hills Presbyterian Church. They performed a concert of sacred and contemporary Christian works flawlessly. The sanctuary overflowed with an appreciative congregation. Rusty and his peers sang with warmth and feeling, their masculine voices cascading from the elegant rafters down over the audience.

After the celebratory final number, the choir and congregation broke for dessert and coffee in the church's Assembly Hall. Rusty went through the buffet line (*'So many choices, so little room on the plate,'* he thought humorously) and took a seat with one of his choir friends. They were encouraged by Reverend Andrews to mix and mingle with the congregation. "No more than two of you Met Men at any one table."

Rusty had barely taken his first bite of a decadent chocolate cake, when an older couple joined the table. Swallowing hard, Rusty wiped his mouth with a napkin and put his hand out in greeting, matching the lady's mirrored move.

"What a pleasure to hear you men sing. My, that was wonderful." Rusty smiled in response. "I'm Janet Walker and this," she pointed, "is my husband Walt. We just can't get over how lovely the music was." Walt shook hands with both choir members.

Over the smorgasbord of desserts, the group at the table discussed the music, the meaning of a few obscure pieces, and the style of several contemporary numbers. Gradually, the conversation turned to personal backgrounds, education, family, and professions as desserts disappeared.

The Walkers reminded Rusty a great deal of his parents down south. They were kind, sincere, and thoughtful. While dressed nicely, they had no airs, and–based on their blue-collar jobs before retirement–they were not especially well-to-do. The Walkers and Rusty continued talking long after the others left.

"I must say, it's so nice meeting a young man like you. And one who likes to sing."

"Well, thank you, Mrs. Walker."

"Call me Janet. No need for formality."

"Janet it is."

"And you say you do computer work?"

"That's right. I've been with Ridgewell for several years. I do mostly software design, but also–when the need arises–some operational stuff."

"I'm always having problems with our laptop. My son suggested getting one, and it's just been a bugger."

"They can be temperamental, for sure. Sometimes desktops are more reliable."

Janet shrugged. "I was just on the phone yesterday with some nice young fellow in India. What an accent! Nonetheless, he stayed right with me trying to clear up–" Janet took off on a long story of her travails. She reviewed the scenario in excruciating detail anticipating Rusty's keen interest. While true initially, by the twelve minute mark, his interest waned.

"So, do you think that made sense?" Janet stopped. Rusty had drifted in the last stretch.

The silence lengthened until Walt stepped in, "Janet, I'm sure Rusty doesn't need chapter and verse on your trials with Dell."

"Look at me, prattling on like that. I'm sorry, making you talk business on your night off. A regular busman's holiday?" chuckled Janet.

"Not at all. I like understanding what end-users experience. You know, if you need some help and India's just too hard to understand or get a response from, give me a call. I'd be happy–"

"You are too kind. That's not necessary."

"No problem. Many times you can talk this stuff through on the phone. Here's my name and number," Rusty scribbled his home phone on his Ridgewell business card. "I hate to eat and run, but it's getting kinda late. So I think, I better–"

"Say no more. Of course, we've talked your ear off. You really are a fine young man."

"Rusty, very nice meeting you. All the best with your career and your singing," closed Walt.

"Thank you. Very nice getting to know you. Do ring me up, if a PC problem warrants. Have a nice evening."

Rusty hustled out to his car and headed back downtown, a thirty-minute drive at night. Despite the hour, he left the church with a warm, satisfied feeling. Following the great music, he had listened (mostly) to the Walkers, tried to give some counsel, and offered some help that would–with little doubt–never be called upon.

SEVENTEEN

Like the eye of a hurricane, a brief respite in the depleting side effects of chemo passed over on Saturday evening and into Sunday. Though not wholly unexpected given the cycle, it proved pleasant nonetheless. In the still of Sunday morning, Bernice enjoyed a warm shower. Standing at the mirror, reviewing her physique and completely hairless scalp in the mirror, she frowned, "How much worse . . . ?" In the closet, she found an unfamiliar robe ("Beverly, no doubt") and slipped it over her increasingly saggy skin.

Still feeling energetic, she navigated the staircase. Tigger and Spider meowed ignored greetings. Bernice paid little heed, beyond throwing some dry cat food toward their dishes. Most landed on the recently mopped floor. She stepped quietly around the kitchen, while followed just as silently by two shadows.

'Maybe some tea,' she thought. She leaned heavily on the counter looking out the window, surveying the frosty snow covering her side yard. The lights in her neighbor's house warmly emitted a welcome. "Haven't seen them in ages," groused Bernice. "They probably think I died. Damn well could've. Couldn't be much worse than this . . . "

Bernice took her cup of tea to the nook and sat. She watched the steam rise as she awaited the next round of sickness to wash across. With no symptoms striking, Bernice sipped some tea. It warmed her, tracing its way down her throat. Her face flushed as she contentedly breathed in the vapors. Finishing the first cup, she poured more hot water and put in a tea bag to steep.

She carried the steaming cup to the study. *'Where it all began,'* she thought. *'Where is that book I was holding?'* She scanned the bookshelves looking for the tome she had been lifting. The misshelved dark blue cover of *Latest Findings of Human Endocrinology – 2001* finally caught her eye. *'Someone's been messing with my study,'* she thought absently. *'What's that next to it?'* A thin book tucked next to a second, thick encyclopedic book, *Poisonous Plants: The Human Reaction* caught her eye. She reached for the ivory-bound book with black print.

She groaned as she stretched. On occasion, her surgery site still felt like someone else's skin. It remained taut, causing her to unconsciously hold it as she reached. She pulled down the unfamiliar booklet, *The Hemlock Society: When Enough is Enough. 'I don't remember this,'* pondered Bernice. *'A gift, I suppose. It's shelved correctly.'* Smirking at the timely black humor, a sudden wave of fatigue crashed across her. She grimaced, setting the booklet down. She collected her cooled tea and returned upstairs to the comfort of her bed.

Barely reaching the bed, diarrhea lashed out, much like the trailing wall of the hurricane's eye. With unexpected force and fury allowing no reaction time, Bernice soiled herself and her bed covers. "Oh, Mother of God," she uttered as the pungent odor rose. She sagged into the bed with the knowledge that she couldn't even control her most intimate functions.

"How will I clean this up?" she moaned. "Oh, shit." Remarkably, she nodded off into a dark sleep. The cats stayed away.

Nearing noon, Carol unlocked the front door and quietly stepped into the house. She listened for sounds and hearing none, remained silent as she walked to the kitchen. She put down her bag and squatted to talk to Tigger and Spider, who surreptitiously entered.

"Hello, kitties. How's Momma?" Noting the cat food on the floor, Carol retrieved a dustpan and brush. "Were you messy eaters? You really need to take better care. Now, let's go see what Momma's up to." Carol grabbed her medical bag and trudged upstairs. "What? You guys don't want to visit? What's the matter?" Carol continued to chatter as she ascended. Both cats watched from the entry hall. "Suit yourselves. I'll just get all the love myself."

The upstairs was still, though the door to Bernice's room was cracked open. On entering the room, the stench nearly overcame Carol. "Oh my, what do we have here?" She looked to the bed where Bernice sprawled atop the covers. Evidence of her accident showed on her nightgown, robe, the fitted bottom sheet, and the carpet next to the bed. "My, you had a whopper, Dr. L."

Past her initial surprise, Carol strode purposefully to the bed. Bernice remained asleep, but Carol checked her vitals. Bernice's breathing was slightly shallow, but otherwise she merely fought the persistent low-grade temperature. "What brought this on?" Carol noted the half-full teacup.

"Dr. Langdon? Let's rouse you a bit. We need to clean you up."

Bernice's eyes flickered open and shut. Disoriented and confused, she looked at Carol through the fog of waking. "What?" she whispered.

Carol enunciated slowly and carefully, as if informing a preschooler, "You had a little accident. We can't let you stay like this."

Bernice gave a start and remembered. "How long have I slept?" she muttered.

"It's noon." Carol paused. "Come on, now. Let's get you up."

She helped Bernice sit up and get her bearings. "Let's get you bathed and into some clean clothes." She held Bernice's eroding waistline and guided her by the elbow. In the bathroom, she helped Bernice into the shower. For the second time that morning, hot water streamed against Bernice. "Doesn't that feel better?" queried Carol.

"Fabulous," muttered Bernice. "Just fabulous."

Carol parked Bernice in a different nightgown on a chair while she changed the sheets. As she worked, she provided a running monologue on her kids' antics and activities. She paused occasionally to solicit an opinion from Bernice, but her patient had closed her eyes and dozed in the chair. Carol took the soiled linens and clothing to the laundry. With carpet cleaner and baking soda, she cleaned the rug. Finally, Carol helped Bernice back to bed. "You rest now. You've had a rough morning."

Downstairs, Carol started the laundry, and after washing her hands thoroughly (for the third time since arriving), she got a glass of ice water. Seeing the debris from Bernice's tea-making efforts, she noted that Bernice had at least two cups of heavily caffeinated tea. *'I wonder if that's what did it? Chemo plus caffeine is gonna pack one heckuva punch.'* Going through the cupboards, Carol found the tea bags and placed all the caffeinated varieties in a sealed plastic bag. *'That should make it more difficult.'*

Before leaving an hour later, Carol took a chilled Ensure to Bernice's side and some cooked rice. "You'll feel better if you get something in you. Rice is good. Vanilla Ensure over ice—well, you know about that already."

Late afternoon, the house tranquil once more, the Ensure had been sipped. The rice stood dry and cold. Bernice lay silently in the growing darkness. *'This is dreadful'* beat in her head as she waited for the next visitation from the dark side.

At dusk, the doorbell rang. Bernice ignored it, but it rang again. She sighed deeply, as getting up required such effort. She finally roused sufficiently to descend the stairs. *'Probably gone by now,'* she thought grimly. She cracked open the heavy front door to the cold January air. Roger Gallo stood patiently.

"Hi, Professor Langdon. My mom suggested I bring you something. Here." His planned speech accelerated as his eyes enlarged assessing his customer. Bernice stared back through heavy-lidded eyes behind her crooked glasses.

Roger handed over a plate of brownies. "I helped my mom make them. They're really good. We put in chocolate chips. I hope you like them. Well, I better be going. Hope you're—uhhh—feeling better." Roger started down the front steps.

"Wait a minute." Bernice opened the door wider. "I'm not feeling well these days. Thank your mother." She breathed with labor.

Roger flashed his trademark smile. "Well, sure, Professor. I'll be seeing you." He turned and, in an instant, faded into the dim light of the approaching evening. Bernice slowly closed the door after watching until he disappeared completely. A tear rolled down her cheek, quickly followed by another and another.

"Why am I crying?" she mumbled. "How will I ever make it through four more months?" She sighed again. "I just don't know that this is worth it."

She carried the brownies to the kitchen island and then retraced her steps. The light from the study remained on from earlier. As she strode into the office to extinguish the desk lamp, she noticed the small white booklet sitting on the edge of the bookshelves.

"Well, that might be an interesting read," she thought, picking up the booklet. "I just might do some browsing." With that quiet statement, she brought the *Hemlock Society* handbook upstairs.

* * *

At home, Roger entered the garage where the bay for his dad's car stood empty. The exposed brick wall separating garage and house instantly riveted him. A burning circle of bluish-white light, like the one in the professor's side patio, illuminated the wall. More quickly than in October, some of the bricks' outlines began glowing. Like before, some started to wink out while others burned eerily.

'It's happening again,' thought Roger. *'What is it? The same message?'* The earlier directive had been odd but became more clear with time. Only 'Choose Life' had proven elusive, but even that fell into place.

He was hanging out with some other freshman football players at a teammate's house. During the afternoon, the guys made bets–egging each other on to more and more edgy stunts. Several of the bigger, tougher guys discovered the cage where the host's sister kept her pet rabbits. Two linebackers lifted the rabbits from the cage and paraded them around the basement.

"Hey, look what we got," grunted the stockier of the two.

"Gonna make ourselves some rabbit stew," chortled the other.

"I'm gonna get me a rabbit's foot," said the first as he squeezed one rabbit's paw. The rabbit whimpered, its nose twitching wildly. It suddenly urinated, spraying the jock's shirt and pants.

"Ya fuckin' rabbit," spewed the damp lineman. "I'm gonna wring your neck."

The football player squeezed the rabbit harder, while the other rolled with laughter. "You got peed on," he spit out. "You're all wet. You turkey."

"I am gonna kill this rabbit. It's a goner," snarled the first as his face reddened with anger and embarrassment. The other players grew quiet.

"You can't do that. It's my baby sister's rabbit. Put it down."

"Make me. The damn thing pissed on me. No one pisses on me, let alone some jerk of a rabbit." He moved his hands to the rabbit's neck and began squeezing.

Not thinking, just acting, Roger sprang across the room and knocked the teammate to the ground. His grip relaxed, and the terrified bunny hopped away with remarkable agility.

"What the hell are you doing, Gallo?"

"I'm saving you some grief. You're gonna be in real trouble if you do something stupid. Just let it go."

"Who you talkin' to? I've got a mind to beat up your scrawny ass."

"That's enough. Stop it, guys," the host stepped forward. While neither Roger nor the host matched the size of the two assailants, they–with the six other teammates–proved formidable enough.

The two linemen put up their hands in mock surrender. The other rabbit jumped and joined the first cowering under a table. "So what about that pool game? You didn't think we were really gonna kill those bunnies?" They snorted and the tension in the room dissipated. Roger didn't stay much longer, but he was glad he'd been there. Choose Life. He hadn't really thought of it in the moment, but it made sense.

Roger wondered if the new words would be a recap. Curious, he studied the twinkling mortar.

PERSIST
GO BACK
KEEP SMILE
SAY UNCLE

This was more ambiguous than going to a dance with Melissa. He smiled. That was some dance, and now he and Melissa were an item. But what was this one all about? The words sparkled and shimmered in the dark garage. As his mom opened the door to the kitchen to suggest he come in, the message faded. The words, however, remained branded on Roger's brain.

* * *

Monday mornings always proved demanding at Dane & Caldwell. Skip left home in a rush after oversleeping. Traffic was slow into town; he felt behind as the day started. He hoped to join Amy and the boys for the evening Epiphany service at church, but the day ahead was a wildcard.

'What a way to start the new year,' he thought, having vacationed from Christmas Eve through last Friday. He twisted his neck uncomfortably behind the necktie's somewhat unfamiliar knot, sighing heavily as he waited at another red light.

Upon arrival, Penny shot him a staccato firestorm. "Good news, your first two meetings cancelled. You have some time to prep for the partners' meeting over lunch. Since you need to update them on Amalgamated, do you need Vince?"

"Thanks, Pen. No, I don't need him; he sent a brief. I would like to talk with Baker, if we can find him. We are making progress on the Mexicani situation and have, apparently, sidestepped the highest risks of litigation. Can you get him on the phone?"

"Sure. Otherwise, no interruptions?"

"Yup. I need to prepare my thoughts on two candidates we're evaluating for partner in the upcoming election. We're doing previews today."

Skip shut his door and settled at his desk, with his back to the expanse of windows overlooking downtown. Working through email, he eliminated the bulk of the internal "all staff distribution" communiqués. Notices on changes in benefit premium schedules, 2003 training programs, and a reminder on appropriate behavior at office parties (catalyzed by rather scandalous behavior at the Christmas gala) quickly became trash.

While reviewing candidate files, Penny buzzed. "Hey, they want to clean windows. Someone complained (probably Mr. Caldwell), and they're coming around to do the insides, okay?"

Skip shrugged. "Sure, but can you clean off the sills? They always make a mess if you leave it."

Penny barely finished moving the piles of papers, books, and folders that Skip kept on his overwide windowsills when a window washer appeared, bucket and squeegee in hand. He smiled a toothy grin and pointed with his squeegee toward the windows.

"Go ahead," Penny nodded.

Penny exited and the young man moved to the windows. As Skip worked, he could hear the man spraying the windows and then the spongy squeak and scratch of the tool moving across the glass. Though moving quickly, the man was in Skip's corner office for some time, working from window to window. When he finished, he quietly departed. Skip barely looked up as he thoughtfully jotted down notes for the lunchtime conversation. Later that morning, Penny buzzed again.

"I have Arnold Baker." The phone clicked.

"Arnold?"

"Good morning, Skip," wheezed Arnold. There was silence as Skip imagined Arnold taking a long drag on his cigarette. "How goes the battle?"

"Doing quite well, actually. I thought it made sense to connect, ensure there are no new developments I should know about."

The men discussed the latest Amalgamated issues. As they talked, Skip swiveled around to look out over the city. Doing so allowed him to avoid distractions on his desk or computer. However, his attention was immediately snared:

BRO LANGDON WILL ATTEND 3 KINGS DROP BAK

Smeared across the cleaned glass, the statement drifted off like contrails of a departing plane. There could be more, but it was gone–perhaps evaporating earlier. Skip stared, half-listening as Arnold outlined the latest Amalgamated initiatives.

"What do you think?" concluded his client, taking another deep drag. The depth and duration of his subsequent cough was concerning. Skip collected his fragmented thoughts.

"Well?" Arnold tapped impatiently.

"I would need more information on the proposed additional acquisition," Skip picked up on Arnold's last few words before the coughing attack. "Given the experience with Mexicani, we must ensure we've done sufficient due diligence so as not to be caught with," he paused, "our proverbial pants down."

"But the Mexicani deal has worked out well. With your help, we've avoided litigation and a class action suit. We still have a lower cost base than the competition. Not surprising. A bunch of wetbacks are willing to take a few additional dollars and keep their mouths shut."

Skip opened and closed his mouth several times. This was not the way he summarized their work together in recent weeks. Had he been duped? Had he been a front man for a shady operation that was continuing, now with an apparent legal stamp of approval? Not good, was all he could think.

"So, we should meet on this next deal. How about Wednesday? Maybe you could come here?"

Skip could imagine Baker's yellow, smoke-stained teeth leering out from between his lips. "Let me do some homework on the target. El Camino Ola Ancha?"

"Yes," purred Arnold. "You do some background. Let's plan for a meeting Wednesday afternoon? Come alone. I'd rather keep this close to the vest for now."

Skip swallowed hard. "I suppose," he weakly countered.

With the commencement of more coughing, Arnold left Skip sitting with the phone at his ear, contemplating the conversation and the strange words still smeared across his windows. As the sun went behind dark clouds, the windows acquired a strange glow, first appearing along the frame. The intensity grew, the edge sparkling and shimmering.

'Was that there all along?' thought Skip. *'Perhaps it's catching some rays?'* That defied logic, as heavy, snow-laden clouds scuttling across the sky hid the sun. As the light exuded the bluish-white cast of a welder's torch, a thought suddenly exploded. *'This is remarkably like my Blackberry.'*

"Penny? Could you come here?" he practically shouted through the intercom. His assistant appeared, catapulted from her desk.

"Shut the door, please," Skip quickly drew Penny across the room. "What do you see?"

She stared at his windows. "Well, isn't that the strangest thing? How'd you do that?"

"Pen, that's not something I did."

"Just pulling your leg, Boss. I can see that. Did the window washer see this?"

"I doubt it. It wasn't there this morning when I arrived. Remind you of anything?"

"Well . . . ." As Penny pondered, the words acquired a similar coloring as the burning white edge. "This looks quite similar to your Blackberry last fall. Remember?"

"Bingo. I thought so too. I wanted an independent perspective. I thought I was losing my mind." Skip laughed. "Then again, maybe I am. The message is odd. Last time was strange too, though remarkably prophetic."

Penny raised a brow.

"I skipped a meeting with Baker and went to Connor's play. He was tickled pink. We still got the Amalgamated deal and it all worked out. All so simple in hindsight."

"Funny, how the message appeared again while talking with Mr. Baker."

"I suppose, though I've had many meetings since. Not a new word or message for any of them." Skip contemplated his smeared window. "I don't like where this Amalgamated deal is going, Pen. It makes me uneasy. You know," a sudden revelation emerging, "I wonder if the first message was bolder than my interpretation. I thought it meant skipping one meeting; maybe it intended for me to forego the entire relationship."

Penny stood incredulous. "Please. And just who is sending you these messages? You sure you're not writing them?"

Skip looked back at her. "Interesting notion, but no. Take this morning: I didn't stand up from the time you were in here clearing the windowsills (thank you) until just now."

With a smile, Penny hummed eerie, but familiar music. "Be prepared. You are about to enter the Twilight Zone," she somberly intoned. They both laughed.

"I'm writing this down and the first message too," murmured Skip. The words continued shining. "Maybe they'll be clearer if I think about them more." Finished scribbling and looking at his watch, he said, "Ah, the group is probably already downstairs. I better hustle. Stand watch on the windows."

The advice proved unnecessary. Before Skip left, the smeary words on the window evaporated. The window frame returned to normal as snowflakes started falling from the cold sky.

As Skip headed downstairs, he wondered: *'Who's Langdon? That's gotta be somebody's name. And what will he do? Attend three kings? And how's he going to drop bak? It's all very odd.'*

'Langdon will' became clear at lunch. Just as the senior partners concluded their advancement discussion, Taylor Caldwell stood up.

"I have one extraneous piece of housekeeping." He paused. "I got a call this morning from Bill Langdon, over at Stoner. You know him?" A wave of nods circled the table, save a few folks including Skip. "His father was William Langdon, the former dean of the business school over at the university. He died ten years ago or so."

Someone piped in, "Had a brain aneurysm. Went instantly."

Taylor continued. "Well, his son is a fine lawyer. That said, Bill Senior's will and estate planning were done here. He was assisted by John Eden, who–of course–has retired to Florida."

More head nodding accompanied fond recollections of the avuncular retiree.

"Bill's mother, Bernice Langdon, is fighting a tough battle with cancer."

"Wasn't she a professor at the university?" questioned a partner.

"Yes, recently retired. She's going through chemo and having a tough time. She asked for her affairs to be put in order. Bill requested a plan update and a consultation with Bernice, as possible, on her wills–living and otherwise." He paused. "Would someone volunteer to take on the Langdon will?"

Skip went numb. How could one of the phrases from his window unexpectedly make an appearance over lunch? Without thinking, his hand rose. "Very good, Skip. That's it, gentlemen . . . and Nancy." Caldwell smiled at the one female present.

On the elevator ascent, Skip reflected on the window's words. He needed to decode the rest and wondered if the implications would be as immediate as 'Langdon will.' He reviewed his notes:

BRO LANGDON WILL ATTEND 3 KINGS DROP BAK

Now knowing that 'Langdon will' was one phrase implied that 'will' was not a verb, as he'd initially thought. If separated, perhaps the other parts were equally discrete ideas. 'Attend 3 Kings' and 'Drop Bak' might be unique actions. He needed more time to think it through, but his afternoon was jammed. Perhaps driving home, he could figure it out. Convinced of his plan, he dove into the afternoon's agenda.

EIGHTEEN

With Epiphany's dawn, Janet looked forward to the evening service at Bedrock Hills. The tale of the wise men—how they followed their hearts, watched the burning sign in the sky, and brought gifts to the baby in a manger—always proved meaningful. It also marked the close of the Christmas season. Janet never looked forward to the change from the holidays to the cold, gray barrenness of midwinter, even though it was a natural affirmation of the continuing flow of life. "If we didn't have the stark plainness of January and February, we'd fail to appreciate the wonders of spring and summer, as well as the beauty of the year-end festivities," Walt annually reminded her.

Janet's day was busy: visiting Hilda at Estate Homes, driving to the Medical Center to see a neighbor and a fellow parishioner, and, finally, calling on Bernice. As she approached Fox Den Road, her mind processed Bernice, *'She is quite the character. It's so unfortunate that chemo is going so badly. I pray that outward appearances are deceptive, and the chemo is beating the cancer's spread. Your will be done,'* Janet fervently finished her long prayer list. Just after two o'clock, Janet rang the doorbell.

The door opened to reveal the Filipino nurse. "I was passing the front door on the way upstairs when I saw you coming up with an all-too-familiar bag. Come in. It's brutally cold."

Janet smiled back at the beaming nurse. "It is good to get inside," she agreed, setting down the Dunkin' Donuts bag. She removed her warm hat and gloves. Her gray hair stuck out in a multiplicity of ways. She glanced in a side mirror and laughed, "Oh, look at me. I'm quite the sight!" She patted her hair down with no great effect.

Carol chuckled as well. "No worries. I like the look. My son would probably say it's all the rage. He and his friends spend more on gels to keep their hair sticking out at all kinds of—Enough. It's Mrs. Walker, isn't it?"

"Please call me Janet."

"I heard your casserole was to die for. It smelled so good. My mouth just watered."

Janet smiled appreciatively. "I can get you the recipe. Almost whatever you have on hand can work. I'm not a particularly big cook anymore."

"Stop. I don't believe it. Beverly raved." Carol turned more serious, "I don't know how much the professor actually ate. Her appetite remains quite light."

"How is she?" inquired Janet. "Does she want visitors?"

"She's been snoozing since I got here. She sleeps a lot. This should be her good week, as she's mid-cycle today. It's taking longer for her to work through each round."

Janet nodded sympathetically. "I've seen others. Oh my, it can be hard."

"It sure can, but you do what you gotta do. That's what I say. It's up to the rest of us to help you get through the battle. Make you as comfortable as possible."

"You nurses are just angels, you really are."

Carol laughed, "My kids would disagree on the halo." She paused. "So, exactly what treat did you bring today? I'm thinking the Dunk doesn't make casseroles!"

Janet shook her head, "I picked up some chocolate chip cookies. I didn't know what Bernice would enjoy, but I thought it might provide a light snack for others or for her grandkids."

"Oh, they'll be eaten. No doubt." Carol cocked her head. "I think I hear the good professor now. I'll zip up and see if she's up for a visit. Could you wait here?" Carol lightly ascended the stairs and disappeared.

As Janet stood in the entry hall, she realized how fatigued she felt. She noticed the study door open and stepped in, remembering the comfortable seat there. She felt guilty moving around someone's home without invitation, but her aching legs and back compelled her. *'I don't think anyone will mind,'* she reflected.

As she perused the built-in bookcases, she heard a door close toward the back of the house. Janet stood and stepped out of the study, startling Beverly who had her first foot on the staircase.

"I wasn't expecting you, Janet." Beverly's eyes bulged from surprise as she came over to give a hug.

"How are you doing, dear? This can be so hard on the family."

"Okay, I suppose. It has its moments. Mother is having such a tough time." Beverly stopped. "Is Carol up there?"

"Yes. I just got here and she was going up. I was waiting a moment to see if she wanted some company. The days can seem so endless when you're ill."

"Yes, they can. Mother has not been in great spirits since chemo started." She paused and reflected, "Though she's always more dour than most. Do you know her well?"

"I can't say that I do. I've seen her at church occasionally, but I don't believe she's a regular."

"No, she's more of a Christmas and Easter attendee," Beverly shook her head sadly. "I do hope this chemo works. I really don't see any improvement so far."

Janet thoughtfully watched as Beverly chose her words. "She seems to get more and more withdrawn. And when there is something to say, it's either harsh and nasty or left unsaid. I'm sometimes at a real loss as to how to help." Beverly welled up suddenly. "It's just so hard."

"There, there. Your being here is a blessing. Bernice can't voice that just now, but it is. I'm sure of it. God has placed you here." Janet stroked Beverly's back lightly.

Tears trickled quietly down Beverly's face, ruining her light mascara. "I guess so. Though it's sometimes impossible to see."

"Stay the course. Your mother-in-law needs you to."

Unnoticed, Carol descended and joined the two ladies, immersed in their quiet conversation. "Not to surprise you, but—" chirped Carol.

Janet and Beverly turned. "How is she?" they chorused.

"She's okay. Resting comfortably is the clinical term." Carol smiled. "She says she wants no visitors, but I think that's an act. I believe we should just surprise her."

"Oh, I don't know. I can just be on my way," Janet uttered hesitantly. "I certainly don't want to impose."

"It's no imposition. She needs to join the living. She can't just hibernate up there."

With a little additional encouragement, the trio headed toward Bernice's bedroom. Opening the door, they found her propped up, watching the almost muted television. With drapes drawn tightly and no lights on, a stuffy, sick smell permeated the room. Bernice paid no heed as they entered. The quiet banter of an afternoon talk show filled the room as they stood semi-circle beside the bed.

"Mother, how are you feeling today?"

Bernice turned her bald, gray head toward Beverly and stared through eyes sunk deep into the pallid skull. She was not wearing her glasses; her eyes appeared small and squinty.

"Dr. Langdon, I knew you'd want some company. The days can seem so long if it's just you, me, and the TV . . . " Carol trailed off as Bernice gave no response, beyond her labored breathing as her torso rose and fell.

She smiled grimly at the group. "I'm feeling just dandy," she uttered, breaking the silence. "Perhaps we should have a party?"

"That can most certainly be arranged. I'd be delighted to pull that together. What theme might we go with? Circus? Tropical Island?" Carol tried to inject some energy, but the words fell flat.

"I don't know whether you've got an appetite, but I brought—" Janet was interrupted as Bernice coughed long and hard. Gasping for breath, she spit out a mouthful of phlegm. She closed her eyes after exerting.

"Mother, can we get you something? Carol brought Ensure. Maybe that would help soothe your throat."

"I don't like the damn stuff." Bernice jabbed her finger toward Carol, "She keeps insisting I drink it. Tastes like shit and looks like goddamn gruel." She stopped. It was the most animation Bernice had exhibited in some time.

"It's good for you, Dr. L. We've been over that. You just want to win the argument on academic merits," Carol winked at the other two. "I was just saying to my mother-in-law this morning–"

"I'm tired. I'm going to close my eyes," muttered Bernice. "You all stay as long as you like. Don't mind me." After listening to four commercials interrupt the talk show, Carol nudged Beverly and jerked her head toward the door mouthing, "Let's go downstairs." The three adjourned.

Bernice lifted one eyelid surveying their departure. With them gone, she sat up more fully and reached for her glasses on the nightstand. Next, she leaned over and opened ever so quietly the little drawer in her nightstand and retrieved the *Hemlock Society* guide. Turning to the dog-eared page, she continued her reading.

Downstairs, the ladies stood around the kitchen island. Janet spoke first, "I don't want to interrupt more than I've done. I can see myself out."

"No interruption whatsoever. I'm so glad you're here. You are so faithful in your visits," responded Beverly. "Please don't go so soon. Stay and visit."

Carol suggested tea and added, "I know of a little treat that's just sitting in the hallway calling us." Puzzled, Beverly looked at her, but Janet jumped up.

"I'll stay just a bit, if you insist. Let me get the cookies." She returned momentarily from the hall as the tea kettle started to heat. She opened the bag, "I'm afraid they're not homemade, but Walt and I just love them."

Moments later, the tea prepared, the three ladies sat. Doctoring their respective cups of tea, each was quiet and lost in her own thoughts. Sipping slowly, they surveyed the snowy backyard.

"I'm worried about her," Beverly finally interjected. "She seems to be getting worse."

"It's very normal, actually. Chemo is no picnic. Many times, I've seen patients go down hill before they pop back." Carol reflected further, "You don't really know what's happening on the inside. We all want instant cures, but all we see is how awful the whole experience is. Some people handle it better than others."

"Amen," nodded Janet. "One of my closest friends had breast cancer badly several years ago. They didn't diagnose it quickly though part of that was Helen. She rarely went for her checkups. I don't know if she ever had a mammogram, until—well, too late. She had a lot of lymph node involvement. She had a double radical mastectomy and then extensive chemo and radiation. My goodness, it was hard." The others listened sympathetically. "But what a trooper. She stayed upbeat and positive, even on the worst of days. Such an inspiration . . . " Janet's voice cracked.

"How is she now?" quietly inquired Beverly.

"She's been in remission for three years. She's not over that critical five-year period, but she's doing really well. Her hair's darker now, but it's also quite curly. She jokingly calls it her 'cancer wave.' The doctors say she's their miracle story. They tell her at each semi-annual checkup that she shouldn't still be here, given how extensive her cancer was." Janet concluded, "She's always at the top of my prayers, even as the list grows. It gets longer the older you get."

Beverly and Carol murmured their agreement. "What a wonderful inspiration. I hope we can say as much about Mother."

"Though I don't think she's going to win the Miss Congeniality award," smiled Carol.

"No, I think not," softly added Beverly.

"You know, I've been thinkin' these last couple of days. Your mother-in-law needs more than just TV and a dark room, especially in the off-cycle weeks. She is just sinking like a rock in that gloomy, smelly room. I've used so many different cleansers and room fresheners and none eliminate that awful 'sick smell.' You know what I mean?"

The others nodded.

"I try and try, and the room still smells like a tomb and has lighting to match. When my kids had chicken pox, their rooms had that awful sick smell. That's what Bernice has going on, only worse." Carol looked at the other ladies expectantly. "She needs something else to focus on."

"I doubt she'd read."

"She doesn't have the stamina to organize her study. It's something she's wanted to do."

"What hobbies does she have?" questioned Janet.

"She always enjoyed her work when she was teaching," responded Beverly.

Janet nodded. "What else does she enjoy?"

"She likes to travel. Another nonstarter."

"No, but she could do virtual travel. That might fit with what I was considering. Is she into computers?" brainstormed Carol.

"She has an old one downstairs. A real dinosaur. I think it was my father-in-law's. He died ten years ago. "

"I can't imagine she's connected to the internet," laughed Carol.

"Oh, I'm almost certain she's not. She may have used email at the university with her students, but I don't believe here at home. My kids complain about visiting and not being able to instant message."

"Walt and I got a laptop a while back," Janet added eagerly. "We enjoy it. We plan trips on it, Walt uses it for stocks, and we actually take it with us when we travel. I would never have believed it years ago."

"I wonder if we could get her intrigued with that. Get her a good computer. Get a speedy connection–not just dial-up, but maybe cable or something. I'm way over my head, but I believe they're faster." Carol accelerated.

"That's not a bad idea," added Beverly. "I don't know enough either, but I'll bet we could find someone who could help us with equipment and the right connection. We could surprise her, maybe install it in the TV room and get her interested in travel and anything else that intrigues her." Beverly enthusiastically gushed.

"Email would be possible too," suggested Janet.

"I like this. What a team," Carol raised her hand to high-five the others.

"We need to get started," suggested Beverly. "This is an off-cycle week, so it's good timing. Do you have any thoughts on how to get underway?"

Janet twinkled, "Walt and I attended a concert at church the other evening. We had dessert afterward with one of the performers, just the nicest young man. He gave me– well, let me see if I have it." She rustled through her purse. "A-ha, here." She placed Rusty's card, with his handwritten home number, in the center of the table.

"A musician?" questioned Beverly before studying the card.

"He's in the Metropolitan Men's Choir, but that's after work. At work, he's a–what's it say?–an applications developer. He offered to help us on any computer issues. I was telling him about dealing with support people in India. He must've thought me a ninny, but he kindly said he'd help if a need arose. I'll bet he'd be willing to help us out."

"Well, we can try. He may not have time, and Glenwood is certainly not downtown. Who knows where he lives?" Beverly slowly added.

"Sounds like a good notion to me. We'll just convince Rusty. If not, we'll find someone else." Carol warmed rapidly to the idea.

"You know, perhaps Bill's office could supply some support. He hates to ask for personal help, but it's another angle. I think this is a good enough reason; I'm sure he'd ask."

"Sounds like we have a couple of possibilities."

"Having an internet connection will give the kids a good reason to visit. They are so reluctant. While I understand on one level, she is their grandmother," concluded Beverly.

Janet and Beverly agreed to follow up quickly. Tea finished and cookies uneaten, the trio stood. "I have stayed much longer than I anticipated," said Janet looking at the wall clock. "Walt will wonder what happened to me." She said goodbye and hastily retreated out the front door.

Carol pulled together a snack for Bernice and returned upstairs as Beverly went to the study to pay bills. With the creak of the stairs, Bernice put her reading away, placed her glasses back on the table, and closed her eyes just as the door to her room pushed open.

* * *

Janet had barely put the car in Drive, when she noted a bright light coming from the radio monitor. In the small space above the buttons, the normally pale green mini-screen typically indicated the CD track or radio station. It now exuded a pulsing, warm orange-white glow around its perimeter. The glow throbbed in rhythm with the car's engine.

"Odd," she thought, immediately recalling the strange experience with the TV. While not precisely the same color, a similar flickering flame-like intensity framed this screen as before. While the TV looked more like a welder's torch, this resembled more the smoky crackle of a campfire. As she slowly drove, she watched the little screen–half expecting it to burst into flame.

As she turned out of the development, the screen lit up more fully. She paused at a stop sign to watch letters–with the same warm hue–move across the screen and stop.

FRIEND ENGAGE RUSTY SKIP B

Merging with traffic, Janet pondered the message aloud. "It looks like the phrase got cut off. I suppose it's obvious. Use Rusty and skip using Bill. I certainly hope Rusty doesn't mind. I wonder why we should avoid Bill. I don't know him, of course–only what Beverly described. He's probably just busy, much like Steve. Finding a different means of doing this without bothering him–perhaps that's the intent. I'll call Beverly as soon as I've gotten to Rusty. Maybe she can just not bother asking Bill."

Pleased with her faster deciphering ability this time, Janet considered raising the strange communications with Beverly. "She'll think I'm a kook," laughed Janet. Out of the corner of her eye, she watched the words silently beaming from the audio monitor.

Parking in her garage, she turned off the engine. The familiar engine noises died, but the screen stayed lit. The message burned with a final intensity. As she opened the car door and grabbed her purse, the screen went dark.

'This thing has a mind of its own, though it sure seems to know what I'm doing. I think I'll call Rusty right away. No point in delaying.'

Janet called out to Walt as she entered the house, but all was silent. Without removing her coat, Janet pawed through her bulging handbag and retrieved Rusty's card for the second time. She called and got his voicemail.

"Rusty? This is Janet Walker from Bedrock Hills Presbyterian. You may recall, we met the other evening after your lovely concert. You had the chocolate cake with cream cheese frosting. I was there with my husband, Walt, and had the little fruit tart. Well, I don't know where to start, but you had mentioned the possibility of helping out with computer issues should they come up and well–" Janet paused. "Well, a situation has arisen where we might use your assistance. I know it's not exactly what we had spoken of, but–let me give you a little background." Janet reflected on where to start.

"There's this member of our church family, Bernice Langdon. She's a retired university professor. Maybe you know her? She taught biology, I believe. Well, she's been quite ill and having a real tough–"

The voicemail tone rudely interrupted. Embarrassed and perplexed, Janet hung up.

"Rusty? Janet Walker again. I'm really not too good on these answering machines. I'm sorry if I'm filling yours up, but Bernice has been having a tough time. A group of us were thinking she needed a distraction and thought the idea of doing research, catching up on the news, and doing some–oh, what do you call it? Virtuous? No. Vital? No. Virtual, that's it . . . some virtual travel using the computer would be just the thing. The thing is none of us know enough about computers to get her set up. There was some talk about not using phone lines–avoiding, let me see, I wrote it down, 'avoiding dial-up connections' because they're slow? Does that make sense? Well, here I go again . . . I'm sure you know much more about this . . . Let me–" She was cut off once more.

"Rusty? Janet Walker. I'll be real quick. We wondered if you could help us out. I know it's an imposition, but you seemed like such a nice young man and I thought, well, maybe you would be willing to lend a hand. If you could, please give me a call. Here's my number." Hanging up, Janet sighed in relief, *'Well, I'm certainly glad that's done. I hate those machines.'* Now, she could think about dinner.

About the time Janet opened her refrigerator, Beverly and Carol both prepared to leave Bernice's house. Carol had an uneventful trip home.

Beverly did not. Before she reached the end of Fox Den, the perimeter of her music system's mini-screen was ablaze with a warm, golden-white light. Similar to the CD player in Bernice's kitchen, words appeared–though this time stationary:

MRS L ENGAGE RUSTY SKIP B

Beverly pulled to the curb, her attention riveted by the memory of the earlier experience and the apparent timeliness of this message.

"What is going on?" she wondered. "The color is different, but it's so similar. It's too odd for coincidence." She sat, trance-like, watching. Fortunately, Carol had driven off first, or she would've assumed there was a problem. "Then again, if she were here, someone else could see this."

Beverly changed inputs from radio to CD to tape; the message remained unchanged. The car's audio remained silent as the flickering yellow-gold words burned gaily from the little beige screen.

Beverly finally headed home. The message blazed away until the car was in her garage. She watched the communiqué for a final minute before getting out and heading into the house. *'Maybe I should call Janet and see if she's had any luck with Rusty, before I ask Bill. It's odd, as I would expect his firm to have more reason to support Bill's mother than this random guy that Janet met.'* She contemplated the messages.

'The message in November proved remarkably prescient. Perhaps this is right too, but where's it coming from? I don't get it.'

Inside, she picked up the phone to call Janet and heard the tell-tale triple tone indicating a waiting message. Before dialing further, she checked voicemail; one awaited her from Janet, indicating she had called Rusty and would keep Beverly apprised. She had a good feeling and felt Rusty was going to work out. So strong was her intuition on this, that she thought they just might "skip Bill's involvement."

"Would you listen to that?" Beverly said to the empty kitchen. "What an odd choice of words! There are so many ways she could've said it. It's got to be more than coincidence. I'll have to tell her next time we're together. She'll think me nuttier than Planters, but she may get a laugh."

* * *

The message light glowed bright red on Rusty's desk phone. He had just gotten back from an "all hands on deck" meeting with Sue and the CIO. They had a new major assignment–"direct from the CEO"–added to the current project list. Then again, the CIO never prioritized the list of urgent, high-impact projects concocted in the executive suite. Initiatives were always additive. "The guy just doesn't have an f'ing backbone in his body," Rusty complained on numerous occasions.

Rusty felt his pager go off several times during the meeting, but couldn't take calls or listen to voicemail with the entire IT leadership group surrounding the table. As the youngest present, he loved the exposure. The money proved pretty darn good as well. His career rocked.

He listened to two broadcast messages, a third message from a colleague wanting help on a software glitch, and then the successive messages from Janet.

He smiled at the first. The grin faded with the second and third stumbling attempts. *'Just doesn't pay to be too friendly,'* he thought. *'I have no time to head back to Bedrock or wherever it is this lady lives. Suck, she sure didn't waste time finding a computer problem.'* He sighed. Given his overwhelming workload in the next few weeks, he just couldn't comply–regardless of the legitimacy of Janet's request. Plenty of others could pull together the necessary equipment. He'd just say no.

Rusty hated refusing; his work ethic centered on, "Yes, can do." However, this should be easy to decline. He'd be respectful, as Janet reminded him of his mother, but a decline would result.

At five thirty in the evening, he looked up again; the Post-it on his flat screen reminded him to call Janet. As he tapped in the last digit and waited, his desktop screen acquired an odd glow.

'Ah, shit, not this again,' he thought as the phone rang, and the perimeter of his monitor shimmered and flickered with the burning colors of orange, yellow, gold, and red. The perimeter widened to nearly a half-inch before holding steady. Rusty watched, fascinated.

"Janet? This is Rusty Stillwagon with Ridgewell. How are you?"

"Oh, Rusty. Thank you so much for calling back so quickly. I was just in the middle of getting dinner and was thinking about you."

"Am I interrupting? I can call back."

Janet jumped on top of his words, "No problem at all. I know how busy you are. You are such a dear for calling."

Rusty watched his screen. Unlike before when words burned into the screen, a ticker tape of words now scrolled from right to left. They shared the flame-like color of the perimeter; however, they were blurry and impossible to read, like looking at a road sign through heavy fog. *'If only the fog would lift,'* thought Rusty. He half-listened as Janet launched into a more detailed description of Bernice Langdon's computer needs.

". . . and so," she was winding up for the request once more, Rusty could tell. "I was wondering. Actually, Bernice's daughter, her nurse, and I were wondering: Could you help?"

She stopped. Silence hung like a wet sheet.

"Well, the thing is, it is just so busy at Ridgewell. I am just getting dumped on, and I'm just not sure when I could get out to Bedrock."

"Oh, it's not Bedrock. Bernice lives in Glenwood. It's a mile or two closer to the City. She will just be so disappointed," Janet added. Recognizing Bernice had no idea this scheme was being hatched, she quickly continued, "–if she knew we were this close to getting her hooked up."

Rusty groaned inwardly. "I hear you." As he watched his screen, the fog began burning off. "I wonder if someone out there–a little closer to Glenwood–could do the trick?" He stopped. Turning down someone like his mom was so hard. Why couldn't he just be a hardass? Chip would have no difficulty. "Blow it off," he would say. "Say yes and don't show. They won't call back." That approach just didn't fit Rusty.

"I just don't know who we'd call," Janet sounded disappointed. Her voice lost energy.

Rusty sighed. "Let me think." He outlined his main responsibilities and projects as well as his calendar for the coming week.

"My, you are a busy man. I had no idea. Perhaps this is just too much of an imposition. I guess I should just look elsewhere. I didn't mean . . . " Janet rambled on apologetically. As she did, the scrolling letters suddenly were crystal clear:

TAKE TASK SEE BERNICE ASAP

Rusty jerked up as if struck by lightning, the words electrically riveting his attention. His last bout of computer hijinks provided great counsel. He thought it either ominous at the time or perhaps just an over-exercised brain, but now–the words were so timely to the conversation at hand. How could he refuse? Regardless of the sourcing (who at Ridgewell could predict the specifics of this conversation beforehand?), he should figure out a way to make it work.

Rusty broke in as Janet closed in on a goodbye. "Janet? Let's figure out how to make it work. I'll find a way to squeeze it into my schedule. Maybe this weekend?"

"Really? You would do that? You're sure?" Janet stumbled in anxious gratitude, so much so that Rusty laughed.

"Yes. I'll find a way. It'll be fun." It felt good to say yes and help someone who needed it.

"Oh, Rusty, you are an angel."

Rusty laughed again but quizzically looked at his computer screen, which continued to burn with the message from . . . well, from somewhere. "Hardly, but I'll do what I can."

"I'll let the others know. You are really a dear."

"I'll get back to you with a precise time. Find out what sort of budget we're working with."

"Of course. I'll talk with Beverly. I believe they come from some money," Janet added in a near-conspiratorial whisper. "I'll bet it's wide open."

With the concluding click of the connection, Rusty watched the screen saver return to his computer screen; the burning perimeter and blazing ticker tape faded away. He couldn't help uttering, "Sickest ever."

When Beverly checked voicemail after dinner, she was surprised to hear Janet's voice again. Consternation crossed her brow as Janet spelled out that she "engaged Rusty. We can skip Bill." Riveted once more by Janet's vocabulary choice, Beverly tuned out the subsequent requests on timing and budget.

'That is just too odd. I can't wait to share this,' thought Beverly as she loaded the dishwasher. She would call Janet back after ensuring that homework was underway.

NINETEEN

Beverly's call went unanswered, as Janet and Walt attended the Epiphany service at Bedrock Hills. Behind them sat Skip, Amy, and the boys. Reverend Andrews shared a thought-provoking message as he considered the visit from the magi, drawing out which gifts each of his congregants might bring to the manger. His energetic voice rose passionately as he prayed for the congregation.

"And so, my friends, as we close the season on this, the twelfth night of Christmas, I hope you have embraced the joy of the Christ child's birth, that you have shared that joy, that passion, and that mystery of the divine captured within the being of a human child. I pray you have not been too caught up in the commercialism and frenzy of the holiday season.

"Certainly, the excitement and the happiness of Christmas should be celebrated and enjoyed. But to get too tied up in knots over gift wrapping, decorating, finding that last perfect present for Aunt Suzie–isn't that right, Sara Hopkins?" he pointedly smiled toward a matronly grandmother, "baking that last six dozen cookies–that would be you, wouldn't it, Janet Walker?–or mindlessly attending the endless parade of Christmas concerts . . . well, that's not the reason for the season.

"We gather to celebrate that wonderful, curious, glorious coming of our Lord and Savior, Jesus Christ. He came as the perfect blend of divine and human. He came with a clear mission and purpose.

"And the three wise men came and worshipped him. They brought gifts–the best they could offer. That is what He asks of you–to bring the best you have. It need not be wealth, it need not be gold; it may not glitter or shine. It is what you can give. Bring your gifts to the manger. And friends, the manger presents itself all around us. As you'll remember what our Lord later said,

> *'I tell you the truth, whatever you did for one of the least of these brothers of mine, you did for me.'* [1]

"Hence, serve those around you with your gifts. Attend to them, just as the three kings came to worship and praise this newborn. Your presence here tonight, as you attend three kings–this service marking the visit of three kings–it can energize your new year. I pray for all of us that we use our gifts in service to our Savior–however and in whomever He presents Himself.

"May it be so for you and for me, in Christ Jesus Our Lord, Amen."

---

[1] Matthew 25:40

Skip gasped when Reverend Andrews moved into his closing remarks. Those three quick words misspoken by the pastor, 'attend three kings,' were no coincidence.

As the congregation sang *We Three Kings of Orient Are*, Skip compared the words on his window with those of the preacher. He barely uttered the lyrics as he considered the sermon more broadly: how might he best use his gifts to serve God and others? Could this all tie together? The Langdon will and now 'attend three kings'? If so, 'drop bak' must intend something as well. He stayed lost in thought as the singing stopped, and his family gathered their things.

"Are you coming home? Or are you just waiting for the next service to begin?" kidded Amy as Skip stared at the vacant pulpit.

"Just thinking," he smiled back. "I'm glad we made the service tonight."

"So am I. It sure was a push to get here."

"It was a hustle, for sure. Guys, hold on just a moment. Don't push," Skip injected pointedly. "We're all going to the same place." He paused and reached down, "Ma'am," he tapped a woman's shoulder lightly. "You dropped a glove."

"My, I believe I have. Wouldn't do me much good in here on such a cold night outside would it?" She laughed. "What a handsome family you are! I don't believe we've met. I'm Janet Walker and this," she pulled her partner by the elbow forcing him to turn from the exit line, "is my husband, Walt."

"Nice meeting you," was shared between the Walkers and the O'Neills as they exited the sanctuary. They shared the observation that in a big church like theirs, families might not cross paths for years. The seven adjacent worshippers dispersed and joined the streams of people heading to the parking lots.

"They were friendly," commented Amy, getting in the minivan.

"Yes, they were. I really like that about our church. Even with people you don't know, they step out and introduce themselves. It's like an extended family."

As the van left the parking lot and Skip eased onto the icy road, the three O'Neill brothers settled into fraternal bickering, a frequent proxy for conversation among them. After two miles of silent driving, Amy leaned over, "You're kinda quiet." She paused, "Whatcha thinking?"

"Oh, nothing, really," responded Skip.

"No way. You may not want to talk about it, but something's on your mind."

"Well, it's odd," Skip said, clearly distracted.

"Try me," insisted Amy though with good humor. "I'll be your sounding board."

"It's strange."

Amy remained quiet.

"You probably didn't notice, but tonight in the sermon, toward the end, Dr. Andrews stumbled on some words. He said, 'attend three kings' and then corrected himself and went on."

"You're right, I didn't notice. So what? We all make mistakes."

"Sure, but the words—'attend three kings': they were written on my office window today."

"Written on your window?"

"Well, like I said, they were written—actually, smeared—on the window this morning. Penny saw them too," he quickly added as if confirming that he was not hallucinating.

"Okay, so someone smeared them on your window. Odd coincidence, I agree, but I'd still say no big deal," Amy concluded. "You think it's weird."

"That's because there's more," admitted Skip.

"Oh?" Amy's voice rose, intrigued. "I like a mystery," she smiled.

"You're going to think I'm nuts."

"Well, I already know that and I still love you, sweetie," she grinned. They laughed as he pulled into the garage. The boys exploded from the rear seats. Amy and Skip took a moment longer to collect the few things they had brought along and followed the boys into the house.

"Tell you what. I want to hear the end of the story, but I need to make sure the boys are finished with their homework. Let's meet in bed for a nightcap and you can tell me your tale," smiled Amy.

With the house quiet at ten thirty, Amy lay in bed reading the day's *Ledger.* Her short brown hair showed moisture where her quick bath had splashed some water. She looked over her reading glasses as Skip entered the bedroom, wine bottle in one hand, two glasses in the other.

"Sorry, I'm a bit late," he said, closing the door. "I got caught up in a brief for tomorrow, thinking about a new angle we might take and—" he sheepishly stopped. "Sorry, too much shop."

"That's okay," smiled Amy. "I don't have any shop to talk for another couple of weeks. English Comp takes a breather."

"I'll join you in a moment."

As Skip disappeared into the master bathroom, Amy called out, "I'll do the wine?" Without waiting, she poured each a glass of cabernet and settled back into bed.

Several minutes later, Skip climbed in bed and reached for his goblet. Clinking glasses, they simultaneously said, "Cheers" and each took a sip.

Skip reached for the remote, but Amy put her hand over his. "No distractions. I want to know what's up: What got you all tied up earlier?"

"Oh, sure. I was just going to check the weather."

"It keeps repeating on the Weather Channel. Talk to me first."

Skip took another gulp of wine. "Well, let's see." He collected his thoughts. "It's from today, but it's actually more than just today."

"Oh?" Amy's eyebrows lifted as she removed her glasses and set them on the side table.

Skip launched into the story of the Blackberry "malfunction" as he recounted the event from the autumn. While unexpected, the message proved relevant at the time. Remarkably, Amy had used the same words when she spoke with him that same day.

"You didn't mess with my Blackberry?" Skip queried.

"I can barely keep up with email and downloading attachments," responded Amy in mock indignation that Skip thought her capable of such technological wizardry and willing to engage in such clandestine activities. "So, some odd words in October . . . and now another weird, coincidental message—what was it, 'attend three kings'—in January?" Amy reflected. "I'd agree. You're nuts."

"There's more."

"Really?" Her alto voice trailed upwards as she lingered, savoring the word.

Skip continued, "Today's message was longer. I've got it down cold: 'Bro Langdon will attend 3 kings drop bak.' When—"

Amy interrupted, repeating the phrase. She added, "That doesn't make sense. I get 'attend three kings,' but 'Brother Langdon will' do what? And 'drop back' where? How?"

" 'Langdon will' became clear over lunch," he paused hesitantly.

Amy eyed her husband and reached over to stroke his arm, implying he should continue.

Skip explained how he initially thought that someone named Langdon would attend something named three kings. The partner lunch convinced him a comma was omitted. Will was clearly the estate planning tool, not the verb. Skip outlined the Bernice Langdon situation. Largely due to the message and his curiosity, he volunteered to update the Langdon estate plan.

"So, you're paying attention to this little messenger?" Amy smiled. "I guess I'm learning how to get to you."

"Perhaps," he pondered. "So, let's assume, the message meant for me to take the Langdon legal work and go to the church service. We barely made it, but we got there. And I am going to do the Langdon will. What's 'drop bak'? I don't get that one." He finished his glass of wine. "Want more?" he questioned as he poured a second, smaller glass.

"No, hon, I'm fine."

"'Drop bak' doesn't make a heckuva lot of sense," he concluded after another two swigs.

"Let me play English professor."

"Well, you do it so well. Be my guest," elicited Skip's first smile in some time.

"Drop back could be reduce, fall back, or—"

"Wait, it's spelled b-a-k."

Amy frowned, "Phonetics? B-a-k is not a word. Obvious, I know, but this message is full of grammatical issues, as we've already assessed. So, let's—for a moment—assume there is legitimate intent. If so, then we have to believe that b-a-k is a misspelled word."

"Could be." Skip paused. "Yeah, it probably is . . . You're right."

"Well, if his—oh, look at me, I assume it's a guy messenger because his grammar's not so good, and his spelling appears equally dreadful," she rolled her eyes. Skip playfully mouthed "sexist," as Amy pushed on, "So, what could it be? Let's assume just one letter is missing: that could be back, bake, balk, bank, Baco—" Skip broke out laughing.

"Baco?" he grinned. "What, Dr. English, is baco?"

"You know Bacos—those artificial bacon bits. They're not good for you."

They both laughed and sipped more wine.

"Let me finish. Bark, bask, or . . . " she slowed. "That's it."

"Process of elimination. We've got them." He looked at his wife admiringly. "You're good." He leaned over and gave a quick kiss.

"Awww, shucks, you could turn a girl on, you know," she shyly looked away but immediately refocused.

"So, let's think about dropping each one of those. What does drop mean, anyway? Let go of, allow to fall, leave behind, want no more of. Right?"

"That covers it."

"So, which of these should you allow to fall or leave behind? I don't see how you can drop another verb . . . so that would seem to eliminate bake, balk, and bask. You could drop back . . . leave the fast track; stop working so hard, so many hours. Shall I continue?" Amy prepared to go down a well-traveled path. She looked at her husband who frowned. "Okay, I thought not. How about dropping a banking relationship we have or that you have at work?"

Skip frowned again. "I don't handle any of the financials at work. That doesn't make sense. You do the banking here. Any issues?"

Amy reflected on their bank: the accessibility of ATMs, the streamlined online banking, and the timely statements. "I don't see it."

Skip shrugged his shoulders.

"That leaves bark. Unless you're going to change professions, I don't see you becoming a tree climber and bark removal specialist. We don't have a dog, so dropping the bark doesn't get us there. I think we're at a dead end."

"Wait a minute. Who said it was just one letter? What if it's more than one? The end of the statement smeared away into the burning edge of the window."

"But the possibilities are endless . . . "

"Well, they could be . . . but what if it's only one or two more letters? What options does that yield?"

Twenty minutes later, two possibilities remained on the paper where many were now crossed out: "Drop Baker" and "Drop Basket." Amy poured more wine.

"It's got to be 'Drop Baker,'" said Skip. "It actually makes some modicum of sense. You've heard about Arnold Baker. He's tough, and if you ask me, he's kinda sleazy. I don't like him, and I don't like what he and Amalgamated are doing. I think they're using us as their *Good Housekeeping* seal of approval. I have to believe the message is saying to drop him and Amalgamated."

Amy remained silent as Skip thought aloud. "Very interesting," he mused. "I wonder . . . "

Several minutes passed as they downed their drinks. "Maybe you should sleep on it," suggested Amy.

"You're probably right, though I don't know if I'll sleep much. It's intriguing but also disturbing. Where are the messages coming from? Who's sending them? Why?"

"I'd like to know who's calling you 'Bro.' We said it's not Brother Langdon. You got some urban backstory in you?" Amy grinned.

"That is curious. No one's called me that since David. And that's been—what—two years already?"

"Just about. David died in April of 2001. So, it's coming up on two." They both remembered David's long bout with leukemia. He left behind a wife, Catherine, and three children.

"You're never going to get to sleep. Odd messages . . . and now thinking about your brother." Amy leaned over and ran her hand over Skip's chest. "Maybe we should take your mind off all of this." She ran her hand down his abs. "Perhaps, I should provide a distraction."

Skip leaned over and turned out his light. "Well, I believe a distraction is just what the doctor ordered . . . the English doctor, that is," he smiled lazily. Thirty minutes later, the couple kissed good night, and their breathing quickly became mirrored and steady.

TWENTY

Saturday, January 11, dawned cold and crisp. Though Bernice rarely slept deeply during the day, insomnia prevailed for long stretches overnight. As a result, she felt perpetually exhausted. Around nine thirty, she rallied to answer the phone, which rang incessantly.

"Hello," she grumbled into the bedside receiver while keeping her eyes closed.

"Dr. Langdon? You're up. This is Carol." The nurse's cheerful enthusiasm burst from the phone.

"No, I'm not up. I chose to answer as the phone wouldn't stop ringing," sighed Bernice, the lethargy in her voice unmistakable.

"Well, I am sorry to get you out of bed, but what a morning–this is a beauty. Open those shades, Dr. L; you'll see. It's going to be cold but gorgeous."

"I do not feel up to opening the curtains," groaned Bernice, sounding related to Eeyore, the forever-complaining Disney donkey.

"What's this? You were doing so well yesterday. A bad night?" Carol tried to jolly Bernice along.

"I slept like shit."

A brief pause in Carol's staccato chirpiness preceded, "I just wanted to let you know I'll be a little late. I need to drop off Kevin at indoor soccer. Usually I'd carpool, but today's not working. Kelly–you've heard lots about her–will be with me, but she'll be real quiet. Maybe she can play with your cats."

"You need not come. I'm fine," mumbled Bernice, sounding decidedly unfine.

"No, I'll be there. If you're fine, we'll just visit," purred Carol. "I'm sure I can find a few ways to make you more comfy."

"Whatever," Bernice went silent.

"Okay then, I'm glad that's decided. We should be there around eleven. Can I get you any groceries?"

"I'm not hungry."

"Well, maybe we'll just pick something up to tempt you," Carol persisted.

"Whatever."

With the phone silenced, Bernice lay in the gloom. Her mood matched the somber hues of her room. She turned on the television and passively clicked through all the channels before settling on CNN and the growing likelihood of hostilities with Iraq. The quiet sound of the anchors filled the room but barely registered. Around ten o'clock, she roused herself for a trip to the bathroom.

Staring in the mirror, she surveyed the ugly bald woman. Without her glasses, the image was blurry (*'Just as well,'* thought Bernice). If more alert, Bernice would have noted deeply bloodshot eyes, black-and-blue bruises at multiple intravenous sites, and increasingly wrinkled, loose skin. "Starting to look like a goddamn Shar-Pei," she grimaced. The surgical incisions looked raw, though not alarmingly. Healing was slow, though the pain of abdominal surgery had passed. Many more debilitating symptoms currently dominated her mind.

Bernice considered washing up but decided against it and returned to bed. She left the drapes untouched. The room brightened slightly as the sun climbed. Back under the comfort of her covers and a glass of water by her side, she put on her glasses and thumbed through a second book by the *Hemlock Society*. The first was now well-worn, and the second was quickly acquiring a similar dog-eared look. Purring contentedly, Tigger joined her on the bed.

Periodically, Bernice closed her eyes and attempted to doze, thinking of the road ahead and reflecting on the growing darkness. She sank deeper in an apparently bottomless hole. The light at the top receded; the voices of others became more distant. She found growing comfort in her reading. Contemplating the long, slow march toward death, that chemo prolonged and consistently aggravated, became increasingly debilitating. Good days had ceased. She'd rather be dead than extend this purgatory.

As promised, Carol breezed into the downstairs hallway just before eleven o'clock. Making no acknowledgement of the vague sounds of conversation between the nurse and young girl, Bernice put away her reading and placed her glasses back on the side table.

"Now, go play with the cats. They're usually in the kitchen looking for food. If they look hungry, put some in their dish."

"But Mom, I don't know where the stuff is." The ten-year-old with long, dark hair and deep brown eyes frowned.

"Don't you roll your eyes! I won't be having that," Carol sharply reprimanded.

"I wasn't rolling my eyes. I've never been here . . . " She trailed off.

"Of course, I'm sorry. I'll show you where the food is. I want to get Bernice a tray, as I doubt she's eaten."

In the kitchen, only Spider was evident–napping on the cushion of the little bench in the kitchen nook and enjoying the warm sunbeams.

"So, where's your brother? Is he hiding?" Carol turned to Kelly, pulling cat food from the pantry. "Here you go, just a cup. The two cats can share," she pointed to the dish.

Kelly stopped petting the sleepy feline who watched her through nearly closed eyes as she walked across the kitchen. After dumping food in the dish, Kelly asked, "Mom? Is it okay if I get them some water? This looks kinda yucky."

"Great idea." Carol absently said as she boiled water for tea and prepared toast with jelly. She made sure to abide by the "I only eat grape" standing directive.

Kelly soon looked bored. "Why don't you get a book out of your backpack?" suggested Carol. "I need to run this up to Dr. Langdon. I'll be down shortly. You wait here, okay?"

"Sure," sighed the girl. "I'll read, I guess." With a pout, she continued, "I don't know why I had to come."

"Don't start. We went over this at home and in the car. We needed to drop Kevin at soccer. Your dad is at the office. You and I are–"

Kelly interrupted, "But I could've stayed at home. I'm ten." She proudly inflated her chest, straightening up to her full forty-eight inches.

"I know, but it would be a long morning. Think of this as some mother-daughter bonding. Maybe we can grab a bite to eat while we're out?" Carol shook her head as she left the room. *'Ten, going on eighteen,'* she thought. Kelly grimaced but retrieved the latest *Harry Potter* book.

Upstairs, Carol found Bernice with eyes closed resting. The TV blared.

"I don't know if you heard us come in, but . . . Oh, there you are Tigger. I wondered where you'd gotten. Maybe you'd like to join Spider downstairs having brunch?" Tigger showed no signs of interest.

"And what about you, Dr. L?" whose eyes fluttered when Carol first used her name. "You should get up and enjoy the day. No wonder you're having trouble sleeping at night. This should be when you're feeling best–near the end of the cycle." Carol chattered nonstop, despite Bernice's feigned sleep.

"Don't remind me," uttered Bernice at last. Her eyes remained closed. "The thought of–" She stopped abruptly.

"I know, chemo is no fun. I was just saying–"

"How the hell do you know? Have you had it?"

"We've been over this ground. No, I've not, but I have cared for many patients who have. Based on that, I would have to say–"

"Just don't say you understand. It is an unending nightmare." Bernice paused, then quietly added, "It's not how I want to live."

Carol stood wordless. "Now don't say that. This is just a short, hard period. You'll get through it. You have to keep the faith."

"Harrumph," growled Bernice, though with decidedly less energy and conviction than she utilized a month earlier.

"I brought you tea—decaf, Summer's Blend—and toast. I made it special for you." Bernice heard Carol from the top of the dark hole but gave no response.

"Can I help you eat some? You'll feel a whole lot better if you get something in you. We need to keep your energy up. Otherwise, your blood counts may fall and prolong the chemo. The docs are getting concerned about those numbers and may delay one of your treatments. Now you wouldn't want that?"

Bernice frowned. "Surely not," she murmured sarcastically. "I want this to continue forever."

"Where's my model patient today? You seem to have woken up with the grumps."

"Stop with the shit. I don't need your goddamned cheerfulness twenty-four seven. Can't you just shut up?" Unseen, Carol frowned back with concern.

"You know, it's not doing you any good feeling sorry for yourself. You've got to take this cancer like a bull by the horns and deal with it aggressively and energetically. I understand you're not feeling ready to run a race, but let's not give up."

"If I want to give up, that's up to me," stated Bernice emphatically. She closed her eyes once more, which had flickered open and burned briefly into Carol's.

"Tell you what," said Carol with tenacity. "I'm just going to open your curtains and get some light in here. You should get a shower or a bath after you eat. You'll feel better, I'm quite certain. I can help."

"You will do no such thing. I can take care of myself."

"Well, that's great," Carol responded with more enthusiasm than she felt. While delighted to see Bernice profess interest in taking some personal initiative, she remained unconvinced. "I just wanted to offer."

Bernice looked carefully at Carol through her sunken eyes and then closed them as she settled more deeply into her pillows. Carol optimistically moved the tray of cooling toast and tea closer. Silently, Kelly had come to stand at the doorway.

"Is she dead?"

"Kelly, you startled me," yelped Carol. "I didn't hear you come in. No, she's not dead. Just having a rough go of it." She said the last in a stage whisper as her daughter moved closer.

"She kinda looks like a gray Shrek."

Carol barely contained a giggle. She shook her head and pointed to the doorway. They barely traipsed into the upstairs hall when the doorbell chimed. "Let's see who that is," she said.

Carol was almost to the door when it opened. In stepped Beverly with Janet.

"I just rang, when who should pull up in the driveway? I hope I didn't disturb Bernice."

The two ladies entered and closed the door on the cold.

"It is frigid out there!" exclaimed Beverly as she unzipped her parka. "The walkway is so icy. I'll have to see if Mother has salt." She hung up the coats. "And who is this pretty young lady?" she smiled at Kelly, who shadowed Carol.

"Oh, you've heard about her. This is Kelly. She's ten and goes to–"

"Mommm," Kelly whined. She looked down and shuffled her feet.

"Kelly, look up. This is Mrs. Langdon and Mrs. Walker."

Both ladies smiled warmly. "It's so nice to meet you," said Janet, while Beverly added, "Are you helping your mom today?"

"I guess," Kelly mumbled shyly.

Beverly turned to Carol. "How is she? We spoke on the phone last night. She sounded low."

"Kel, why don't you go see what the cats are up to?"

"Mommm, can't I just stay and listen?"

"Kelly. Now." Carol turned directive, as Kelly trudged toward the kitchen.

"She's not so good," began Carol. "She's tired. She says she didn't sleep well, but I'm actually more concerned about her mental state."

Alarmed, Beverly leaned in, "How so?"

"She seems down. You know what she said? 'If I want to give up, then I'll just give up' or words like that. She's not sure the chemo is worth it. 'It's no way to live,' she said."

"Oh, that is concerning," worried Janet. "I've heard chemo can bring on depression."

"Yes, it's common, especially with older patients. It's usually a passing episode, but–"

"Do you think that's true here?" Beverly's voice broke nervously.

"That's where I was going. It just feels to me–call it a sixth sense–more serious."

"So, what can we do?"

"Well, it depends, but drugs can be prescribed. There are so many good, effective antidepressants out there. Of course, a doctor needs to diagnose and prescribe medication."

"She won't want that. It's a struggle to get her to see Dr. Esch every other week, even though she liked him . . . at least when we started." Beverly paused. "Interesting, but she doesn't talk about him much at all anymore. Even when we see him—sure it's brief—but she doesn't engage. She's just flat—even with him."

"Could he prescribe something to help?" wondered Janet.

"He specializes in oncology, but I bet he deals with complications including depression."

"Don't you need a psychiatrist?" asked Janet.

"Many times," agreed Carol, "but Dr. Esch probably has enough exposure that he could prescribe meds."

"Well, it sounds like you have a lot to discuss and I don't want to overstay my welcome. I just wanted to check in and see if there was any way I could help. I baked a little something." Janet pushed forward a plate of blueberry bread.

"Must you go?" inquired Beverly. "I want to hear about when Rusty might stop by," she paused.

"He said either last night or today. I gather he didn't make it yet."

"Well, if he did, he would've surprised Mother."

"We should've nailed down the details better." Janet smiled ruefully. "I'll give him another call. He is such a nice man. I did pass along your message on budget. I only got his voicemail, but—"

A knock on the front door interrupted. Through the side windows, they could see that the waiting visitor was heavily burdened plus a large box sat on the step.

"UPS? I didn't order anything," Beverly hesitated. She opened the door. Clad in a dark red down vest, a plaid flannel shirt, and jeans, Rusty held several boxes.

Beverly smiled. "Come in. We were just talking about you, I wager!"

Janet came closer to the door. "Oh my, so good to see you again. Can we help?"

Rusty gave a wide all-American smile. "No, ma'am. Let me set this inside and get the other two boxes. They're heavy."

Kelly wandered to the hallway to see what was causing this new wave of loud conversation. Two big computer boxes, several smaller cartons, and a folder of papers later, the ladies shut the door. Introductions were shared.

They agreed to set up the computer in the TV room upstairs. Earlier in the week, Rusty arranged initiation of internet service and sweet-talked the provider into forgoing their normal "service visit" if guaranteed a one-year contract.

He carried the equipment upstairs and set to work. Kelly joined him as did the cats. While he worked, Beverly and Janet went to Bernice's bedroom.

"What the hell is going on out there? So much noise," complained Bernice. "How am I to sleep?"

"Mother, we had an idea. We thought–knowing your interest in research and travel, but recognizing it's impossible to do right now–"

Bernice peered through her smudged glasses, as Carol brought in a tray with four cups of steaming tea. The professor said nothing.

"Well, we thought it would be quite interesting to get you a fast connection to the internet. That way you could do some virtual travel, or look up topics of interest, get email more easily here–"

"Why?" sneered Bernice.

"We thought you could use a diversion."

"I am sicker than a dog. I can hardly walk from the bed to the bath. I don't think having internet access is going to heal me." A loud noise interrupted as something fell down the hall.

"What the hell was that?" Bernice demanded. "What are the cats into now?"

"Oh," Beverly looked sheepish. "We–uhhh–we wanted to surprise you. This fellow–"

"I met him at a church musical. Rusty Stillwagon. I don't believe you'd know him–"

"There's someone else here?" Bernice groaned in frustration. "Are you having a party?" She sighed in disgust and shook her head slowly. "You don't ask; you just have some guy show up to do what? Redesign my house?"

"No, he's just setting up some new equipment. It will tie into the cable service you already get. It should be done very shortly–"

"I really don't give a damn how quickly it's done. I didn't ask for it. I don't want it. My life just isn't my own anymore, now is it?" She scowled once more.

Rusty appeared in the doorway. "Excuse me," he rubbed his unshaven stubble. "I didn't mean to interrupt, but I could use some help lifting the entertainment console. I need to get to the cable box in back to splice the line."

"No apology necessary," responded Beverly. "Do you need one or more of us?"

Rusty smiled broadly. "Well, it just depends on how strong y'all are."

Carol pumped up a bicep as she pushed up the short sleeve of her blue polo shirt. "Me: Supernurse. Able to lift furniture with a single heave-ho." She laughed.

"I'm always helping Walt. I'm happy to lend a hand."

"Before you leave, let me introduce you. This is my mother-in-law, Dr. Bernice Langdon. This is Rusty Stillwagon." Rusty edged his way toward the bed. He stuck out his hand. Bernice ignored it.

"Pleasure to meet you, ma'am. This won't take long." Bernice surveyed the young man.

"When you get sick, you have no privacy. Forget modesty. The world shows up at your bedside."

Rusty blushed. "Ma'am, I didn't mean to disturb you. I'll just do my thing and get on out of here. Course, if you want–" he looked at Beverly, "I'd be happy to spend some time showing you some tricks to make surfing the net that much easier."

"Just what I want to do: surf the net," snarled Bernice.

"Oh, Mother, really. We believe this will be–"

"Who is this 'we'? We this, we that. Is the 'we,' you, Beverly?"

Embarrassed, Rusty stepped back and waited to be dismissed.

"You can blame me if you want, but it was a brainstorm with Carol and Janet. I ran the idea past Bill, and he agreed. You know, if you don't use it, so be it, but at least the option is there." Beverly's voice rose in volume and strength.

"The annoyances are endless," grumbled Bernice. "Do what you will. It doesn't concern me." The fight left her as quickly as it had erupted. She closed her eyes.

"Dr. L, how 'bout a little more tea? I made it fresh; we've been enjoying ours."

Bernice kept her eyes tightly closed. With no apparent movement toward the tea, Carol and Janet followed Rusty from the room.

"She's tough. Are you sure this is what you want?" inquired Rusty, wondering whether he was wasting his Saturday: first a trip to the Computer Depot to get equipment, then the slow drive on icy roads to Glenwood, and now a recalcitrant end-user. He tried hard to avoid showing frustration.

"Oh, my yes. This is precisely what she needs. Walt and I use ours all the time. It's a godsend."

"Janet is right. She's having a tough morning. Monday's chemo is pulling her down."

"Oh, I'll bet it is. I can't imagine it week after week," concluded Janet.

"If you think so. It won't take much longer, and we'll fire this puppy up."

Kelly giggled. "I wonder what the cats will think when a puppy gets here."

"Figure of speech, little lady," Rusty somberly nodded. "No puppies at this cat-house." He smiled for Kelly's benefit.

After helping access the cable box, Carol and Janet left Rusty and his able assistant to finish the connections. They descended to the kitchen where Beverly joined them.

"What a bad mood today!" exclaimed Beverly. "She can be tough on good days, but she's reaching a radically new level today." She pondered further as Carol reheated their tea in the microwave. "I see what you mean, Carol; there's a darker tone in her language."

"I'll bet it's anxiety over another chemo round. It might not be anything more."

"I'm thinking a conversation before treatment, between you and Dr. Esch, might be good."

"I feel so far out of my element," responded Beverly to Carol's suggestion.

"It can't hurt," offered Janet.

"All right, I'll try him this afternoon. My goodness, look at the time; here it is almost one. How about something to eat?"

"I can't believe it's so late. I'm not sure I can . . . " Janet trailed off.

"I insist. You both must be famished. Give Walt a call. Plus, I must tell you about the oddest coincidence."

The ladies pulled together a light lunch. Detecting food and accompanied by both cats, Rusty and Kelly appeared in the doorway.

"Mom, Mom," Kelly burst out. "It is so cool. You should see the new computer. Can we get one just like it?"

Rusty smiled, "It's up and running. The cable company–remarkably–got their act together. I had a little trouble with protocols between servers, the cable modem, and the new desktop. But," he reached over and tousled Kelly's hair, "with your help, we were able to figure them out. You're in business."

"She really will appreciate it. Trust me," commented Beverly.

"So, I can show you a few things and be off–"

"You must have a bite to eat. It's the least we can do," responded Beverly.

"I'll get out the blueberry bread I brought. No use letting that sit, unless you think Bernice will eat all of it."

"I doubt it," Beverly shook her head.

As the group headed to the table with sandwiches, Kelly interrupted, "Can we go back on the internet? I want to show you a really cool website," she smiled at Rusty. "Mom, can we?"

"Oh, Kelly, I don't know that Dr. Langdon wants crumbs all through the house. Can't you eat and–"

"Pleeease, Mommmm. Pleeease. We'll be really careful, won't we Rusty?"

"It's okay, Carol. I don't see any harm."

"Okay, but no crumbs and bring your dishes back."

Rusty and Kelly retreated upstairs with lunch in hand. "I think someone has a crush," smiled Beverly.

"Kelly is easily smitten. I'm sure with Rusty just nodding her way she has concluded they will marry." Carol laughed.

As the women dug into sandwiches, Beverly repeated, "I must tell you about this strange coincidence. Last Monday, when we were all here, we discussed how the internet was such a great idea."

"I'm certain it will be," commented Janet, taking a potato chip.

"We ladies move fast," smiled Carol. "It's only Saturday, and we have a computer up and running."

"Well, that evening you left me two voicemails."

"I'm so sorry to do that. I wanted to talk live, and–"

"No apology necessary. I was out and then we were having dinner. We don't interrupt dinner for phone calls, so you got voicemail."

"That is so nice that you don't take calls. I wish more families would do that," quietly commented Janet.

Carol lit up, "We're always jumping for the never-ending phone calls. Only once in a–"

"Let me finish. In your messages, you used very specific phrases. You talked about engaging Rusty and skipping Bill's involvement."

"Just like we discussed," Carol chorused. "What's so odd?"

"I'm getting there."

With the sudden illumination of a light bulb, Janet said, "I don't know where you're going, but I've got a strange one to share as well. I hadn't thought about it, but–oh, there I go, interrupting. Sorry."

Beverly smiled. "No worries. Here's the odd thing. When I left here that afternoon and pulled away in my car, I happened to look at my car radio. And you'll never guess."

Janet suddenly paled causing Carol to become concerned. "Janet? Are you all right? You look really washed out."

Janet stared at Beverly. "It can't be." She murmured. "The same?"

"What?" Beverly stopped. "I was just about to say, suddenly on the little screen is a string of words, rather like a–"

Janet jumped in, "Kind of like a ticker tape." She added excitedly. "One of those running strings like at the bottom of a TV show?"

Beverly turned silent. "Well, it didn't keep moving, but . . . You saw something like it?"

"In fact, I did," Janet paused. "And you're more accurate. Mine stopped as well."

"Well, I'll be. I thought it was just me. Maybe it's from the radio station– an advertisement or something."

"What did your message say?"

Before Beverly could respond, Carol piped in, "You're pulling my leg, right?"

"Wait, listen to what mine said. I memorized it. It was so odd . . . even before I heard Janet's voicemails. The words read, *Mrs. L Engage Rusty Skip B.* I figured the B meant Skip Bill, of course."

What little color had returned to Janet's cheeks disappeared. "Oh, my."

Beverly and Carol turned her way with expectant looks.

"Mine was very similar. *Friend Engage Rusty Skip B.* Like you, I concluded Bill was cut off."

"Are you sure you weren't having the same dream? Stranger things have happened."

"No, it wasn't a dream. I'm convinced now, more than ever. The oddest part was when I heard Janet's voicemails. She used the same language– engaging Rusty and skipping Bill. Now, I understand why." Beverly paused, "But where'd they come from?"

"I think from whom is the better question," observed Carol.

The three ladies sipped their drinks and picked at their respective lunch plates.

"'Who' is an interesting way to think about it," Beverly finally said.

"You know. They're exactly the same message," commented Carol. "You both used the precise same words right down to the interrupted B."

"Except the greeting."

"True." The trio contemplated in silence.

"Why would whoever sent the message use Mrs. L in one case and Friend in another? Wouldn't you be Mrs. W if you're Mrs. L?" Carol pointed at each assertively.

"You would think." Beverly paused, uncertain whether to introduce the other message. "What the heck," she finally said aloud.

Curious, the other women looked her way.

"There's more."

"Your message was longer?" Janet raised an eyebrow.

"No. I got another message earlier."

Janet abruptly broke in, "I wasn't going to say anything, but so did I."

"On your car radios?" Carol questioned.

"No," they startled each other simultaneously. Silence prevailed, broken only by muffled laughter emanating from upstairs. Bernice was temporarily forgotten.

"I hate to screw up the mystery any further–and with knowing neither where your messages appeared nor what they suggested. I'm going to add a new wrinkle," Carol stopped. "Your other message wouldn't have been in a teacup by chance?"

"No," they chorused.

"Mine was on my TV."

"Mine was right here–" Beverly pointed above the counter. "Playing across the CD screen."

"Why did you think the message was in a teacup?" Janet and Beverly looked at Carol with curiosity. Shaken, Beverly blinked hard with realization and stuttered, "You got one too?"

Carol nodded. "This is so intriguing. I've only gotten one message–ever–from God knows where . . . but it showed up in my teacup, written in the tea leaf residue at the bottom."

"Really?" Beverly was incredulous.

"I've heard of the Lord working in mysterious ways, but I'm certainly not familiar with this approach where messages appear so explicitly." Janet was curious but reassured by the others.

Questions cascaded quickly, "When was your other message?" "What did it say?" "How could they be sent?" "How could the message still appear when the electricity was no longer connected?" "Have you heard of others?" "Do you think they're all related?" "A teacup?"

"Wait a minute," Beverly forcefully broke in. "Let's discuss this more methodically and write down what we know." She retrieved a pad and jotted the first two messages dating them January 6.

"Now, what are the other messages and when did we each get them?" she quizzed. "I'll start with mine. It was here in the kitchen. It said . . ." and here Beverly hesitated. Should she state exactly what it said? It seemed so sensitive at the time. Given the apparent overlap with the others, she plowed ahead. " . . .*Mrs. L No Job. Confront Bill.* Let's see, it was just after Mother's first chemo, so that would be the first week of November. She had chemo on Monday, and I stayed until Friday. It was probably Thursday evening."

"Isn't that interesting? The same greeting twice," Janet observed the similarity. "It wasn't the same for me. My first message . . . " Janet paused in thought. "When was it? Oh, I know; I wrote it down in my datebook. I thought it so odd at the time. I didn't tell anyone about it–not even Walt!"

Janet went to her purse and pulled out her 2002 datebook. She smiled, "Still carrying around the old one. Haven't quite gotten to 2003!" She paged back, finally stopping in late October, "Here," she said. "The night before Halloween. I stayed up late watching the news. When I awoke–I can doze off so easily anymore, words burned from the screen: *Colleague C Bernice AP $ Tell Andrews Soon.*"

"Did you say burned into the TV?"

"They were a flickering, glittery light, like a flame burning behind the set. As I recall, the whole edge of the TV was lit up–rather like a picture frame, only this bright flame-like light." The others gasped.

"That's just like mine," exclaimed Beverly.

"You know, it was the same in my car–that odd border, the same burning light," Janet whispered conspiratorially.

"You're going to think I was drinking something, but my teacup had a burning edge. I thought I was dreaming, but now that I hear you two . . . it was precisely the same," Carol concluded excitedly.

"What did it say? When was it?"

"It was also October. I was still at the Med Center and that would've been . . . probably a Friday night. The cup had a glowing perimeter. My tea leaf message was not nearly as high-tech as you ladies: *HH good Fam 1st Take job.* No name. I sure won't forget seeing those tea leaves."

"So, three messages within a month and now two more. The burning light around them sure makes me think they're related. The fact that two of them were, in essence, the same confirms it."

Janet raised the obvious question, "So where does that take us?"

"It appears we're getting messages to help."

"Make decisions? Guide us, perhaps?"

Carol injected, "Mine was pretty clear. I was debating the merits of HomeHealth. 'HH' couldn't have been more direct."

"Isn't it interesting that all the messages brought us here? Carol through HomeHealth, me very specifically, and, Beverly, you were going to be here anyway. Odd, that our paths have now crossed, don't you think?"

"Was it to bring us together?"

"Perhaps to work as a team–helping each other."

"Helping Bernice, it would appear."

"Of course." The women reflected individually. "But where are they coming from? And why?" Carol's question broke the silence.

"I'm still intrigued by the content. The Bernice angle is evident, but there's always more–and in some cases, it's a pretty thin hook to Bernice. Carol, yours to HomeHealth to my mother-in-law could clearly just be coincidence. We could easily have chosen a different organization."

"You could've, but you didn't," observed Janet.

"True, but still . . . it could just be probabilities."

"But, then why are the three of us together, receiving messages? Do we think lots of people get messages?"

"Well, we don't know that they're not," reflected Janet.

"Who have you told?"

"I told another nurse. At that point, he wasn't getting any. I also told Jay about the teacup. He humored me but certainly didn't suggest then (or since) that he's a recipient."

"I told no one. I half believed I dreamed it."

Beverly concluded the poll, "I didn't tell anyone else either. It slipped my mind the first time . . . and this time, well, it was so recent that I figured I'd tell you, Janet. I can't imagine these messages showing up for everyone. I think they're selective."

"So, we're back where we started. Where do they originate?" queried Carol emphatically.

"It's all very curious," Janet chimed in. "But if we're following the counsel, does it matter?"

Beverly observed, "If the actions seem logical, maybe it really doesn't matter. But what if they don't or they continue and they appear to 'sense' intuitively what we're about to do? That's unreal."

"From another world," laughed Carol. "Maybe we've entered the Twilight Zone."

Janet looked mystified, but Beverly chuckled. "We're overthinking. Maybe it's just change of life."

"Speak for yourself," cackled Carol. "While I don't want any more kids–two is plenty, and I love 'em–I'm not ready for hot flashes and night sweats."

Janet smiled. "I'm pleased to report that's behind me . . . and they're really not as bad as those ladies' magazines would make you believe." The three laughed again.

"You know, I ended up following the advice," began Beverly. "Let me tell you. I was quite intrigued with the call from Max Diamond. But, oh my, did he turn on the sleaze, agreeing with everything I said, making everything I had done sound comparable to climbing Mount Everest or writing an epic novel. Really. He was too much. I turned him down. It just didn't make sense."

"He does sound unprofessional," noted Janet.

"A slimy used car salesman, I'd wager," nodded Carol.

Beverly continued, "With Bill, we had a heart-to-heart conversation. I simply told him how I was feeling. It may not have been his intent, but I was reacting to his behavior. It really helped reduce the growing tension I felt between us."

"Sounds like a good first step," agreed Janet.

"I think so," concluded Beverly.

Carol quickly filled the momentary silence. "The HomeHealth choice was consuming me. HH had to mean that. While Jay–I'm sure–thought I was smoking something, I decided to take the plunge. It really has worked out pretty well, so far. I can put our own family first, and I'm trying to establish a more manageable work-life balance. It's not easy, but I'm trying," she smiled. "I can't believe how tight I've gotten with you and your family," she nodded toward Beverly. "With others, it's still so new . . . but shoot, I really feel like I'm helping them–in ways I never could before."

Janet took a rambling approach, recalling every detail of her evening: Jay Leno, his guests, and her troubles with the jumbled cords and cables. Carol and Beverly patiently listened as Janet's tale reached her consistent visits with Bernice. She shared an edited version of her church investigation. "All of this is a bit speculative," she somberly spoke, "and I don't want to sully the poor man's name, but . . . " She paused.

"To feel more confident, I took three additional weeks to monitor the money. On the last weekend, Pastor Bob and Rita attended a conference and, sadly, the monies balanced. When they got back, the deficit returned as well, to the tune of a little over $150." Janet shook her head regretfully. "I just couldn't hold off any longer. I went to Reverend Andrews and let him know what I had found. He indicated he would follow up from there, expressing gratitude for my effort." She concluded, "You know, I really felt at peace based on that discussion. Better yet, within two weeks, the receipts aligned!"

"So the counsel has been clear, and we've followed it–consciously or not."

"And the outcomes have been good–though not necessarily what we would anticipate beforehand," commented Beverly.

"It's all very interesting, isn't it?" added Janet.

"You know, my family line traces back to the Philippines," smiled Carol. "They believe all kinds of voodoo. This could be some ghost story–"

"I don't believe in the supernatural," Beverly shook her head.

"Well, tell that to my great-great-grandfather. He might have words on the subject," countered Carol.

"Maybe not the supernatural, but God can do all things. Why wouldn't He send messages in whatever form He chose?" Janet suggested.

"I buy God's power but so explicitly? I believe He works more behind the scenes, not quite like this." Beverly remained skeptical.

"We can't understand the Lord's ways, but we need to believe." Janet persisted.

Carol was stymied, "But He'd have some greater purpose. Why just the three of us? How did we get chosen?"

"And why does He use no name for Carol and Mrs. L for me? I think He'd be more personal."

"I can't explain it," concluded Janet. "I'm merely saying it's within His reach."

"I'm going to have to sleep on this," concluded Beverly. "I don't know what to think."

"Let's promise to share if we receive anything new from the Great Beyond." Carol chuckled, just as Kelly entered the room.

"Mommm, I thought you were coming. You should see the coolest website ever. It is awesome. Come on." She spun on her heel to return upstairs and then paused. "Oh, and Mrs. Langdon–the one in bed–she was moaning and coughing."

"My goodness, I'm afraid I've been derelict in my duties," exclaimed Carol, hustling upstairs.

Glancing at her watch, Janet said, "I can't believe how late it's gotten. Walt will be wondering what happened."

With the first floor quiet, Beverly poured two glasses of iced tea for herself and Rusty. *'He must be parched,'* she thought. *'This has proven so much more complicated and time-consuming than I expected. I think I'll just see what's up.'*

TWENTY-ONE

Rusty continued to labor in the TV room. Once satisfied with the software installation and the desktop placement of applications, he turned to Kelly.

"So, little lady, where shall we surf? This cable modem rocks."

Kelly shyly looked back. "I don't know," she whispered.

"You must have some favorites. Doesn't your mom or dad go on the internet with you?"

"My brother does. Sometimes Dad."

"Great," smiled Rusty. "Where do you and your brother visit?"

"I don't know." Kelly's lips lifted in a small goofy smile.

"Sure, you must. How about Disney?"

"I like Cartoon Network."

"That's a good one. Let's go there. Why don't you pull over that chair?" Kelly rolled over a desk chair as Rusty googled Cartoon Network. Starting there, they zipped among websites; cascading movie trailers and videos filled the screen.

"Didn't I tell you this was going to rock?" noted Rusty.

"Wow. This is cool. I have to tell my mom," yelped Kelly as she ran from the room. Moments later she came back, "They're still talking," she said, rolling her eyes. "I think my mom will be up."

Because the two were deeply absorbed by their exploration, Beverly entered the room unnoticed. She lifted her tray, "I thought you might like something to wet the whistle. How's the computer coming?"

"You've got a great set-up. It took a little longer to get the modem working, but it is—to quote Kelly—'awesomely cool.' I hope your mom enjoys it."

"I'm sure she will. It should be a great distraction for her." Beverly watched as another movie trailer ran across the screen. "Wow! That looks like TV. That's really just the computer?"

"Yes, ma'am. The tech rocks. If I were buying another desktop, this is clearly the one I'd get. It's not top-of-the-line, but it has a huge amount of storage, the RAM processor is super quick, and the sound card . . . well, let's just say—"

"Enough," laughed Beverly. "As soon as you get beyond the keyboard and the on/off switch, I'm lost."

"Okay," Rusty smiled. "I won't bore you, but let me show you a couple of things." He diminished the current window of movie premieres and turned to the rather plain desktop. He demonstrated a variety of applications. Windows popped with rapid abandon as he flew through the software. Wordless, Beverly looked increasingly dazed.

"That's a whole lot to take in. I'm not sure I'm getting it all."

"It's pretty much self-explanatory. You just have to nose around."

"I won't blow it up?"

Rusty laughed again, "I've set the no-explosions control on the inside. You can't blow it up or burn it down. Just have fun."

Beverly responded, "I sure hope Mother will use it. You've done such a nice job. Thank you."

"No sweat. Happy to help. Hey, I sure hope your mom feels better soon."

As Beverly left, Kelly and Rusty maximized the website window they had been visiting and resumed their cyber scavenger hunt. Pausing outside Bernice's room (Carol cheerfully cajoled Bernice into the bathtub), Beverly heard the doorbell.

'It's like Grand Central. People coming and going.' She descended the stairs. Opening the heavy oak door, she found Roger Gallo.

"Oh, hello," he hesitantly sputtered out, visibly surprised to find someone other than Bernice. "I didn't think anyone would be home, but then I saw the cars and figured . . . " His voice faded.

"Hello, I'm Mrs. Langdon. My mother-in-law lives here. Can I help you?" Beverly was courteous but close-lipped. With no interest in buying light bulbs or magazine subscriptions or participating in the latest candy-bar fundraiser, she prepared to close the door as quickly and politely as possible.

"I'm Professor Langdon's paperboy . . . "

"Of course. I thought you were selling something."

"No, Mrs. Langdon. I'm collecting. I couldn't get any answer over the last couple of weeks, but when I saw the cars today, I thought–well, maybe–" His voice dissolved again.

"Come in. It's cold out," welcomed Beverly.

Roger stepped across the transom. "I also brought this for the professor." He held up a pound of Dunkin' Donuts coffee. "My mom thought she might like it."

"That was so nice of you. Completely unnecessary," gushed Beverly. "What do we owe you?" Without stopping, she continued, "and I didn't catch your name?"

"Roger," he answered. "It's two months of seven-day delivery. I collect for the whole week, even though I don't deliver Sundays," he explained. "So, that would be thirty-two dollars."

"Let me get my purse and I'll pay you. Hold on."

Beverly disappeared, taking the fragrant package of coffee. Roger swayed between feet waiting. He could just barely hear voices from upstairs. At one point, he heard a directive voice ordering someone into a chair. A moment later, he heard a distinctly male voice: "Would you look at that?" and a younger child's whoop and laughter.

Beverly returned. "I'll bet you didn't get your Christmas tip, did you?"

"No, but it's not necessary, Mrs. Langdon."

"Don't be silly, you provide a real service. We want to ensure you're taken care of." Beverly smiled. "We can't have everyone else giving a tip and the Langdons don't, now can we?"

"If you say so," Roger nodded.

Beverly pulled out a crisp fifty dollar bill. "Here, you take this. That should cover the bill and give you a little extra spending money."

"Thank you very much, Mrs. Langdon," grinned Roger. He pocketed the fifty. "I hope she's feeling better soon."

"I'll tell her you stopped by. I'm sure she'll appreciate the coffee. Now you bundle up."

As the door closed behind Roger, Carol, Rusty, and Kelly descended.

"Well, how goes the battle?" queried Beverly.

Rusty answered first, "All set. Your mother can zip around all day and night without leaving the house."

Kelly nodded enthusiastically. "We were showing Mom a couple of really cool sites."

Carol laughed. "I can barely keep it together on email and there's my ten-year-old daughter flying through space. What a computer!" she concluded.

Rusty laughed. "Hey, the world keeps advancing. Kelly is just getting there first."

After sharing a few more internet adventures, Rusty departed. Getting in his Miata at the curb, he paid little attention to Roger's profile receding on the street ahead. Otherwise, Fox Den Road was deserted. As he rolled down the street, he shivered involuntarily. *'Sure hope this thing warms up fast. It is wicked cold.'* Reaching Interstate 82 with the stereo blasting and the heat cranking, Rusty started feeling ready to party.

Disregarding Kelly's whining, Carol collected their coats, "No, hon—no more internet. We have to run errands and get home. Kevin will be there, and I don't know what time Dad is getting back. Let's hustle." Carol turned to Beverly, "Are you sure you don't need any additional support this evening?"

Beverly vigorously shook her head. "No, you've been here so long already. You're a real angel. Go home. Enjoy your family."

"And tomorrow? What time will you be here?"

"Good question. We'll probably swing by around lunchtime. I suspect we'll spend the afternoon. The kids can do their homework," she smiled, "or surf the internet on the new hotrod." The women chuckled.

"Then maybe I'll pass on tomorrow. It sounds like she'll have plenty of company. I'll come Monday after chemo. Okay?"

"Absolutely. You haven't taken a day off. Mother appears stable at the moment. Having you here Monday would be great."

* * *

"Mother, how are you?" Bernice rested in bed mindlessly watching the television, turned down so low, it proved hard to hear.

"I'm still here."

"Can I get you anything?" met silence. Beverly plunged forward. "Everyone's left now. Just you, me, and the cats. I hope it wasn't too much racket."

Bernice lay stoically, propped up on her pillows.

"I don't know if you sensed what the young man was doing . . . " Beverly trailed off expectantly. Bernice relented and looked toward her daughter-in-law, shrugging her shoulders and rolling her eyes. Beverly chose not to be rebuffed.

"His name is Rusty Still—"

"I heard his name. He stood right here. I have cancer, not deafness. I am goddamn sick and tired of being treated like an incompetent old fool."

Beverly's cheeks burned. "You didn't appear to be listening to what he—"

"I gather I'm to be a computer junkie. Just what I need. Spend time in front of a computer screen looking for God knows what." Bernice's eyes blazed briefly. Beverly held her ground.

"Mother, we honestly thought you might find this fascinating. You have always enjoyed travel. Research has been a big part of your life. Having access to a slice of the world through the computer, well . . . we anticipated . . . " Beverly stopped.

"Jesus H. Christ. I am sick. I can barely care for myself. I have a goddamn nurse here nearly twenty-four hours a day. And now, I'm supposed to go sit in front of a computer and do research? I just can't stand this." Silence hung over the room like a heavy black shroud. "I don't want to talk about it anymore."

"I'll just say one more thing. I watched Rusty visit some websites. That computer really zips along–remarkably fast. You can see movie trailers–just like on TV. I just may want to do a little exploration myself."

"Well, you go right to it. Be my guest." Bernice sarcastically snapped. Her closed eyes sank further into her bony skull.

Beverly stood watching intently, wondering how the chemicals coursing through a body could affect the emotions so intensely. Moments ago, Bernice raged and now she lay there–deflated, like a punctured balloon after spinning erratically around a room. Hearing the clock strike downstairs, Beverly quietly exited as dark shadows filled the room.

An hour later, Beverly returned with a tray of hot tea, an English muffin with peanut butter, and some fruit cocktail. She included two chocolate chip cookies, a perennial favorite of her mother-in-law's.

"About time I got something to eat," she grumbled. Beverly gritted her teeth and set the tray down. "Get me a glass of wine." Bernice looked up. "Red."

"I don't know that wine is a good idea. You're not feeling that well and you have chemo to–"

"You ask how you can help and then you argue. I know full well tomorrow's schedule. Since I won't be up for wine anytime soon, I would like some tonight." A long silence ensued. "Please," Bernice cynically snarled.

Beverly left silently but returned–despite her misgivings–with a modest glass.

"Is that it? I meant a healthy glass. This is not communion, you know."

"Why don't we see how this agrees with you first, before pouring more?"

"Suit yourself." Bernice ate a few bites of the English muffin. "Oh, God," Bernice swallowed. "What's on this?"

"Peanut butter. It's some protein. I thought–"

"If I wanted peanut butter, I would've asked. I'm gagging on it."

Beverly's face went red once more. "Shall I get you a plain one?"

"That would be lovely," a tightlipped Bernice responded.

Beverly returned with the buttered muffin. "Here, try this," she directed.

Bernice bit into the still warm-from-the-toaster baked good. "It's stale."

Beverly exhaled loudly in exasperation. "I got those muffins yesterday. I can't imagine they're not fresh."

"They're not," a grim-faced Bernice responded. "It doesn't taste right."

"Is there anything I could get you instead?"

"No, this will do."

Silence hovered oppressively. Bernice nibbled more muffin; the rest of the tray went untouched, save the glass of red wine.

"Get me more."

"Do you think you should?"

"I can tell. Get me more," commanded Bernice. After a pause, she added, "Please."

After a trip to the kitchen, Beverly returned with yet another modest glass.

"Jesus. Another two sips and I'm done again. What are you, my nurse?"

"I don't think you should overdo it."

"You are not the doctor. Esch said wine was fine. It's good for the heart. I might just as well keep something in working order."

"I don't believe on the night before chemo–"

"You don't know. I've got a degree in human physiology. If I want a goddamn glass of wine, I will damn well have it."

Beverly refilled the glass once more–but maintained her stance on moderation. She left the bottle downstairs. As she returned, the clock downstairs struck five-thirty. She grimaced. Setting the third glass down on the end table, she said, "Mother, I have to leave. Bill, the kids, and I are celebrating Caitlyn's birthday. Are you okay?"

Bernice shrugged her shoulders and sipped her red wine. "I'll live, I imagine. Though what kind of life this is, who's to say?"

"Don't say things like that," Beverly shot back. "Obviously, chemo is not something anyone wants, but in the long run, it will make you well again."

"How can you possibly know? I feel like shit, and I look worse. And the way I feel? I'm not improving." She finished her thimbleful of wine.

"It's hard to assess how the treatment is progressing. Dr. Esch–"

"No more." The back of Bernice's hand waved dismissively. "Get me another glass on your way out."

"I think you've had enough. Why don't you just rest?"

Bernice glared, but remained silent–watching through the slits of her eyes behind her glasses. Beverly stared back but broke away first. "I'll be on my way. We'll be back tomorrow."

"Whatever."

As Beverly's car pulled away, Bernice cautiously descended to the kitchen. Collecting the bottle of wine, she returned upstairs. Tigger and Spider playfully followed every step. Stopping in the bedroom, Bernice picked up the now empty glass and headed to the TV room. The computer's aquarium screen saver showed fish swimming across the flat screen.

"God, how much of my money did they spend?" Bernice remarked to her cats. She sat down and moved the mouse, causing the fish to immediately disappear. Rusty arranged the desktop with very few icons, but each was well-marked. He guessed on what might be most useful to a former university professor, with the exception of a link to the American Association of Retired Persons ("What the hell is this for?" Bernice reacted).

She clicked on the university icon and launched the homepage where she moved the cursor to the entrance link for faculty members. She tried her old username and password but was denied access. "Goddamnit, they think I'm already dead," she muttered, trying repeatedly to enter with no success. "Damn."

She closed the university window and tried AOL, the screen moving like greased lightning. She perused the Welcome page and toggled through several News windows. She paused only briefly on the WebMD bookmark, "Don't need to learn more about what's killing me." She hesitated, as her mind turned. "I wonder . . . " she began.

She returned to the desktop where she opened Google's search window. She typed, "Hemlock Society." The screen instantly filled with more than 65,000 entries. The first sites she visited presented legislation and philosophical approaches to 'end of life' issues. "I don't need politics; I want practicality. I want tactics. Ones that are painless," muttered Bernice.

Increasingly intrigued yet simultaneously frustrated, Bernice tried different approaches to find an appropriate website. She tapped her way through a plethora of possibilities: right to die, euthanasia, suicide, options for suicide, and committing suicide. Google delivered voluminous lists, but the links frequently took her to suicide prevention sites, ultra-conservative Christian sites on "the life worth living," and radical political platforms on right-to-die legislation and movements. As the wine in the dark green bottle slowly descended, so did Bernice's hopes of finding a website to complement her recent reading.

"I understand the mechanics well enough, for God's sake," she thought. Her mind wandered aimlessly through a host of dark and dreary corners, contemplating how much more dreadful chemo might become. She considered her continuing downhill slide like a wild toboggan ride into a long, dark tunnel. Shuddering with the enormity of the continuing treatment path, she knocked over her nearly empty wine glass and watched in slow motion as the liquid cascaded across the desk and drop by drop fell to the carpet. "Damn glad it's a dark rug," she thought grimly. "God, I do not want to keep living like this. I'm tired. I feel awful. This could continue endlessly."

Her internet search proved futile. Conversely, she found nothing that convincingly suggested an alternative. Despite her best efforts, nearly one-third a bottle remained when she finally closed the windows on the computer and painstakingly stumbled back to bed. Without closing the drapes, she fell asleep with the TV purring in the background.

TWENTY-TWO

Overnight, nine inches of fluffy white powder coated the towns of Glenwood, Bedrock, and Bedrock Hills. All four Langdons spent the morning clearing snow with Bill on the snowblower and the kids shoveling the walkway to the front door. Beverly swept the front porch and cleared a path from the back door to ease the dog's outside excursions. A spontaneous snowball fight punctuated the morning; laughter and shouts crackled through the cold air of the neighborhood. Later, gathered by the dancing gas fire, they enjoyed hot chocolate in the oversized kitchen.

"That was fun." Brad and Caitlyn thoroughly enjoyed the morning. Being more measured and controlled, their dad rarely participated in such spontaneous family fun.

"It sure was," he echoed. He even gave Beverly a hug and a kiss. "We should do this more often."

Beverly smiled, "We just need to ensure the snow will fall, huh?"

"So, what's everyone got planned today?" Bill questioned.

"Before you all answer, we should go see BeBe," asserted Beverly. "I told her we'd stop by. We should clear a path to her front door and–well–it's been a while since you've been over to visit . . . "

"Ahh, Mom. It's so boring. BeBe doesn't talk or anything. She just lies in bed."

"She looks awful," frowned Caitlyn.

"Do we have to?"

Bill weighed in, "Mom's right. Maybe we can take a DVD over and watch it with her."

"BeBe doesn't have a DVD player."

"A mere technicality. We can take a video instead."

"Actually, you may be able to play DVDs. We got her new computer hooked up yesterday. I know I don't understand it completely."

"It's a computer, Mom. What's to understand?"

"You'll see. It's got–what do they call it? A cable–"

"A cable modem? Really? At BeBe's? They're supposed to be wicked." Brad was suddenly interested, even excited, about the prospect of a visit.

"Can I do my History on it?" questioned Caitlyn.

"I'm sure you both could do a bunch of things on it." Beverly paused. "I doubt your grandmother's going to use it much. Somebody should benefit from it," she sighed.

An hour later, the all-wheel-drive SUV was loaded with videos, backpacks, snow shovels, and a cooler of food ("Perhaps your mother will join us for a meal," Beverly noted optimistically). The roads were icy but passable, and they made good time getting from Bedrock Hills to Glenwood as few people were out.

On arrival at Bernice's, they found Roger shoveling. He watched the SUV come to a halt. He recognized Beverly and walked down the partially shoveled front walk.

"Hi, Mrs. Langdon. I got done at our house and just thought, well—maybe Professor Langdon could use her path done. My mom thought it was a good idea."

"You didn't need to do that. We'll pay you."

"Oh no," stammered Roger. "That's not why I'm here. I just—well, I just . . ."

"Nonsense." Beverly paused. Her family joined her. "At least we brought more troops to help out. This is Brad and Caitlyn. This is Roger," she hesitated. "I'm forgetting your last name."

"Gallo."

"Guys, this is—"

"We got it, Mom," interrupted Brad. He eyed up Roger, who stood nearly a head taller.

Looking at Caitlyn, Roger said, "I didn't put it together that you—" he nodded toward Beverly, "were Caitlyn's mother. We have geometry together."

Caitlyn smiled. "You know Melissa, Mom. She and Roger, well . . . " Roger blushed in the little skin that showed between knit cap and parka collar. Beverly caught the tone and smiled. "I see. Well, why don't the three of you finish the walk? Bill, could you help me get this stuff inside and then maybe some of us can start on the drive?"

After unloading, Bill suggested, "Why don't you look in on Mom? I'll start on the driveway. Hopefully, Mom's got enough gas for the snowblower. Don't know the last time that was used."

"Okay. I'm happy to get in from the cold, but call if you want help."

By the time Bill returned outside, the kids had completed the walkway. While not as clean a job as he would like, the walk was passable. Remarkably the snowblower fired up easily and allowed rapid progress on the driveway. While Bill worked, the three kids stood watching.

"Hey, Dad? Does BeBe have any snowboards or saucers or anything?" shouted Brad above the racket.

"You can look. She had some years ago, but I'll bet they're gone."

In the garage, no contemporary snow accessories waited, but the three found a stack of cafeteria trays and decided to try them on the hill behind Bernice's back property line. Bill watched–with envy from age-old memories–as the kids careened down the hill dodging trees and shrubs. Each pass made the emerging trail smoother and slicker.

"Hey, let's ice it. It'll rock." Brad suggested. Without waiting for the others, he ran over to his grandmother's house for a container of water to splash on the trail. The icy slope worked even better than anticipated and the trays soon sailed.

"Dad, you have to try this," coaxed Caitlyn, as Bill finished the driveway. "It's so cool."

"Yeah, Dad. Try it out. Here, use my tray."

"I don't know. I probably won't even move. I'm so much bigger." Bill laughed but hesitantly settled on a tray at the hilltop. With a big push from Brad and Roger, he zipped down the slope faster than he would've dreamed possible. Falling off and rolling in the snow, he got up laughing, his heart beating fast and hard.

"You're right. That was pretty cool!" he shouted back up the hill.

After many more runs, the group decided they were cold and wet enough to go in.

Roger hung back, "I should probably be going."

"No, you have to come in. Maybe my mom will make us some hot chocolate. She did this morning. It was great."

Bill insisted. "By all means, unless you need to get home, come on in. Dry off, get a hot drink. Maybe you guys can watch one of the videos we brought."

"I've got a better idea," suggested Brad. "BeBe's got this new, awesome computer. We can surf the web."

"I don't know about that. I don't want you getting into websites you shouldn't . . . " Bill's voice, while not definitive, inserted a cautionary note as they entered the house.

"Awww, Dad. We know better."

Caitlyn agreed. "You can sit with us if you want."

Brad grimaced. Bill saw the reaction and smiled. "Okay, I won't sit with you, but let me know where you've been. And don't stay on too long."

Beverly joined them in the front hall. "I wish we had a change of clothes for you guys. You must be cold. Did you have fun?"

"Awesome, Mom."

"Yes, ma'am."

"Can you make hot chocolate? That was so good this morning . . . " Caitlyn sweetly smiled.

"That's a lot of chocolate in one day, but I suppose . . . What are you going to be up to?"

"We're gonna try out the new computer."

Beverly nodded, "BeBe's dozing, so don't make too much noise–particularly walking past her room. Close the door to the TV room."

The kids tromped up the stairs and with exaggerated stage whispers tiptoed down the hall. They shut the door to the TV room with a louder thump than planned. Bernice opened her heavy eyelids.

'Another full house,' she thought with disgust. *'I just can't be alone.'*

Brad, Caitlyn, and Roger clustered around the large monitor. Before long, they tooled through countless websites and rapid downloads.

"I've never moved so fast online," Roger observed.

"It's a rocket," added Brad.

"What a great computer," enthused Caitlyn.

They remained engrossed in the web tour, savoring the hot chocolate and cookies Beverly served.

"Hey, could one of you come down and help me with dinner?" hollered Beverly. "I could use a hand."

Hearing her mom request help in getting dinner ready, Caitlyn agreed, having grown tired watching the boys. As she shut the TV room door, the aroma of ham swept through.

"Wow, that smells good," smiled Roger. "I'll leave when you eat, but let's keep exploring."

The boys moved through a variety of sites eventually finding classic rock music. They linked to Pink Floyd where they listened to several huge hits from the best-selling seventies album, *Dark Side of the Moon.*

"Awesome. I never even heard of these guys."

"Me neither."

"What else do they do?"

Brad's finger ran down the titles of other Pink Floyd best sellers. "I don't know any of 'em."

"So pick one."

Brad double-clicked on *The Wall.* A white brick wall filled the screen.

It pulsed and moved with the music. As the music's intensity grew, the wall rotated and shimmered like a kaleidoscope.

"Is that cool, or what?" The shifting screen mesmerized the boys. The wall faded away, replaced by video scenes. As the song ended, the pulsating bricks reappeared.

"Almost looks like it's on fire or something, doesn't it?" observed Brad, causing Roger to get a funny look. "What's with you? You look like you ate something bad."

"It's nothing. Just kinda odd."

"What?"

"The brick wall. It reminds me of a weird thing that happened . . . "

"So, tell me. I mean, this wall video is kinda cool, but so–?"

"It was here at your grandma's house. Last fall."

Brad looked at Roger quizzically, clearly encouraging Roger to continue. Pink Floyd moved to the next tune on *The Wall.*

"I was delivering papers. It was late afternoon. I don't know why, but I went around the side of the house to that little patio, you know, with the bricks."

"Yeah?"

"Some of the bricks–their outlines–glowed. They were in a circle . . . and this is even more weird . . . " Roger stopped.

"You can't stop there."

"The outlines spelled out words. When you said the wall almost looked like it was on fire, well–that's the way the bricks looked. The words were like burning."

"Cool." Brad reflected momentarily. "Are you sure you weren't dreaming? What did the bricks say? Are they still burning?"

"They burned that evening but were gone the next time I stopped. A friend of mine saw 'em too. I don't think we both dreamed it."

"So, what'd they say?"

"I can't forget: '*Choose Life Go Dance Coffee Not Free.*' "

"Wicked cool, man."

"Yeah . . . but you know what's even weirder? They actually fit stuff that was going on."

Brad's mouth hung open as Roger recounted the series of subsequent events. "No way, man." He finally added. "No way," he repeated.

"Way, man," echoed Roger. "But that's not even the end."

"You're putting me on, right?"

Relieved, Roger continued with the message from the garage wall. "I can't figure this one out: '*Persist. Go Back. Keep Smile. Say Uncle,*'" he concluded. "It's not as clear. I don't know."

"You are so lucky. You know, if that first message meant something, this one must too. I wonder if–"

Beverly interrupted, "Time for dinner."

"Hey, I better be going . . . You don't think I'm nuts?"

"Nah, no way. Weird story, but not nuts." Brad shifted subjects quickly. "Hey, why don't you come back sometime? We found some excellent websites."

"That'd be awesome. I better hustle."

* * *

After dinner (which Bernice declined, "I'm not hungry. Stop asking."), Bill retreated to Bernice's study to read her newspaper. Caitlyn stayed in the kitchen doing homework. After cleaning up and taking a tray of food to Bernice (which remained uneaten), Beverly joined Brad in the TV room. He bounced among three pro basketball games simultaneously, which gave Beverly a headache.

"Can you show me what you found on the internet?"

"Okay." With a flick of the mouse, the swimming fish dissolved into the white bricks of Pink Floyd.

"What's this?" asked Beverly.

"It's a music site, maybe from your era," grinned Brad. "Some group named Pink Floyd . . . "

"Sure, they were big. Aren't they around anymore?"

"Aw, Mom. I don't think so."

"So what's the site do?"

Brad clicked on the music title and the wall began to shimmer and pulsate to the opening beats.

"That's pretty neat. It looks like the wall is alive . . . "

"Yeah. Hey–" As if a light bulb suddenly turned on, Brad interrupted himself, "You should've heard the really awesome thing that happened to Roger. He was telling me about it."

Beverly looked at her son quizzically. She grew increasingly focused as he recounted Roger's stories.

He finally stopped, "Well, aren't you going to say anything? That's pretty weird, isn't it?"

Breaking her concentration, Beverly responded, "Yes, indeed. I don't quite know what to make of it."

"Think it's magic? Maybe something extraterrestrial?" Brad hesitated, as Beverly said nothing. "Could be a ghost!"

"I really don't know, Brad."

"Do you think it's like a modern Moses? He got a message on stone tablets."

Beverly smiled, "I guess it could be, though the Ten Commandments were more explicit than what you've described."

"I guess."

"Have you ever seen any messages like these?"

The twelve-year-old looked at his mother as if she suddenly sprouted a second head. "Of course not. Why?"

"Oh, I just wondered. It's so odd. Why Roger? Why this message?" Beverly paused. "And what did you say they said?"

"I'm not sure exactly, but something like–" as Brad rattled off the two communications with remarkable precision, Beverly jotted them down. "What are you doing? Why are you writing them?"

"I'm just curious. They're rather extraordinary; maybe seeing them on paper will help me think about them. That's all." Successfully projecting a neutral innocence, Beverly slipped the paper in her jeans. "So, what else have you found online?"

Ten more excruciatingly slow minutes of surfing passed as the scribbled words burned in Beverly's pocket. She desperately wanted to study them further. After the fifth sports website, she excused herself to go to the bathroom. She collected the pad of paper holding the other messages and rewrote the words from Brad onto the pad. The pad now held seven messages. And all four recipients, coincidentally, now visited Bernice's house with growing regularity.

'I wonder if anyone else is getting messages?' she pondered. *'And why? And from whom?'* She extended her bathroom visit as her mind swirled with confusion, phrases, and words from the various communiqués. She looked forward to catching up with Janet and Carol. Roger might need to join them for a discussion, odd as that might sound to him. She placed the pad in her purse and opened the bathroom door just as an exceptionally loud thump resonated from the second floor.

"Bill, come quickly. It sounds like Mother has fallen," Beverly shouted as she shot to the staircase, only to find Bill's backside disappearing at a rapid rate into the hallway above.

TWENTY-THREE

Rusty awoke Sunday with a thumping hangover. The room still spun as he opened and closed his eyes multiple times. Even with half-shut eyes, he could tell he had forgotten to close the shades. The reflection of off-white, cloud-covered winter sun cast an eerie illumination across his bedroom. The warmth of the covers caused him to burrow deeper.

"You awake?" His bedmate rolled over and threw an arm across Rusty's chest.

Rusty groaned, "Barely."

"Hey, last night was great . . . You know . . . "

* * *

Rusty was showering when one of his housemates pounded on the door, "Hey, phone's for you." Rusty remained unaware, but his new friend–a thirty-something plumber– retrieved the cordless extension beside the bed and brought it to the adjoining bathroom. He opened the frosted glass where Rusty was rinsing shampoo from his hair.

The tradesman reached in and tapped Rusty's wet stomach, startling him as his eyes were closed to avoid streaming shampoo.

"No more," Rusty groaned.

"Stud, the phone . . . for you."

Moments later, Rusty held the headset to his ear.

"Did I get you at a bad time?"

Rusty tried to place the voice. "Sorry, I was in the shower."

The older voice paused. "It's Janet Walker."

"Janet, of course. I didn't recognize your voice."

"Should I call back? Maybe a better time? It sounds like you've got company."

"No, this is fine . . . What's up?" Still dripping, Rusty smiled across the room at his companion.

"I hate to bother you yet again. You've been so dear, helping out Bernice. I really think she is going to get such good use from her computer. Thank you so much. I could just go on . . . "

"No problem. It was kinda fun, but that's not why you called."

"No, it's not. This is just silly, I'm sure. Now you just tell me who I should call."

"Is there a problem with the Langdon set-up? Everything seemed okay."

"As far as I know, it's just fine. It's my computer at home. We've had it nearly five years. Walt thought we should get a new one. He was worried that this one would crash."

"It crashed?"

"Well, I don't think so. It's just not right."

Rusty's exasperation grew. Despite his best efforts to be patient, his voice showed an edge. With a white towel wrapped around his waist, he walked across the room and stood by the window.

"Well, last night, I was working on my minutes for the Sarah group at church. We meet every two weeks and have just been getting deeper and deeper into the New Testament."

Rusty closed his eyes and sighed.

"Listen to me; I am just prattling on . . . "

Rusty shivered. "No, not at all. Tell me more." Rusty felt lightheaded–a combination of last night's liquor and standing, dripping wet in the chill.

"Well, last night, I was typing. I use Microsoft Word. Are you familiar with that?"

"Yes, ma'am. Of course."

"I knew you'd know it. Well, there I am writing away when suddenly the edge of my screen changes color–almost like there's a picture frame around the screen. I don't know where it came from. It almost looked like fire or something."

With no response, she optimistically raised her voice, "You've seen this?" Rusty remained wordless. "Well, even though it looked like flames, the screen was cool when I touched it."

His mind racing, Rusty stuttered, "Yes, no, of course, it would've been cool. I can imagine how you felt watching the screen."

"You know what else?"

"No, I can't guess," he rolled his eyes.

"There were words." Rusty extended the receiver from his face like an alien object. "Words burned across the screen . . . same flaming texture and color. Mostly red, a little yellow. Flickering and dancing. It was actually quite pretty."

Awestruck, Rusty squeaked, "Words? Familiar words?"

"Oh yes."

"What'd they say?"

"I won't forget:

SEE BERNICE
GET RUSTY
SKIP CHURCH
ROGER"

"That's more than odd, I'll grant you."

"Would you come and look? I'm half afraid to do anything. Why would it do that? I'm worried there's something wrong, and I thought you might have some idea as to what was causing this."

"I wish I did, but this is way outside my expertise. Unless you programmed something in there . . . "

"Most assuredly, I did not. Granted, I am going to see Bernice, but I didn't type her name in there. And I'm sure Walt didn't . . . "

"Did you ask him? Maybe he was writing you a reminder. You should ask."

"Maybe. But could you . . . "

"I don't think I'd add much. Getting burning messages from –well, from wherever . . . I just don't know."

"Please."

Rusty frowned. His overnight companion rose and walked to the bathroom. He glanced over his shoulder at Rusty still standing with the phone propped between ear and shoulder.

"I suppose I could take a look. No promises."

Before he finished, Janet interrupted, "Thank you. I just knew you would. I'm sure you can get to the bottom of this. Would this afternoon work? I'll make dinner."

Rusty begrudgingly accepted. He'd be there by late afternoon, provided the roads were passable. Hanging up, he heard the shower. Perplexed, he looked out his windows overlooking the snow-covered park. His eyes took in the yet unmarked snow and the glistening ice outlining each and every tree branch with artistic perfection. A photographer's dream morning! His mind tumbled through facts with confused intrigue.

'What is this all about? Why would this church lady receive a message in such a similar way? I don't get it. It's not normal. And yet, she did. It's almost identical, and I didn't say a thing to her about mine. Fuck, this is unreal.'

* * *

As Janet prepared dinner, Rusty sat in front of her PC assessing various Office software. No evidence of a flaming border or unsolicited text materialized. After an hour of fruitless testing, Rusty wandered to the kitchen.

"I don't know, Janet. I can't get it to do anything close to what you saw."

"How disappointing! I hoped you'd see the same thing."

"I can't replicate what you described. Are you sure you weren't just tired? Or maybe imagining the screen shot?"

Janet looked at him bewildered, "Oh no, I'm most certain. I would've called Walt to see, but he had already gone to bed. It was definitely there. You know why I know?" She lowered her voice conspiratorially.

"Now, you'll think I'm some old kook, but . . . it's happened before."

"What do you mean?" Rusty was skeptical, but intensely curious.

"Not on my computer, but almost the same."

"Really?" Without his own experience, he certainly would've thought Janet nuts.

"Well, it happened twice. Once on the TV. Once on my car radio."

"What happened?" Rusty sat down at the kitchen table; Janet–after checking her preparations on the stove–took a facing seat.

"The same burning outline. The same burning words. Well, the car radio had that burning edge, but the words were gray. They moved like a ticker tape on CNN and then they stopped. But the edge was identical."

"The same words?"

"Oh my, no. They were different each time. But you know, a funny thing, they were oddly appropriate at the time." Janet described the two situations in excessive detail, though she skipped the connection with Beverly and Carol.

Rusty remained silent, a fierce internal debate raging. "Janet?" Rusty finally said, as she stood at the stove stirring spaghetti sauce.

"Yes?" Rusty remained awkwardly wordless, so Janet continued. "I figured you were thinking it all through. I can't decipher the message this time. See Bernice seems clear. The Get Rusty–well, I didn't initially think of you, to be honest. I thought more about getting old and worn out on my visitation skills. Getting rusty, you know? But maybe it is about getting you. You are here. Skip Church? That doesn't make any sense. Roger? I suppose it could be a sign-off."

"Actually, I think the 'Get Rusty' is about me. You see–"

Janet interrupted, "Why? I mean–"

"I know this will sound odd, but . . . " Rusty launched into his tale of burning borders, shimmering, flame-like letters and words, and comparable directives. Somehow the words fit with what he should be doing. Coincidentally, they pointed toward Bernice.

Janet asked no questions. She appeared lost in her own world.

"There's something more you need to know," she whispered to his puzzlement. "We're not alone. Others get messages too."

"No way. Who?" Rusty speculated that they were both headed for the loony bin.

"Beverly and the nurse, Carol. The four of us must talk. Maybe we can figure out what this means: who's the sender and why. The Lord certainly works in mysterious ways, but this is all new for me."

Rusty laughed. "You and me both. I sure hope whoever this is has a good master plan. I don't want to drive off a cliff or something."

"My goodness, of course not, but I think this is something bigger. But why us? And who else–if anybody–is getting communications?"

"I don't know, but I'm curious enough to want to find out. Maybe talking with the others will help us figure it out. Put all the information on the table, you know?"

"That Beverly, she's a sharp one. She was doing exactly that: laying out all the messages side by side to see what we could learn. Now, we can add yours. This is quite the mystery! And at my age?" Janet chuckled, "I'm beginning to feel like Jessica Fletcher."

Rusty looked quizzical.

"Surely, you know Mrs. Fletcher? From the TV show, *Murder She Wrote*?"

He shook his head.

"I'm showing my age." Janet jumped up as they heard the single chime of the grandmother clock from the dining room. "Why, it's six thirty already. Where did the time go? I don't even have dinner on the table. Walt will be starved. I'm surprised we haven't heard from him. Could you go downstairs and let him know dinner will be in ten minutes?"

A modest Italian dinner of pasta, meat sauce (from a jar), and red wine (from a box) served as the backdrop for conversation. Dialogue never touched the supernatural or messages from unknown origins. Rather, they discussed Walt's old hardware store, their respective hobbies, and favorite travel destinations. In parallel, Janet and Rusty continued attempting to interpret the growing array of odd communiqués.

TWENTY-FOUR

As Beverly reached Bernice's bedroom, the doorbell chimed.

"When it rains it pours," she sighed loudly in Bill's direction, who was leaning down toward the pile of graying flesh.

"Hon, can you help me before you go downstairs?"

"Sure. I was going to do just that," nodded Beverly.

The couple struggled vainly to lift Bernice back onto the bed. Unresponsive, she proved deadweight, as Bill and Beverly wrestled to get her upright against the sideboard.

"Mom," Bill insisted. "Are you okay? What happened?" The older woman's head sagged on her chest as her body scissored into itself. She breathed raggedly.

"I'll get some water." The doorbell rang again. "Brad? Caitlyn? Could someone please get the door?" yelled Beverly, hustling toward Bernice's bathroom. Thumping feet pounded down the stairs.

"Sorry, Mom, I didn't hear the bell," Brad yelled back.

Beverly brought back a cup of cool water and a damp washrag. Bill sat on the floor trying to keep his mother from sliding any further. Both mother and son looked awkwardly uncomfortable.

"Mom?" Brad shouted from the foyer. "It's for you."

Carol stepped into the house. "Where's your mom?"

"Oh, she and my dad are upstairs. BeBe conked out on the floor," Brad mindlessly added.

"Oh my," hung in the air as Carol took the stairs two at a time, reaching the bedroom door just as Bernice opened her eyes and groaned.

"Oh shit," Bernice moaned. "Are we having a party again? Who the hell else is here?"

"Mom, it's just us. You fainted. Do you remember anything?" Bill spoke.

Carol, still cloaked in a hot pink parka, squatted down and placed two fingers on Bernice's wrist, studying her own watch. Simultaneously, she felt Bernice's forehead, now cool from the washcloth.

"Pulse is erratic, but quite slow. I can't tell much from her forehead.

Let me see if she's running a fever; her hands and arms feel clammy." Carol paused. "Dr. L? Can we get you up in bed? You'll feel more comfortable."

The three adults together hoisted Bernice's limp body back up. Her dull gray coloring was paler than usual. Not moving and with eyes glazed over, she sat silently on the bed's edge.

"I bet she fell going to the bathroom," cited Carol. "Has she been eating and drinking since yesterday?"

"Not especially well," Beverly shook her head. "We can barely get her to consider food or fluids. Other than some red wine last night."

"Wine?" the nurse raised an eyebrow. "During chemo?"

Beverly sighed, "I tried to tell her, but you know my mother-in-law. I believe she drank quite a bit. I saw a near-empty bottle in the TV room when we got here earlier. It may have been from a couple of nights, but . . . "

Bill turned to his mother, "Did you really? That can't be good . . . "

"I'll damn well drink a glass or two of wine if I want. No one–not even a perky nurse in comfortable shoes–will tell me otherwise." Bernice groused with surprising strength.

"But Mother, I don't think–"

Bernice cut in rudely, "I don't really give a damn what you think. Now, if there's nothing else, I'd like some quiet."

"Dr. L, let's get you under some covers and propped up. You would benefit from additional fluids. Having wine last night," Carol winked at the others, "may have dehydrated you. We need to get you well-hydrated. Otherwise, you start making worse problems than just chemo side effects. Beverly, could you get some Ensure?" Carol grinned. "I sense you're feeling nutty today and might enjoy some Butter Pecan."

Bernice frowned as Bill and Carol repositioned her in bed.

Moments later, Beverly reappeared with a cup, "Here, sip this." Bernice remained still. Carol, rounding the bed, took the drink.

"I insist. You are drying up." She brought the straw toward Bernice's lips. "Here, I've got it all set." Carol brushed the straw against Bernice's lips. "If you won't drink or eat, we will visit the ER for intravenous. You will not dehydrate right before us."

The threat of a trip to the hospital a day early prompted the retired professor to take a modest sip.

"There you go; now doesn't that feel better?" Carol spoke in a sing-songy voice. As Bernice drank, Carol turned to Bill, "I've heard so much about you I feel like I know you . . . "

"I'm sorry. I didn't make any introductions. What with all the excitement . . . "

"Carol, you've been great," responded Bill. "I'd shake your hand or give you a hug or something, but . . . " he motioned toward the cup of thickened fluid the nurse steadied. "Beverly has told me all about you . . . "

"Beverly, could I bend your ear for a moment? It's actually why I stopped by," Carol interrupted. Bill cocked his head inquisitively. "Perhaps you could help your mother with her drink? We'll only be a moment. I'd just rather—" Carol stopped, motioning toward the prone professor, as if to say, "—get out of earshot."

Expressionless, Beverly's interest rose as the two ladies strode to the guest bedroom and shut the door.

"I couldn't believe it. Just this afternoon." Carol's words accelerated with growing excitement. "I was frying bacon for brunch. The kids just love bacon." The nurse laughed, "And me: the health care professional acquiescing to their demands.

"Well, I drained off the bacon, and set it on paper towels to dry. Taking frozen bagels from the freezer, I put them in the microwave to thaw, and returned to the skillet. That's when I saw it."

"Saw what?"

"The skillet should've been cooling," Carol ignored Beverly's interruption. "But the pan was looking hotter, as if the bottom's edge was on fire. Its blue-white tone shimmered and flickered. At first I thought it was the angle of the ceiling lights; I assumed one of them must be reflecting off the pan. The more I watched, the more I became certain— particularly after talking with you and Janet—that another message was emerging. I could just feel it. The house grew silent as I watched the skillet's glittering circumference grow. It was the oddest thing.

"I thought it had to be in my head after all those stories of the supernatural. I rubbed my eyes, I even lifted the skillet off the burners, but the light kept intensifying."

"Unbelievable," Beverly finally interjected.

"The pan actually wasn't hot, so I lifted it. That's when I noticed the bacon residue. What do you call that stuff? It's the odds and ends of bacon—little dark pieces and burnt crud—caught in the grease."

"I have no clue, but I get it."

"Well, the residue formed letters. They weren't super sharp or well defined, but I could absolutely tell they were letters."

"You don't think you were just looking for letters given our earlier conversation?"

"No, I couldn't believe it, but with the glowing circle, it was too similar to that crazy teacup and the communications you and Janet got."

Beverly acknowledged the strong coincidence, especially given the burning edge. "So, what did they say?"

"They were cryptic, but clear:

C BL ASAP
A FALL
ROGER

Beverly absorbed the words. "Really?" she emphasized the first syllable, momentarily drifting in thought.

"So, I said to Jay and the kids, 'Guys, I have to go. I have a sixth sense Dr. Langdon needs me.' And I got in the car as soon as I could and here I am."

"And Mother had, indeed, fallen. She did need your help. We all did. I am so glad you came, but how eerie . . . and so," Beverly stopped, at a loss for words, "timely. Our communicator is in multiple places simultaneously and knows so much." Another long pause ensued.

"I don't get it. Who is it? Why us? Why now?"

Beverly hesitated, "Wait a minute. Did you say it ended with Roger?"

"Yeah, kinda like 'Roger and out.' Why?"

"Well, there's someone else."

"What do you mean?"

"Someone else getting messages. He doesn't know I know, though."

"But I thought you hadn't told anyone?"

"I didn't. But my son, Brad,–"

"He's getting messages?"

"Not at all. By happenstance, he was talking to Mother's paperboy this afternoon

and . . . " Beverly quickly recounted Brad's story.

Moments later, Carol excitedly responded, "The paperboy? As in, bacon bits Roger?"

"Could be."

"I questioned why take all that bacon to write 'Roger.' Just ending the message would've been fine."

"True, but maybe there's a connection. Maybe–whoever this is–he's trying to connect the dots."

"Could be a she. Whoever heard of a man using bacon residue to send messages? Please." Carol laughed. "This really is out-of-this-world."

"We must get all four of us together. I wonder if Janet and Roger could join us."

"Right now?" Carol was surprised, but excited.

"No time like the present, though I'm not sure what we'll tell Roger's parents. If I were them, I'd be skeptical. I bet, if Roger's like the rest of us, he's not been telling his parents about the messages."

"This is mind-boggling," added Carol, just as someone pounded on the door. "Hey, I could use a little help. Mom just threw up."

The ladies sprang from the room and followed Bill back to Bernice's bedside. "Bill, this is nothing. She has some phlegm. No sweat." Carol focused on Bernice whose coloring was returning to its more typical shade of gray. "Are you feeling any better?"

Keeping her eyes scrunched shut, Bernice said nothing, willing the trio to vanish. *'Leave me alone,'* repeated endlessly through her brain; they remained parked, watching her sip. The three quietly talked about the wind-down to the holidays, the upcoming Super Bowl, and the challenges of parenthood as the clock downstairs ticked with excruciating slowness.

At eight o'clock, Carol stood with the chime of the grandfather clock. "I think you're all set. I'm glad I was able to help out."

"And then some," quipped Bill. "Did you two get your business resolved?"

Carol and Beverly looked at one another and nodded. "Yes, we're working through the continuing arrangements for Mother."

"I hope there's no chance we're going to lose you," Bill looked at Carol with alarm.

The nurse chuckled, "Like a bad dream, I just keep coming back. Can't get rid of me that easily. I've been called to be here." She shared a knowing look with Beverly. "Do you want to take the lead on gathering the group?"

"I'll check around," agreed Beverly. "See what I can arrange. Thank you again for all your help. You are an angel."

"Well, someone sure is," received a curious glance from Bill to his wife to the nurse. However, Carol was already attired in hot pink and on her way out the door. "Dr. L, I'll stop by tomorrow" drew no response. A short time later, the Langdons packed up and left, despite misgivings on Beverly's part.

"Do you really think we should leave? I worry about her. She doesn't look good."

"She's fine. She has the phone by her bed, with our number on speed dial. She's mostly sleeping. You'll be here first thing in the morning. You're taking her to chemo, right?"

Beverly shrugged but agreed. Bernice wasn't accepting their help and didn't enjoy their company. Having a quiet house so she could sleep might help. When asked directly, Bernice barely acknowledged their departure.

TWENTY-FIVE

Bernice rose from bed around ten o'clock as sleep had proven elusive. Remarkably alert, she padded downstairs, pushing past Tigger and Spider who no longer received any love. In the still, dark house, she trudged to the kitchen, where she turned on the hanging light, bathing the room in a soft, eerie glow. Surveying the refrigerator, she found little appetite for anything there. A half-finished bottle of white wine stood with its vacuum stopper on the lowest shelf. She contemplated having a glass and stood transfixed in the light from the icebox weighing this monumental decision.

At long last, she reached down and lifted the bottle, despite minor misgivings around white wine keeping her awake. "How much worse could insomnia be?" she said aloud. She splashed some into an everyday juice glass, spilling a bit, unnoticed on the island. She gulped the cold liquid and grimaced, "How long has this been in here?" She continued splashing the coolness toward her parched tonsils.

She carried the bottle and glass to the table. "Perhaps a cracker would help," she said to Tigger who watched closely. She retrieved a box of Wheat Thins and sat, her mind a foggy pool as she indulged. Before long, she poured another glass. The fog settled in like a dense cloud over a marsh, the air still and stagnant. Meaningless thoughts drifted slowly like heavy gray clouds.

Eventually, her mind migrated to the next round of chemo, which she remembered was scheduled for the next day. Her body and posture turned inward, like an evening lily closing up as the sun finally sets. Her thoughts swirled and circled, growing deeper and darker as more alcohol crossed her lips.

Leaving the open box behind, she collected the near-empty bottle and her glass, climbed the stairs, passed her bedroom, and navigated the hall to the TV room. The computer's soft blue light filled the room like a ghostly presence. Settling into the desk chair, she moved the mouse. The screen saver instantly evaporated and returned to the last screen used earlier. A long series of unanswered messages scrolled along the left side, likely an acquaintance of Brad's who also had abandoned the game involving dragons, knights, and substantial blood and gore. The inappropriate nature of the game barely registered. Bernice opened Google and returned to her earlier search. Quickly immersed, she found several sites that provided cold comfort: relief was possible.

Well after midnight, Bernice wound down. The wine anesthetized her, deadening the pain—both mental and physical—and dulling her logic. She was increasingly confident in her emerging contingency plan—a more compelling proposition with each passing day. Incongruous, though oddly supportive, the hell of chemo provided an additional argument toward final resolve. The computer's swirling screen saver emanated dull blue light as she left the empty bottle and glass beside the monitor. She lay in bed, catatonic but awake . . . unable to sleep, unable to force her eyes to close and her mind to shut down. She barely moved, she barely breathed, but she lay there—turning partial thoughts and snippets of research over and over in her mind. The faint light of dawn was just breaking behind the shades when Bernice's breathing became regular and even.

TWENTY-SIX

Skip woke up Monday thinking about his late brother, David. He couldn't quite figure out why. Nothing from the exceptionally full weekend jogged his mind in that direction. The boys were deep into winter activities, requiring endless chauffeuring and carpools. Throw in church and the unexpectedly heavy snowstorm on Saturday night, and the weekend had been jammed, simply exhausting. Now he lay with David on his mind and a nagging loneliness. Strange. David would have loved the snow.

Still in a reflective mood, Skip went through the motions of his morning routine: shower, shave, shirt, tie–the works. He shared a cup of coffee with Amy. She loved the extended break between semesters and maintained a long list of things to do. Sensing his somberness, Amy reached out and stroked his arm. "Hey you," she smiled, "No recent messages from the other side?"

Skip's mood broke and he laughed, "No, I guess I've been out of touch. Maybe the line is disconnected. Sure was odd."

"Keep me posted," she chuckled. "I'm always up for a mystery." They stood together and hugged, a little longer than usual in his morning dash to the door.

As he drove to the office on the slick highway, he considered the messages for the first time in nearly a week. He'd made no movement to drop Arnold Baker, nor had he dealt with the Langdons. He forcefully scrunched up his brow. He must resolve the estate matter this week. Another partner meeting would be on the calendar shortly and Caldwell would undoubtedly ask on its status.

Penny greeted him with a pile of paper as he walked in and hung up his coat. "You must've been here at dawn to get all this organized."

"No, Chief. Just twenty minutes ago. I prewired a bunch on Friday. How was your weekend?"

"Dandy. And yours?"

"Excellen-tay. My sister and brother-in-law were out of town, so I stayed with my nephews. We had great fun in the snow, and then I introduced them to *Casablanca*. We closed off the weekend with *The Wizard of Oz*."

"Sounds like fun." Skip paused, "So, what's hot?" He pointed to the documents piled on his desk.

After prioritizing where Penny could do additional work, she left and closed the door. As his computer fired up, he absently paged through the standard windows until he reached the desktop view. Double-clicking Outlook, he perused the minimal new messages from the weekend. *'Clearly, people were consumed by the snow,'* he mused.

He worked his way through fifteen emails, listened to eight voicemails, and then shifted gears to the papers on his desk. As a senior partner, he vigilantly maintained the one-touch rule on his desk: "Delegate it, resolve it, or file it" was his mantra.

As he turned to his papers, out of habit, he glanced at the darkened voicemail light–nothing new had arrived–and his email in-box, which showed three new messages. He didn't recognize the third one. Its subject was *Follow Up* and came from himself, *oneill.* He failed to recall why he had sent himself a delayed transmission. While he did this periodically to manage his activities and in-box, he couldn't recall *Follow Up.* His subject lines were typically more descriptive.

'I'm losing it,' he thought, double-clicking the cursor. The message popped up rapidly, but the normalcy of email evaporated immediately. The new window exuded a warm, red-orange glow framing the text. The message was short and was written in vacillating flame-like font. It was bigger than normal and appeared burned into the background of his screen.

WHY DELAY? ASAP BRO
LANGDON WILL DROP BAK

Skip's heart jumped as he blushed. Embarrassment washed over him similar to what he once felt when a teacher called on him and he hadn't completed his homework.

'Those messages,' he thought quietly. *'It's like I willed one onto the computer.'* He pushed his chair back and pondered again the meaning. Thoughts of who, why, what, and how tumbled erratically through his brain. Eventually, his screen saver subsumed the open window. When he realized the message was gone, he moved the mouse. The burning letters immediately rematerialized.

"Hey, Boss, you want a cup of coffee from Java Jane's? I'm going downstairs and I could–"

Penny noticed Skip looking dreamily out the window. "Hey, there . . . you okay?"

"Yeah, sure. Pen, I got another of those messages."

Penny walked over while staring at his window. "I don't see anything. Window is dirty, but clear."

"No. Look here." He pointed.

"Ah-ha. There it is. Another burning message. Maybe God is speaking to you. Though it's flames; maybe it's the devil," Penny chuckled.

"It's gonna put me in the nuthouse. What do you make of it?"

"Well, it's basically the same message as last time. That was only a week ago." She smiled wickedly, "You didn't do your assignment, did you?"

Skip blushed again. Why was he embarrassed? "Well, I didn't get to it," he hesitantly uttered.

"I believe you should get to it soon. Seems like your friend is getting annoyed with your lack of compliance."

"Like I told you, Amy and I worked our way through that one. Three Kings was the Epiphany service. We went and that phrase is gone."

Penny said nothing.

"The Langdon will: I volunteered to review and update the estate plan."

"Have you done it?"

"Not yet. Drop Bak remains more puzzling. The only explanation is Arnold Baker. I know you think that's far-fetched, but I can't come up with anything else. The problem is: on what basis would I drop a major client? Getting messages from the great beyond is not especially credible."

His assistant remained silent. "Probably not, but what if you passed the client?"

"On what basis? I don't care for the guy that much, but still–I've had plenty of clients I don't connect with. If I can help the organization, putting up with a . . . " Skip paused. "With an eccentric lead guy is probably something I can stomach. I've done it before."

"Sounds like you're rationalizing."

Skip stayed deep in his reflections. "Perhaps. Baker is sleazy. I would feel a whole lot better if I didn't have to work with him."

"Life's short, Chief. You got to make some choices. Look at your brother," Penny quipped.

Skip's eyes widened and stared deeply at Penny.

She reddened. "Hey, I didn't mean to–" she started, but Skip interrupted.

"No, no problem. It's odd you bring up David. I was thinking of him this morning. Just a funny coincidence. You know what else is odd?"

"I'm standing here thinking this whole deal is kinda odd, and you want to tease out something specific?"

"The only person who's ever called me 'Bro' is David. Is that odd or what?"

"Maybe he's talking to you."

"Listen to yourself. He's been dead nearly two years. You'd have to believe in ghosts," Skip paused.

"And you have a better explanation?"

"Okay, so it's inexplicable. But why now? Why is David suddenly engaging in my life right now? Wouldn't he have just started talking right after he died?"

"Well, I'm no expert on ghosts, but I'm not sure they follow the same logic that you–in your lawyerly kind of way–might follow. That's all. Who else could it be?"

"Why not just some random spirit?"

"Listen to you. A random spirit? Maybe it's a defendant you've worked with. A crazy frat brother perhaps? " Penny laughed.

Skip smiled as well. "This is way outside my experience."

"Listen, I am going to Jane's. I'll get you something to clear the head. Regardless of what you do or don't do with your brother's directive," Penny made up her mind, "you better get ready for your afternoon meeting with the associates working on Thornberry. The briefing is right there." Walking to the door, she turned upon reaching the transom. "And Boss?" She waited until Skip looked up, "I'd act on Langdon and Baker. What do you need? A house to fall on you?" They both laughed as she exited.

Based on Skip's request, Penny arranged a Friday afternoon meeting at Bernice Langdon's Glenwood home. He would meet her daughter-in-law there. Bill would potentially join them. Minimally, he would conference in by phone. Beverly was open to whatever timing would best fit Skip's schedule.

That evening, Skip spent a quiet hour in his study penciling the pros and cons of dropping Baker as a client. The list proved significant on both sides as he analyzed the situation. Like Penny, Amy believed the messages would become more compelling if Skip delayed action further. The directives to date had been perfectly fine things to do, though not earthshaking. This one held more consequential implications.

He closed his eyes, considering his list. It made no sense. While he didn't have great feelings about Amalgamated and harbored misgivings around Arnold Baker, this move would be radical. His indecision caused a rare feeling of paralysis.

* * *

The article appeared below the fold on the front page of the Marketplace section in *The Wall Street Journal.* "Insider Trading Rampant at Amalgamated" screamed the headline. At the center of the controversy were two men–the chief financial officer and the Senior Vice President of Human Resources, Arnold Baker. While only alleged charges, the two men apparently coordinated a series of huge Amalgamated stock option plays predicated on a string of acquisitions, including Mexicani. They bought options with remarkably coincidental stop loss protection, collaring expected gains post acquisition. After each buyout, the stock rose dramatically on the promise of strengthening profitability while simultaneously growing revenues. In the period shortly thereafter, the stock's price fell–in a pattern that only those closely following Amalgamated could see.

The CFO and Baker traded with an uncanny knack for knowing precisely when the stock would turn; they exercised options or placed stop losses all too perfectly each time. The Mexicani acquisition tipped SEC investigators, due to the potential class action suit, which focused undue attention on Amalgamated. The pattern of option buying, impeccable stop loss placement, and option exercise proved too consistent and unerring to be fortuitous. Company counsel, Dane & Caldwell, had no comment for the morning edition.

"What is this?" a startled Skip yelped to Amy as they sipped coffee. "Who is giving no comment? Why am I not even aware?"

"There's got to be a good explanation. I'm sure you'll find out."

"I cannot believe this crap," Skip retorted.

Amy sat silently, as Skip fumed. "I have to get downtown and find out what is going on."

"Of course. Call me, when you figure it out." Skip leaned down to kiss Amy before storming out. "Love ya" hung in the air unanswered.

"Why'd Dad slam the door?" inquired Matt, entering the kitchen, hair disheveled and looking ready to return to bed.

"Just some work issues. He'll work it out." Amy changed subjects despite Matt's astute eyebrows being raised. "Let's get you guys out the door. I can drive you to school, if you want."

One uninvited thought plagued Skip as he sped downtown; yesterday's message was remarkably prescient with the overnight events. Perhaps he had stalled too long on the decision. *'Water under the bridge,'* he grimaced as he pulled the Beemer into his parking space under the elegant Dane & Caldwell tower.

He strode rapidly into his office, dropping his overcoat on a side chair, and starting his computer. Penny flew in. "Chief, Mr. Caldwell has called a special meeting for nine. All senior partners are asked to attend. I figured with the morning headlines and the sudden meeting with the guy in the corner office, well . . . I've got your files on Amalgamated, as–" she stopped and looked at Skip with concern. "The place is buzzing already, and it's not even a quarter after eight."

"Thanks. This whole thing ticks me off, but we'll deal. Get me Vince Weigand as soon as he shows. He's been following the market and business dynamics on Amalgamated since the fall. I want a current update. His paperwork trailed off just before the holidays."

Twelve new messages crammed his in-box, since nine thirty last night when he last checked. Several delivered this morning were from his closest colleagues in the senior partnership. Each expressed surprise yet ardent support. Caldwell's message outlined the morning agenda, which–as Penny had surmised—focused on the firm's exposure and position on the emerging Amalgamated situation. The last email caught his eye: a note from "*oneill*" with a crisp subject line.

SEE? ACT QUICKLY DON'T DELAY BRO

A similar burning perimeter surrounded the message window's blank white space. All that needed to be said was—apparently—in the subject line.

Skip felt a sharp pang of anxiety. *'I should've dropped him. I knew it. I had a gut feel, but I went with logic. I procrastinated, even though I knew the decision was clear. And now this.'* He chastised himself a few moments longer, but the meeting was in less than forty-five minutes.

When Vince appeared in the doorway, a quick conversation revealed that Caldwell had directed him to cease ongoing research on Amalgamated. He inferred that the eponymous managing partner of the firm and Skip debated and agreed this course of action and, as a result, never raised it directly with Skip. He was immensely apologetic when he saw that Skip was not informed. Visibly nervous, the lanky associate discussed his analysis, which mirrored the *Journal*'s report. Despite Caldwell's directive, Vince continued watching the stock and its options, puts, and calls. He only stopped writing them up and circulating his daily report.

Skip became direct, "What happened isn't your fault. You followed directions and made some assumptions as to who knew what. Let's fast-forward. Basically, the report in the *Journal* is a fair one. These two guys moved stock positions at a rapid pace, out-predicting the market and making a killing."

"Yeah, but it's not just them. They appear to coordinate a buying syndicate. There may be as many as two dozen other executives involved."

"You must be kidding."

"Actually not. Look at the insider trading activity just since the Mexicani purchase."

Analyzing Vince's printouts made the extent of the activity and the number of people who were "guessing" on market dynamics very clear. While not every name was recognizable, the number of people or institutional investors involved in the apparent scheme was the order of magnitude Vince speculated.

"Unbelievable. How could I have been played?" Skip said to no one in particular. Vince stood helplessly watching.

"I need time to review this before I join the meeting. Thank you for your candor and responsiveness. I'll let you know what I can, when I can." Vince beat a hasty retreat.

Penny poked her head in. "Hey, I brought you java. Just figured you'd want it before heading down the hall." Skip nodded, but said nothing. "Anything I can do to help get ready?"

"No. Thanks for the coffee." Skip buried himself in Vince's papers and scribbled notes on his legal pad. He listed questions he wanted addressed when he joined the partners. Penny quietly closed the door and played guard, denying access to several colleagues who stopped.

Promptly at nine o'clock, Skip marched to the conference room where he joined the other senior partners, taking the last seat at the long, mahogany table. Sharply attired, Taylor Caldwell called the meeting to order with the lawyers uncharacteristically drawing still with remarkable speed.

TWENTY-SEVEN

Dr. Esch made a rare appearance, surprising Beverly and Bernice during chemo on Monday afternoon. Sharp-tongued and quick-witted, he failed to engage Bernice who remained lost in her own world. Sullen with eyes closed, she allowed the pharmaceutical cocktail to drip intravenously into her left arm.

"I'm worried," whispered Beverly following the physician from the curtained treatment area. "I think she's depressed. I know this is hard, but she seems to withdraw more and more each week. It's tough getting her to talk . . . not that she's Miss Congeniality on her best days."

"Different people react unpredictably to the rigors of chemo in varying ways. Seeing how feisty she was when we started, I expected more of a fight, but you never know."

"She doesn't eat much. She rarely gets out of bed, even toward the end of the cycle. The only thing she enjoys is wine, and I'm not so sure that's a good thing."

Jeremy chuckled, "Well, I wouldn't prescribe alcohol, but given what she's fighting, a little–as we discussed earlier– shouldn't hurt."

"But she drinks a lot once she starts. Just this morning, there was another empty bottle in her study. I don't know if it was full when she started, but I'm suspicious. I could barely rouse her when I arrived around ten o'clock."

The doctor grinned again, "Sleeping it off?" Seeing Beverly's somber look, his smile faded. "You're right; full bottles of wine are not the best. Although there's little research, few people in chemo have any taste for alcohol. I suspect her interest and tolerance will diminish with each passing week. The alcohol will affect her more quickly."

"Should I get it out of the house?"

"You could, but that might irritate her." He paused reflecting, "Of course, showing a little life could be good. But–again–wine in moderation shouldn't do any real harm. There's no reason for draconian measures."

Beverly nodded. "Okay, let me shift gears. How's her progress?"

"It's still early. As you know from Drs. Gerhart and Elway, your mother-in-law was in pretty rough shape when she had her surgery."

"No one ever came out and precisely said what the prognosis was."

"She's dealing with a damn aggressive cancer. It showed up in multiple sites and metastasized rapidly. Without the chemo regimen she's enduring, I think she would've—well, I think her prognosis for recovery was limited. Perhaps as low as ten to twenty percent."

Beverly blanched.

"Yes, but Dr. Gerhart did a masterful job."

"Yes," Beverly nodded.

"Chemo is harsh on the body and on the lingering malignant cells, if any. It's a war zone inside, and her body is the battlefield. She's suffering collateral damage."

"I didn't realize how much her appearance and personality would deteriorate."

"Bernice had excess weight, which gave her insurance—some body fat to live off while she fights. Her weight loss was predictable. The psyche—well, that's harder to anticipate. She's suffering more than expected." Dr. Esch paused. "Much as I'd like this to be an exact science, it's not. It's much more of an art with some chemistry thrown in."

"I see. But," Beverly persisted, "how is she doing? Do you have any sense?"

"I planned to do blood work and another CT scan next week. Do it on her off-week so she can stomach the idea better. If you think she's up to it, we could schedule some preliminary work today. I can—"

Beverly interrupted, "I just want to give her some good news. I hope this dreadfulness is worthwhile."

"Well, I suggest early next week. Why don't you bring her in on Tuesday? She should be clear of side effects by then. We'll do some lab work, shoot some scans, and I can see her . . . say sometime late in the afternoon," he smiled broadly.

"Thank you, Doctor. Mother isn't showing much gratitude at the moment, but I'm certain she's appreciative. You have been a bright spot in this experience."

"Just doin' my job, ma'am," quipped Jeremy as he turned to leave. "Takin' it one step at a time. See you next Tuesday." His white lab coat billowed behind him as he zipped off to his next patient. Beverly returned to Bernice's side and mindlessly turned magazine pages as the pump dripped slowly but surely into the somnolent body.

* * *

Carol preceded Beverly and Bernice's return late Monday. She changed the sheets, vacuumed the upstairs thoroughly, and cleaned Bernice's bathroom. "The things I don't get paid for," she chuckled.

After Bernice was dozing in bed with a nearby bucket, Beverly and Carol retreated to the TV room.

"We should hang up here. She'll likely be feeling ill shortly. I want to stay close."

Beverly agreed and got two steaming cups of tea from downstairs. They barely touched on Wednesday's predicted snowstorm before Carol changed topics.

"So, we need to get this group together?"

"Yes, I hoped to do that last evening, but it got crazy. Maybe we should call around and see if Janet has time and if Roger's parents would let him visit."

"What if you didn't share the topic—precisely—with Roger's parents? Just pose it as, 'Bernice is asking for him. She enjoys his energy and youth.' You know, just a little, tiny, ever so small, white lie?"

Beverly smiled, "It is a strange one. Perhaps doing some sidestepping is not really a complete falsehood; Mother might be thinking just that. She really isn't offering up much these days. We could try the youthful exuberance angle. A visit from Roger just might boost her spirits."

"That's good. I like it."

"First, let's see if Janet is available."

"One other thing: Dr. Esch." Beverly almost completed the update when Bernice gagged loudly.

"Let me see to her. You call Janet," directed Carol.

As Carol hustled off, Beverly reached Janet just as she and Walt were preparing dinner.

"Oh, I can't really talk right now. How is Bernice?"

"Well, it's going to be a hard couple of days. She had chemo today."

"Please remember me to her."

"Of course. Janet—just a moment more, would you have time to stop by this evening? Carol is here and, well, we'd like to figure out these communications." She paused dramatically, " . . . and we've discovered another person receiving messages."

"Really? Well, I know," responded Janet.

"You do? But how?"

"I was talking to him."

"You spoke with Roger?"

"Who's Roger?"

"Mother's paperboy. But why, you said you knew?"

"That's not who. I meant Rusty."

"The guy who worked on Mother's computer?"

"One and the same." Janet paused in the middle of tossing a green salad. "So there are two more involved in this—whatever this is?"

"I guess so. We do need to talk. You're sure Rusty is involved?"

"Most definitely. He must join us."

Beverly swallowed. "Of course. This is just so much to digest."

"I would love to chat, but Walt is ready for supper and I have a church meeting. Perhaps tomorrow? I'm free."

"An evening makes most sense, as Rusty works." Beverly continued, "Shall we try to convene around seven o'clock at Mother's? I'm sure she wouldn't mind and we might as well meet where we all see one another. I don't want to go too late, as Roger is only in ninth grade."

"That should be fine. I'll contact Rusty. You'll connect with the others?"

Janet scooted off the phone to finish meal preparations, though her mind was clearly elsewhere as she arranged the myriad puzzle pieces that kept multiplying in complexity.

After sharing the newest wrinkle, Beverly and Carol each attempted to sort through the same set of intriguing but confusing facts. Reluctantly, they agreed to delay continuing their conversation until the next evening, when the group—hopefully—would convene.

TWENTY-EIGHT

Tuesday evening didn't work, but Wednesday night did.

Receiving his invitation, Rusty was skeptical. After leaving the Walkers' home on Sunday, doubts arose in his mind about the credibility of the messages. He easily declined Janet's request for a follow-up discussion, based on his growing disbelief and a heavy workload. He and Chip were collaborating on an early stage prototype that would go in front of the CIO on Wednesday morning. After leaving his regrets on Janet's answering machine, a subsequent voicemail from the church elder suggested heightened urgency mixed with disappointment.

"You really must join us," Janet insisted. "We will just find a different time."

"Laying on the guilt. It's like talking to Mom. This just isn't going to go away," Rusty muttered. He didn't respond.

Late Tuesday, Rusty and Chip finished. The new application rocked, with enhancements and features well beyond the likely expectations of the CIO and CEO. They high-fived one another and closed down.

"Hey, I just need to close up," Rusty had recently moved into an office, away from the sea of cubes. "Meet you at the elevators?"

Rusty returned to his desk and spun his chair, rotating past the windows with a quick glance over the increasingly quiet city street and lurched to a stop in front of his flat-screen. With an uncomfortable growing familiarity, the perimeter of the screen glowed.

'God, it's back,' he thought. Staring at the growing border, Rusty watched as letters materialized at various points on the screen and then kaleidoscoped toward the middle, slowly coming to rest, shimmering from the center.

CONNECT DOTS
TIME HAS COME
GO MEET

"Why is this no surprise?" he murmured. "It's the sickest. Pretty damn obvious." He grimaced.

"Hey, Bud. You coming or not?" Chip, tired of waiting at the elevator, stood in the doorway. "Whatcha looking at?" He stepped behind Rusty. "Cool. I've never seen that font before. Isn't that kinda similar to that shit you had happen . . . when was that? Last fall?" Rusty remained silent. "You remember, don't you? You ever figure that out?"

At last Rusty responded, "Nope, never did. Don't quite know where it comes from, but . . . " he trailed off.

"So, what's it mean? 'Connect dots. Time has come. Go meet.' Messed up, if you ask me."

"No clue. Let's get outta here. I'll figure it out in the morning."

"Whatever you say." As they headed out, the words faded.

"Wanna grab a cold one?"

"I'm bushed. I'm gonna crash," responded Rusty.

"Yeah, you're right. I could use some shut-eye. Share a cab?"

"Course." Moments later, the taxi disappeared up the quiet street.

* * *

In the morning, Rusty placed an early call and quickly got to the point.

"Listen, I can't talk long. I have a huge meeting in less than an hour. When are you guys getting together?"

"Well, I've not spoken with Beverly yet. It's not even nine o'clock. Perhaps this evening," Janet paused. "She was disappointed not to meet last night."

"Well, I'd like to–uh–join the group if we can find a time." Rusty stammered, uncharacteristically inarticulate.

"Wonderful news. I'll talk with Beverly and see if we can get things organized for this evening. Shall I leave a message?"

"Yeah, that would be great. Anytime after six thirty should work. Traffic may be a bear, but I'll try to be on time. Drop a voicemail. And Janet . . . ?" Rusty paused. "I got another message last night. It's the strangest." Relief surged as he told someone who might understand.

"Really? What did it say?"

"Connect dots. Time has come. Go meet." Rusty looked at his notepad. "You know, I wasn't going to come, but it's almost as if this messenger sensed my reluctance. It sure doesn't make sense."

Janet's voice became resolute, "I'll leave you a message shortly. Now hurry along to your meeting."

Within the hour, Beverly sprang into action. Carol planned to spend the day and could easily extend through dinner and into the evening. Beverly next dialed Roger's house. After providing Elaine Gallo with an update on Bernice and appreciation for the gifts, she shifted gears.

"There's actually another reason for my call. I was wondering if Roger would be up for a visit this evening. Do you think he might stop by, perhaps after dinner, to visit my mother-in-law?"

When Elaine remained quiet, Beverly quickly continued.

"I know how much Mother enjoys him. She has such a passion for engaging with young people. Probably why she became a teacher. Roger's becoming such a fine young man. You must be quite proud."

"Well, yes, but I'm not sure why . . . "

"Mother's not eating that well. We thought if a few of us gathered with her and had a bite of dessert, she might feel more motivated. Maybe Roger . . . " Beverly awkwardly stammered.

Elaine looked quizzically at the receiver. "I'm not sure that Roger would motivate anyone beyond watching just how much he can consume!" She laughed, changing the conversation's dynamic. "I can certainly ask. As best I know, he's got an open schedule tonight. He can't stay out long, as he'll have homework."

"Naturally, I've got kids too. Both in that tweenster stage."

"Roger met your son the other day. Is he coming?"

"I will see to it," Beverly agreed, thinking on the fly.

Elaine worried needlessly about encouraging her son to visit. Arriving home, Roger entered through the garage where a circle of virtual fire beckoned. Intense and vibrant, the circle radiated a blinding white light. Brick outlines flashed on and off like a highway construction sign. Squared off letters were readily apparent.

CONNECT DOTS
TIME HAS COME
GO MEET

More intrigued than alarmed, Roger watched the letters shine in the gloom.

"Awesome. I wonder what it means." As the words appeared static, Roger instantly remembered his after-school starvation. "Hey, Mom. I'm home!" he yelled.

"Roger, don't slam the door," responded his mother. "How was your day?"

"Fine."

"Anything happening?"

"No."

"Any homework?"

"Not much." Roger shrugged his shoulders. "What's to eat?"

"I made chocolate chip cookies. They're still warm."

Roger inhaled the first cookie before Elaine finished speaking.

"They're good," Roger grunted, downing another. He got some milk and gorged on another half-dozen. "I gotta go do papers."

"Hey, Roger?"

"Yeah?"

"What do you think of dropping off some cookies for Professor Langdon?"

"Awww, Mom. I hate carrying extra stuff."

"Actually, Brad's mom called inviting you to visit this evening for some dessert with the professor. Professor Langdon would like to see you."

"Really?" Roger grimaced. "Do I have to?"

"It would be nice. She hasn't been eating well. Beverly thought that if a few people–including Brad–came over for dessert, maybe she would eat." Roger was silent. "It's doing something nice for her. She's been quite sick, you know."

"I know," Roger rolled his eyes. "She doesn't look that great. I don't know about hanging out with her . . . " He consumed another cookie.

"You should go back. Plaster a smile on your face. Sometimes you just need to persist at things you find distasteful."

Roger rocked on his heels. "What did you say?"

His mother looked at him perplexed. "You heard me."

"No, I just wondered." Roger paused. "What did you say?" He pushed.

Elaine sighed. "Just go back. Keep smiling. Persist."

"Did you want to add, 'say uncle'?"

"What are you talking about?"

"Never mind."

"Brad will be there. Maybe you can play with him."

"Mom, I don't play with kids anymore," Roger sighed.

"Don't be disrespectful."

"Sorry," Roger exaggerated, as he considered the coincidental consistency of the first message in the garage, '*Persist. Go Back. Keep Smile. Say Uncle,*' with his mom's language. Maybe today's message was about going to the Langdons'. Maybe that was who he was to meet. Maybe the time really had come.

"Okay. I'll go. When?"

"Tonight. After dinner. You can take cookies."

Roger hustled outside. Though the forecast called for evening snow and the skies thickened with threatening clouds, no precipitation fell. Invigorated by the brisk January air, he walked with his paper bag over his shoulder. Riding a bike would prove too treacherous given the lingering ice. Puzzled, Roger contemplated the alpha-bricks as he went from house to house.

* * *

The grandfather clock in Bernice's front hallway chimed seven times. The doorbell coincided with its last chord. Beverly strode across the hallway from the staircase, bucket in hand, having just left Bernice in her bedroom. Carol remained upstairs attending to the professor and her retching, dry heaves.

Roger stood at the door tapping his foot, a container of cookies in hand. His exhalations created misty clouds in the frigid night air. His mother waited in the car at the curb.

"Roger. Come in. You must be frozen." Beverly let him slide past. "Did you walk?"

"No, Mrs. Langdon. My mom–" Roger jerked his head back toward the street, "drove me over. She said you offered to bring me home."

"Absolutely." Beverly leaned out the door and waved at the dark station wagon, which slowly pulled away.

"Now, what did you bring?" she asked, taking his coat.

"My mom baked cookies. Said we were having dessert and that Professor Langdon might want some."

"I'm not sure if she'll be up for a cookie just yet." The sounds of a forceful round of gagging wafted down the staircase.

"Oh? I thought that's why–" Roger stopped.

"I hoped so, but there's something else I'd actually like to talk over with you."

Roger looked at Beverly curiously.

"Brad told me about the unusual messages you've received. I hope you don't mind, but they may be more important than you realized."

"He told you?" Incredulous, Roger stood, embarrassed and angry. "Why did he tell you?"

"He thought it was interesting and I suppose . . . " Beverly stopped. "It actually doesn't matter. Listen, other people have been getting messages too."

Roger was still processing the broken trust with Brad. Embarrassment won and he blushed, his cold face getting rosier. Only then did he realize what Beverly had said.

"Other people? Who?"

"That's what I'd like to talk about. That's really why you're here. I couldn't tell your mother, because I suspected you hadn't told her."

"No way. She wouldn't understand."

"Brad doesn't know about the other messages either. He just helped me connect with you. Rather like that old game of whisper down the lane?" Beverly tried unsuccessfully to connect with Roger as he looked back blankly.

"Never mind." She paused. "I've been getting messages too."

Roger's eyebrows rose with surprise. "Really? You saw a message in the courtyard?"

"No, mine arrived differently and were equally odd. But, there are others."

"Who else? Brad?" Roger's brain spun excitedly.

"No, in fact, he didn't come. I thought you'd understand."

"Well, who else then? How did you learn about anybody else?"

"As with you, it happened by accident. You know the nurse upstairs?"

"Not really." Roger thought for a moment. "I guess I've seen her."

"Her name is Carol. She's gotten two messages as well. Just like you. And me."

"No, ma'am. I've gotten three." Roger puffed up with the news. "I got another one this afternoon. I wondered if it had something to do with coming over here tonight."

A breathless excitement entered Beverly's voice, "Another one? Just this afternoon? My goodness, it must be related. I wonder if–" but the doorbell interrupted her. "More visitors."

Janet and Rusty, who arrived and parked on Fox Den simultaneously, stood outside. Bundled up and looking like the Michelin Tire men, they stamped their feet.

"Hurry in," Beverly gushed. "Get out of the cold."

"My goodness, it feels like snow. The air is so brittle but dense. We could get a doozy tonight."

"They say heavy accumulation if the winds stay right. I don't want to get caught out here in the 'burbs."

"Worst case, you can always stay over, but we'll keep an eye on the weather." Beverly smiled.

Hanging back by the door to the study, Roger surveyed the new additions and wondered how many others were getting communications from some curious source that spoke in riddles.

Janet and Rusty shed layers of outerwear as Beverly directed them toward the study.

"Hi, I'm Rusty Stillwagon." He raised his hand in a casual hello.

"Hey," smiled Roger, awkward and shy.

"And I'm Janet Walker. I gather we all have something in common."

"And Carol Kneffler, too. She's upstairs and will join us momentarily."

The sound of another round of gagging reverberated into the vestibule.

"Oh my, she is having a tough time of it, isn't she?" frowned Janet.

"Carol says it's rough today. She got here first thing this morning. Mother has kept nothing down all day. It seems that each round is worse. I sure hope it's working."

"We continue to pray for her at church," murmured Janet.

Feeling out of place, Roger stared at the floor while Rusty analyzed the wallpaper pattern in the hallway leading toward the back of the house.

"Sorry, guys. I imagine you're not into gag reflexes and prayer lists. Shall we move to the kitchen? I have decaf coffee brewing. And, Roger, I can make something for you."

"I brought some cookies I picked up earlier today."

"Wonderful. Roger's mother baked chocolate chip cookies as well. We'll put them all out."

The foursome moved to the kitchen and stood around the island as Beverly arranged cookies on a large plate. Roger agreed to hot chocolate, "if it's not too much trouble, Mrs. Langdon," he politely added. He snuck two cookies immediately as she prepared his drink.

"Do you have something with more of a kick to it?" asked Rusty. "I sorta think with what we're gonna discuss, I could use something with some higher octane." He smiled broadly.

"Well, let me see what's in here." Beverly perused the dated inventory of liquor bottles in her mother-in-law's pantry. "We have wine, though none of the white is chilled. There's also some old stuff in here—probably from when my father-in-law was alive. I don't believe alcohol goes bad, does it?"

Rusty cast his eye across the bottom shelf. "You know, red wine sounds fine."

In no time, Rusty uncorked a bottle and poured a hearty glass for himself. "Anyone join me?" he inquired, to which Carol, entering the room, responded enthusiastically, "Fruit of the vine sounds real good about now."

Beverly agreed to join them with a modest glass, while Janet stuck with the decaf. Roger contentedly sipped his hot chocolate. Bringing the plate of cookies and the bottle of wine, the group took seats at the kitchen table.

"So, where should we start?"

"Actually, do we all know each other?"

"Good point. Maybe as we do a quick round of introductions and share our messages, I could write them down on my pad of paper," said Beverly as the guys looked at her quizzically. "Just so you know, I started transcribing the messages Carol, Janet, and I received. We can add yours."

"Makes sense. Maybe we'll see a pattern," nodded Rusty.

"Maybe," nodded Carol.

Though everyone else was talkative, Roger remained quiet until they got to him. Then, he shared his newspaper job and the way he received his messages. Beyond that, he was overwhelmed but intrigued.

With all the stories shared, Rusty poured more red wine for himself and Carol. Beverly declined. "I can't believe this. Why us? I wonder if we're the only ones."

"Well, we don't know if we're it or not. How could we?" Janet added.

Carol nodded, "Though don't you think if there were others, they'd find us?"

"True–we did find each other," agreed Beverly.

"So what do we have so far?" Rusty asked, sipping more of his drink.

The group leaned in to review Beverly's notes. She had added Carol's newest message as well as those of the guys.

Janet	Oct 30	*COLLEAGUE C BERNICE AP $ TELL ANDREWS SOON*
	Jan 6	*FRIEND ENGAGE RUSTY SKIP B*
	Jan 11	*SEE BERNICE GET RUSTY SKIP CHURCH ROGER*

Beverly	Nov 7	*MRS L NO JOB CONFRONT BILL*
	Jan 6	*MRS L ENGAGE RUSTY SKIP B*
Carol	Oct 18	*HH GOOD FAM 1ST TAKE JOB*
	Jan 12	*C BL ASAP A FALL ROGER*

Rusty	Oct 18	*ENGAGE PRODUCTIVELY. WORK WEEKEND. FOREGO PARTY.*
	Jan 6	*TAKE TASK SEE BERNICE ASAP*
	Jan 14	*CONNECT DOTS TIME HAS COME GO MEET*

Roger	Oct 25	*CHOOSE LIFE GO DANCE COFFEE NOT FREE*
	Jan 5	*PERSIST GO BACK KEEP SMILE SAY UNCLE*
	Jan 15	*CONNECT DOTS TIME HAS COME GO MEET*

"Wow," Roger uttered.

"What's the deal, Bro?" exclaimed Rusty. "Whatcha thinking?"

"How cool is that? My last message is exactly the same as yours. And, it came today . . . just one day later."

The group silently focused on the list. Only the dull, rhythmic ticking of the grandfather clock broke the tranquility. Rusty poured the scant residual wine into his glass.

"More, anyone?" he inquired. No one spoke, as their private contemplation continued. Rusty rose and uncorked a second bottle of merlot. Roger munched quietly on another cookie as Rusty filled his glass and, without asking, poured more for Carol and Beverly.

"You know, Janet, Carol, and I spent some time on ours already. We agreed on a few things."

"Yes, indeed," effused Janet.

"Whoever–whatever–is sending them is a force for good and is able to see the future."

"They seem to give direction, which–intentionally or not–the three of us have acted on and things have turned out well."

"Give an example," prodded Rusty, to which Janet and then Carol quickly complied.

"And you can see what a huge asset she has been to us, I imagine," Beverly jumped in as Carol wrapped up.

"Mine are equally clear in what they suggested and what I actually did." Rusty gave the run-down on his choices in recent months. In fact, he attributed his recent promotion, new office, and much broader visibility across Ridgewell to following the advice, whether he admitted it or not.

He closed, "I have to say, I didn't really want to come out here again. I was a little spooked by the conversation with Janet on Sunday–no disrespect or anything," he quickly added.

"None taken," smiled Janet warmly.

"Then late last night, another message arrived as clear as day. I tossed and turned all night thinking about it. I thought at first it was about the meeting with Ridgewell's CIO earlier today, but I couldn't patch together what 'connect dots' could be. I thought it could've been the storyline we're going to tell about the prototype . . . " Rusty delved deeper into the technology presentation. Finally, he smiled sheepishly, realizing the group was lost.

"Hey, guys, I'm sorry. I get a little carried away with this stuff."

"It certainly sounds fascinating," gushed Janet, a little too enthusiastically. "It's just, you're so far beyond us, that well . . . " She stopped.

"It's obvious now that I was directed here." Rusty jammed his index finger forcefully into the kitchen table. "Roger's writing on the wall confirms it."

Roger piped up. "Yeah, that's what I think. I had no idea what the message meant. The first one was pretty clear. Then that second one–well, I couldn't figure it out. But my mom helped me. She used almost the exact same words today."

"She did?" Beverly raised an eyebrow.

"Yup." Roger shared his story, including the rabbit rescue.

"You're a real stand-up dude," Rusty responded, giving a high-five. Roger blushed, his dimple showing deeply.

"I don't know that I can do too much, but if I can, I will," Roger concluded.

"Connecting dots, well . . . you have to believe we're the dots, right?" Carol observed.

"No other explanation. That's why we're here. The time has come, and we've met . . . connecting the dots." Janet agreed.

Beverly looked perplexed as she took another sip of wine. "Again I wonder, is this the whole group?"

"If there is someone else, they'll show up, I imagine," noted Janet.

"We've all ended up helping Bernice in some way, right?" Rusty pointed out. The group nodded. "Has anyone else been showing up or helping her in some way?"

"That's an interesting angle."

"I sure haven't been here much," said Roger quietly.

"Maybe not, but I've been here even less," observed Rusty.

"My husband has been here off and on, but I'm sure if he received messages, I'd know. He's been an open book lately," added Beverly. "Ever since our little heart-to-heart, we've been more of a team again. It's been great."

"That's so nice to hear," murmured Janet.

"So who else?"

"How about her doctors? Any of them show up?"

"Or what about the nurses at the university? Does it need to be here at the house?"

"No one else has been in the house. The doctors don't make house calls. And other than you, no nurse has been by."

"Any other visitors?"

"Well, Brad and Caitlyn, but I think if they were seeing messages regarding BeBe, they'd let me know. Particularly Brad, given that he told me about Roger."

Roger nodded, "Yeah, he definitely would've said something."

"A couple of other people have been by from the church, though none as faithfully as you, Janet."

"What about the pastors?"

"Pastor Andrews has been twice but not recently. The messages have led us all here recently."

"There's another: Albert, probably her closest colleague from the university, stops by consistently. In the last few weeks, he has taken to dropping in–usually with some soup around lunchtime." Beverly paused. "Like Mother, Albert's retired. He's ga-" Beverly stopped abruptly.

"What? Something relevant?"

"No, he's a grand friend of Mother's. I know they're close." Beverly looked down.

Rusty sensed what she planned to say and wondered why she stopped. A sense of privacy? A desire to avoid unnecessary gossip? He found it intriguing.

"So, where does that leave us?"

"I believe we're a Party of Five," chuckled Rusty as he refilled his bottomless glass. More flushed than earlier, the wine warmed him from within. Beverly and Carol also floated pleasantly. "More?" Beverly pushed her glass forward, which Rusty obligingly splashed with some red.

"So, who's at the center?"

"I think the way we're addressed is key," Rusty said. "I've been studying the list. Don't you all think it's kinda interesting that we're addressed in different ways?"

"We thought so too," agreed Janet. "But what does that tell us?"

"I think it's from God," Beverly opined. "Who else could send them?"

"Why would God greet each of us so differently?" posed Rusty.

"Why not?" Beverly sipped more wine.

"I think we'd all have a more intimate relationship with God–whatever form each of us believes God takes, of course," Carol suggested.

"You know, I'm not a deeply religious guy. Why would God reach out to me?" Rusty shook his head.

"Why not? Jesus engaged with all–the rich, the poor, the high and mighty, the low and weak. He talked with believers and nonbelievers. He offered hope and salvation for all. Why not you?" Janet inserted.

Rusty nodded, "I hear ya, but I just don't buy it. It strikes me as an odd way to spend your coin if you only have so much to give."

"But He has infinite power and capacity," Janet anchored the faith corner.

"I don't think it's God. I agree with Carol. He'd call each of us by something more familiar. He'd use friend, disciple, or believer," Rusty suggested.

"Why wouldn't He just use our names?" asked Roger. "He knows 'em."

"Good point," applauded Janet quietly. "He certainly could, but He wouldn't need to. Jesus didn't necessarily use people's names."

"But it seems like whoever is leaving the messages has limited space or time to write. So he–let's just use 'he' for a moment–has to convey a lot in a small space."

"That's a good point too," agreed Janet, nodding in Beverly's direction.

Carol remained uncharacteristically quiet. "I really think it's someone different. He hasn't used any name with me. What am I: Chopped liver?" Her question drew a hearty laugh around the table. "Even so, I agree: the names he's chosen are a clue. Maybe that's part of the deal."

"Interesting," Rusty piled on. "He has limited space and time. He wants to communicate a message–whatever it's going to be–and he's trying to clue us in on who he is."

"Fascinating."

"So, where does that take us?"

"Well," Beverly moved the pad closer, "he's using uncle with Roger–though in an odd way, he uses Mrs. L with me, he uses Colleague and Friend with Janet. For you heathens," another round of laughter resulted, "he uses nothing. No clues."

"Wasn't there a theory somewhere that everyone knows everybody somehow? I vaguely recall something from some class in college." Carol grimaced.

"Six degrees of separation. We all can connect to everyone else–"

"Yes, that's it." Carol nodded enthusiastically. "We all know this person somehow, someway. There's got to be a connection."

"That makes sense," agreed Beverly. In the background, the grandfather clock chimed.

"My goodness, is it eight o'clock already?" Janet said.

"It's nine!" yelped Rusty looking down at his metallic watch.

"I can't believe it. We're just getting started, and there's so much to discuss," noted Beverly.

"Well, we're not going to nail it down tonight, but we've got a start and some real food for thought. Maybe we should reconvene soon."

Nods of agreement suggested all were amenable. Rusty sipped wine.

"How about Sunday afternoon?"

The group agreed, though Roger quietly acknowledged he'd have to check at home.

"Of course, and we need to get you home, don't we? Your mother is going to wonder what's keeping you."

Carol stood up. "I'm going to check our patient. She's been quiet for awhile, and I'm hoping she's been able to sleep."

Beverly showed the others to the front study where they collected their coats and prepared for single-digit temperatures.

"Hey, Bud?" Rusty nodded toward Roger. "How ya getting home?"

"Mrs. Langdon said she'd drive me."

"Let me take you. It can't be far, right?"

"No, not at all. Mrs. Langdon, is that all right?"

"Are you sure, Rusty? That'd be great as I'd like to ensure Mother is settled for the evening, and it's gotten later than I anticipated."

"No sweat."

"You're feeling okay to drive?"

"Ahh, sure. No problem at all. I've been far worse." Rusty laughed a little too loudly, as he opened the front door. Janet and Beverly rolled their eyes with concern.

"Now, you take care and don't get run down. Bernice needs you."

"Thank you. I'm doing my best."

"This was a fascinating evening. I look forward to continuing."

"I hope it proves to be for good."

"I'm sure it will. While we may not think it's God, He most certainly has His hand in it. And His hand is a loving and powerful one."

Janet exited to the street where Rusty and Roger finished scraping her car of a very light dusting of snowflakes that foretold the now fast-approaching storm. They moved to Rusty's Miata as she neared.

"Why thank you, gentlemen. Be careful driving home."

"Yes, ma'am," echoed both guys.

Within the hour, all four cars—which stood like guards in front of Bernice's house—pulled away, as big, fluffy flakes of cold, white beauty swirled and blew in the night air. Before midnight, they changed to an infinite tapestry of hard-driving minuscule flecks ending at sunrise. The night's snowfall accumulated to well over fifteen inches, one of the biggest snowstorms to hit the metropolitan area that winter. It slowed commerce and general traffic to a near standstill as Thursday, January 16 dawned.

TWENTY-NINE

Not surprisingly, on Thursday morning schools were closed. Since no one showed from the snow plow service, Skip and the boys worked on the long, curved driveway from the road to their brick home on the crest of the snow-covered hill. Their cold, visible exhalations punctuated the crisp morning air. The gray sky remained foreboding, though no additional snow fell.

Matt manned the snowblower, while Skip shoveled the front walk. Connor and John cleared snow from the walkway to the mudroom. Their progress inched along, due to frequent snowball fights, which returned snow to recently cleared places.

Lost in thought, Skip barely noticed as he worked. His top priority–to get downtown to his office–accelerated his pace. The Amalgamated mess was spiraling out of control. His mind drifted back as he grunted and perspired, lifting the heavy snow.

* * *

Tuesday's partner meeting resolved little. Taylor Caldwell spun a complex story that essentially explained nothing. He never made eye contact with Skip, which was perplexing. Curiosity evolved to annoyance and then hot-blooded anger as Caldwell increasingly focused on Skip's handling of the client.

The managing partner of the firm artfully raised questions about how Skip could've missed clear signs that the insider trading scandal was brewing. Skip attempted to interject on several occasions but was shut down by Caldwell raising his hand and suggesting through his body language that he did not wish interruptions. Caldwell admitted serving Amalgamated in a very low-key way during the Mexicani acquisition. Though he advised the senior leadership team, he never met Arnold Baker. He engaged with the CFO as part of Amalgamated leadership but did not meet with him one-on-one. As he understood it, Skip established a close relationship with Baker. With little doubt, Baker shared his thinking and strategizing. It appeared possible that, " . . . unintentionally of course," Taylor's voice dripped sarcasm, "Skip may have opened Dane & Caldwell to some legal exposure."

Skip seethed. When Taylor stopped talking, all eyes turned to Skip.

"This is pure fabrication. All of you know me too well to believe I engaged in some insider trading scheme explicitly or implicitly. I don't know why you're suggesting otherwise, Taylor. We have an issue with the Amalgamated relationship. Our client– and I use "our" explicitly–has a bloody, black eye this morning. Rather than attempting to allocate blame, I suggest we determine how to best aid and advise them moving forward."

Caldwell smirked grimly as he tented his two hands, playing the fingers of one off the other. His smug demeanor radiated a diabolical aura.

"Skip, I certainly don't intend to malign your character. We all get caught in some—shall we say—difficult circumstances on occasion." Taylor's eyes finally burned into Skip's. "I believe, with hindsight, we all can see where you may have run aground on this one."

Skip exploded. "Run aground? What are you talking about? If I were so incompetent, why was there no discussion prior to convening the entire partnership to witness this inquisition?"

"Precisely. I sensed you would take a defensive posture, disputing where fault must lie."

The conversation unraveled further. Other partners, many of them close friends of Skip's, looked increasingly embarrassed. After an hour of heated remarks, another gray-haired elder interceded, his deep baritone cutting through the debate. "Gentlemen, I believe we've heard quite enough. We are past the point of productive discourse. As such, we have next steps to attend to and a client who—under any circumstance—needs serving. I propose you return to your respective corners," which elicited a nervous chuckle around the table, "and we determine an appropriate course of action."

The partners moved to a more constructive, full-partner discussion of how to best help Amalgamated, if at all. After another hearty debate on protecting the firm's reputation and credibility, they agreed how to engage with the CEO and the board of directors. Additionally, Skip would withdraw to an advisory role for the reconstituted client service team. The new lead partner would contact the CEO immediately after the partner meeting. Skip and Nancy would craft a note to Arnold Baker, disengaging from service to him as an individual. Their decision would be framed as "making the necessary and appropriate choice of rendering legal services in support of Amalgamated. Inasmuch as he, Arnold Baker, would likely have personal legal needs, he should seek independent counsel to advise him, to avoid any further perceived conflict of interest."

The meeting ended on a somber note as the partners left the conference room. Nancy followed Skip to his office. Together, they finished drafting the letter to Baker, expanding on the initial outline. Finishing, Nancy turned to Skip.

"You doing okay?"

"Sure, great start to the day."

"You know, if you want to talk, we can. I'm here for you. I know most of the others feel the same. It's inexcusable that any of us should be called out for public flogging. It's just not the way we do things." Skip sighed and his shoulders sagged. "Chin up. This is going to pass, Skip. And, we—the partners—will get to the bottom of what's going on. This is not just about you; it's about all of us."

Always professional, always buttoned up, yet with an incredibly good eye for human emotion, Nancy was an awesome litigator. She could acutely sense where the landmines were buried, accurately identify the underlying issues, and then brilliantly strategize on how to move forward. Skip felt deeply reassured as she left.

Before lunch, he received additional quiet calls and visits from other partners who attended his evisceration. All expressed similar sentiment. None could believe that Skip was the culprit; rather, Caldwell in his oddly eccentric fashion was looking for a scapegoat. Legend had it that in the early days of the firm—a much smaller firm—he veered wildly from guardrail to guardrail in steering the practice and in championing colleagues one day and then skewering them the next. All believed with age, he was returning to some old habits.

In the early afternoon, a silver-haired elder encouraged Skip to leave for the day. "Clear your head; get out of here. I'll keep you covered. Keep your cell on. If anything comes up, I'll let you know." Skip heeded the advice and enjoyed the drive. He cranked up both the music and the speed and went twenty miles past the Bedrock/Glenwood exit, deciding he needed more alone time. When he walked through the door at two thirty, Amy was surprised.

"Hey, handsome. Home so soon?" She smiled.

"Yeah. Outstanding day at the office."

"Oh? I can't imagine. I figured with the awesome start, it was going to be a peach of a day."

Skip stayed grim. "Taylor's a lunatic. He opened fire. I'm surprised I'm still with the firm. Let me tell you . . . " Twenty minutes later, he sighed, "Did I miss something? Should I have seen this coming?"

"I don't see it from what you've said. And your partners seem supportive. There's something else."

"Nancy says he's an eccentric old coot." Skip snorted. "Maybe I should be doing something different? Maybe go out on my own."

"Now hold on. You love this work. You also appreciate your partners. Let's see where this lands first." Amy paused. "You know, it sure is interesting when you think about your quirky messages. They certainly line up with what's going down, you know?"

"And I didn't even tell you: I got another one today."

"Really? Now that's better than the meeting. What did this one say?"

"'See? Act quickly. Don't delay, Bro.' More than a coincidental email, eh?"

"I'll say. It's actually pretty neat. I wonder what they'll suggest next."

"If anything," uttered Skip. "Maybe they'll stop. I didn't take the advice. This could be goodbye."

Amy laughed. "You've learned your lesson and will–no doubt–be more responsive going forward."

Skip shrugged.

"It ended with 'Bro' again? Very interesting."

"It came from my mailbox."

"Do you think this is somehow related to David? You know, you're not the only O'Neill. We said he was the only person who called you Bro, unless you have some urban guardian angel." Amy chuckled again. "A member of a gang. A band of brothers."

* * *

Skip spent Wednesday quietly studying the Amalgamated files in his office. The overnight letter to Arnold Baker elicited no response. Several partners now advised the unimplicated CEO. Many of his executive team were being tried in the court of public opinion by both local and national press. While not named in the insider trading, the press acknowledged, how could the CEO be unaware of what was happening on his watch?

That afternoon, Skip leaned back in his chair and closed his eyes. He recalled meeting Baker and his surprise at learning of Caldwell's involvement in the Mexicani deal. *'How did that start?'* he wondered. He had never really pursued that thought. *'What was the original connection between Caldwell and Amalgamated?'*

Skip googled Taylor Caldwell and received an expected list: managing partner of the firm, founder of the law practice, leading philanthropist in the region, and member of the university's Board of Trustees. Nothing inappropriate popped out, nor did any apparent connection exist to Amalgamated. Nothing added up.

'Then again, I'm not the best techno-geek,' he acknowledged.

He tried another search on Amalgamated and the CEO. Again, no connections materialized–though he reviewed only the first three pages of more than five hundred results. He tried several search strategies, hoping for different results. He got nothing.

Frustrated, Skip spoke into his speakerphone, "Hey, Vince? Could you see if you can find any connection between Caldwell and Amalgamated? I'm curious, in hindsight, how we got the client, and, in particular, how he came to first serve them–even before you and I got involved."

"I don't need to do that."

"Why's that?"

"I already know the answer."

"You do?"

"I figured you knew. Mr. Caldwell indicated it was common knowledge, so there was no need to be surprised when I discovered it."

"What are you talking abou–" but Skip interrupted himself. "Why don't you come down and fill me in?"

Minutes later, Vince and Skip were behind closed doors.

"Mr. Caldwell and Amalgamated's CEO serve on the board for a community trust partnership–it's private and very low visibility. Both work hard keeping their names out of the news. I only found the link, 'cause I was bored one evening and kept digging through a Lexis/Nexis search."

"I don't get it."

"They serve on this board, raising money and doling it out for neighborhood revitalization."

"How did you learn that?"

"Well, I backed into it."

Skip raised an eyebrow.

Vince eagerly continued. "When I pulled that report on insider trading for Amalgamated, I couldn't help but notice that all the names were legitimate–not that I really expected anything different. All traders were members of the Amalgamated Board or executive officers, except one. That was T.C. Graybill."

"So? Who's T.C. Graybill?"

"That's the name of the community trust led by Mr. Caldwell and the CEO, William Gray."

"Who else sits on this community trust?"

"I figured that out. I went searching for T.C. Graybill. I turned up the community trust, and there were the two guys. I couldn't find anyone else. The trust holds a seat on the Amalgamated board."

"Does T.C. Graybill fit the same trading patterns as the rest of the executive syndicate?"

"To a tee."

"No way. Really?"

"No question. I figured you knew."

"Absolutely not. I don't think anyone knows." Skip collected his thoughts. "Do you know what you're sitting on?"

"Well, I'm hoping it's not what I've been worrying about these last couple of days."

"Vince, don't share this with anyone. It's explosive for Mr. Caldwell and–potentially–for our firm. We need to do the right thing and do it in the right way. Unbelievable."

"I haven't said anything to anyone. I'm sure glad to finally tell someone. I've been losing sleep . . . "

"Rest easier. You've done the right thing. Let me take it." Skip paused. "Can you pull together an airtight brief on what you've just outlined? Show the linkage between Amalgamated, Gray, Caldwell, and the insider trading debacle? Even if done for philanthropic purposes, it's wrong and we need to resolve it."

"Sure. I'll have it for you tomorrow morning."

"Great. We'll discuss it live."

Vince nodded vigorously and bolted from the room.

* * *

With Thursday having dawned with another twelve inches of snow, Skip assessed the boys' progress on the walkway. They were nearly done.

"Guys, can you wrap up while I shower? I have a meeting downtown, and I'd like to make it on time."

The boys nodded as the cacophony of the bright red snowblower filled the air.

Inside, Skip updated Amy.

"You're still going in?" She looked concerned.

"Yeah, I'm meeting Vince. He's pulling that report together and–"

"I know, I get it. You want him to know his efforts are worthwhile . . . " Amy trailed off. "But, hon, it's really slick out. I don't think it's safe."

"I'll be fine. And while I do want to indicate I value his work, it's more about ensuring the partnership is doing the right thing. We must get on top of this as we are potentially exposed."

"If you think so, but call when you get in."

"Of course," Skip hollered back down the stairs.

Two hours later, as the morning waned, Skip finally pulled into the parking garage. While more sparsely populated than most weekdays, a surprising number of vehicles still sprinkled the parking spaces.

Shedding his parka and boots in his office, he dialed Vince. He hoped Vince was in but ominously got no answer. Skip left a voicemail and booted up his desktop as he zipped through several voicemail messages. No new emails waited, correlated with the severity of the overnight storm. Finishing his quick scan and scowling at not seeing anything from Vince, the unshaven associate appeared.

"Pretty brutal storm last night, huh?" opened Vince.

"Yeah, I'll say. Hey, I just called."

"I saw. I went for another cup of coffee. Java Jane is closed, so I'm just drinking the office sludge."

"I'll spring for something better, when Jane's is open," encouraged Skip. "I could use something hot."

"I'll get you a cup. Here's the brief."

"Excellent. It's the big reason I came in. Thanks for pulling out all the stops to get it done."

"Yeah, late night. No big deal. It was actually kinda interesting to summarize what I'd learned. A little different than the norm."

"For sure. Why don't you get that cup of coffee for me, and I'll take a quick read. We can discuss it when you return."

Skip still read when Vince got back. Wordlessly, he took the cup of coffee and sipped as he digested the brief. Vince sat patiently.

Finally, Skip put the paper aside.

"What do you think?"

"It's well done. Just like you told it yesterday, but with more detail and substantiation than I would've imagined. It's a very well-written, well-documented piece."

Vince glowed.

"I thought there might be questions or places where the story didn't hold together, but it's all there. Caldwell is deeply involved in T.C. Graybill. In fact, he is T.C. Graybill, and, through it, is deeply immersed in the insider trading scandal that keeps growing. You need to continue keeping this on the Q.T." Vince nodded. "You've not told Caldwell that you're doing this, right?"

"No, I knew–given the content–that this was one of those times . . . "

"You got that right. I'll share your work with a couple senior partners to determine how to best proceed. With that in mind, I'll keep you apprised to the extent possible." Skip paused and looked seriously at Vince. "Given the sensitive nature, I may not be able to share every–"

Vince cut him off, "I know, no worries. Tell me if you can, and if you need anything else done, well, let me know how I can help."

"You're the man."

Vince exited quietly past Penny's empty desk. Alone, Skip sat determining his next steps. He walked the halls to see what senior partners were present. Though very few secretaries had battled their way in, numerous associates dotted the shared offices along the corridors as Skip wandered the four floors that comprised the law practice. He stopped at several offices inquiring about the associates' work and thanking them for their diligence and perseverance, in light of the storm. "Make sure you don't get caught here, if it starts to snow again," he warned on several occasions. The skies outside continued growing dark and threatening.

Not surprisingly, the senior partner offices were dark, save Taylor Caldwell's. Beside his closed door, the frosted glass panel gave evidence of the brightly lit office beyond. He appeared to be the only other senior partner in attendance. Skip bypassed a visit with Taylor. He wasn't ready to share what he knew.

Returning to his office, he keyed a brief email to several partners in which he proposed a Friday morning meeting, inviting Nancy, the elder statesman who had eventually interrupted his debate with Taylor, and three others. He made copies of Vince's brief, filed them in his locked cabinet, and placed the original in his briefcase.

Pulling out of the parking garage, snowflakes started falling once more. By the time he reached the Bedrock/Glenwood exit, snow covered what had earlier been plowed. Glad to have borrowed Amy's minivan, he appreciated its all-wheel traction as he navigated back roads, eventually reaching his driveway, which clearly needed more shoveling. He examined it as the garage door descended. *'I suppose it can wait; might as well let the snow fall before blowing it too soon,'* he thought. He took his stuffed briefcase and entered the warm house, finding Amy and the boys having a midafternoon snack of hot chocolate and just-baked cookies.

"Now, that will hit the spot," he grinned, joining them. "I'm in the mood for chocolate."

THIRTY

Bernice shivered uncontrollably as a chill set deep into her being. Throughout Thursday, she couldn't shake the bone-penetrating cold. She burrowed more deeply into the blankets and comforter in the dim room to no avail. Outside, no footprints disturbed the white crystal powder from Wednesday night's snowfall. Bernice neither knew nor cared.

Having a quiet, undisturbed house was a pleasant respite from the ongoing circus that her daughter-in-law deemed necessary at every possible turn. Her increasingly thin cats wandered into the bedroom. Receiving no acknowledgement, they slunk back downstairs to watch over the backyard from the kitchen table.

The phone rang and went unanswered. Weeks earlier, Bernice had unplugged the answering machine. If someone were desperate to talk, they'd find another way. She couldn't tolerate listening to recordings of sympathetic voices. Despite Bill and Beverly's encouragement otherwise, the machine remained unhooked. The phone rang each hour Thursday morning. At one o'clock, the phone rang interminably.

Bernice propped herself up and mumbled, "Hello?"

"Mother, I was worried. Is everything all right?"

"Fine," clipped Bernice.

"Bill and I are coming over to shovel you out."

"Did it snow?"

"Yes, the kids are home from school. We got well over a foot."

"I see."

"Can we bring anything? I made broccoli soup. Perhaps that would warm you up?"

"Whatever."

"We'll swing by after we finish shoveling here."

"Great," snorted Bernice.

"Has Carol been over?"

"I don't know."

"How are you feeling today?" Beverly ignored initiating a pointless debate.

"Dandy."

"You don't sound so well. How's your nausea?"

"Simply lovely, if you must ask."

"I'm trying to help. Perhaps I should see if Carol can stop by."

"Wholly unnecessary," groused Bernice. "I'm fine."

"I wish–" but Beverly stopped. "We'll see you shortly. Maybe you'll try some soup."

Bernice hung up, abruptly cutting off further discussion. Hurt, Beverly stared into the receiver.

Bernice sipped water and shivered again. She felt like she'd not slept last night. Her empty stomach, surprisingly serene, showed no signs of generating an appetite. Her colorless skin hung in loose, wrinkly folds around her midsection as she lay in bed. It hung from her arms, like tired, sagging sails on the weathered frame of an old ship.

At long last, she gathered sufficient energy to shift to a sitting position. Her head swam in a sudden wave of lightheaded dizziness. Sparkles of light danced in front of her eyes, as with sudden unexpected violence, her stomach rolled and tossed. She moaned softly–a series of low baritone groans, vibrating across her body. Her torso cramped badly. With fury, her stomach spasmed and forced its acidic backwash up her esophagus, scorching her throat.

She heaved and coughed, trying to catch her breath. Gagging and grimacing, the retching continued. Her nose burned; her eyes watered. Her cheeks reddened as she attempted to quiet the caustic eruption.

An hour later, Bernice lay back. Her stomach was sore, her food-pipe singed. Pervasive discomfort now counterbalanced the chill that filled every muscle. She closed her eyes and tried to sleep but was denied. Easy, restful, even dreamless sleep eluded her. Despite her efforts, she couldn't avoid thinking about the poisons in her, the continued march of malignancies traversing her body. With pained fascination, she visualized opposing forces flowing through her body–translucent neon streams moving up, down and sideways. The vicious armies of Cancer were winning, overwhelming the equally aggressive Chemos. The war of combative insurgents depleted her, day by day. She could sense the change. She just wanted the fighting to stop.

* * *

When Beverly, Bill, and the kids arrived, Bernice feigned sleep. After refreshing her water glass and putting new Saltines near her bed, the four went outside. Roger's arrival with the newspaper disrupted their shoveling rhythm. He smiled knowingly at Beverly and chatted with Brad and Caitlyn, both eager for a break.

With Roger's departure, the Langdons returned to snow removal. When the four trooped inside, Beverly fixed hot chocolate, and Bill went to sit with Bernice. She continued to rest, with eyes closed.

"Is BeBe going to die soon?" asked Caitlyn, alone in the kitchen with Beverly.

"I hope not," replied her mother. "We're supposed to find out how she's doing this coming week. Dr. Esch wants to do some tests to see how things are going."

"Does she still have cancer?"

"We don't know. We hope the chemo has eliminated it, but it takes time."

"She doesn't look so good."

"She's looked better, that's true, but appearances can be deceiving. Chemo is very hard on the body. Sometimes you have to go through some pain to get to a good outcome."

"I hope I never get cancer," concluded Caitlyn definitively.

"I hope you don't either," murmured Beverly.

Bill entered the kitchen. "She's quiet. I guess she's sleeping, though not deeply. Her breathing's not heavy." He paused. "She doesn't look so good."

"That's just what I said," nodded his daughter.

"I'm no doctor, but you have to wonder if this is working. Her coloring is dreadful."

"I can't disagree. Caitlyn and I were just discussing it. We should know more next week. Dr. Esch seems optimistic."

"I'll bet he's optimEschtic," giggled Caitlyn, cutting the concern, which blanketed the room.

"Perhaps," smiled Beverly. "I bet he'd like that: optimEschtic. He's certainly a character." She moved to the microwave. "I'm going to warm some broccoli soup for BeBe. Then we should probably get on our way."

"Is her nurse coming over?"

"I'll call Carol, but I doubt it, with more snow predicted tonight."

Not much later, the Langdons departed. As they turned onto the main road out of Glenwood, unknowingly they followed Skip O'Neill in the forest-green minivan. Very few other vehicles joined them on the road. Several miles further, Skip turned toward the tonier enclave of Bedrock, while the Langdons continued toward upper-middle-class Bedrock Hills.

Bernice opened her eyes when she heard the door close. She had maintained her snooze profile for–generally–the entire visit. Only when Beverly brought the soup had Bernice modestly rallied to perform. She looked at Beverly and Bill (who accompanied the delivery with a plate of warm, buttered bread) through thin, squinty slits peering out from her pale skull. They placed the spread next to her bed, where it remained untouched. She acknowledged their presence and then closed her eyes. She wasn't moved to have a conversation. Moments after they left the room, she heard

Brad's footsteps stomping down the staircase–two steps at a time–in the rush to leave.

She switched channels once again and defaulted to a news network, which warned of more terrorist threats and another imminent storm targeting much of the eastern United States. She grimaced, and returned to contemplating the war raging within. *'Let it be over soon,'* she thought. *'I just want it done.'*

Late-afternoon shadows lengthened across her room, as the new snowfall accelerated. The wind whistled and blew once more as snow pelted the house. While the racket grew outside her windows, a somber orchestra played inside, increasingly drowning out the wind, the snow, the icy mix, and the newscasters telling her just what and how much to expect. Her brain slid downward–neither awake nor asleep, merely an icy state of perpetual suspension–much like cable television malfunctioning, with a screen of black, white, and gray snow. A shapeless, deadening malaise matched her gray presence.

THIRTY-ONE

Snow fell the rest of Thursday and through the night. Flaky white crystals laced the frigid air for hours, sometimes falling in a fury, other times gracefully drifting through the cold gray sky. Traffic, what little ventured out, again slowed to a crawl. The overnight hours were periodically punctuated with the sound of cinder trucks and snow plows; heavy metal grated against roadway surfaces and bright yellow revolving lights cascaded out in slow, perpetual rotations across houses and lawns.

Daybreak on Friday coincided with the falling flakes slowing in their graceful ballet. A quiet settled over Glenwood, Bedrock, and other suburbs surrounding the city as people woke for the second time that week to an unplanned schedule shift. No one needed to listen to the endless list of school closings. More than two feet of accumulated snow lingered across the valley.

Rusty woke with a start. Given the unusual quiet of the street outside his apartment window, without looking, he realized last night's snowfall must have been substantial. He lingered, enjoying the warmth of the down comforter as he contemplated his day.

Ridgewell would be hopping even with snow. Senior management frequently arranged a spontaneous snow party to engage the twenty-somethings, yet still motivate a prodigious level of productivity. He finally sat upright, listening to the sounds of his roommates through the walls. He continued pondering today's party, as he entered the shower. If Ridgewell failed to produce, he would convince a gang to head off to the Waterfront for an early weekend kickstart. *'I mean, with more than two feet of snow on the ground, people should allow plenty of time to get home safely,'* he grinned as the hot water steamed up the bathroom. With the heat's pounding saturation, his thoughts migrated to the necessary work preceding any partying.

Sixty minutes later, Rusty was chilled to the bone. No available cabs forced a one-mile march to the office. The typical fifteen-minute walk required more than thirty, due to piles of snow filling walkways and intersections. In his office, he unpeeled his gloves, ski jacket, and scarf. Having brought no alternative, his heavy snow boots remained on his feet. No one was going to see them and he doubted whether Sue or his three new direct reports would care. He smiled, *'Being the eccentric, but gifted program designer has perks!'*

On his desktop computer, he tapped in his username and password and soon blew through email, while simultaneously listening to voicemail messages. His day rocked, and twenty minutes still remained before his first team meeting. Connecting with Chip, they headed to Java Jane's in the building lobby. Playfully horsing around getting on and off the elevator like in their frat days, they agreed to meet as soon after five o'clock as possible, to head to the Marina Grill.

"Cool, bud. I'll give a shout when I break free," concluded Rusty, returning to his office, where his team hovered.

"Excellent-tay," concurred Chip, splitting off.

* * *

Bernice awoke just after seven thirty on Friday. The extreme quiet of her neighborhood proved disorienting as she slowly pulled up from the depths of slumber. Overnight sleep continued to prove elusive; gratefully, she had fallen into an unbroken stretch around five thirty. Consistent with recent days, she felt groggy and heavy-headed. Her nausea was not as debilitating but maintained an off-stage presence.

Given how parched she felt, she hesitantly sipped some lukewarm water. The flat, metallic taste gagged her, which immediately yielded a round of deep, wrenching heaves as she valiantly tried to collect herself and return to the more peaceful state she enjoyed moments earlier.

She sighed deeply, after allowing waves of rising nausea to subside. Her eyes glistened with tears. She returned the glass of tepid water to its perch next to the untouched, foul-looking broccoli soup. She lay back down and allowed her mind to return to the snowy, undefined images of recent days. The feelings of profound loss and hopelessness returned, like a dark cloud blanketing her completely, as the minutes moved by in excruciatingly slow motion.

Mindlessly, she turned on the television set. She was uninterested in the news, couldn't care less about the weather, and was oblivious to the perky morning chatter of Katie and Matt. Bernice rallied sufficiently to visit the bathroom. While wholly reliant on Carol for bathing (who really cared?), she maneuvered very slowly to the commode where she sat uncomfortably for a long time. She rose and surveyed the mirror's image. While not especially prone to a weak stomach, even Bernice was shaken by the continuing erosion of her physique. *'How much worse can this get?'* she pondered, while gazing distractedly through tired, gray eyes at the dreadfully sick woman staring back.

Brushing her teeth proved a bad idea. The gritty taste of toothpaste initiated another round of vigorous dry spasms rippling across her torso and through her upper chest and head. She gripped the sides of the vanity as best she could. As the wrenching waves continued, she eventually slid to the floor, lying down on the pale pink floor mat. The clock downstairs chimed ten as she crawled back into bed.

Not finding the remote, she blindly searched around with her right hand. *'Maybe I put it in the drawer,'* she thought. "I need to stop the noise. All of it," she mouthed desperately as *TODAY* faded into a Jerry Springer slugfest.

She pawed open the end table drawer with no luck. She did, however, put her hands on the modest little pamphlet from weeks ago. "What's this?" she muttered as she tried unsuccessfully to read the blurry title. She dropped the little *Hemlock Society* booklet as she found the remote, which she punched aggressively, plunging the room into silence. "Better," she moaned. The clock downstairs ticked along its slow journey.

* * *

Janet awoke to the sounds of shoveling. Walt was clearing the walkway. She reluctantly left the bed's warmth and headed to the kitchen to find freshly brewed coffee. She got a cup and went to the side door, which she opened.

"Hon, don't overdo it," she called out.

"Good morning," returned Walt. "It's gotta be done. Really can't wait."

"Now you know what Dr. Elway said."

Walt sighed, "Yes, dear, but we need to clear the walk. I'll use the snowblower on the drive. Don't want someone falling and breaking their neck."

"I'm going inside. It's frigid out here."

"I'll take a break in a minute. Join you for breakfast."

Janet closed the door and turned on the little kitchen TV to watch *TODAY*. She puttered around, getting out fruit, cereal, and milk. Entering moments later, Walt unwrapped his scarf, pulled off his omnipresent Russian peasant hat, and unzipped his coat. Having discussed the probability of additional snow and Janet's decision to skip grocery shopping, they ate in quiet contentment with Katie and Matt providing a lively backdrop.

The Walkers' morning passed quietly. Walt finished shoveling and blowing snow. Janet filled the outdoor bird feeders and swept a path to the mailbox. Inside, she brewed more coffee—mostly decaf—and eventually settled on a recipe for vegetable-stuffed cornbread she could create for the church supper on Sunday, making ingredient substitutions in light of her cupboard inventories. The sounds of Walt's woodworking equipment and the aroma of baking soon filled the air.

* * *

Bernice's morning dragged. The dim translucent light filtering in through her shades reinforced her gloomy mood. The phone rang at ten thirty; it went unanswered. At eleven, when its piercing jangle refused to stop, she finally reached over, lifted the receiver, and immediately hung it up. Moments later, it rang again. On the third round of her routine, she could hear Beverly practically yelling.

"Mother! Don't hang up."

"What is it?" groaned Bernice into the phone.

"I just wanted to check on you. We can't get out of our driveway yet. The snow has turned icy. Despite Bill and the kids' best efforts, the end of the driveway is like rock . . . " Beverly yammered.

"I'm fine," a flat-voiced Bernice intoned.

"Are you sure? I hate to have you sitting over there by yourself. Carol's not been over yet?"

"No, no one here but me," Bernice grumbled.

"We'll try to get there later, but the roads are quite bad. I'll see if Carol can have any better luck."

"Don't bother," grunted Bernice. "Nothing going on here."

"I'll call back in a bit. See if you need anything."

"Whatever." Bernice abruptly punched the off button and returned the cordless handset to its base. The "no reception" screen remained encamped behind her closed eyes as she attempted, fruitlessly, to will sleep's embrace. Her head pounded and nausea crept back in intensity.

Bernice lay as still as possible, attempting to force the growing upset into an isolated corner of her mind. She was unsuccessful. As the downstairs clock struck noon, she found herself once more spluttering and gasping as she dealt with wave after wave of miserable toxicity. The clock's inexorable journey droned on.

* * *

Carol was outside with Kevin and Kelly. Thoroughly enjoying the day off from school, they sailed down the hill in back of their house on saucers and snowboards. Jay was at work, despite Carol's misgivings. "Why go, Pud? Who's worried about environmental regulations right now? There's two feet of snow on the ground."

"Babe, you know we're on call to help clear roads. While I doubt I'll be driving a plow, I may be manning the ops center. You know the drill."

"Sure," acquiesced Carol. "But I may need to go to the Langdons'. I missed yesterday, which I didn't intend . . . but with Kelly getting sick, I couldn't leave. I don't think HomeHealth sent anyone else, but I need to check. This is chemo week."

"I'll see if I can leave early, but it'll probably be late afternoon before I get home."

Carol sighed. "Maybe I can take the kids . . . "

"I wouldn't try. The roads are a mess. The jeep should be okay, but I'm not keen on you taking the Saturn. It's okay in the snow, but on ice . . . "

Jay left shortly after breakfast. Now, midmorning, Carol and the kids took advantage of the wintry weather. Their laughter and shouts shattered the frigid air, as they rode time after time down the steep incline.

"Enough, already," shouted Carol at long last. "I feel like an Eskimo and need to warm up at the igloo. What about you two?"

Kelly, newly recovered from a twenty-four-hour bug, chimed in, "Hot chocolate."

"I said nothing about hot chocolate. I'm not sure how that would be on your stomach."

"I'm fine, Mom."

Kevin joined them at the base of the hill, having just rolled off his flying saucer coating himself liberally with fluffy white powder. "Did I hear you're making hot chocolate? Awesome."

"You guys!" grinned Carol. "How 'bout we make it together? You're old enough to take care of your doddering old mother. This is why I had kids–to help in my old age."

"Mommmmm," wailed Kelly good naturedly. "You're not that old."

"And just how old am I?"

"Well, you're not falling apart," Kevin paused, ". . . yet."

"You!" Carol threw a fistful of snow in his direction as he took off. The powdery substance broke apart in midair. "Let's go inside. I'm like ice."

Soon, a fire burned on the kitchen hearth, hot chocolate steamed on the stove, and their wet clothes hung around the laundry room.

"How about a movie?" suggested Carol.

"I don't know," said Kevin, as he sipped hot chocolate.

"Let's see what we've got."

Carol looked through the shelf of flicks. "*Forrest Gump*? *Mrs. Doubtfire*?"

Kevin interrupted, "How about *The Terminator*?"

"No way. I want *Harry Potter*."

"I don't think so. I'm outta here." Kevin slurped down the rest of his hot chocolate and departed for the basement playroom and his video games.

"Looks like it's just you and me, Kel. What do you say?"

"*Harry Potter*."

"Okay. Why don't you pop it in, while I clean up? We can watch part of it before lunch." As they watched Harry and his friends, the movie and the mysterious messages intersected in Carol's mind. She fleetingly considered the possibility of magical communications, but smilingly dismissed it. *'If only this were as easily explained as Harry's issues,'* thought Carol. *'If only we had Dumbledore's watchful eye on us . . . '*

* * *

Early afternoon, Bernice absently ruffled the pages of the pamphlet.

She wondered what she was thumbing and held it up to her face again. She scrunched her eyebrows together trying to focus without her glasses.

"Aha, the little Hemlock treatise," she concluded. Unbidden thoughts trudged through her brain, dropping silently but relentlessly into place.

Around one thirty, nausea forced her–once more–to lean over the side of her bed. She gasped for air as tears streamed down her cheeks.

"This is so dreadful. I just don't know how much more I can take," she moaned. "I must stop the nausea." She rallied and–for the first time in quite a few days–headed to the staircase. Tigger followed.

In the kitchen, she pulled a bottle of merlot from the cupboard. "Maybe, this will help." With effort, she methodically uncorked the bottle. She poured a small slug in an everyday juice glass. She swirled it and tasted. It didn't taste quite right, having a slightly metallic flavor. "Everything tastes like shit these days," she muttered, but she forced another small sip and grimaced again. Fighting through the distaste, she slowly sipped the liquid from the little juice glass.

With the last drop gone, she sighed, "That tasted better toward the end. Maybe a tad more would prove beneficial."

No severe gastric reactions resulted. "You know, Tigger, we'd be more comfortable upstairs." With that, Bernice, the bottle, the little juice glass, and the cat made their way back upstairs. Over the next hour, Bernice slowly consumed nearly half the bottle. The pleasant buzz warmed her, for the first time in a week. She felt better than she had in days. *'This is very nice,'* she thought.

She even turned the television back on. She periodically sipped as the clock downstairs moved toward three.

* * *

Roger loved snow days. He and Jesse spent most of the morning outside shoveling neighbors' sidewalks for spending money. Next, they hung out at the Stauffers', playing computer games and trading instant messages with friends before moving to Roger's.

"So, what are you boys up to?" smiled Mrs. Gallo, as the boys finished lunch.

"I don't know," replied Jesse.

"How 'bout we go to the park? We can use my snowboard," suggested Roger.

"Cool. We'll get mine on the way."

By two thirty, their cheeks flushed with the outdoor air, the boys were cold and tired. They were caked with snow from rolling off their snowboards multiple times. Back at the Gallos', they peeled off their outerwear and attempted to warm by the fire, which crackled in the family room.

"I made peanut butter cookies. They're still warm."

They contentedly munched on the fragrant goodies as they watched the flames. With permission, the boys returned to the computer and were soon chatting with several friends, while they waited–and Roger hoped–for Melissa's online arrival.

* * *

As Bernice nursed the bottle, she once again fingered the little white booklet. The mellow intoxication from the red wine soothed her; she floated in a world beyond her bedroom. At times, she observed herself from a heightened vantage point–watching and waiting.

She contemplated the booklet with more clarity. The idea of stopping the pain, ending the brutal suffering of chemotherapy, and achieving a pleasant, sustaining euphoria like that induced by the wine was increasingly compelling. And, the idea grew more acceptable, even if she didn't know what waited on the other side. The wine eased her logic and thinking.

'Death is merely another part of life. We all die,' she thought. *'It's not like it's never been done before. It would put a decisive end point on what apparently is interminable. I can't accept that this will go on and on, with no change.'* She became more belligerent. *'Well, why not? Who's really to worry about this anyway? It's my life and I can damn well do with it what I want.'*

She sipped. *'So, if I were to do this, how? That's the question.'* The wine helped fill the nooks and crannies of her mind. *'It can't be painful and it must be certain. Landing in a more debilitated state is intolerable.'*

The wine's warmth pleasantly surprised her. *'I'm actually feeling quite good, but it will pass. I'll be back in the pit soon enough.'* Her mood darkened. *'I'm ready for this chapter to end.'*

Finishing the bottle, she wondered if more wine was in the house. She hated to stop feeling so good. *'No one's coming out in this weather. They couldn't even get out of the driveway, for God's sake.'* Bernice staggered from her bedroom to the TV room. *'I wonder if that little stash is still up here?'*

In the cabinetry under the bookshelves in the TV room, delightedly she found three bottles: two cabernets, one merlot. "Plenty," she smiled grimly. Unsteadily, she uncorked one and carried it to her bedroom, replenishing her juice glass. "Nice," she said aloud. She settled into her pillows, her eyes looking toward but not focused on the TV. "Here's to me," she slurred and awkwardly raised her glass. Her mind continued turning, contemplating techniques and timing, as the clock downstairs tolled four thirty.

* * *

'Where has the day gone?' Skip thought, looking up at three thirty. Despite the snowfall, Dane & Caldwell hummed. While willing to be cavalier about the first snowfall, relaxing through a second one in the same, billable week was unthinkable. Each partner had pushed on teams of associates to be in the office Friday. The partners made three concessions to Mother

Nature: staff arrived late, they wore casual, winter attire, and they received a free pizza lunch, accompanied by beer. As a result, a festive atmosphere blanketed the office throughout the day.

Skip met with his colleagues early. Some shock and initial disbelief met Skip's presentation, but Vince's brief proved convincing. Taylor Caldwell was clearly implicated. The partners needed to plan for his exit from the firm and manage their potential exposure. The group coalesced behind Skip, giving him their full support as a plan emerged. He no longer felt like the lone castaway on an island.

Based on their planning, Skip and one of the elders of the firm–a generational contemporary of Taylor's–would approach him on Monday afternoon. They would lay out the evidence and listen to his side of events but then move quickly and decisively, requesting his resignation and exit from the firm. Preceding that meeting, the small group of partners assembled would visit with all other senior partners to apprise them of the facts, share the plan, and address any questions they might have. They debated having discussions immediately, but worried that word might leak–unintentionally or otherwise–to Taylor. The facts were clear: the situation was unambiguous and the need for his resignation nonnegotiable. Taylor Caldwell, despite many fine attributes, must go. Otherwise, the entire firm and its future were at risk.

Skip now sat in his office, attired in his plaid shirt, v-neck sweater, and corduroys, drafting the outline for Monday's discussion. He committed to sharing a draft with the collaborating partner before the close of business. Skip made good progress, but hit some roadblocks as he considered how best to tell someone he had admired and respected for two decades that he must step down and leave the practice.

He stared at the monitor, willing words onto the page, but none materialized. Writer's block prevailed. Rarely at a loss for words, he decided to walk around the floor with a stop at Java Jane's. He paused at Penny's desk, collected her order for a double latte, and wandered down the corridor, stopping periodically to talk with associate lawyers, administrative staff, and fellow partners. Conversational and upbeat, he relished what he was best known for: being a top-notch lawyer with a keen eye for engaging talent. Skip inspired the best and brightest to achieve far more than they thought possible and to develop strong bonds of loyalty to the firm and to himself. Energized from his walk and fully caffeinated, he decisively completed the outline before five o'clock.

THIRTY-TWO

Carol and Kelly stopped the movie to eat lunch with Kevin. Shortly after and with the kids momentarily absent, Carol returned to the family room and flicked on the TV. As she searched for the best place to restart *Harry Potter*, she noticed the screen's perimeter begin glowing with the all-too-familiar flickering flame border.

COURAGE 9-1-1 DR L TODAY

The words shimmered as they moved across the bottom of the screen. Carol stood transfixed. "Oh God," she whispered. "It's back."

"What's back?" Kelly asked as she entered the room. Carol pointed at the screen, but the words had vanished. The flame-like border remained.

"Wow, that's cool. How'd you do that?"

"I didn't." Carol considered sharing more broadly. "I can't figure out what's wrong with the set."

"It's cool. Think it will stay like that?"

"I don't know." Carol anxiously processed the new message. 9-1-1 was a clear call for help, but how urgent? It was already after three o'clock, and while she had considered going to the Langdons' today, evening rapidly approached. Maybe this was a not-too-subtle reminder of her responsibilities, though she couldn't go much of anywhere without the jeep. Earlier, Jay said the town was having a difficult time making the roads passable.

"Shall we finish the movie, Kel?"

"Yeah, maybe the border is some DVD special effects." Kelly grinned. "They're always doing something."

"Perhaps. Why don't you get it started . . . ?" Carol trailed off. The movie returned, but as she watched the flaming border, she couldn't focus. The missing words remained branded in her brain.

COURAGE 9-1-1 DR L TODAY

* * *

Skip stared at his screen on his return from Jane's, his cup of coffee firmly in hand. The perimeter danced with a bluish-white light. It flickered and faded, moving from pale to brilliant. The edge framed a ticker tape display across his draft outline.

BRO 9-1-1 LANGDON TODAY

"Jeez," Skip said aloud. "I know I intended to go today. I wonder if Penny had the foresight to reschedule. They must still expect me." He paused. "Hey Pen?" He yelled across the open office.

"Yeah, Chief?"

"Is the Langdon thing still on? I know we made the appointment, but I don't see it on my Blackberry and I wondered . . . "

"Well, I figured with the Caldwell mess . . . " Penny stood in the transom. While not fully apprised, she had put together most of the story. "I suspected you'd want to postpone. I left a message yesterday and told them we needed to delay. I suggested calling me to reschedule, but I've not heard back. Why?"

"Well, I—uh—got a message which makes me think they're expecting me."

"On voicemail?" Penny was indignant. "I said to contact me, not you. I will just— "

"No, Pen. It's not that. Look." Skip gestured to his computer.

Penny came over. "Well, I'll be. It's back." Skip nodded. "And you think this is about the estate planning? What could make that an emergency?"

He shrugged, "Did she die?"

"Not that I heard . . . and I think they'd have the decency to call, if she had." Penny grimaced. "Though you couldn't do much updating at that point anyway. Maybe it's something else."

"What could it be? It's gotta be Bernice as I'm familiar with no other Langdon. But you're right: estate planning is rarely a crisis. Maybe you should call again and see what's up. I suppose I can swing by on my way home."

"Fine. I'll find out what's going on." Penny paused at the door. "What time's workable?"

"I don't know. Six thirty or seven?"

"If it's on, I'll let Amy know you'll be late."

As Penny left, Skip returned to his draft. The goose-stepping letters still burned on the page. He struggled to focus as the words danced their way into his brain:

BRO 9-1-1 LANGDON TODAY

* * *

Roger and Jesse were IMing back and forth when SweetFox227 came on line.

"Hey, she's ba-a-a-ack," Jesse sang as Roger blushed. "You're getting red, you dawg."

"Get off it. Ain't nothing."

"Sure is. You two are sweet."

Roger shoved him, but Jesse laughed. "Go ahead, talk to her. You know you want to."

Roger typed in "hey" and hit Send.

"That's it?"

"It's a start. Get off my case."

SweetFox227 wasted no time. Roger and Melissa moved through a monosyllabic exchange before shifting to full sentences. He and Jesse continued dialoguing with others as well.

"That's it, chat her up. You missed seeing each other two days this week."

"Cool it."

"Hey, dawg. What's it doing?" Jesse pointed to the screen's perimeter.

Roger looked more closely. "Don't know," he reflected momentarily as he recalled his fellow compatriots at the Langdon house. He'd not shared the conversation with anyone including Jesse. He thought fast, "You know, it's sorta the same color as that brick message from Professor Langdon's. Remember?"

"Whatever. I guess so." Jesse went quiet. "Why? You think this is related."

"Yeah, I think it might be."

Despite pings from their friends, including Melissa, Jesse and Roger sat transfixed and returned no IMs. They watched as words slowly materialized. They emerged in their own window–a short, wide, rectangular black space near the bottom of the monitor. Across it, the words slowly trudged, just like the others had described.

ROG 9-1-1 PROF L TODAY THINK UNC

"Is that cool or what?" exclaimed Jesse. The flickering, flame-colored lettering accelerated, conveying emotion and urgency.

Roger thoughtfully watched. "Yeah, I guess," he finally mumbled. Despite his alleged disinterest, he couldn't take his eyes off the message. "I wonder . . . " he began half-heartedly.

"You wonder what, man?"

"What it means."

"It's pretty clear to me. 9-1-1–that's an emergency, bud."

"I know that," Roger curtly replied.

"Well, it is. It's saying that old professor . . . Well, she's got an emergency of some kind. Today."

"I guess. Maybe I can find out when I deliver her paper."

"What's 'Think Unc'?"

"No clue. One other message included uncle too. Maybe it's from my uncle?"

"Whoa, wait a minute. I saw the message in the fall–it didn't say any uncle. You mean you've gotten others?"

Roger reddened. "Yeah, a few."

"A few–and you didn't tell me about 'em?"

"I figured you'd think I was nuts or something."

"But one of 'em said uncle?"

Roger nodded.

"Cool, then this one must be from your uncle too. Which uncle can do this? I'd love to learn."

"No clue."

"You don't know much do ya?" Jesse laughed. "Just raggin' on you," he added as Roger flashed annoyance. "So, what are you going to do about this one?" Before Roger had a chance, Jesse continued, "And I want to hear more about the others. You got your own communication thing going on here, man. Very cool."

"Yeah, it's great," said Roger resignedly. "My papers will be here pretty soon. Maybe you could ride along . . . see what's happening."

"This is wicked sick."

As the words scrolled across the screen, Roger and Jesse went back to their IM buddies. As the dim afternoon sun arced toward the western horizon, the boys pounded out IMs, awaiting the afternoon *Ledger*'s arrival. Periodically, each watched the flaming words:

ROG 9-1-1 PROF L TODAY THINK UNC

* * *

Janet pulled the last two pans of cornbread from the oven. The piping hot aroma wafted through the first floor. Her experiment seemed successful even with all her improvisation. She had made multiple batches ("you better hope the dinner takes place," Walt laughed as more and more cornbread cooled on the counter).

Three thirty neared, and she was exhausted. She poured some ginger ale and sat, closing her eyes for a moment, inhaling deeply and half-listening to the afternoon talk show that played on her small television. As Oprah moved to a commercial, she looked up as a familiar jingle promoting dishwashing detergent attempted to make housework appear enjoyable.

The edge of the TV burned, much like three times prior. Ever vigilant, Janet watched the border grow and then stop, as its odd, reddish-golden flame took hold–like a candlewick sputtering and finally gaining traction in sustaining a flame. The border glittered and danced. Within moments, a personalized ticker tape appeared—just above the fiery border. The words moved slowly but gradually picked up speed. Their color matched the border and contrasted brightly against the stark band of black they moved across.

ELDER 9-1-1 B-L TODAY

Janet sipped her soda, wondering if the words would change. Other than speed, nothing differed as Oprah returned.

"Walt? Do you have a moment?"

"What's up?"

"Just come up. It's the TV." Janet paused. "Again."

Walt hustled upstairs. "What's up?" He stopped abruptly. "So this is the kind of thing you've been seeing?"

"Yes," Janet quietly murmured, deep in her own thoughts.

"What do you think this one means?"

"I can only imagine. It's not good. 9-1-1—must be an emergency of some kind. But today? Right now? Maybe I should go over. Maybe Bernice needs me."

"Hon, the roads are a mess. All these messages seem to have a lengthy fuse. None have seemed particularly earthshaking. You probably have plenty of time to contact Beverly and figure out how to be helpful." Walt had given up attempts to demystify the messages.

"You're probably right, but I am going to give her a call." Janet dialed the number and got voicemail. She left a message asking Beverly to call back as soon as possible. "I'll bet one of her kids is online," Janet noted brightly as Walt returned to the basement.

Janet cut cornbread loaves into portion-size squares and then wrapped them. She planned to freeze the entire batch until Sunday morning—assuming the dinner was not postponed. She periodically looked up at the scrolling words moving across Oprah and then Dr. Phil. The words burned into her being and dialed up her anxiety.

ELDER 9-1-1 B-L TODAY

* * *

Rusty worked hard to wrap up the top-priority project assigned early in the week. The weekend couldn't come soon enough. He was ready for a couple of drinks. He hoped that one of the sales associates he had seen on the floor several times would be at the Marina Grill. He had seen him there before but only recently figured out the Ridgewell connection. While rarely choosing to "fish off the company pier," sometimes—for the right reasons—one made exceptions.

Recently, this guy literally took Rusty's breath away when they ran into each other. The sales guy, an obvious gymrat, unexpectedly bumped into him in a crowded corridor. *'Could be nothing or just clumsy,'* thought Rusty. They each smiled, as the young sales aide offered profuse apologies. Each went his separate way. *'Don't read too much into it,'* smiled Rusty remembering the incident.

His phone lit up with Chip's name. They quickly agreed more beer was in order to maintain the residual lunchtime buzz.

"Give me a shout when you're ready. Sounds like you've got more to do." Chip exaggerated, "Plus, you are a manager with a windowed office, and you do need to be a role model."

Rusty laughed. "Dawg, stop with the shit. I'll call." Hanging up, he turned back to his monitor which had morphed during his conversation and now visibly burned at the edges.

"You must be kidding," murmured Rusty. "No more directives. Not now. Let me just finish work." Curious, he watched as the bluish-white border shimmered. This time it sparkled with silvery undertones but, as before, the border blossomed until it framed the whole screen. Explosively, a window popped open and a stream of words flew across the black.

RUST 9-1-1 DR L TODAY THINK UNC

"This is driving me nuts. What the hell?" Rusty stared. In his gut, he knew his evening was taking a new turn. "What the fuck?" he said helplessly as the words scrolled across the monitor.

He processed the message aloud. "Okay, not much doubt on the names. 9-1-1–likely an emergency. Of course, it could be something with terrorists, but it seems unlikely if the sick professor is involved. She doesn't appear to have Al Qaeda roots." He laughed grimly. "So an emergency involving the professor and happening today. Maybe I just call 9-1-1 and send them over?" He reflected, "But that would cause an uproar if nothing's going on. Plus, if I were a cop, would I go to someone's house in the middle of a snowstorm based on a call from some guy downtown?" He shook his head, "They'd dismiss it."

"What's Think Unc? Could be unclear. Could be uncool–definitely the case on a Friday night. Could be unconscious. Shit, I wonder if she's knocked out–lying in a heap on the floor or something? I guess it could be uncle like Roger's message. Could be the same. What am I supposed to do with this?"

Rusty thought long and hard. *'Uncle makes no sense. Roger and I would be cousins. It's not like 'father of the country' or something. That could be more broadly interpreted. But uncle? 'Just say uncle' suggests you're giving up . . . maybe that's it. Maybe I should throw in the towel!'*

He kept watching, but no new changes materialized. *'I'll call one of the others. They're a lot closer. I'll bet they can just handle this.'*

Rusty left Beverly a voicemail saying he'd gotten another communication and wanted to discuss it quickly, as it dealt with her mother-in-law and a problem of some sort. He returned to his computer. After unsuccessfully attempting to minimize the ticker tape, he moved it to the bottom of his screen, so he could resume work. "What a fucking detour," he uttered as he reengaged in his project. Already four thirty, Chip was going to be waiting. The brightly burning words served as a reminder for the remainder of the afternoon.

RUST 9-1-1 DR L TODAY THINK UNC

* * *

"Aren't you guys offline yet?" inquired Beverly. "Where's Caitlyn?" she asked Brad, who now sat alone at Bill's desk rapidly moving the mouse and cursor keys.

Without missing a beat, he replied, "She went upstairs to watch TV."

"And you? You've been on there all afternoon. We should check and see if there are any messages."

"Sure, Mom. I'm just in the middle of a–wow, that was close," Brad interrupted himself as the plane he piloted through a series of online competitors nearly crashed. "I need to finish this round."

"Come on, let's wrap it up."

"Okay, give me a couple minutes." Beverly returned to the kitchen as she prepared dinner and meals for Bernice. The next time she looked up, another forty-five minutes had passed.

"Brad! Come on. You're well past what we agreed," Beverly asserted.

Moments later, Brad reached his hand into the warm Chex Mix Beverly had made.

"Did you turn off the computer?"

"No."

"Good, I want to check email. Can you . . . " Beverly stopped. "No, don't log back in. I should check voicemail first. You've been on for a long time."

"Whatever."

"Why don't you set the table for dinner? I'd like to eat early. Maybe after your father gets home, we can go over to BeBe's. I still can't believe he went out in this."

Beverly lifted the phone's handset to hear the telltale tones of messages waiting. Wading through voicemail, Beverly wondered about the close coincidence of Janet's and Rusty's messages though only Rusty indicated receiving another communication. *'I'll bet she got one too,'* she thought. She dialed and Janet picked up on the first ring.

"I hoped this was you," she responded. "I'm worried. I don't know why, but I've got a bad feeling and it's grown over the afternoon." With that, Janet launched into the details of her day, ending with the newest message.

Beverly expressed concern, but–like Walt–thought 9-1-1 might not be as urgent as a typical 9-1-1 call. "Tell you what. I'm going to try and get over to Mother's this evening. I'll give you a call. I spoke with her earlier, and she sounded fine. Well, at least as fine as she's been sounding."

After hanging up, Beverly talked to Rusty and felt rising concern as he shared essentially the same message. She promised to update him as well following her evening visit.

She next responded to Penny. Beverly indicated Skip should not break his neck coming out this evening. With the snow, she had anticipated a postponement. On the other end of the line, she heard a sigh of relief. They easily rescheduled for the following week.

With no other messages, Beverly walked to Bill's study to check email where the newest arrival–from oneill–surprised her. She suspected Skip O'Neill wanted a follow-up confirmation, redundant with her conversation just moments ago. However, the subject line was blank. Upon opening the message, she gasped at the burning edge. The border glittered with the intensity of an arc welder's torch. Similarly, the words brilliantly radiated.

DEAR 9-1-1 MOTHER ASAP

Nearly verbatim, this mirrored Janet's and Rusty's. Something critical was indeed happening. Importantly, her directive arriving later included a meaningful change. The urgency had risen. ASAP was notably different from today. Maybe Bernice had fallen. Maybe she had suffered a stroke. God forbid something had happened when no one could get there due to weather.

She watched the burning words. The tone of a new arrival dinged quietly. She moved the windowed message from oneill to the corner–it wouldn't minimize–and went back to the inbox. Another entry from oneill waited.

She opened it nervously. The same burning border and letters beckoned, however now the words moved across the screen at breakneck speed. The lightning-fast pace caused Beverly to be stymied momentarily as she worked it out.

DEAREST WASTE NO TIME GO NOW NO DELAY

THIRTY-THREE

Bernice was bombed. The clock struck five and her head was spinning. Somewhere, buried in the deep recesses of her brain, she knew she'd consumed far more wine than prudent, but she didn't care. The floating sensation, the absence of nausea and pain, and the warmth she felt were all very pleasant. Over the course of the last hour, she talked with Tigger and Spider: a slow-firing monologue that increasingly made sense.

"So, my little friends, the time has come. Let's go downstairs."

Bernice collected the second bottle–still mostly full–and the juice glass and left her bedroom. Her pale blue terry robe flowed freely at her sides as she continued her regal processional to the first floor. Like royal servants, the cats attended their queen.

Stopping in the office, she collected a favorite CD: the soundtrack from *Les Miserables*. She walked to the kitchen and surveyed the freshly organized and decluttered room.

After sipping another dose of her favored medication, she reached under the kitchen counter to find another bottle ("Just in case we need more, my little friends," she muttered). In doing so, she lost her balance and sat down suddenly on the floor. The tile felt cool as she leaned against the island.

She drank another slug directly from the open bottle; the room began to spin. "No need to keep up appearances, now, is there?" she slurred to the cats who patiently watched.

It took Bernice time to get back to her feet and move both bottles to the countertop. She uncorked the newest addition to her collection and then reinserted the cork. ("Safer to carry," she explained, as Tigger and Spider watched with interest.) Splashed evidence of her difficulties blemished the counter in sharp contrast to the spotless kitchen. Bernice neither noticed nor would've cared.

Bernice stuffed the CD in her pocket and collected the two bottles. The juice glass was left on the island, next to the splotchy stain. She moved across the kitchen toward the door to the garage. Over the next hour, under the watchful eyes of her pets, she carefully and methodically completed her preparations–between periodic sips. The second bottle's level fell steadily, though Bernice's pace slowed, becoming more unsteady. The frigid garage helped her stay awake, counterbalancing the growing fog of alcohol. Her game plan was unequivocal, though her movements clumsy. She smiled grimly as she worked. At one point, she returned to the kitchen to warm up. ("Spider, my fingers are numb. This is much more challenging than I expected.")

Finally, she finished. The Honda Accord sat quietly with its new accessory: a dirty green garden hose from a long-ago Father's Day roped its way from the tailpipe to the back passenger window. Duct tape held each end.

Bernice got in the driver's seat. "Want to go for a ride, kitty?" she inquired sweetly. Both cats jumped into her lap and quickly moved across her to the vacant passenger seat. Moments later, Spider jumped between seats and settled in the back as Bernice closed the door. She tightened the belt on her pale blue robe. Unbeknownst to Bernice, the hall clock chimed six o'clock as she turned the key in the ignition. Honda, known for reliability, did not disappoint. As the car began to warm, the retired university professor slid her CD into the car player. The musical's *Overture* kicked in as Bernice sipped her red wine and closed her eyes. She lay back heavily into the contoured seat, a small smile affixed to her face.

* * *

Beverly tried unsuccessfully to reach Bill. He was attending a meeting, his assistant indicated, but the group had adjourned to grab coffee. Beverly's anxiety grew minute by minute. She placed a phone call to see if Carol was going to Bernice's.

"Really? You got a message as well?" Beverly was only slightly surprised. "I'm worried. I'm going to try to get there. The roads are probably better by now, don't you think?"

"Let me just turn to the five o'clock news," responded Carol. "Though I'd like to get there, our Saturn is no good in snow. Hey, here's TrafficWatch." She held the phone so Beverly could also hear.

"Oh, but wait . . . "

"What is it?"

"The TV—the border is beginning to glow."

Excitedly, Beverly couldn't restrain herself, "Carol, what's it say?"

"Hold on, it's really big letters this time. a . . . "

"A-what?"

"A . . . s . . . "

"A-S-. . . , A-S-. . . ," Beverly repeated.

"A-S-A-P. That's it," Carol paused for a nanosecond. "What is going on?"

"I don't know, but I'll call again and then I'm going over."

"I'll try to get there."

"Don't kill yourself."

The women hung up quickly. Beverly speed-dialed Bernice. Not unexpectedly, the phone rang unanswered.

"Mother," uttered Beverly. "For God's sake, pick up the phone."

"Oh my God, what's happened?" an anguished Beverly murmured. Quickly, she called out, "Kids! I need to go to BeBe's."

"Yeah, I know. I thought we were going after dinner."

"I've decided to go now."

"Why?"

"I need to. Call it intuition."

"Do we have to go?" Brad whined.

"Stay here, and I'll call when you can start dinner. If Dad calls, tell him where I went." Beverly's words shot out staccato style as she donned outer garments.

"Say hi to BeBe," Caitlyn smiled.

Beverly didn't hear the last sentiment as she pulled the door shut hard behind her. The kids looked at each other mystified. They watched as their mom cautiously guided the car down their front driveway, over the icy snow-plow residue at the end, and onto the street. The taillights slowly made their way down the snow-covered roadway until disappearing around the curve of their lane.

* * *

Skip sat in the van at a traffic light, the engine purring smoothly as the vehicle gradually warmed up. He had left the office in a hurry after another message on his desktop monitor completely obliterated the discussion outline.

A S A P BRO
NO DELAYS NOW

Penny looked at him quizzically as he strode purposefully from his office.

"What's up, Chief?"

"Gotta go. The Langdons.'"

"Huh? I told you they were okay with postponing. They expected a delay given the snow. In fact–"

Skip cut her off, "No, Pen. Something's not right. I'm being bombarded. I don't know what these messages are all about, but I've been slow to act in the past. I can't ignore them this time."

"You got another?"

"'ASAP. No delays. Now.' It's gotta be Bernice. I'm heading out."

"Be careful."

"I will," responded Skip grimly. "Don't stay late. I'll finish the outline over the weekend. Can you send a quick email to the group? Let 'em know when to expect the draft. Couldn't quite wrap it up today. Something's come up. Etc."

"Sure. No problem."

Now, waiting in the minivan, Skip flipped through CDs landing on a Michael W. Smith favorite and allowed it to ease his escalating anxiety. While scanning CDs, the time— 5:35 p.m.—stuck in his brain as traffic began moving.

* * *

The afternoon *Ledger* arrived late. Jesse had disappeared soon after his mom called asking that he come home to help with chores before weekend company. When the papers finally landed in front of the garage, Roger wrapped them in tight plastic bags and prepared to walk. The bag already felt heavy.

He put on his bright yellow parka, boots, hat, and gloves. "I'll be as fast as I can," he yelled to his mom and was out the door. Elaine involuntarily looked up at the clock. The time was five thirty.

"We won't eat until close to seven, I bet," she sighed.

* * *

At six-fifteen, as Roger turned the corner onto Fox Den, a neon blue two-seater zipped past him. *'That looks like Rusty . . .'* he thought. *'I wonder why he's out here.'*

Rusty didn't see Roger, even in the brilliant parka. Wholly focused on his destination, he could barely see straight, given his annoyance at this entire inconvenience. "Why in God's name am I in Glenwood and not at the Marina Grill?" he exhaled loudly. His hands fiercely gripped the steering wheel as he careened down the road.

Thirty minutes earlier, he was all set to power down and kick-start the weekend, when the 5:32 message nearly exploded on his screen, proving simply unambiguous.

ASAP KILL GRILL SAVE BERNICE

He tried to reach Beverly but only got her kids, who said she was out. He called Janet, but Walt was surprised to learn that his wife was not in the house. Just where was everyone? Despite his thirst for barhopping, he couldn't ignore the communiqué. With no one else to talk to, he decided to go to Glenwood. Hopefully, he could catch up with Chip and the others.

"A fucking wild goose chase," he grumbled, though a core part of his Tennessee upbringing would be unforgiving if something happened while he partied. As he drove—with too little caution for an icy January night, he couldn't imagine anything more he could do to help the professor.

He braked hard and pulled to a stop at the curb, behind Janet's car. She was getting out as he hopped from the sports car and slammed his door.

Another pair of headlights appeared down the street.

"Rusty. I'm so surprised to see you—but, then again, maybe I'm not."

Before he answered, a green minivan pulled up behind the Miata. As the driver turned off the engine, another car could be heard, though the curve of the road prevented visibility beyond the foreshadowing glow of headlights.

Skip stepped from the van, just as an SUV pulled up. Carol exited the passenger side and the SUV pulled away. She gestured, "My next-door neighbor. What a trooper. I knew the Saturn wouldn't make it, and I needed to be here. Looks like a party."

"Just what I was about to say," nodded Rusty.

"Where's Beverly? Is she in the house?" inquired Janet.

"Your guess is as good as mine," Rusty responded.

"And look who else is here: Roger," smiled Janet. The teenager joined the group gathered on the unshoveled sidewalk.

"Hey," Roger added to the conversation.

The group turned and looked at Skip.

"I don't think we've had the pleasure . . . " Janet's voice faded.

"Skip O'Neill." He stuck out a gloved hand, as the group hustled up the walk.

Carol's eyes twinkled, "And you just happened to be in the neighborhood?"

"I'm helping Dr. Langdon with her estate planning. I had an appointment . . . " he hesitated.

"Oh great, a lawyer," chuckled Carol as they reached the door.

"On the snowiest night of the year?" Janet raised an eyebrow.

"That's way dedicated," frowned Rusty.

Skip surveyed the foursome, "But why are you here?"

"Enough already. We all were summoned. At least, I was," the nurse inserted.

"Me too," added Roger enthusiastically.

"Ditto," exclaimed Rusty, who like the others, ignored the attorney. "Another message on my computer. 9-1-1, an emergency—more or less."

Skip stared dumbfounded at the group as Janet pushed the doorbell. "You all got messages to come?"

"It's a long story," Janet offered, as the group studied him quizzically.

"I'd love to hear it sometime."

Looking at his watch which read 6:20, Rusty interrupted, "Time's a-wastin', folks."

The doorbell echoed hollowly and drew no sounds from inside the house.

"Beverly must not be here."

"I've got a key. Let's just go in," injected Carol.

"Odd. I thought she was coming," Janet added with concern.

"I spoke with her kids before I left work. They said she was on her way."

"How long ago?" asked Carol, rustling through her bag.

Before the response, she found her key and inserted it. Smoothly the door opened and the five trooped in. The house was silent.

"She must be sleeping."

"I hope so."

"I'll go check," Carol murmured. Without dropping her coat, she sped upstairs.

The others stood anxious, but quiet in the hall. In moments, Carol called down, "She's not here."

"Maybe Beverly took her to the hospital. She could've taken a turn for the worse," Janet speculated.

"How quickly could her daughter-in-law arrive and get her out the door?" Skip grimaced.

"Not likely," Rusty agreed.

Roger stood quietly next to the front door. "Where are her cats?"

"Good point. The cats would be here, even if Beverly took her to the hospital. Where are they?" Janet started looking.

"They've got to be around. Carol, look upstairs. We'll split up across the first floor."

"Skip, can you check the basement? Just in case?" Janet pointed him toward the recessed doorway.

Not sure what to think, Skip agreed while Rusty went to the kitchen with Roger.

"There's a spill here," he yelled.

Janet slipped in from the living room where she had looked behind the sofas and under the furniture. "Did you find the cats?"

"No, but look: red wine."

"Wine? Why?"

Carol called down as she checked each room upstairs, "Not here. No sign of cats or Dr. L." She paused in the little TV room. The cupboards below the bookcase were open and empty. *'Curious,'* she pondered.

Carol took one additional look around Bernice's bedroom, spying the wine bottle on the floor. "Oh my," she sighed. "She's been drinking." The little *Hemlock Society* pamphlet stayed hidden in the folds of the covers.

Reconvening with the others in the kitchen, Carol observed, "This bottle and your spill tell the story."

"Nothing downstairs," cited Skip.

"So where could the cats be?" Roger wondered.

"And where is Bernice?" Janet was increasingly anxious.

"What about Beverly?" Rusty questioned.

The group remained momentarily lost in thought and then began covering the same ground. Despite the growing volume of excited conversation, Roger's ears perked up; he sensed a persistent humming. He tried tracing its origin, which was neither the refrigerator nor any other appliance. He wandered around the kitchen trying to determine its cause. When he got close to an apparent closet, the humming was more pronounced and the door vibrated slightly.

"Does anyone know what's in here?" he questioned.

The group at the island paused.

"It's the garage door," confirmed Carol.

"We didn't check there."

Roger opened the door and flicked on the light. The sounds of a car idling filtered into the room.

"Oh my God!" yelped Carol.

"Oh shit!" screamed Rusty.

"Hey, it's a hose," observed Roger.

"Oh my God, get her," Carol crisply directed as she nearly fell down the two small steps into the garage.

Janet went white. Carol sprinted, quickly followed by Skip and Rusty. Roger stood at the doorway, pointing at the hose and the car. "Professor Langdon's in the car. She's trying to drive herself."

"No, it looks like she's trying to take her life," murmured Janet as she pulled Roger toward her.

Carol yanked open the driver's door. The sounds of *Empty Chairs at Empty Tables* suddenly filled the garage and kitchen. Bernice looked peaceful, her eyes closed. A green bottle lay on its side and a pool of red wine spread on the floor between seat and pedals. The cats appeared equally tranquil. Spider lay in the rear seat; Tigger curled up in the front.

"Is she breathing?" coughed Skip.

"I don't know. Get her out. Help me!" yelled Carol.

Gagging from the fumes, Rusty and Skip reached in and got hold of Bernice and lifted. She was a deadweight as they awkwardly tried to move her. While attempting to extricate Bernice's bulky figure, the men blocked any further access.

"Roger, go in the other side. Turn off the car." commanded Carol.

Roger obeyed instantly. The garage plunged into silence–save the grunts and groans of the men. The faint, slightly sweet smell of car exhaust filled the space.

Carol suddenly exclaimed, "Roger, now: the big door. I don't think there's an opener. Get some air."

Roger hustled. He slowly lifted the door, despite the heavy snow on the outside. The temperature dropped precipitously; fresh air never felt or smelled so good. The men finally succeeded in dragging Bernice from the vehicle.

"Lay her on the ground. I'll try CPR," Carol ordered. "I don't feel a pulse. Shit."

"I hope we're not too late," Skip shook his head.

"The message said ASAP. My goodness, I can't get over this. Why would someone–?" Janet said quietly, dabbing a trickle of tears. She held a cold washcloth and a cup of cool water. "Let me know when you're ready," she voiced to Carol.

Carol forcibly performed CPR. While not her first time, she had never done so with such passion. "Come on, Dr. L. Don't leave us."

"In, out. In, out. In, out." Carol forcibly blew air into the woman's body.

"She needs oxygen, good air. We need help."

"You." Skip pointed at Janet. "Call 9-1-1. Get an ambulance. If she's going to make it, she needs life support as quickly as possible."

"Let me take over," Rusty offered. "I know CPR. What about external heart massage? Can we do both?"

"We can try. You do CPR, really?"

"Yes, ma'am. I'll try to stay out of your way."

Minutes were passing quickly. "I still don't feel anything. We may be too late," grimaced Carol. "She just couldn't wait it out. I think she was getting better, even if it didn't look like it."

"Ambulance is coming."

Carol pounded on the professor's chest. "I think I feel something." She pounded once more. "Keep blowing, Rusty. Blow for God's sake." She forcibly compressed Bernice's chest again. "I'm gonna crack a rib, but . . . " They worked in growing rhythm. "We're getting her. Yes, I feel a slight, thready pulse. It's not much and she might be in bad shape, but it's something. Keep it up, Rusty."

"I hear the ambulance," added Roger.

"Yes, I hear it too," nodded Janet, leaning against the door frame to the kitchen.

"Can't come soon enough," Skip said, as he paced. Unhooking the garden hose, he wrapped it back up in a coil. He also removed the duct tape from the exhaust pipe.

"Should we do anything with the cats?"

"Are they dead?"

"Smaller bodies. They couldn't take as much. They succumbed more quickly, I imagine."

"They were okay cats, as far as cats go," Roger noted seriously.

Flashing red lights could be seen as an ambulance made its way up Fox Den Road. It stopped in front of the unplowed driveway and a pair of paramedics ran with a stretcher and an oxygen tank. Several neighbors looked out from their windows.

"Where is Beverly?" Janet pondered anxiously.

Rusty and Carol stepped back as the paramedics took over. Despite all their efforts, Bernice's eyes remained closed, her breathing barely evident, and her heartbeat erratic. One of the attendants zipped back to the ambulance for a defibrillator. As he retrieved it, Bernice gave a quiet little gasp and went into cardiac arrest.

"Hurry, man. She's seizing."

The guy with the shock-kit flew up the driveway and landed next to his partner and Bernice's chilled body. They quickly opened up her garments.

"Clear!" The shock rippled across her body as the contacts delivered.

"Step up."

"Clear!" More voltage entered Bernice.

"I got a beat. She's got a pulse."

"Get her on oxygen. Don't know how long she's been in the car."

An oxygen tube was inserted nasally. "Okay, let's pop her on the stretcher. She needs an eval. Yes?"

While one paramedic continued external compressions, his colleague appeared to be asking Carol for permission to transport Bernice.

"I'm sure that's what her family would want."

"You're not family?"

"No, we are . . . "

"We've been helping her through her illness . . . " inserted Janet.

"She's sick?"

"Yes, cancer. Most recently, a heavy regimen of chemo. We're hoping she's on the other side of it."

"Guess she didn't think so?" said one attendant as he strapped Bernice onto the gurney.

"She just may be on the other side," the other paramedic responded grimly.

"Yeah, anybody who offs themself isn't thinking too clearly." The men talked in staccato shorthand as they wheeled out the unresponsive body.

"Well, let's get her to the ER and see where she stands," urged Carol.

"Is she stable?" Skip inquired.

"Enough to move," noted the lead paramedic.

"I'll come with you. I'm her nurse. Just in case there are questions on meds."

"Good. Let's roll."

Within moments, the ambulance accelerated toward the Glenwood ER satellite of the University Health Center. The lights revolved frenetically, though—at Carol's insistence—the siren stayed mute. The remaining foursome retreated to Bernice's kitchen.

THIRTY-FOUR

The ambulance passed Beverly twice on its trip to and from Bernice's house. Trying to make better time, she had accelerated into ice and skidded off the winding country road, landing in a ditch two miles from Fox Den Road. Despite her head crashing into the ceiling, she felt fine. Unfortunately, in her haste, she had failed to bring her cellphone. With the frigid temperatures, leaving the vehicle's warmth to walk in either direction was decidedly unappealing. The icy roads resulted in exceptionally light traffic. The occupants in the first two cars to pass simply drove by.

The revolving light of the ambulance heightened Beverly's nerves. Just after its second pass, a young man in a pick-up stopped. Enthusiastic though inexperienced, he wanted to try out his towing apparatus and hooked up chains and cables. In a few short moments, she was–delightedly–back on the road. Despite his protests, she gave the barely twenty-year-old two crisp twenty dollar bills.

"Awww, shucks, ma'am," the pick-up cowboy stammered. "You needn't do that. It's still the Christmas season. You weren't gettin' outta there without some assistance. I was jest happy to oblige."

"Nonsense. I insist. I would've been sitting there for a good long while. I don't even have my phone to call Triple-A. You saved my evening. Thank you."

When Beverly pulled in front of her mother-in-law's house, she was surprised to see the line-up of cars. She recognized only Rusty's Miata. The footprints leading to the garage escaped notice. She hustled up the walk and entered the front door, hearing hushed but insistent voices from the back of the house.

"Hello?!" she hollered across the foyer as she doffed her outer garments. "Is Mother all right?"

Janet hurried out to the foyer. "Oh my dear, come into the kitchen. I've made tea."

"Where's Mother? I want to see her. I'll just go upstairs and be right down," Beverly asserted, heading to the staircase.

"She's not up there."

"What?" Beverly looked alarmed. "Where is she? Is she okay?"

"Please, come to the kitchen. We'll fill you in."

Beverly's color plummeted as Janet walked away, sharing no information.

Following the gray-haired matron, she entered the kitchen causing the three males to go quiet. She nodded at Rusty and Roger and then focused on Skip.

He stood up and walked over to meet her. "Skip O'Neill. We've spoken by phone. You've also spoken with my assistant, Penny."

"Of course. But where is Mother?" Beverly was becoming annoyed with the lack of information. The group just looked concerned and worried.

Janet came over with tea, "Here, sit. Bernice isn't here. She just left for the hospital–"

"The hospital?!" Beverly yelped with alarm.

"Well, actually the ER. Glenwood."

"I should get there. I really must go," Beverly began to stand.

"A moment, please," insisted Janet pressing her hand on Beverly's forearm. "We need to tell you . . . "

"Her nurse is with her. They went by ambulance," Skip added.

"By ambulance? But how . . . " Beverly stopped, processing the information and speculating on the ambulance she had seen.

Skip stared at Beverly closely, "No doubt this will come as a shock, but your mother-in-law attempted to take her life this evening."

All eyes watched as Beverly sat back down suddenly. Her eyes welled up and her color drained. "She did? Oh my, I knew I shouldn't have left her alone . . . "

"Don't chastise yourself, dear," Janet whispered. "If someone wishes to take such drastic action, they will always find a way."

"I know," moaned Beverly. "In hindsight, you could see this coming. I never would've thought she would, but–" She stopped in mid-sentence. "How exactly . . . ?"

"In her car in the garage. Carbon monoxide. Quite a set-up she engineered," Skip began.

"I'm surprised she had it in her," Janet shook her head sadly.

"It took real effort," Skip continued.

"She was drinking," added Rusty.

"Oh my," Beverly paused. "I've got to call Bill. She is still alive?"

"Yes, but barely. Carol and Rusty got her breathing again and her heart pumping, but it was quite tenuous."

"They used a defibrillator when the paramedics got here," Janet noted.

"Cardiac arrest," nodded Skip.

"I knew something bad was happening. The messages." Beverly sagged.

"I must call Bill." As she got up, Roger handed her the cordless phone. "Thank you. This must be quite a shock for you. I'm sorry you had to be here . . . "

"Roger found her," Rusty acknowledged. "We searched the whole house, and came up empty. We were here in the kitchen, and Roger heard the car running. He opened the door and well . . . "

"Oh Roger, you are a real treasure."

The teenager blushed. "It was nothing. Really."

As Beverly dialed Bill, she walked to the front hall. The others remained at the kitchen table, sipping lukewarm tea, except Roger who drank ice water.

"What about the cats?" Roger couldn't forget the rabbit. He had missed another opportunity here.

"I'm not sure what you do with deceased pets. The ground is–no doubt–hard as a rock, so we can't bury them. On a Friday night, I doubt a vet will be open."

"Let's wait for Beverly. She may know what Bernice would want," reflected Janet.

"You know, I could use something a little stiffer than tea," observed Rusty. "I'm thinking a shot would steady the nerves."

"Oh Rusty, now?" cautioned Janet.

"The young man is right. I could use a good stiff belt as well," added Skip. "Do you know where the Langdons keep the hard stuff?"

"I don't know, but I'll find out," quipped Rusty, leaving to check the small office. Roger trailed along.

Skip peered at Janet. "So, we've met. Church maybe? You look very familiar."

"I thought the same. I go to Bedrock Hills Pres."

"Of course! The Epiphany service. I'm sorry, I didn't recognize you immediately."

"No worries. I should've known. I'm Janet Walker. David's your brother?"

"Yes, but he passed away."

"I know. I served with him on the church council. Such a nice man. You look a bit alike. I can see the resemblance now; I didn't put that together when we first met."

"He's missed. He was a real saint."

"He truly was an inspired leader, spreading God's word."

"Amen." Skip took a breath. "So, what are these messages people are talking about? I only caught part of what–"

Janet interrupted, "Such a story, but so interesting. The people here tonight are connected by messages we've each received over the last several months. They focus on actions we should take." Janet paused, lost in thought. "It's all quite fascinating. The recommendations have all been just perfectly appropriate. We figured it out–at least in part–over the last week or two. It's all quite cryptic."

"Messages? How do you receive the–?"

"That's the most curious part. For each of us, it's been different but similar. You'll think we're nuttier than Planters, but they show up rather magically in the course of our days."

Skip scrunched up his brow. "I don't get it. And everyone's been receiving them?"

"Well, myself, Carol–that's the nurse, Beverly–who you just met, Rusty–he's such a nice young man. I'd like to introduce him to . . . "

"And what about the boy?"

"Roger? The paperboy? Yes, him too. As I said, they're all delivered a bit differently, but . . . " Janet reflected. "Well, they have similarities. Each appears within a flaming border–it's illuminated, flickering and shimmering like a roaring fire. I've gotten messages on my TV and my computer. Roger gets them on the brick wall of his garage, of all places. I–"

"Did people get messages today?"

"Why, yes. We all did. That's what brought us all here at the same time. Each of us was told–as I sense it, anyway–that there was an emergency. Mine said 9-1-1. I believe others got something similar." Janet looked carefully at Skip. "Why do you ask?" Suddenly the nickel dropped and Janet's eyes widened. "Are you saying that you got one as well?"

Skip paused. Reluctantly, he nodded. "Yes, I've been getting them since the fall as well. I recently connected them with Bernice, but today's clearly suggested I come quickly."

"And Bernice is alive because we all did."

"Remarkable, isn't it?"

"What's remarkable?" asked Rusty, entering the room with a bottle of Kentucky bourbon in hand. Roger shadowed him.

"Janet told me about your messages. As I just shared, I've been getting them too."

"Really?!" Both young men chorused.

"I didn't know what to make of them. I'm relieved to know about others."

"That's six of us," noted Roger.

"Do you think there are more?" questioned Rusty.

"I wonder," sighed Janet.

"So, what do you make of them? Looks like we all have Bernice in common." Skip hurriedly tried to catch up with the group's thinking.

"That's what we thought when we spoke earlier this week," Janet nodded.

"Was it really just this week?" Rusty tossed back a double shot. He grimaced briefly as the harsh liquor hit the back of his throat and burned down his esophagus. "Wow, that's potent. Wonder what Dr. Langdon was doing with this in her liquor cabinet?"

"Here, I could use one." Skip reached for the bottle.

Beverly walked back into the room. "Bill is heading to the ER. He'll meet me there. I'm wondering if one of you could give me a lift, as I'd rather not drive again this evening." After recounting her earlier travails, Skip agreed to chauffeur.

"So, I sense you also receive these strange communications?" asked Beverly looking at Skip who nodded.

"It still fits: helping Bernice brings us all together," murmured Janet.

"Yes, that's what they were saying," motioned Skip. "So, where do the communications come from?"

"There must be a common denominator," noted Rusty. "Someone who knows all of us."

"A person?" Skip was curious.

"How could the sender be inanimate? It must be a person," frowned Rusty.

"Even suspending disbelief, I can't imagine we're all connected," Skip pushed back.

"Why not? We're all here," quipped Rusty.

"Sure, but that's happenstance," Skip was unprepared to acquiesce.

"And it's happenstance we each got a message today?" Janet joined the debate.

"Touché." Skip thought some more. "So, who is the sender?"

"Well, do you have any suggestions? What have your messages said?"

"Guys, can we go?" Beverly was increasingly agitated by the discourse.

"Of course, I'm sorry. I am just immensely curious as to what is causing this . . . and how it knows what to send and when," said Skip standing up. Moments later, the minivan pulled away from the curb, replicating the ambulance's earlier journey.

Janet, Rusty, and Roger remained at the table. The clock in the hallway chimed. "My goodness, it's seven thirty already."

"I would've guessed later, actually. So much has happened."

"My mom is going to wonder where I am. I better be going."

"Of course, you run along. Though it's dark. Perhaps you want a ride?"

"I'll take him. No sweat." Rusty stood. "I was supposed to meet some friends tonight, but maybe I'll just head home. I'm not sure I'm up for a night out."

"Whatever. I'll just clean up a bit and then be on my way."

Rusty and Roger got their coats and headed out to the street.

"This is an awesome car."

"Hey, thanks. It's really cold when you first get in during the winter. I nearly froze my ba-" Rusty grinned, "–my butt off coming out here tonight. Can you believe Dr. Langdon?"

"No man. That was scary. I sure hope she's okay."

"Modern medicine. Pretty awesome what they can do."

The guys took off down the street as Janet scrubbed the wine stain from the countertop and put the teacups and shot glasses in the dishwasher. She hummed tunelessly, thinking about the evening's events and how the six could possibly be connected. She wondered why Bernice wasn't getting messages directly. Before eight o'clock, Janet's snow-covered compact car pulled away as she headed to the warm familiarity of home.

THIRTY-FIVE

The last thing Bernice recalled was hearing *On My Own*, a lovely ballad from the Broadway hit. As she slid away into darkness, the young woman's song echoed through the car. *'That's the way it ends,'* she thought. *'On my own: how fitting.'*

Later, Bernice remembered more. A feeling of warm familiarity, a lifting, embracing light filled the car . . . and came to visit with her. Did she actually see light? She couldn't open her heavy eyelids, yet the presence was so clear and inviting. She could see the contours of the light. A glittering, vibrating white glow rested adjacent to her. She felt drawn, much like a lantern illuminating a path beckons.

The light took shape and gradually metamorphosed into an older man—in his fifties or sixties—sitting in the Honda. He was of slender build, compact features, and thinning hair. In fact, he was balding quite clearly on top. He exuded kindness and friendship. He provided companionship as invisible, poisonous fumes filled the car.

Dressed entirely in casual white clothing, the man appeared translucent. His misty body provided a three-dimensional projection screen on which Bernice saw scenes, much like fuzzy clips from a movie. People and scenery were evident, but she watched through a Vaseline-infused fog. She remained entranced.

The light pulsed and radiated around the man like an all-body halo. Bernice considered asking questions, but couldn't speak. She could only experience. He reached out and stroked her arm. She couldn't tell if her eyes were open. Her cats slept, showing no interest in the light.

She wanted to ask who this man was. He looked familiar, but she couldn't name him. Could this possibly be Bill, dead ten years? Even in her slowed mental state, she knew it was not. The twinkle in this man's brown eyes never existed in her late husband's. Bill's pools of blue always seemed so shallow, where these reflected deep and profound love. This being exuded grace and a peace that she could not fathom. Somehow, it gave her great comfort and confidence for the journey ahead.

Bernice could not say how long the gentleman of light sat with her, but the scene abruptly shattered with a shout from beyond the intimate space they shared. As Roger opened the door and flicked on the overhead fluorescents, Bernice was only vaguely aware of the commotion. The light beside her was so inviting, so engaging. She hated to see it leave, but the man gave her hand a squeeze. "Not yet, Bernice," he mouthed as his presence evaporated. The car's interior went dark and Bernice felt nothing.

* * *

The ride to the ER was noisy and frenetic as Carol and the paramedic tried to stabilize Bernice. Her breathing was ragged; her coloring remained exceptionally poor, her pulse barely evident. Like the ambulance skittering down slippery roads, her grasp on life careened along a perilous course uncertain of outcome or direction.

At the Glenwood ER, Bernice was rushed into triage on the wheeled gurney. They lifted her near lifeless body onto an examining table and hooked her up to myriad monitors. Fluids were drawn, blood gas analysis quickly completed, and warmed blankets enveloped her. As part of the ER ballet, an intravenous tube and more oxygen were connected. When Beverly arrived with Skip, Bernice had not regained consciousness.

"Mrs. Langdon, I think we got her back," opined the doctor. "We've stabilized her. She's getting fluids and her CO levels are decreasing. Oxygen is up," he pointed at a monitor. "I believe she's out of the woods, but the complication of heavy alcohol intake with carbon monoxide, on top of an already depleted physical condition . . . well, you can't wholly predict outcomes. Pulmonary side effects from chemo may exacerbate how this plays out. We'll keep her sedated tonight for observation, given that she's suicidal. I anticipate sending her to the Medical Center in the morning."

"Are we doing enough? Is there more we should do?"

"Nothing more to be done at this point. It's a matter of watching and waiting. We don't know if there's brain damage. We can't tell, of course, how long she was in the vehicle. We can only go by the toxicity in her bloodstream and the oxygen counts. Neither is good, but they can be misleading."

"She's feisty, and if she wants to come back, she will," observed Carol joining them.

Beverly smiled, "Yes, that's true." She turned and embraced Bill as he arrived. "I just can't believe it." Tears finally cascaded down Beverly's cheeks.

The two broke their quick hug and Bill turned to the doctor. "Well? Will she make it?"

"We won't know 'til she wakes. It may be a while and that actually is a good thing–in part why we're keeping her sedated. Let her work some of the poison out."

"So, it's just watch and wait?"

"Yes. You can sit here with her, of course. We'll monitor constantly. It may be a long night."

Beverly and Bill sat down next to Bernice's bed, while Skip and Carol hovered nearby.

"You two should go home. There's nothing more to do here. You heard the doctor," Bill suggested.

"We'll keep you posted. And Carol, thank you so much. You saved her life."

Carol smiled, "A team effort. I'm glad I could help."

"Does seem like we all showed up when we needed to."

"Skip, it's a pleasure meeting you. I'm sorry it's under such–" Beverly's throat caught. "But, welcome to the club."

Skip smiled. "I didn't know what I'd been missing."

Bill raised an eyebrow, "What are you talking about?"

"It's a very long story," commented Carol.

"But we have a long night ahead and I can fill you in," nodded Beverly.

Beverly walked Skip and Carol to the exit. After saying goodnight and calling home, she returned to Bernice's bedside. "Kids are okay. I also called Roz, to fill her in. The kids know she's next door."

"That's good. Thanks, hon."

Beverly sagged into her husband as tears cascaded once more. "Why would she do this? We're supposed to find out this week how the treatment is progressing. Why now?"

"I don't know. I've been deeply remiss. You've been shouldering the load. I've only been engaged at the periphery. I'm so sorry."

"No regrets. She'll hate being back in the hospital again."

Bill sighed. "So tell me a bedtime tale." He smiled gently, "What's this long story?"

Beverly smiled back through her drying tears. "You have some time?"

Bill looked at his mother. "Her coloring seems slightly better. But, yes," he stared at Beverly, "I've got time. You've piqued my curiosity."

"Well, sit back and I'll tell you." Bill was intrigued and asked many questions as the clock ticked its way toward midnight. Together, they made no new headway and eventually both sat quietly, attempting to interpret the evening's events and the growing collection of people and stories that were being artfully woven together by a hand, greater than theirs.

After midnight, Bill convinced Beverly to return home–taking the car. He would remain all night. The kids needed a parent in the house. They agreed to talk in the morning before she drove back.

THIRTY-SIX

Rusty awoke alone Saturday morning. He luxuriated in the feel of the warm sheets and heavy comforter. Piling up the pillows and sitting against them, Rusty pushed the covers down. He punched ON and CNN filled the TV. He enjoyed the proposition of a wide-open Saturday: no pressure, no meetings, and no tasks that required attention.

At a commercial break, he padded to the bathroom. After brushing his teeth, he returned for a few more minutes under the warmth of his covers. The rest of his apartment was quiet. Either his housemates still slept–it was just past nine–or they were not home. When he returned last evening, the place was his own which was just as well. He had much to contemplate.

Rusty couldn't comprehend Bernice's suicide attempt. While never being that close to a nearly dead person, he was glad to help, but the experience shook him. *'You just never know what people are thinking,'* he reflected. Everyone coming at the right time to help save Bernice was pretty remarkable. That was something he would wonder about for a long time. Was this why they'd all been receiving the messages? Was this all about saving Bernice? But why the six? And who was the sender? Were the messages done? Rusty shook his head. "So many questions, so few answers," he finally uttered aloud.

He slid out of bed again and slipped on a pair of Abercrombie lounge pants. With a pot of coffee brewing, he collected the newspaper from outside the apartment. He turned on the TV in the living room and sat down, while sipping coffee and perusing the paper.

Opening the *Metropolitan* section, he noticed a box at the bottom-left corner. Normally in that spot, the newspaper held a cartoonish chart depicting a random factoid, but not today. The all-too-familiar burning border boldly outlined a square space of deep sapphire blue. Words the consistency of clouds drifted across the space, disappearing into the fiery border:

CONNECT 6   TODAY   BE THERE

"Ahh, shit," Rusty said aloud, nearly spilling coffee on his lap. "I cannot believe this. More?"

Nonetheless, he watched fascinated. A repeating pattern of clouds crossed the eerily burning sky box.

"I wonder where we're meeting?" he frowned. Curious, he aggressively punched in a telephone number and listened.

"Hello?"

"It's Rusty. I gather we're meeting today. It's in the paper."

"I've not seen."

"Well, I just got up . . . and it's there. I guess yesterday wasn't the end."

"I suppose not."

"I thought saving Bernice might be the reason for the messages."

"That thought crossed my mind as well."

"So, you don't know about a meeting?"

"No one else has reached out. I'll call Beverly."

"Well, if something's going on, let me know. I'll see if I'm available."

"You'd have to be! And Rusty? Thank you for your gift last night."

"Huh?"

"The gift of life. You gave that to Bernice, you know."

"It wasn't just me. I'm glad I could help."

"The Lord works in mysterious ways. He clearly has His hand in all of this."

"I suppose."

"Perhaps we'll see each other later today."

With a click, the connection went dead, and Rusty sat holding the handset. *'Well, I'll be . . .'* he thought as he watched the clouds change their wording,

GO MEET COMMIT SOON

'Ain't that the damnedest? It's like having a guardian angel looking out for me,' Rusty grimaced. *'Wonder what's next in this little adventure?'*

* * *

Hanging up, Janet collected the prior evening's newspaper. She'd read it upon returning from Bernice's, but likely she'd been distracted. Sure enough, a flaming box filled the bottom left corner of *The Ledger's Living* front page. The interior of the box exhibited the clearest, bluest sky she could remember; crossing clouds spelled out a message:

CONNECT 6 SATURDAY BE THERE

"Would you look at that? I don't know how I missed it." She frowned, "Though, maybe it wasn't there. Walt?" she called out. "I may need to go out later today."

Janet called Carol to avoid rousing Beverly too early. As they spoke, Carol picked up *The Ledger* and opened to the same page and the same message.

"I hope this doesn't mean Dr. L took a turn for the worse," chattered

Carol excitedly.

"I hope not, but Beverly would call if things weren't good."

"Perhaps. I was going to check, but figured they wouldn't need help today, especially if she is transferred to the Medical Center." Carol paused, "I suspect they'll want to keep her a few days."

"Why don't I call Beverly? See how we might help."

"That would be great. I've got to get Kelly and Kevin to indoor soccer this morning. They each have practice 'til noon."

"Carol, thank you so much for what you did last night."

"All part of the job. Goes with the turf. Cleaning up poop one minute, saving a life the next. Seriously, I'm glad we all were there."

"Funny how God works."

"He must have some mighty big plans for Bernice!"

Janet laughed. "It very well could be!"

* * *

"Bill?" The unshaven, deeply fatigued thirty-something looked up.

"Yes?"

"Look at this." Beverly held up the *Metropolitan* section and pointed to the bottom left corner. Just as when Rusty scanned the page, the same azure-hued editorial box with cloud-like words drifting across caught her attention.

CONNECT 6 TODAY BE THERE

"I'm amazed there's another message with all we've been through."

"Hon, I don't know what to make of it, but Mom needs us. She's still not awake. I'm worried."

"The doctors said it might take some time given the sedation. Her vitals appear good. Her coloring is so much better today, though it's still off."

"I'd just like to know she's going to be okay."

"Wouldn't we all?" Beverly watched the newspaper. The cloud words moved effortlessly as if pushed by a gentle breeze. She hesitated, "I'm going to call around and see if others are getting messages."

"You do that." Bill closed his eyes again.

Beverly's first call confirmed that the kids were having breakfast and that Janet had called.

"She said it was important," concluded Caitlyn offhandedly.

"I appreciate your taking the message. Now you two behave and stay inside. It is brutally cold out. I'm sorry that Dad and I are out again, but we need to see how we can help BeBe."

"How is she?" Caitlyn's voice caught.

"About the same, though she looks a little better."

"Has she woken up?"

"Not yet."

"I hope she doesn't die."

"I hope not."

"Why'd she do it, Mom?"

"I can only guess. Like I said last night, she's frustrated by how long her treatment is taking. She's been depressed. She probably doesn't know whether she's getting better or not. She anticipated the worst. It all must've just gotten to her."

"Will she try again?"

"I hope not, but we'll watch her."

"Mom, I'm scared," sobbed Caitlyn.

"It scared me too. I'll be home as soon as I can. Don't you worry."

"Don't stay out too long."

"I won't, hon. Now, go finish your breakfast. It's probably cold by now. Nuke it . . . but just a little."

"Is Daddy okay, Mom?"

"He's fine. Just tired."

"He won't try to kill himself will he?"

"Oh no, of course not. This is something that just BeBe is dealing with. I know it's very scary, but it doesn't mean that Dad or I would ever—" Beverly's voice wobbled. "It's the last thing in the world either of us would—" she trailed off again. "Don't worry, Caitlyn."

"Okay. I guess I'll go finish my breakfast." Caitlyn sniffled loudly.

"Good idea. I love you. Very much."

Beverly called Janet. They compared notes and decided to gather at Bernice's. "While I suspect 'connect six' means the six of us, we should be doubly certain. Call me superstitious, but let's meet at six o'clock."

"You're right, dear. I believe it does intend the six of us, but adding an extra 'six' certainly can't hurt." Janet hesitated. "I know you've got so much going on. Why don't I call the others?"

"That would be great, though I'll call Roger."

"Not to worry. I've already spoken with Rusty and Carol. I'll get hold of Skip."

"That's so sweet of you."

"I'm only doing what you'd do if the roles were reversed. Go back to Bernice."

By the time Beverly returned to the little curtained room, Bernice was sitting up, sipping apple juice through a straw. With unfocused eyes, she nodded at Beverly, as Bill held her hand and stroked her forearm. She did not resist.

"Mother, you're awake. You had us so concerned. I am so happy to see your eyes open," Beverly swallowed hard.

"She asked for you when she first woke. I said you would be right back."

"Really?" Beverly's eyes burned and a lump inexplicably filled her throat. "I'm so pleased to see you," she finally choked out.

Bernice stared at her, while continuing to sip slowly. Though silent, the retired professor seemed more at peace than she had been. Even her coloring appeared better than in the preceding weeks. As Beverly and Bill sat with her, she periodically closed her eyes and dozed lightly.

In the late morning, Bernice uttered, "My head hurts . . . " and closed her eyes again. The nurses gave her Tylenol, which appeared to take the edge off. Around noon, the doctor authorized a move to the University Medical Center.

"We're not equipped to handle an extended stay here. Her blood gases look good. Her electrolytes are stable. Given her state, I'd like to have her observed for several days. Have her see a counselor."

The ambulance transfer downtown was far calmer than the prior evening's ride. Bill rode with her, while Beverly drove the family van. Bernice silently accommodated the move. She looked groggy and wrung out.

In her new room, Beverly helped Bernice shower and dress in a clean nightgown. All the effort and the events of the last day proved exhausting. She quietly lay down and closed her eyes.

"Do you need anything?" Bill asked.

She subtly shook her head.

"I'm going to run home, shower, and change. Then I'll be back." Bernice gave no acknowledgement.

In the hallway, Bill and Beverly whispered. "I'll stay for the day. I expect the group around six o'clock at her house. Perhaps I'll order pizza?"

Bill cocked his head. "I'll bring the kids over. They can have pizza and hang out upstairs while I come back down to Mom. New subject: we need to take care of the cats."

Beverly grimaced, "I guess. Fortunately, it's so cold, they're probably frozen."

"Regardless, we need to dispose of them. I hope it's not too big a loss for Mom."

"I hope not."

"I'm thinking I should stay with her tonight, maybe tomorrow."

"She will receive plenty of care here. I don't want to see her alone. Not after–" Beverly broke off.

Her husband nodded, "I know. I just feel like I should stay at least tonight."

"Maybe later in the week when she gets home, either Carol or I can stay with her."

They kissed and Bill departed. Beverly got herself a cup of strong tea, while Bernice rested–comfortably and quietly–in her room. The digital clock on her monitor blinked steadily across Saturday afternoon.

THIRTY-SEVEN

The blue Miata zipped up to the Langdon house at 5:59 on Saturday evening, completing the set of cars at the curb. Beverly opened the door as Rusty came up the walk.

"Come in. The rest are in the kitchen getting drinks. Pizza should be here any minute."

Joining the others, Rusty laughed as he shook hands, "Heckuva party we're throwing."

"You bet," smiled Skip. "When Janet called and suggested getting together, she asked if I'd gotten my invitation already. When I said, 'no one had called,' she responded, 'look at your newspaper.' Unbelievable: bottom left, *Metropolitan* section. Clear as day."

"I gotta admit, it's got me a little spooked. You wonder what else this guy has up his sleeve for us," nodded Rusty somberly.

"I told Jay, 'Pud, you won't believe it. The messages keep coming; I've got to act on them.' He could see the sky-box in the paper and the cloud words; he just shook his head."

"Roger, you got the message in the paper?"

"Yeah, though I didn't see it 'til today. I was looking for yesterday's NBA scores and there it was in *Sports*. I had to convince my mom I should come over, but . . . "

"You were sent yesterday as well," smiled Beverly.

"I guess. But that box: the burning edge, the dark blue background, and the words made out of clouds, blowing across . . . " Roger recalled vividly.

"Pretty awesome way to deliver a message," agreed Rusty.

Roger kept talking. "You know, I was curious whether it was in other copies. So, I went through some of the extras for customers who were away."

"Interesting. I wouldn't have thought of that."

Beverly shook her head, echoing Janet's comment.

"You know what?" Roger held the group's attention. "None had the box. Not in *Sports*, not anywhere." He paused dramatically. "I went back to our copy. The cloud words were still floating there."

"Rather convincing. The message was intentional," agreed Skip.

"I wonder who else received it."

"'Connect Six' is definitive," argued Skip. "I was the latecomer, but I sense we're it."

"The fact that we were all here yesterday when Dr. Langdon really needed us: for me, that nails it. We are the group," noted Carol.

"Though I didn't make it," commented Beverly.

"You were waylaid in a snowdrift." Janet patted Beverly's arm.

The doorbell chimed. Four hot pizzas soon perfumed the room as the group gathered around the island to snare slices.

"Before we eat, shall we have a word of prayer?" suggested Janet.

Everyone paused while reaching for pizza.

"Well, okay," shrugged Carol. "I guess that would be appropriate after what we've been through."

"I'll bet you're pretty good at praying, unlike me anyway!" Rusty added. "Go ahead, Janet, you pray, but don't take too long. The pizza's hot."

The others laughed, but all bowed their heads as Janet began.

"Gracious Lord and Creator. You've given us so much to be thankful for: material possessions and gifts, but more importantly a relationship with you and with those around us. Bless this gathering. Help us to understand Your will as we seek the purpose driving us as individuals and as a group of Your followers. Bless Bernice as she struggles against the physical, emotional, and spiritual challenges wracking her earthly body. Be with us this evening–both here in fellowship and in our journeys home. Bless this food to our bodies and help us deliver on Your promises and Your expectations. As always, we are Your faithful servants. To Your name we raise our praise, Amen."

"That was beautiful," commented Beverly, lifting a slice of broccoli pizza.

"Amen," added Carol. "I'm not much of a prayer giver."

"Me neither," noted Rusty, just before taking a mouthful of pepperoni pizza.

"We all pray in our own ways. Some are more glorious and artistic. Most are short and informal. Pray in the way that feels comfortable to you. Don't use others' style as an obstacle."

"I'm doing well if we recite some memorized verse at dinner without someone choking on a partially eaten piece of food going down unblessed," Carol's eyes sparkled. "I can sure learn from you, Janet."

"We all learn from each other."

The group contentedly made their way through the pizza in short order.

"I brought cookies," Janet said. "I just knew we'd have some hearty appetites here tonight, and I didn't think you'd have time to bake!" She smiled in Beverly's direction.

"I brought over Nutter Butters and Oreos: big favorites and always on hand at my house," added Carol.

Brad, Caitlyn, and Roger grabbed the first handfuls. "Now, before you three disappear upstairs, we're going to need Roger to stick around. We have some business to discuss."

Brad grimaced, "Can't we just go online for a coupla minutes, Mom?"

"It's already seven o'clock. I don't want to keep people here all night."

Roger nodded, "I told my mom I wouldn't be late. I'm kinda interested in what's going on."

Brad shook his head, "Whatever." He disappeared and loudly clambered up the staircase. Caitlyn lingered briefly, but then followed him quietly upstairs.

"Shall we move to the dining room? There's more room."

"Nah, let's stay here. It's close to the cookies and the drinks."

The group migrated to the alcove table, as Beverly collected her pad from the earlier discussion. Curious, Skip studied the pad. "Let me add mine at the bottom," he said, penning his messages.

"Don't we all have some new ones to add?" queried Beverly. With that, the pad circuited the table as each appended new additions. The complete list ran onto a second page.

Janet	Oct 30	*COLLEAGUE C BERNICE AP $ TELL ANDREWS SOON*
	Jan 6	*FRIEND ENGAGE RUSTY SKIP B*
	Jan 11	*SEE BERNICE GET RUSTY SKIP CHURCH ROGER*
	Jan 17	*ELDER 9-1-1 B-L TODAY*
	Jan 18	*CONNECT 6 SATURDAY BE THERE*

Beverly	Nov 7	*MRS L NO JOB CONFRONT BILL*
	Jan 6	*MRS L ENGAGE RUSTY SKIP B*
	Jan 17	*DEAR 9-1-1 MOTHER ASAP*
	Jan 17	*DEAREST WASTE NO TIME GO NOW NO DELAY*
	Jan 18	*CONNECT 6 TODAY BE THERE*

Carol	Oct 18	*HH GOOD FAM 1ST TAKE JOB*
	Jan 12	*C BL ASAP A FALL ROGER*
	Jan 17	*COURAGE 9-1-1 DR L TODAY*
	Jan 17	*A S A P*

	Jan 18	*CONNECT 6 SATURDAY BE THERE*

Rusty	Oct 18	ENGAGE PRODUCTIVELY. WORK WEEKEND. FOREGO PARTY.
	Jan 6	TAKE TASK SEE BERNICE ASAP
	Jan 14	CONNECT DOTS TIME HAS COME GO MEET
	Jan 17	RUST 9-1-1 DR L TODAY THINK UNC
	Jan 17	ASAP KILL GRILL SAVE BERNICE
	Jan 18	CONNECT 6 TODAY BE THERE
	Jan 18	GO MEET COMMIT SOON

Roger	Oct 25	CHOOSE LIFE GO DANCE COFFEE NOT FREE
	Jan 5	PERSIST GO BACK KEEP SMILE SAY UNCLE
	Jan 15	CONNECT DOTS TIME HAS COME GO MEET
	Jan 17	ROG 9-1-1 PROF L TODAY THINK UNC
	Jan 18	CONNECT 6 SATURDAY BE THERE

Skip	Oct 17	BRO – DETAILS MATTERS FAMILY 1ST FOREGO MTG
	Jan 6	BRO LANGDON WILL ATTEND 3 KINGS DROP BAK
	Jan 13	WHY DELAY? ASAP BRO LANGDON WILL DROP BAK
	Jan 14	SEE? ACT QUICKLY DON'T DELAY BRO
	Jan 17	BRO 9-1-1 LANGDON TODAY
	Jan 17	A S A P BRO NO DELAYS NOW
	Jan 18	CONNECT 6 SATURDAY BE THERE

"It's incredible seeing all the messages," observed Skip.

"Even when today's was basically the same for everyone," Beverly nodded.

"It does seem like we're connected," agreed Rusty.

"So, what's the point? Why are we here tonight?" Carol piped up.

"Bernice is certainly the heart of our mission to date," Janet observed.

"It would appear," agreed Beverly.

"But they're not all about her," Rusty pushed back. "All of us have gotten other messages."

"But now, having gotten our attention, we're all focused on Bernice," analyzed Skip.

"Not me. My most recent one–'Commit'–I don't see what that has to do with the professor."

"What makes you so certain? Maybe Mother needs more from each of us . . . including you."

"I don't buy it."

"On Wednesday, we thought that how this fellow refers to us was important," Janet redirected the conversation.

"Interesting point. How do my entries help?"

"Let's see: the sender refers to you as 'Bro' six times," Beverly contemplated.

"You have any bros in the 'hood?" smirked Rusty. "I'm thinkin' you're lookin' like a leather dude. Maybe you got an issue with a bro."

Skip snorted, "You never know. My wife and I talked about that. We also thought about my late brother, David, but he's been gone nearly two years. He fought a tough battle with leukemia, but it was just too aggressive. Even after a bone marrow transplant, he couldn't do it. He passed away in April of 2001."

"As I mentioned to you, I knew David. We served on the church council. He finished his term in the late nineties, but we spent a lot of time together. You know how church board meetings can go . . . " Janet paused. "In fact, several of us attend Bedrock Hills, don't we?"

"Not me," interjected Rusty quickly.

"Nor me," said Carol.

"So it's not the church angle, and I suspect we all need some connection to the sender. Church only connects you two."

"That can't be it. The guy calls himself uncle for me." Rusty paused. "Well, maybe not precisely . . . "

"Me too. He used uncle with me twice."

"It may just be a figure of speech. You two aren't related are you?"

"I don't think so, though Roger's a cool dude," Rusty playfully punched Roger's abs.

Roger smiled. "Rusty would be okay as an older brother."

"Or cousin?" laughed Carol. "Well, our mystery guest doesn't refer to me by anything."

"And why am I so formal? Mrs. L? And then later a shift to Dearest? It's downright Victorian!"

"It's certainly intriguing. I can't make it out," added Skip.

"Out of curiosity, what did your brother do?"

"He taught English. When he died, he was at the junior high. Earlier, he was at the high school."

"No way," Carol yelped. "I had him. Eleventh grade. Mr. O'Neill. I just didn't put it together." She paused as the others looked at her expectantly. "I am connected."

"It may link me as well," exclaimed Beverly. "I'm nearly positive he taught Caitlyn. I would never have remembered his name, but her English teacher–she loved him, by the way–died during the spring. He only taught for a month or two in the fall and then got ill. She was so disappointed. I met him several times even in that short period. I helped out on a class project regarding Shakespeare and the Globe Theatre."

"His web touches four of us." Skip assessed the emerging clues. "How does that tie with the names?"

"It works great for me. Suddenly, calling me Mrs. L . . . short for Mrs. Langdon, of course, is precisely the way we'd engage. You know that odd way you talk with teachers. I called him Mr. O'Neill; he called me Mrs. Langdon."

"But Dear? And Dearest? That's a little off," noted Rusty.

"Yes, but he did have an affectation in his speaking sometimes," Beverly commented.

"Maybe it's that Shakespeare project?" speculated Carol.

Skip smiled, "You could be on to something. David had a certain stilted formality on occasion. Don't really know where that came from."

"Very interesting. And you, Carol?"

"Like I said, he doesn't call me by name. So, I don't see any real connection in the words–" She stopped suddenly. "Whoa. Wait a minute."

"What?" ricocheted around the table.

"The message from yesterday. I hadn't thought about it in years, but . . . "

The group all looked back to the list and saw nothing. "What do you see?" asked Beverly.

"You know, I thought 'Courage, 911' was a means of saying, 'Buck up, be brave. This is an emergency and you need to be strong.' Given what happened, that fit. Now, I'm thinking back to English class. We had an assignment at the start of school." The group around the table leaned toward Carol expectantly.

"We each wrote a short narrative essay about ourselves, our goals, and aspirations."

"So?" Rusty rolled his eyes.

"We titled the essay using an alliteration of our name and an adjective that helped define our life goal. I chose 'Carol Courage.' As Mr. O'Neill said, many of us would end up with a name that would stick for the remainder of the year. While most did not, mine did; I was known as Carol Courage for the rest of eleventh grade. In fact, it stuck through senior year. It's even in my yearbook."

"Really?"

"Sometimes, Mr. O'Neill would just call us by our nicknames. For me, that was 'Courage.' Boy, I haven't thought of that forever."

"It's gotta be more than coincidence," observed Skip.

"Sure sounds like it," added Beverly.

"But where does that leave us cousins?" frowned Rusty, pointing his thumbs toward Roger and himself.

"Roger, can you think of any connection to Mr. O'Neill?"

"I definitely didn't have him for class in junior high. I remember him; he was kinda thin. White hair. Bald on top. No offense, Mr. O'Neill," Roger looked at Skip, "but he looked like you–just older." Roger blushed.

"David looked like my father, particularly toward the end of his life. The ravages of leukemia wore badly."

"But I didn't have him."

"Never?" asked Carol.

"Maybe for a study hall or as a test proctor or something, I guess."

"That's mighty tenuous," Skip commented.

"Nothing really. Why would he pick you out of an inconsequential study hall?" Beverly put out on the table.

"And why would he suggest uncle?" Rusty persisted.

"It doesn't make much sense."

"What a fine gentleman David was. He did such a nice job at church. He helped put out the weekly bulletin. He could always find a way to turn a phrase; he could communicate so artistically and in so many creative ways."

"Listen to your description. It fits with what he's doing: creatively communicating. Turning phrases in interesting ways . . . " Beverly sagely noted.

"I hate to say this, guys, but this is bullshit. He's dead. Long gone. God rest his soul. I'd like to believe it, but–come on. Communicating from beyond the grave?" Rusty kept his arms tightly crossed.

"So what's your take?"

"Okay, I have to admit, I don't know, but it's kinda surreal to think some ghost is sending messages."

"So wrack your brain. Who else?"

"You too, Roger. None of us think the study hall connection–if one even existed–is sufficient. The rest of us have a stronger relationship."

"Though honestly, Beverly, your connection is rather light also." Beverly reluctantly nodded with Skip's assessment. "Now before we go too far down this path, we should see if there are any other options–any other forces–that could send messages," Skip propositioned the group. "We may be jumping the gun to the first plausible connection."

"It seems so promising," responded Beverly.

"If you believe in ghosts," Rusty countered.

"I prefer to think of this as angels, rather than ghosts," observed Janet reflectively. "Angels are often around us. You know, angels unaware."

Looks of skepticism rippled around the table.

"Perhaps in this instance, this angel needed to provide more explicit help than being unaware allows."

"But why here? Why now?" Rusty shook his head.

"There are plenty of people out there who are sick or contemplating suicide that could be helped," Carol nodded her agreement.

"Certainly, but there's a reason why we're together. Perhaps we're a means to an end. This angel, if we believe, needed some human intervention. Maybe it's Bernice's attempt on her life. Perhaps that's just a beginning."

"You mean we may be like superheroes? Saving people from trouble and danger?" Roger warmed to the idea as the group chuckled.

"Well, I don't know about that, but we should think more broadly. It truly is incredible to be part of God's plan."

Skip shook his head, "It's rather remarkable, whatever is causing–"

Rusty interrupted, "I want to know why I'm at this party. It doesn't fit. I'm not that religious. I don't believe in angel stuff. I just don't know." He winked at Roger. "I came to help Ber –I mean, Professor Langdon–and here I sit with a group getting off-the-wall messages. While cool, it's kinda bizarre."

"We are all amazed by this apparent miracle. There's no other explanation," agreed Janet.

"I go to church regularly, but I don't think of myself as deeply rooted in my faith. This may prompt me to change," reflected Skip. "I've been searching for something more. Maybe this will push me in a new, meaningful direction."

"It's been years since I was Courage, and yet, it is so compelling. I'm now back on a path more explicitly tied to my earlier aspirations. Awesome."

"So, what about me? Where's the uncle?"

"Yeah, me too," nodded Roger.

"It requires more thought, but we're on the right track. It's the only way this all fits together. No other soul–living or deceased–could connect the four of us in the way your late brother has," observed Beverly.

"You know what else is odd. One of my email messages was tagged 'oneill.' I thought at first it just dealt with me as the recipient, but now I wonder if it was from my brother."

"I thought the same thing. I figured the message I got was from your office and never reconsidered the sender. It could've been your brother."

"Very interesting. I wonder where this whole thing goes next," Carol injected quizzically.

"Stay tuned," intoned Skip.

"Same bat time, same bat channel," announced Rusty sonorously. His proclamation was greeted by the others' laughter as they stood collectively.

"Can we get together again? This has been fun and, who knows, maybe there is something more coming," noted Carol.

"I need to return to work on the estate plan."

"Of course. Perhaps we could do both on the same day. Save a trip?"

"I'll see what my schedule looks like. No promises. I know I've been getting the same string of messages, but I still don't see the connection. Maybe I'm getting them by mistake," frowned Rusty.

"No," said Skip, resting a hand on Rusty's shoulder, "I don't think it's coincidental. You're meant to be here." He rubbed Rusty's shoulder affectionately. "I really think you are." He gave Rusty a playful slap on the shoulder blades and smiled a broad, white-toothed grin.

Rusty exhaled sharply, "If you say so."

Roger disappeared upstairs to find Brad.

"I wonder how Bernice is doing . . . " raised Janet gently.

Beverly nodded. "We should give Bill a call and check. I'm sure he's with her. Why don't we call from the study where Mother has a speakerphone?" The three ladies left the room, leaving Skip and Rusty alone in the kitchen where they started taking plates and glasses to the sink.

"You know, you look familiar. Have we met before?" inquired Skip. "I've looked at you all evening . . . and you just seem so familiar."

"I don't think so. I'm pretty good at remembering faces, but I don't recall meeting." Rusty's blue eyes stared deeply into Skip's. "Anything's possible, I guess."

"Maybe I'm just looking at too many signs and odd coincidences tonight."

Rusty laughed. "Maybe." He paused. "You do any work with Ridgewell?"

"No, can't say that I do, though I've met your CEO. He's sharp."

"He sure is. It's unbelievable what he's been able to accomplish. He's not even forty."

"Careful. Don't go down that over-the-hill-at-forty road. You're in sensitive territory."

Rusty smiled. "Nah, not with you. You're in good shape for an old guy." He play-punched Skip, who returned the jab, mirroring Rusty's move. Each smiled.

"I need to head out. My wife and the boys will wonder what happened to me . . . I told 'em this would just be a short discussion, and here it is going on nine."

"Yeah, me too. I'm hopin' to hook up with some friends. Last night got a little out of control. I just crashed after leaving here."

"That kind of excitement I can do without. I've got a long day tomorrow. Busy week at work coming up."

The men headed to the foyer where they collected their outdoor gear. Hearing the ladies talking quietly on the phone, they just waved through the study doorway to say goodbye.

"We'll be in touch soon," mouthed Beverly.

"Yes, pick a date. We'll drag Rusty along." Skip winked at Rusty.

"Whatever. Night y'all." Rusty's southern twang echoed across the foyer.

By ten o'clock, the house was quiet after Beverly and the kids left for home. At the Medical Center, Bill settled into the recliner next to his sleeping mother and closed his eyes, pondering the last twenty-four hours.

Periodically, he looked at her monitors. Optimistically, he looked for a burning border and a ticker tape to appear. Through heavy eyes, he watched for a long time, until he gradually floated off to a distant place as the message-free screen blinked.

THIRTY-EIGHT

"Hey," Roger called out as he stepped into the kitchen from the garage.

"We're in Dad's study."

Roger stuck his head in the doorway, "I'll be downstairs. I want to catch *SportsCenter* before I hit the sack."

"Wait a minute. Tell us about your evening."

"How's Dr. Langdon doing?"

"Fine."

"That's it. Fine?" Elaine questioned. "The poor woman spent the night in the ER and today she's fine?"

"Well, yeah, Mom. She's doing okay. She actually wasn't at home. I hung out with Brad and the others."

"She wasn't there? Where was she?" Mike Gallo's eyebrow arched.

"At the hospital. She's doing okay. They said she needed to stay for observation or something."

"But I thought you were going to visit her?" Elaine was mystified.

"Well, it didn't turn out that way. It was the same group that was there last night . . . plus Brad and Caitlyn," Roger added.

"I'm not understanding . . . why did the same people get back together?"

"How are you doing, Roger? That was quite a scare," his father interjected.

"Fine. No big deal." Roger was pleased to respond to the conversation's new direction.

"Being at the scene of an attempted suicide is—in fact—a big deal."

"I didn't have any nightmares or anything."

"With Dr. Langdon recovering, I'm sure that helps," noted Elaine.

Roger shrugged, "I guess."

"So I'm still curious. What in heaven's name were all these people doing at the Langdons'?" Elaine refueled. "And who are they again?"

"Well, Mrs. Langdon and Mrs. Kneffler—that's Professor Langdon's nurse . . . "

Mrs. Gallo arched her eyebrows.

" . . . and Mrs. Walker, and the Langdons' lawyer and a computer guy."

"Mrs. Langdon didn't mention a party when she called."

"Okay, I'll bite. What was this all about?" His dad looked over the top of his glasses.

"It's kinda a long story," Roger squirmed. At breakneck speed–barely stopping to catch his breath, he brought his parents up to speed.

"Why didn't you tell us?" Elaine asked.

"You're yanking my chain, right?" His dad gazed sternly at his son, while wrinkling his brow.

"Oh, it's the truth. Get Friday's newspaper. See if the box is there."

Moments later, Mike returned with the rumpled Friday paper from the recycling bin. "Where?"

"*Sports*, bottom left."

"Nothing there but an ad. No box with cloud letters."

"I'm not surprised. The other messages faded away too."

"I'm unconvinced."

"Then how did everyone know to show up and save Professor Langdon?"

"A nice, timely coincidence."

"I don't know, Mike. It sounds like something more to me," Elaine piped in. "Beverly Langdon seems like the level-headed type."

"For sure, Mom. But there's something odd."

"Just one odd thing?" His mother smiled.

"We tried to figure out who was sending the messages. The only good idea was an English teacher at my school, Mr. O'Neill, who died."

"David O'Neill?" interrupted Roger's dad.

"Yeah. But the odd thing? Four people had some connection to him, all but Rusty and me."

Elaine gasped, "But, Roger, you do have a clear link. You're related."

"What?" Roger sat down abruptly.

"Sure, he's the father of Mitchell, Seth, and Polly."

"Who?" Roger asked incredulously.

"Oh, you've heard of them–your second cousins. They're older than you. They're probably in college now. Maybe even out. But we've spoken of them."

"For real? How could I have cousins I've never heard about?"

"You've just forgotten. You know your dad's family. They're not the most communicative."

"Well, yeah, but . . . " Roger paused as his dad grimaced gently.

"It's just the way they are. They keep to themselves. Your parents are lovely. You know I love them like my own, but your siblings? They are–shall we say–an interesting group."

"But who are Mitchell, Seth and Polly?"

"Don't you remember us talking about Seth? He's a wrestler. Went to State."

"No, nothing."

Mike continued, "Grandpop's older brother, Joseph had one daughter, Catherine. She was–actually is–my cousin. She married David O'Neill. They had three kids. Had them pretty young, as I recall."

Roger and his mother silently listened.

"My Uncle Joseph was an odd duck. I didn't know him well. He kept to himself, after his divorce from Aunt Linda. She tried to keep the family together, but she wasn't blood. Uncle Joseph drifted away. The family didn't exactly disown him, but we never really reconnected. I think he traveled cross country for awhile."

"Catherine turned out okay," Elaine paused. "I always liked your Aunt Linda."

"She died a while back, though I couldn't tell you the cause."

"Wow. I'm related to Mr. O'Neill, and I thought he was just a teacher at school." Roger's world rocked. "The messages must be coming from him. Even the way he referred to me, 'Think Uncle.' "

"Well, Rog, he's not exactly your uncle. He's the father of your second cousins."

"But it's kinda cool that if you think cousins, their father is kinda like an uncle, right?" nodded Roger, putting the pieces together. "If we've found this connection between me and David . . ." his voice drifted.

"David and me," his mother quickly inserted.

" . . . David and me," Roger emphatically voiced, "I wonder about Rusty and him. All the rest are linked. He must be too."

"Who's Rusty again?"

"Rusty Stillwagon. He works downtown. Drives a Miata. Really sweet car."

"And he couldn't find a connection? How about to anyone in the group?"

"Nothing."

"Certainly a very curious tale, but look at the time. We have church in the morning. Let's head up."

"Awww, can't I watch *SportsCenter*?" Roger whined.

"'Til eleven. No later. You're too wired to settle down anyway."

Roger sprang up to ensure no protests to the contrary emerged. "Deal. Thanks." He bolted from the room; his heavy feet thumped down the steps to the basement.

"What do you make of all that?" Mike questioned.

"I don't know, but I guess we go with the flow. He's engaging in a mature way with some adults. Interesting how they showed up when Bernice Langdon needed help the most."

"It's all rather curious." Mike tented his fingers and played them off one another. "I found that part most intriguing. The tie with David is pretty remarkable. I'm surprised Roger didn't think of it."

"He's fourteen and not particularly interested in keeping up with cousins twice removed and black sheep relatives."

"Who's this you're calling a black sheep?" Mike chuckled. "I'll have you know there are no black sheep in my family. None." He added with emphasis.

"Whatever you say. You're the boss," smiled Elaine. "Shall we go upstairs?"

"Sure. Here's hoping our fourteen-year-old will go right to bed and not look in on us to say good night."

"Why, you devil! Did you have something in mind?"

"Perhaps a little nightcap without the liquor. This white sheep would like to visit the farm."

"Well, I always liked spendin' time at your farm. Shall we?" Elaine smiled, finishing her southern drawl with a curtsey.

Mike gave Elaine a quick hug and a kiss as they walked up the staircase together. When Roger came up later, he paused outside his parents' room and raised his hand to knock. Hearing soft murmurs and seeing the blue light under the door, he realized his parents had already fallen asleep with the TV on. He smiled as he shut the door to his room.

THIRTY-NINE

Taylor Caldwell stepped down on Monday as Dane & Caldwell's managing partner. When Skip and his fellow partner arrived for the meeting, Taylor intuitively sensed the nature of the discussion. While he vigorously defended his innocence, Skip was persistent and firm. The facts were clear: Taylor had overstepped, at minimum, ethical lines. The firm could not sustain having him as its leader. Resignation was the only choice.

By noon on Monday—a quiet Martin Luther King Jr. Day at the generally closed office—Taylor had drafted his letter of resignation. By the end of the day, the remaining senior partners were apprised. A meeting of the full senior partnership was called for Friday to agree on the best route forward.

Skip left the office in midafternoon. He wanted time to clear his head. Several partners were encouraging him to step forward as the firm's leader. He needed time to consider what was best for both the firm and his family. Leadership of a large, growing enterprise could be all-consuming. Not one to shun large roles, this would increase both stress and hours significantly.

The week accelerated with a rapid cascade of communications and planning at Dane & Caldwell. Wednesday afternoon, Skip decided to leave the office early and get some 'think time' at home. On his outbound commute, he enjoyed the Beemer's acceleration on the expressway, now completely clear of snow with only light midafternoon traffic. As he drove, he hummed along to Casting Crowns' latest offering. He decided—on a whim—to stop at Bernice's. "I'll see if I can at least get started on this estate work," he noted.

"Come in, Skip. It's so nice to see you. What a pleasant surprise."

"How's Bernice?"

"Just home this morning. She's actually doing pretty well."

"I'm glad to hear."

"She is hooked up with a caseworker who will be visiting every few days for the next several weeks or so. They want to keep an eye on her—particularly the depression, but—remarkably—she is physically quite good. She ate some chicken noodle soup today and enjoyed it."

"Hey, great news!"

"There is something different I sense in her. It's actually a good thing, if you can believe it! She just seems more tranquil or something. I can't quite put a finger on it." Beverly paused, "Would you like to say hello?"

"Sure, if it's not a bother. I thought I'd see if you had any of the preliminary paperwork . . . "

"Of course. Let's visit Mother first." Skip doffed his coat, leaving it on the banister as they ascended.

"Dr. Langdon. So good to see you," Skip's hearty baritone filled the room. Bernice looked up and reached for her glasses. Putting them on, she focused.

"Have we met?"

"Skip O'Neill, Dane & Caldwell. Bill asked that we help out on some estate planning."

"I inquired about that some time ago. Certainly took you long enough to respond." Bernice sniffed over the top of her glasses, which hung precariously at the tip of her nose.

Skip smiled as Beverly cringed. "You had us worried, you know."

"How so?" A smirk crossed Bernice's face.

"Well, several of us happened to stop on Friday and . . . "

"So, I gather. Ending a perfectly lovely death scene." Bernice cut to the point as Beverly rolled her eyes. "I'm feeling more myself today. Perhaps we all need a little death to shake us up sometimes."

"I'm glad to see you rallying, Dr. Langdon."

"Please. If you're working on my estate, call me Bernice." Bernice pointed her thumb at Beverly, "She coddles me. She's worried I'm going to off myself again." Bernice stopped. "I did it so well the first time."

"You nearly did. You scared us."

"It's wonderful that you're here sitting up, talking and kidding about—"

"There's no point in being maudlin and depressed over death. Move on." She flipped her hand regally. "And they think I need a caseworker?"

Skip opened and closed his mouth twice. No client matched Bernice.

"So, how long will this take?" Bernice plowed forward.

"Depends on how far along the work is," Skip paused. "And how many changes you'd like to make."

"The last meaningful iteration was while my late husband was living. A few changes will be in order, no doubt."

Skip smiled, "Quite possibly. I'm glad you hung around for us to get the work done." He bantered easily with his new client.

Bernice smirked, "It's why I'm back."

"Mother, really."

Skip couldn't help chuckling. "I'm sure glad to meet you in such rare form. Maybe I should extend this work, ensure you won't go anywhere too soon."

"Not to worry. I've seen enough of the dark side. I believe I'll stay," she paused dramatically, " . . . for the moment."

Beverly grimaced. "May I show you the files we pulled together? I hope we've got what you need."

Skip said goodbye to Bernice ("Now, we're not paying you some king's ransom to update this, are we?") and followed Beverly downstairs. She handed him three folders.

"This is what Bill suggested." Beverly became more thoughtful. "She is one-of-a-kind, don't you think?"

"I'd never guess she'd attempted suicide on Friday night. You'd almost think it was a stunt done just for effect."

"She got much more energized with you. With me, she's been rather dour. I sure hope this represents a turn for the better. I worry about her. I sure don't want her to try again."

"Doesn't sound like she's about to."

"Bill and I've decided to make sure someone's in the house with her all the time for now."

"Are you getting some relief?"

"Carol will be by later. Tomorrow, we have an appointment with the oncologist. I hope we get good news."

"I hope so." Skip reached for his coat. "Well, I'm off. I'll look this over today, while I've got time. I'll cycle back."

"You should contact Bill. He's more knowledgeable. Then again, there's Mother. If she continues looking up, she'll want a voice."

"Of course. Let me see what suggestions I've got, and we'll go from there."

As Skip opened the door, Janet materialized.

"I wanted to stop while I was out. I hope I'm not interrupting."

"Heavens, no. Skip's just leaving. It's like Grand Central."

Skip said hello and goodbye as he headed out.

"How is Bernice?"

"Actually, remarkably good. Skip stopped for the estate materials. She really warmed up. You would never know on Friday—" Beverly stopped, a lump caught in her throat.

"There, there, dear. It's going to be all right. I sense it." Janet reached over and gave Beverly's forearm a quick squeeze.

"I know, it's just so much, so fast." Tears suddenly ran down Beverly's cheeks. Janet pulled an ever-present tissue from her purse. "It's clean," she murmured. Beverly smiled, dabbing the tissue at her eyes.

"I could cry at any moment. I'm so on edge."

Janet nodded, "I remember that feeling. When I went through the change, I always felt like my emotions could unexplainably burst out any time, any place."

Beverly smiled, "Yes, that's it. She can be so harsh at times, and then she goes and does what she did on Friday. I just don't understand."

"None of us do, but she's here now. It sounds like she's doing well—all things considered." Janet reached again into her purse. "I didn't want to raise this Saturday night, but I found this—" she revealed *The Hemlock Society* booklet, "on Bernice's bed Friday evening. I was changing the sheets and it fell out."

Beverly took the booklet. "Well, I'll be."

"What people publish motivates crazy ideas."

"I wonder where she got it. Regardless, can you take it? I don't want it in the house."

"Are you certain? I don't want Bernice thinking—"

"I doubt she'll be asking about it. Please."

Moments later, Bernice looked up as the women walked into her bedroom. She stared at Janet, mentally placing the face with a name.

"What? You didn't hear? I didn't die. I won't be needing the services of the church just yet. Thank you."

"Bernice, it's so good to see you," Janet smiled as Beverly frowned.

"I believe in drama. Go out with a bang." Bernice paused. "But I couldn't find a gun."

"Please, Mother. Stop. That is just not funny. You scared us to d—"

"What? Cat got your tongue?" Bernice abruptly stopped. "Where are the cats? I've not seen them for—" She thought long and hard. The women watched as realization dawned.

"The cats were with me." She hesitated, her eyes getting teary. "Did they—"

Beverly's eyes also filled as she wordlessly nodded.

"Oh my God. Really?"

"It wasn't your fault, Bernice. You weren't thinking straight. The cats simply followed."

"Oh dear Lord."

"Mother, what's done is done."

"Oh, shit." A lone tear slipped down Bernice's pale, wrinkled skin. "I'll be damned. I really screwed the pooch on that one Friday night, didn't I?" Another tear followed the wet trail of the first.

Janet leaned forward, "Things happen. It's certainly not what you planned, but you pulled through. And we're praying for your continued recovery."

"Shit." Bernice took off her glasses, settled back into the pillows and closed her eyes. Janet and Beverly watched.

"I suppose I'll be going. I'll stop again soon." Bernice said nothing.

The two women returned to the first floor silently.

"I'm so sorry that came up. We didn't know how to tell her. I hope this isn't a setback."

"Dear, she'll weather the loss. We need to keep propping her up. She will grieve and move forward."

"I hope so, Janet."

"You could see a little of her spunk up there, before the subject of the cats came up."

"We haven't seen that in weeks. Maybe months." Beverly thought more. "Funny how an attempt on her life could actually in some odd way help her recovery. I hope it continues."

"I pray that it does. Something good will come of Friday."

"Goddamn cats," Bernice uttered as Beverly returned to sit in the chair opposite the bed. "I can't believe the goddamn cats followed me into the car."

"They did what's normal. They shadowed you."

"I killed them."

"Revisiting this isn't going to bring them back."

"I damn well know that. It just pisses me off . . . Where are they?"

"Bill disposed of them. He dropped them off with the vet yesterday."

"Not just the trash?"

"No, of course not."

"Good," Bernice sighed. "You know, it wasn't my time to go. Not yet."

"No, hopefully not for quite some time."

"No, not yet. That's for sure."

"Can I get you anything?"

"Perhaps some crackers. Something with a little taste. Not just Saltines. Can you find something?"

"Well, I'll see what I can rustle up," smiled Beverly.

"You do that. I'll be right here." Bernice stared at her daughter-in-law's back as she exited. Another tear formed as she watched the empty doorway for a long time. The tear initiated a stream from each eye that continued as the clock in the front hall chimed four o'clock.

FORTY

Thursday dawned cold and gray. The air hung heavily as forecasters again predicted significant snowfall. Beverly had stayed overnight once more. When Bill and the kids ate dinner Wednesday at Fox Den, the kids shyly greeted BeBe, though they were even less talkative than was their norm. The suicide attempt took BeBe to a place they didn't understand.

Bernice ate a small serving of the casserole Beverly made for the family. She nibbled part of a biscuit as well. She was denied a glass of wine ("You have a doctor's appointment tomorrow; let's hold off tonight"). Bernice started to protest but decided against taking up the battle.

Wednesday evening, Carol had called apologizing for not stopping at the Langdons' that day and agreeing to swing by Thursday when Bernice returned from the doctor.

Beverly and Bernice sat in Dr. Esch's waiting room. When they first arrived, a nurse ushered them to the lab for bloodwork and then a CT scan.

Beverly flipped distractedly through an old *Redbook*. Bernice stared straight ahead. Time passed slowly as the wall clock continued its journey. When called shortly before ten o'clock, Bernice and Beverly traipsed through the labyrinthine maze to a tiny, windowless space strongly smelling of disinfectant. A nurse practitioner took vitals and asked routine questions. Bernice answered with minimal energy that things were fine, chemo was dandy, and she had recently begun eating from a trough. "Mother!" Beverly exasperatedly interjected and then volunteered more pertinent facts for the nurse. No one mentioned Friday night.

At ten fifteen, they entered Dr. Esch's book-lined office.

"Good morning, Bernice. And Beverly, so good to see you both," he smiled. "I see from the notes that you are doing better since last we spoke. I'm hoping you've turned a corner."

"Me too," nodded Bernice.

"I hear you created some excitement on Friday," cited Dr. Esch, watching Bernice closely.

"I tried to off myself, if you consider that exciting," Bernice stared at the young physician.

"Now just why would you do that? We're past the halfway point. You're in the homestretch."

"It just felt right," responded Bernice. "Though I sense it wasn't my time.

Not yet."

"Well, I think not. I'm glad you didn't succeed."

"I'm usually quite successful in what I undertake," Bernice sat up straighter. "I was foiled."

"I'm glad."

"As are we," Beverly affirmed. "How are Mother's reports?"

"We don't have all the reports back yet, but I do have some preliminaries from this morning. Given the research funding, we're able to get downloads pretty quickly online. I know I kept you waiting–"

"We've been here since eight. It's now ten thirty. You know, if I kept a class waiting that long . . . well, they wouldn't have been there to greet me on arrival. You physicians–playing God with us lowly patients . . . "

"It's great to see your spirit coming back. I like that. You must be feeling better. I know we're in mid-cycle, but it's a good sign. Give me as much grief as you want." Dr. Esch smiled at the women.

"So? What's the news?"

"It's good. In fact, it's very good. The initial reports show no sign of cancer. That is actually remarkable, given your case and the specific characteristics of your adenocarcinoma. At this point, we see no recurrence. I believe Dr. Gerhart got it all, and the chemo is working. I couldn't be more delighted."

"The bloodwork too?"

"All very consistent. There is residual oxygen deficiency, but I suspect that this is due to Friday night."

"I wanted to give you something to talk about. Couldn't have a completely clean bill of health, now could I?" Bernice smirked.

Jeremy laughed. "I suppose not. The carbon monoxide exposure clearly impacted the O-two numbers significantly, but I suspect you're on the uptick. If we tested again later today or tomorrow, we'd see an increase. I'm not especially alarmed. But hey–"

Bernice looked at him over the top of her ever-sliding glasses, "Yes?" she uttered with a gravelly tone.

"Don't go sittin' in any more cars with a hose piping in the exhaust, okay? It's not good for my test results."

"Well, if that's all I've got to worry about, I imagine I can keep myself clear."

Beverly couldn't decide whose comments proved more alarming: Bernice or her physician, but she held her tongue.

"I'm pleased with how you're doing. I know chemo can be debilitating, and you've still got more, but you're doing well. Keep focused on the goal. Even when it's really tough." Dr. Esch looked across his desk, riveted on Bernice.

"I'll try, Doc. It's been hell. A real battle, but hearing that we're winning is promising."

"Do you think Mother will need the entire duration? That takes us out through early May."

"Hard to say. For the time being, I'd continue, even though I recognize how draining it is. You had such an aggressive malignancy, that–even with promising results at this stage–I'd like to ensure we put up a real wall against future metastases."

"I get it. I don't like it, but I hear you."

"We'll see where we stand in another couple of months. By mid-March, we'll have another four rounds of chemo behind us and–"

"Stop with the royal us. No one else is doing chemo in this room, save me. I'm the one having four more infusions of poison. I'm the one dealing with the side effects."

"Touché, Bernice. You will have completed four more rounds. If we continue to see the results we're seeing now, we may choose to end sooner. It's three parts art, one part science as to when precisely we conclude."

"Now I'm an arteeste! For God's sake, perhaps I should cut off an ear!" quipped Bernice.

The oncologist laughed. "You are certainly one of the most unique patients I've ever enjoyed."

"Well, I hope so. I am one-of-a-kind," Bernice parried back. "And did you hear? Now I have a therapist; I'm so trendy."

"Mother, it's an outpatient caseworker."

"Caseworker? Therapist? We argue over such trivialities . . . "

Beverly simply shrugged and looked to the physician for guidance. He shook his head. "Bernice, hang in there. My schedule is such that I should be able to see you more consistently looking forward than in this first stretch. I'd give you the run of why, but . . . "

"No harm, Doc. I'm still kicking."

"Good for you. I'm feeling excellent about your case and your prognosis. For now, I think we're done . . . unless you have any more questions."

"I do have one," Bernice winked at Beverly. "How do you feel about wine these days?"

Jeremy grinned. "I believe I know where this is going. I like a good cabernet. California, Napa. But, regarding you and wine, I think–if you have an appetite for it, a bit in moderation is probably fine. It's not something we've studied, but there's no reason to expect a bad interaction between your meds and alcohol. But Bernice, at this point, no more than one modest glass daily. Period. Your organs will be too quickly stressed with more."

"Thank you, Doc," Bernice slightly bowed her head and lifted her hand, palm raised in his direction, while looking at Beverly. "I wanted us all on the same page. I do enjoy a splash of the grape occasionally."

"Just not the whole barrel. Not even a whole bottle. A modest glass, at most. No make-ups for days missed either."

Bernice grinned wickedly, "You know my devious ways, Doc."

Finally, Beverly smiled as well. "So be it, Mother."

The ride home proved uneventful. Bernice even insisted they stop at Wegmans for a few things including some flavored crackers and frozen yogurt. They continued homeward, listening to classical music on the local radio station. The excursion had been good.

FORTY-ONE

Late Thursday, Beverly placed a round of calls inviting the others to a Sunday potluck dinner. They could visit with Bernice on the eve of her next treatment.

Though she quickly received RSVPs from Janet and Carol, the men proved more elusive. Elaine wasn't convinced that Roger should be out for another school night. Additionally, the Gallos typically enjoyed family dinner together on Sundays.

Skip was concerned about his workload. The partner group was meeting on Monday to discuss the candidacies of the men running for managing partner. After carefully weighing the pros and cons with a colleague and with Amy, he had chosen not to tender his name. However, the decision on who should next lead the firm weighed heavily. Regardless of outcome, he knew the week would be intense. Losing an evening of preparation and family time didn't feel viable.

Rusty said no. When he received Beverly's call, he had a strong visceral reaction to the notion of reconvening. While he couldn't dismiss the unusual string of coincidences, the idea of another "night in the 'burbs" held no appeal. He planned to party this weekend; no more monopolizing his discretionary time with Bernice. Though unspoken with Beverly, he anticipated being in full recovery mode on Sunday. Furthermore, all the others–except Roger – seemed related to the sender. He saw no meaningful connection.

Friday morning, Elaine let Beverly know that Roger, surprisingly, insisted on attending. "What can he bring?" she inquired as the conversation ended.

Neither Skip nor Rusty sent any word all day Friday.

* * *

When Rusty awoke Saturday, the cold light of another gray January day streamed through his windows, as he'd left the shades up. He looked across the dark skin of the guy's chest sleeping soundly next to him. He smiled as he recalled the prior evening. Meeting Drew at the Railroad, going to the Sanctuary, and then coming home for a nightcap. *'And my head doesn't even hurt that bad. Sweet,'* he thought, listening to Drew's steady breathing.

Rusty slid out of bed and headed to the kitchen. As he reached the door, he glanced at his monitor, where a message streamed via his continuous DSL connection to the internet. He reversed course and walked over.

JOIN 1ST CIRCLE   STOP 1 NIGHTS   COMMIT

"Ah, fuck," he muttered quietly. As he watched, the border burst into flame–the perimeter jumping with animation as the warm, golden-red flickers of the deep beyond boldly framed the increasingly rapid scroll.

"I cannot believe this." He shook his head.

"What's up, Dude?" Drew propped himself up on the pillows. "Whatcha lookin' at?"

"Ahh, nothing . . . You want coffee?"

"I like mine tan," Drew grinned. "And hot."

Rusty laughed. "I like it black."

"Well, why don't you get some?" Drew flashed his white teeth, contrasting sharply with his dark brown skin.

Rusty turned, but then recalled the message. "Shit." He paused. "I think I'll put the coffee on, bro. I could use a little wake-up java."

"Suit yourself. I'll be here."

In the kitchen, Rusty collected his thoughts. The most important message immediately preceded Bernice's suicide attempt. The messages saved her, however unbelievable. Now when they should be done, a new one arrives. Worst of all, it referenced the exact phrase–First Circle–Beverly laughingly mentioned on Thursday.

"I was thinking we should all get together. Something easy: a potluck. You know, we've become Mother's 'First Circle' of support. Won't you join us?"

With no doubt, he was being summoned. Rusty wondered if the messages would ever terminate. As the coffeemaker gurgled to life, one of his apartment mates joined him.

"Hey, sounded like you scored last night . . . "

Rusty smiled, "Man, keep your voice down."

Eric laughed. "So, where is he?"

"Lounging. I'm gettin' coffee."

"Can I grab a cup?"

"Sure. Let me get two first."

"Whatcha up to today? I was thinking about a movie. Couple good ones playing at the Astoria."

"Maybe. I may go out to the 'burbs this evening."

"You hanging with that church group again?"

"Not exactly a church group. But, yeah, it's the bunch that saved that old professor from doing herself in."

"I can't get over that. How'd you end up there?"

"It's a long story, and—well, it just happened."

"Cool. You don't want to say, don't. Must be some hot—"

"Hey, are you bringing that coffee or not, bro?" Drew appeared in the doorway wrapped in a towel and wet from an obvious shower. "Oh, 'scuse me, didn't know we had company."

"No sweat. This is Eric—it's his crib too. We were just starting up some chow."

"Nice meetin' you. Be right back," Drew responded.

A short time later, the three enjoyed a leisurely brunch and Drew departed. Rusty showered and returned to his computer where the message still scrolled, and the burning frame lingered, though looking more like long-standing fireplace embers.

'Commitment again: what's that all about?' mused Rusty. *'I know I move around a lot, but I've stayed at Ridgewell quite a while.'* He unsuccessfully tried to avoid considering his rather fluid relationships. *'That's what this is about. Shit. I don't want to hear it. I get enough of that from Mom.'*

He sat watching the streaming words. "*STOP 1 NIGHTS*: there's only one interpretation." He thought again of last night and got the same warm sensation at his core. "Shit," he said aloud.

After a long time watching in a near-hypnotic trance, he compromised. "Okay, I'll join the group tomorrow. Beyond that, well, we'll see . . . " To ensure he didn't lose momentum, he left Beverly a voicemail indicating he would join the so-called First Circle. He would bring wine.

* * *

Skip and Amy woke early Saturday. She leaned over and ran her hand down his chest. She tickled his abs and gave him a quick peck on the lips. Kissing her back, he brought his hand to her breast, cupping it through the warm flannel of her nightgown.

"Only the sexiest for my hubby," she smiled.

"Oh, I think it's plenty sexy," he softly murmured. Amy's hand lightly ran along his torso, as his caress became more intentional.

"Plans for today?" Skip asked as they lay in bed later.

"I've got papers to grade."

"Already? The semester barely started."

"I know, but I like to assess where we're starting from."

"'Where we're starting from?' And you're the English prof?" Skip grinned.

Laughing, Amy smacked a pillow across his chest. "You . . . I'm off duty. Give me a break." She paused, "You still feeling good about the decision?"

"Yes, it's the right call. I've got more than enough to do with my clients even without Amalgamated."

"You know we would've supported it either way."

"I know, hon. I worry about the firm's well-being as we navigate this stretch. I imagine we're in for a stressful run."

"Just keep your sanity. We need that! You would, of course, be awesome as the managing partner."

"I think so, but I have a bias . . . "

"Not me. As objective as the day is long."

"Days are pretty short around now."

Amy laughed. "No way, sir."

After breakfast, Skip reviewed the Langdon paperwork. He drafted recommendations integrating input from Beverly and Bill. By noon, he finished and once again considered Beverly's invitation. Over lunch of yogurt and fruit, he raised the dinner proposition with Amy.

"Well, I think you should go," she responded without hesitation.

"Really? I'm surprised. I was merely a bystander last Friday."

"You were there, and like the others, you've been getting messages from—it sounds like—David. While unimaginable and anyone else would think we'd lost our minds, who else could send them? It is beyond nature and certainly outside this world."

"You're starting to sound like Nancy Reagan or something."

Amy smiled broadly, "Give me a different explanation."

"So why Roger and Rusty? They don't have a link."

"You just haven't found it. That's all. It'll show up."

"But I have a brutal week coming up. I may be out late. I hate spending time away on something like this."

"This is family. It's your brother. You always say you wish you'd had more time. Maybe this is a way of getting it."

Despite worries over his coming week, Skip acquiesced and became the second affirmative voicemail Beverly received. When she listened to them both, a warm tingling filled her: the First Circle was reconvening and that just felt right.

* * *

The First Circle came together shortly before six o'clock. Once again, cars lined the curb and Beverly's van sat in the driveway. Snow had fallen during the early morning hours, recoating everything with four more inches of white powder. Earlier in the day, Beverly placed hospitality candles in each window facing the street. Unnoticed by Bernice, the little white flickering candles filled each of the nine windows.

Bill, Brad, and Caitlyn joined the group, though Carol declined Beverly's suggestion that she bring Jay and the kids.

"No way. This is my evening out! Jay is making some bachelor surprise. Heaven only knows what that is, but he and the kids have their 'Mom's Away' favorites. Let them (and me!) have our fun," chuckled Carol.

Buffet style, the group circled the island to take servings from the colorful array of dishes. The mixed aromas of honey-baked ham, vegetable-stuffed cornbread ("Sorry, it's leftover from the church supper"), macaroni and cheese, spinach salad, and warm crescent rolls filled the room. Hearty conversation and laughter bubbled merrily. Knowing one another better, they more easily poked fun at each other–at least, the men and Carol.

In the dining room, all nine bowed their heads in prayer. No one seemed ready to take the lead after Janet politely declined, so Beverly asked Caitlyn to start the family prayer, to which all joined smoothly.

God is great, God is good.
Let us thank Him for our food.
By His Hand, we all are fed.
Thank you Lord for daily bread. Amen.

Conversation quickly resumed the same familiarity and rhythm from the kitchen. Skip and Rusty were first up for seconds, joined by Bill.

"You know, I think I'll see if Mom wants anything. I'll bet she can smell it upstairs."

"No doubt. How's she doing?"

"Pretty well. I'm amazed. It's been just over a week since she –uh, well . . . " Bill got suddenly tongue-tied. "She sure seems to be doing okay. I'm no doctor, but the news this week was good. The caseworker also is upbeat–though decidedly more circumspect, not knowing my mom or us very well."

"That's great news on both fronts."

"Pretty cool that she's coming back around," Rusty nodded as Bill left the kitchen.

"Sure is. I didn't know if she'd make it after last Friday."

"Me neither. She looked dead."

"You did a nice job on CPR."

"Not a skill I want to use often. I learned at work. They wanted someone trained on each floor. I guess I drew the short straw."

"The Langdons are glad you did."

As Rusty and Skip returned to the table, Bill appeared with Bernice on his arm. Clearly, Bernice had spent a few minutes cleaning up. A bright blue-and-white scarf covered her bald head. Her glasses appeared clear, the omnipresent smudges eliminated. She wore a dark blue robe, with her initials embroidered; her slippers were soft deerskin slip-ons. The group quieted as she entered but then warmly greeted her.

Bernice at last held up her hand. "Thank you. I should sit."

"Of course." Beverly moved her chair providing easy access to the head of the table. Bernice slowly lowered herself. Her gaze fell on each dinner party attendee one by one.

She smiled wickedly. "Well, I'm not lookin' at the brown side of the grass just yet." She paused. "And it's thanks to you." Again she stopped. The group, particularly Roger and her grandchildren, twitched uncomfortably.

"And, I am grateful," she said with a long sigh. "Truly." The group around the table beamed.

"I'm not the best at thank-yous, but . . . " Bernice stopped and looked around again. Her eyes welled up, as did Beverly's and Janet's.

"It's good to be here. This isn't easy. Chemo is hell, and there's more coming."

"But you're handling it . . . "

"And the word is good. Your reports are looking up," Carol added energetically.

"For that, I'm grateful. This bloody war would not be worth it otherwise. This is not something I'd wish on anyone. This damn poison is enough to kill y—" Bernice let out a small chuckle, "Well, I guess it nearly did, huh?"

No one quite knew how to respond and just continued staring at the aging professor. Bernice looked down the table and spied the bottle of red wine tucked between Rusty and Skip.

"I'd like a glass please," she flipped her hand regally.

Rusty blushed, "Do you think it's okay to—"

Bill interrupted, "A fair question, but the doc has said 'in moderation.' So, Mom, if you'd like a glass, I believe we could persuade Rusty to pour you one."

Rusty obliged and poured a generous glass of cabernet.

"Oh, I don't know. That may be too much," cautioned Beverly.

"Nonsense, I've not been to a party for some time. Let's live like we're dying," quipped Bernice.

Beverly shook her head, as Bernice took her first long, slow swig of the wine proffered. "Very nice, son. Very nice, indeed."

The group sat expectantly, awaiting Bernice's direction. When she realized the cause for silence, she prodded, "Well, you were having a fine time before I showed up. Carry on. By all means."

Nothing of great consequence was shared, until well into dessert: a decadent Death by Chocolate cake. Rusty, Skip, and Carol anchored one end of the table, enabling them to more easily share the red wine; they were well into a second bottle. Rusty's face in particular was becoming more flushed.

"I still haven't figured out a connection."

"What's that?" Skip looked more closely at Rusty.

"You know–why I'm here."

"My wife feels certain it will show up."

"Is she a medium or something?"

"Hardly, she just has a feeling."

Others in the group sensed the dialogue shift. Bill, Caitlyn, and Brad moved to the living room. Bernice sat quietly sipping her wine.

"I figured out mine," piped up Roger. "My parents helped."

"More than the proctor?" nodded Beverly expectantly.

"Tell us." With the group's encouragement, Roger divulged the relationship to his second cousins' father, Uncle David. Concluding, he blushed, "Like I said, we're not tight with my dad's family even though they live in the area."

"Some families are like that," agreed Janet.

"That just puts the nail in the coffin," observed Carol. "Oh–" Now, she reddened, "A rather awkward phrase . . . "

All eyes turned to Bernice who appeared unfazed. "I've heard of death before. It's not new. I've got some experience." She sipped her red wine and waved for the group to continue; they needed little persuasion.

"So now all of you have a relationship with David, except me," Rusty grimaced. "I don't get it."

"But you're getting messages, same as us," pointed out Beverly.

Inquisitively, Bernice raised an eyebrow, "Messages?"

"It's a long tale. I'm happy to share it, but . . . " began Beverly.

"I like stories. Give me the abridged version."

Though Beverly started, others quickly chimed in, adding their own anecdotes. Twenty minutes later, Bernice raised her hand.

"So, you all believe you're receiving messages from some unknown sender . . . in some remarkably unusual ways." The group nodded. "And you think this man," she pointed at Skip, "his late brother is sending them from beyond the grave?" The group nodded vigorously.

"And you think I'm crazy? You should all be committed!"

"It's pretty remarkable, but not otherwise explainable," Skip responded.

"But why? Why are you getting messages?"

"Our hypothesis? They're being sent to help you. All of us have gotten communications in some form to help you through a tough time." Skip concluded as Bernice listened intently.

"Why wouldn't this 'person'–as it were–send messages directly to me?"

"How? In all truth, you've been too sick to be receiving messages."

"Perhaps, but still . . . " Bernice's gravelly grumble acknowledged Skip's logic.

"Plus, Dr. L, if you needed help, you needed others, not just you." Carol nodded aggressively.

"Maybe . . . "

"I don't see my link," Rusty retread old ground. He'd finished another glass of wine and refilled as he spoke. "I don't have any tie to this guy."

"You know, Rusty, I've been thinking about that." Janet, long quiet, spoke up. "David was quite a singer. He was in our church choir for years."

"He loved music. Especially classical and show tunes," commented Skip.

"I recall him being in an outside choral group. Beyond the church."

"I sing," acknowledged Rusty.

"I know. That's where we met," agreed Janet. "What's your group's name?"

"The Metropolitan Men's Choir."

"Why, that's it. That's where David sang. Weekly rehearsals. Lots of concerts," Skip enthused. "That's where you two connected."

"I don't remember him."

"It's got to be."

"When was he in the choir?" Rusty asked.

"For years."

"Really? But when?"

"Let's see. He died in April '01." Skip reflected, "I don't think he participated after his diagnosis. He probably stopped in 2000. Maybe even late '99."

"There you have it," Rusty took another big swig. "I tried out in mid-2000, but didn't get selected until late in the year. They bring new people in just after the Christmas concert season. I started in January or February, two years ago. 2001."

"I thought we had it," Skip sagged as did the others.

"I don't think we met there," Rusty punctuated his statement with more wine and stabbed the table forcefully with his index finger. "We don't have it. Maybe it's just not there."

"If the rest of us have a connection, you certainly do. We've just not found it," Janet added with great sincerity. "I'm sure we will. Like Skip's wife, I have a feeling."

Bernice continued listening but said little else. She thought about her vision in the car, which clearly was related. She hadn't thought of David in years. Suddenly, he was thrust back into her life again. She needed to ponder this odd coincidence on her own. Delightedly, she'd have something to think about during chemo; she grimaced at the thought. Watching her, Beverly worried, as she saw a frown pass across her mother-in-law's countenance.

An hour or so later, after more dessert, red wine, and decaf coffee, the party drew to a close.

"You okay to drive?" Beverly looked at Rusty.

"Ahhhh, sure thing," Rusty growled playfully. "Ain't nothin'."

"Be careful," Beverly warned. "We have to watch out for each other."

"No sweat. I will exercise great caution on the roads of our fair city," Rusty stepped out the door with great exaggeration and nearly slipped off the front stoop. "Watch your step on the first one; it's a real beaut." He laughed as he slightly staggered toward the Miata.

"I worry about him," observed Carol, donning her parka.

"Such a fine young man," noted Janet.

"I just hope he's a safe young man," nodded Carol.

Bernice insisted that Beverly and Bill sleep in their own bed. She was fine; they need not babysit her. Despite some concern, the two decided it felt safe to do, though Beverly poured out–unnoticed–the remainder of the third bottle of red wine that was largely untouched. Much as she hated such waste, she didn't want temptation lingering.

The twinkling candles in Bernice's windows illuminated another long, cold January night, conveying the warmth and inviting hospitality which grew in the house.

FORTY-TWO

Monday dawned with windchill temperatures dipping well below zero. Bernice awoke early. A sense of foreboding sat heavily with her. She contemplated another round of chemo and reflected on the events of the past ten days. David O'Neill's ghost seemed to haunt the prior evening's dinner party. Curiously, all these unrelated people were finding links with a dead man. Unbeknownst to the group, she too shared a link.

"Must be a coincidence," she harrumphed quietly, though a small smile crossed her face fleetingly. "Even so, it's a nice memory."

She stalled a little longer under the warmth of the covers. For some reason—even with chemo ahead, she didn't feel as ill. She focused on moving forward. New spirit breathed energy to climb the mountain, break through the wall of chemo, and get to the other side. The thought of ending her life rapidly receded, even though chemo was far from over. Again she spoke aloud, "Odd. No reason whatsoever to feel any differently."

She slowly sat upright. The rush of blood made her lightheaded for a moment. With reluctance, she trudged to the bathroom. *'Perhaps today won't be so bad,'* she thought. *'Maybe I'm on an uptick.'*

Shortly after ten o'clock, the doorbell rang. Leaving her cup of tea in the kitchen, she labored to the door.

"Where the hell have you been?" she growled as she opened it.

"Good to see you too, Bernice," smiled Albert. "May I?" He stepped in without waiting for a response. He doffed his cap—a rather stylish black beret—and pulled off his scarf and earmuffs.

"You staying?"

"In fact, I am—for a few minutes. I just got back in town. St. Kitt's, you know." He looked closely at his former colleague.

"What are you staring at?" Bernice snapped.

"I heard." The tanned, silver-haired professor paused. "I was shocked. How could you?"

Bernice smirked. "How could I? Be bold. Go out with a statement."

Albert huffed. "I couldn't believe it."

"It's been a tough haul. Goddamn chemo takes the life out of you. I wouldn't wish this on anyone." Bernice hesitated but couldn't avoid a small, but wicked grin. "Then again, I would consider—"

Albert interrupted, "Say no more. I brought biscuits. Shall we have a spot of tea?"

"I just made some." The two retreated to the kitchen.

"You never could make a decent cup of tea, Bernice. What do you have here?" Albert went looking in her cupboards. "This is it? What sort of selection is this?"

"Didn't know I was entertaining this morning. Otherwise, I'd've baked a cake." Bernice savored each word sarcastically as she sat at the table.

"I would expect nothing less, though your culinary skills rival your tea-making."

Bernice laughed for the first time in many weeks.

"When is your next treatment?"

"This afternoon. This is about the best I'll feel for some time, I imagine." Bernice shuddered involuntarily. "This really has been rather ghastly—far worse than I imagined."

Albert reached over and rubbed Bernice's hands. "I can only begin to understand. What a battle. Is the news promising?"

"Actually, yes. My doc says the cancer appears to be in remission."

"That's simply wonderful."

"The regimen is largely prophylactic at this point. No one knows for sure what's going on."

"How long will this—"

"'Til the spring. Originally they said six months. If things remain good, they may stop earlier." Bernice paused, before grinning devilishly, "I'm looking forward to my girlish good looks returning."

Albert guffawed. "You!" He exclaimed, gazing at the gaunt, bald-headed woman.

"Hard to imagine getting all that back but here's hopin'." Bernice raised her teacup. They clinked cups and silently sipped.

"Where are Tigger and Spider? I was sure they'd have come—"

"Gone. Dead. Buried. I killed them. Unintentionally. Trying to off one's self, in this case, had collateral damage."

Albert looked crestfallen. "I'm so sorry."

"Me too. I miss them. I've not been much company lately, but they provided some movement in the house."

Albert wordlessly shook his well-coiffed head.

"Move on. You have to." Bernice sipped more tea. Albert nibbled on a biscuit, which Bernice declined. The two colleagues spoke until Bernice started looking fatigued.

"I must be off," Albert stood. "You could probably use a little downtime before your date. You have a way of getting there?"

"Yes, Beverly is taking me. She's been a big support." Bernice stood up slowly. "Thank you for stopping. I know I don't always tell you, but–"

"Stop. I am unaccustomed to niceties between us. This is hardly the time to start. Perhaps when I next take you to St. Kitt's. It's lovely this time of year."

"I just–"

Albert shook his head vigorously, "I understand and you needn't say anything. I feel badly that I've been so absent."

During chemo that afternoon, Bernice closed her eyes routinely. Seated adjacent, Beverly feigned interest in a magazine. The poisonous cocktail coursing into Bernice's veins yielded an especially graphic vision–nearly hallucinogenic in clarity and vivid color. The neon hues of the fluids created a vibrant roadmap of her body's circulatory system. As she watched, fascinated, the bloodlines morphed into pathways and she found herself floating along one of them.

She traveled in slow motion, yet the neon walkway accelerated ahead. Concurrently, her feet felt locked in quicksand impeding rapid progress. She wondered whether she could lift her eyelids, but as quickly as the thought entered, it left.

Suddenly, she floated in a new place: a grassy courtyard where a series of buildings beckoned at the end of a pathway. They could be low-rise office buildings or an elegant housing complex–perhaps condos or apartments. No people seemed to populate any of this space, she realized, as she navigated the courtyard. *'Where am I?'* she wondered dreamily.

The place looked recognizable, but she failed to identify it. It wasn't a place she'd been, she was fairly certain, and yet, it felt familiar. Everything seemed strangely comfortable and inviting. A particular set of doors in one of the buildings drew her. She drifted toward them, as if blown by a gentle breeze. The doors opened and a kaleidoscope of doorways, rooms, hallways, and furnishings starburst before her. Intertwined amongst them, unrecognizable faces emerged. The people smiled, but, as with photographs that fade with time, these faces dissolved into the constant movement of the space.

Floating through this house of illusions, Bernice had no choices. A personal trade wind, earmarked by color and viscosity, nudged her forward. As she progressed further into the building, the intensity of the colors changed. Neon transitioned into bolder reds, oranges, golds, and yellows. They flickered and shimmered. *'Like being consumed in a beautiful fire of light,'* she speculated. She was drawn by the fire toward double doors and drifted–like a living ember– into a room filled with empty chairs around a table. Each chair carried an elegant carved letter: *D, B, W,* and three question marks. Toward the front of the room a brighter, white light glowed. Involuntarily, she was pulled toward this brilliant incandescence.

As she moved closer, she realized a figure created the light. A man, cloaked in brilliant white garments, stood with one hand resting on the *D* chair. With the other, he reached out. She realized this was the same presence from ten days earlier. Yet, his face—while familiar—was clouded, partially hidden by light and mist—just like in the car. She felt she knew him, but like the surroundings, she couldn't name him. The man—an older man—smiled warmly.

'Am I dying?' Bernice thought. *'The light?'*

The man shook his head, clearly yet kindly. "Not yet, Bernice," he mouthed insistently. She could see his facial features more clearly. "It's not your time. You have more to do."

"What am I to do?" Bernice scrutinized his features and his movements for some sign. None was forthcoming. Rather, he exuded warmth and care, a great kindness and love. Bernice tried to move closer, to more fully inspect his profile and face, to clear the fog with her hand, but found she was frozen. The prior breeze had evaporated. And with its disappearance, so had her ability to move. She desperately wanted to understand both the man's identity and his message.

Time stood still. After an enjoyably long, yet immensely frustrating period, Bernice found herself moving toward a different corner of the room. Looking back, the illuminated man watched and lingered. The room gradually faded into the earlier colors of fire. First, the outside edges of the room erupted in flame—glittering and sashaying in sparkling reds and oranges. The borders relentlessly consumed the room as Bernice watched. The fiery mix of vibrant colors comprising the room faded away. She closed her eyes to the light, just as she felt the tube being pulled from her arm.

"Dr. Langdon?" the medical technician touched Bernice gently. "You dozed off. We're already done."

Beverly looked over. "Mother, your eyes are watering. Is everything okay?"

"Yes, I'm fine. I just—" Bernice stopped. She wasn't sure what to make of her dream. It was so real, so vivid. She felt sad leaving the vision, but thankfully, the chemo proved more tolerable. At least, so far. They rode home quietly, as was their norm. Interpreting the vision riveted Bernice unlike the usual dread she felt awaiting the first waves of nausea. Nearly an hour passed at home before the rising tsunami began hitting the shores. Apparently, the man of light was powerless to stop the repercussions of chemo's physical assault.

Beverly stayed until Carol arrived. They alternated getting cool washcloths and lukewarm, fizzless fluids to bring Bernice some relief. Bernice said little the remainder of the week. Beverly got the clear impression that her mother-in-law focused elsewhere. She prayed it wasn't on suicide.

* * *

Beverly and Caitlyn stayed Friday night—as the side effects continued to wreak havoc. On Saturday morning, Caitlyn answered the doorbell. Albert stepped across the threshold just as Beverly entered the foyer.

"How is she? She was due for another round of chemo . . . " Albert trailed off.

"She's resting. Chemo weeks are hard. This one was critical, as the last time, well . . . " Beverly looked at Caitlyn. Albert noted the glance and nodded.

"Of course. I thought it might be prudent to hold off a day or two before stopping by."

"She'll be delighted to hear you stopped by. I can see if she's—" A sharp meow coming from Albert's bag interrupted.

"It's a kitten. I can see it," yelped Caitlyn, spying the screened opening of the pet carrier.

"Oh, I don't know if—"

"Nonsense. I heard that Bernice lost her cats. I know how much they meant to her."

"I just don't know that she's ready for a new one." Albert's forwardness annoyed Beverly, despite knowing how much her mother-in-law enjoyed him. "She was not doing much to care for the others before—" Again, Beverly stopped uncomfortably.

"I propose we see what Bernice thinks."

"Thinks about what?" came a strident and remarkably strong voice from the top of the stairs.

"Oh, you're up. Albert stopped by."

"He's seen me in my robe before. Send him up. He doesn't bite."

Caitlyn giggled. Beverly pointed toward the stairs and Albert, still wearing his outer garments, ascended with the cat in tow. Caitlyn and Beverly followed.

"I see you've brought company." Bernice pointed at the carrier. "What's that?"

"I sensed you could use a new companion." Albert lifted a very hesitant gray kitten. "Meet Bernice, my good sir," Albert dramatically made introductions.

"Oh, he's a cutie," purred Bernice with a gravelly undertone.

"BeBe, what're you going to name him?"

"Albert, have you named him?"

"That's up to you."

"Caitlyn, what do you think?"

"He's kinda invisible, you know. He blends in with his gray fur, sort of like a ghost. Maybe you should name him Ghost."

"That's morbid. Please, something more appropriate," Beverly cautioned with dismay.

Bernice held the gray kitten close to her face, looking deep into his eyes. He stared back. "Good idea, but I'm not sure about a Ghost in the house. What about Spirit? Same idea, better name."

"Spirit? I rather like it. It's got some life to it, shall we say?"

"I don't know. What about Boots? Or, Snickers? Or, Shadow?" Beverly stammered. "What about–"

Bernice interrupted, "Spirit it is. I like it. Spirit, come to bed." And with that Bernice led the entourage back to her bedroom, still shadowed from the drawn curtains. She tossed Spirit through the air. He rolled onto the bed and immediately dove under the covers, seeking the lingering body warmth. "The Spirit has landed." Bernice paused and looked at Beverly. "Perhaps a spot of tea for our party?"

"You're feeling up to it?"

"In fact, I am, thank you." Bernice looked directly at Beverly who stood considering the request. "Please."

Beverly shook her head as she stepped from the room. While delighted to see Bernice feeling better and happy to make tea, the naming of the cat stung. Bernice's suicide attempt was too near. A new cat was surely not a good idea; the novelty of his arrival would wear thin quickly.

The tea party with Albert was successful, even though Spirit tipped over the pitcher of milk causing a minor flood. Albert drove the conversation, recounting stories of his recent Caribbean expedition. Though based in St. Kitts, he traveled throughout the islands. His pale blue eyes danced as he told stories–some surely created to lift the spirits of those in the room, whether fully grounded in truth or not. Bernice smiled and even laughed several times–much to Beverly's delight and surprise–as Albert's monologue ebbed and flowed, like the trade winds and tides in the lands he described.

FORTY-THREE

Beyond periodically changing the desktop screen image, the O'Neill males frequently found great humor in sending messages with the scrolling screen saver. On Sunday after church, Skip found a new note.

LEAD WITH GRACE & HUMILITY

The font's flame color was fuzzy, appearing singed along the edges and constantly changing, as if the letters continued to burn. Despite no distinctive border, David's fingerprints appeared evident. Skip stuck his head out of the office and gave a yell.

"Hey, did anyone change the screen saver last night?!"

With no response, Skip found Amy in the kitchen. "I think David's back," he remarked. She accompanied him to his office and watched as the message scrolled across the monitor.

"So, what's he suggesting?"

"I don't know. It could be any of several clients. Seems more general than specific."

"What about the Langdons? The other messages dealt with them. Could this one as well?"

"But then the meaning's even more unclear."

Amy shared the silence with Skip. "What's happening with the election?" she raised hesitantly.

"We've covered that ground before." Irritation entered Skip's voice.

"Don't snap. I just wonder–"

"We concluded it was not the right step."

"Perhaps David suggests otherwise."

Skip exhaled loudly. "He was an English teacher."

"I know; he just may have a different perspective."

Skip grimaced resignedly. "I can't fight heaven, but there are many ways to lead. It's sure not just the managing partner who leads the firm."

"True. What about leading the band of six?"

"Doing what?"

"I don't know," Amy shrugged. "Maybe you'll have to see what else transpires . . . or if more messages appear."

"I guess. You know the election is this week. I think either Don or Gary will get the nod."

"Have you decided–"

"No, it's a tough choice. They are both strong at client-building. Don does more government work. Gary is the consummate corporate guy. Both are well networked. If everything were equal, I'd say Gary. I think that's the way we'll grow most rapidly and build a more distinctive practice. Now with the potential of scandal looming, well . . . having great ties with the government may be what's required."

"Would one of them lead with greater grace and humility?"

"That's intriguing. Perhaps David is suggesting a way to vote," Skip reflected. "That's tough. Both are great outside guys, but they are brutal on staff. Associates don't want to work with them. The pain is too high."

"I'm sure glad you're you. People beg to work for you."

Skip smiled, "My incredibly biased fan club?" He gave Amy a tight hug. "I should get some work done. This week is gonna be a bear."

"Go get 'em, Tiger."

* * *

Sitting with Walt in their pew at Bedrock Hills, Janet prayed for a long list of shut-ins, elderly parishioners, and friends that she visited consistently–including Bernice. Janet felt in her heart that Bernice was on the road to recovery. She would stop and see her this week. Her prayers included Steve and his family. Her daughter-in-law seemed increasingly frazzled raising four young children as an apparent soloist, at times. Janet hoped Steve would see the light and rebalance his priorities. She closed by lifting words of blessing for herself and Walt–to sustain and strengthen their relationship and maintain their good health. She bowed reverently and looked up as the prelude faded and Reverend Andrews ascended the pulpit to extend his welcome. The sun shone through the stained glass windows behind him.

Listening to the announcements, Hilda Baumgartner's passage into eternal life mildly surprised Janet. She had visited Hilda on Thursday. While her health clearly was failing and she didn't respond much, her eyes twinkled as she listened to Janet. Thinking of someone as vibrant and alive one day and dead the next always moved Janet.

"It's just another transition," she once told Steve. "You're not always certain what's on the other side of a doorway, but you step through and find yourself in a different place. I believe death is much the same. It's a transition to something we don't wholly understand or know but will fully embrace when it's time."

Janet refocused on the service. After the choir sang the Introit, the congregation stood to sing the opening hymn. As the voices rose, Janet noticed a change in the stained glass window. She turned slightly toward Walt to see if he noticed, but his eyes followed the bass harmony line in the hymnal. Janet knew the window faced south–to capture as much light as possible each Sunday. The morning sunlight, while brilliant, had not changed significantly during the opening minutes of the service. Certainly not enough to change the window's appearance!

The longer she watched, the more she realized that a panel of the richly hued window was starting to glow. She knew that each pane in the southern bank of windows represented a Bible story. She watched as the fifth pane on the right became more brilliantly illuminated than any other.

As the panel flickered, its contrast with other panes became so significant that nighttime could have fallen behind the others. Though she knew the stories behind most panes, the lower fifth panel required a look-up in the hymnal. *'Sign of advancing age,'* she thought.

Walt finally looked over, as Janet's warm soprano no longer provided counterbalance to his voice. He peered over his reading glasses. She nodded back, and he returned to singing.

As the hymn concluded, Pastor Scott commenced the Prayer of Confession. Janet turned to the front of her hymnal. *'Apologies, Lord,'* she thought.

Walt watched from the corner of his nearly closed eyes. Janet quickly thumbed down the window interpretations.

> ***St. Stephen*** *– The bread, stones and fire all have special significance.* ***Bread*** *connotes Stephen's distribution of bread to the needy,* ***stones*** *represent his martyr's death, and the* ***fire*** *symbolizes the Holy Spirit's presence in his life*

She closed the hymnal and her eyes simultaneously, listening to the congregation finish. Pastor Scott shared the Words of Forgiveness and the congregation responded in song. Following the Passing of the Peace and a brief Minute for Mission, Janet refocused on the Stephen pane–which glowed brightly. During the Offering, the panel edges stood out, a burnished orange glow.

Janet couldn't help smiling. *'David. Here? Now? You should know better.'* Embarrassed, she blushed with curiosity. "Completely different this time: a picture."

"What, hon?" Walt leaned over and whispered, as the choir's voices rose with the anthem.

"Sorry, thinking aloud."

"You okay?"

"Yes, I'll tell you later," Janet mouthed. Walt watched closely as her gaze returned to the stained glass windows. Unable to determine what she studied, he retreated to the service as a church elder blessed the offering and began the first scripture reading.

Janet remained riveted. Much like Roger's bricks, some of the individual pane edges radiated continuously; others flickered on and off, eventually staying off–as if the light within had burned out. She tried to discern letters. Midway through the sermon, her eyes suddenly picked out words within the odd angles of stained glass.

L I S T N
E N G A G
B A S T E P H

"Interesting," she reflected. "It must be abbreviated. The first two lines make sense. But Basteph?" She wrote the three lines on her bulletin. Dr. Andrews energetically preached, but–unlike most Sundays–he failed to hold Janet's attention. She remained absorbed by the window's message. *'If only I were equally illuminated.'*

After the final prayers of the church, the pastor announced a hymn change. "We have a misprint in the bulletin. Please stand and join me in singing hymn number 324: *Open My Eyes That I Might See.*"

"Oh my goodness," murmured Janet, skimming the opening lines. "Uncanny."

Open my eyes, that I might see. Glimpses of truth Thou hast for me
Place in my hands the wonderful key, that shall unclasp and set me free
Silently now I wait for Thee. Ready my God, Thy will to see
Open my eyes, illumine me, Spirit divine.

She smiled as her soprano voice joined with Walt and the congregation in a vibrant rendition. She watched the window as the final refrain closed. During the Benediction, the window's lighting flickered twice more and then faded to match the other panes.

"So, what's up with you?" Walt touched the small of Janet's back as they made their way down the long center aisle to shake hands with the pastor.

"Later," Janet turned to greet others waiting in line.

Hearing Janet's excited download on the way home, Walt agreed with her speculation that this communication was intended for her. Though not studying them carefully, he had noticed nothing different in the panes. "What else could it be? You weren't feeling ill?"

"Not at all. I actually feel full of life. I also think I've made the connection. It's actually quite clear. Listen and Engage fit with the last line. Basteph. It's actually Stephen. Be A Stephen. It must be. It was in the St. Stephen pane. It can't be anything else."

"Rather ingenious angel you've got," chuckled Walt.

"It's so interesting, don't you think?" nodded Janet.

"Indeed. So, you've figured it out, but what are you supposed to do?"

"I need to think about that some more. I don't see the connection to Bernice . . . " Walt stayed quiet. Janet resumed, "I wonder if Bernice is not involved. Perhaps it has something to do with this new program Pastor Bob is trying to launch."

"What's he doing?"

Janet paused, "It's been in the bulletin. Stephen Ministry. He's looking for folks to develop a program much like other churches in the Presbytery."

"I'm not familiar," Walt raised a quizzical eyebrow as he parked the car.

"As I understand, Stephen ministers support people going through hard times: illness, grief, or other crisis."

"Extending the reach of the pastors?"

"I suppose. Now I don't know for sure, but I believe they're listeners and sounding boards. They give people someone to talk to when they're not sure where else to turn."

"Sounds like you. You already do that."

"But with no real training. Maybe this is a way to engage again. Not being on the council any longer, I've wondered how to best contribute."

"Could be quite a commitment."

"But if it's something I enjoy, what else are we doing in our retirement?" Janet laughed quietly. "Maybe David is onto something."

"I'll just follow your lead. Maybe I should do it with you . . . "

"That would be wonderful, Walt. Would you?"

* * *

When Beverly emailed the First Circle, she was not surprised when they all quickly agreed to gather for a casual dinner on Sunday, February 9. The newest skybox in Wednesday's *Ledger* guided her expectations. Once again, clouds floated across the sapphire sky bordered in a glowing frame.

CONNECT 6 PRAY GROW FAITH

She imagined–and later learned–that all of the First Circle saw a similar box. Over brownies and ice cream at Bernice's house, the group caught up on the last two weeks, with the biggest news being Skip's election as managing partner of Dane & Caldwell. He was as surprised as anyone.

"I didn't tender my name. In short, none of the candidates could cobble together a super-majority vote as required in our by-laws. The issue: a lack of credibility on internal staff leadership, despite their prodigious talents at client development and service. Following a three-ballot stalemate, my name was raised. I pushed back, but there was overwhelming support. In very short order, a formal nomination was made, seconded, and a vote taken. I was elected on the first ballot." Skip smiled broadly.

"Congrats, Old Man," proclaimed Rusty as he poured large glasses of cabernet. "I'd pour something stronger, but this'll have to do."

Echoes of congratulations circled the table.

"Why weren't you suggested earlier?" asked Beverly.

"Others wanted the position badly. With the voting impasse, the group needed to think outside the box. My role in professional development and culture-building across the firm helped. I have a good client record, though not as strong as the other candidates."

"Surely you're being modest," smiled Janet warmly.

"You're the man," Rusty chimed in boisterously.

"We are in the presence of leadership," laughed Carol.

"And one of such grace—" added Janet.

" . . . with humility to boot," observed Beverly.

"Interesting," Skip noted. "I got another message, by the way. Before the election."

"Really?!" A collective reaction rippled around the group.

"On my computer. Same flaming letters."

"What'd it say?"

"'Lead with grace and humility.' Were you clued in?" he looked at Janet then Beverly, who vigorously shook their heads.

"I got another as well. Oddest thing," interrupted Carol.

"You? Me too." Rusty offered.

"I thought it was just me, this time. It was so different," added Janet.

The group looked to Roger and Beverly. "In fact, I heard from David as well," nodded Beverly.

"Whoa, I'm not saying mine are from David . . . " Rusty shook his head.

"Well, I will. Mine was on the garage wall again. Kinda weird but cool." Roger finally got a word into the accelerating discussion.

It took time for all the stories, but all six had heard once again. After Janet told of signing up in the inaugural group of Stephen Ministers, Beverly followed.

"My kids have me addicted to a little handheld computer game: Yahtzee. I was sitting in bed, waiting for Bill to come up Tuesday. I had just rolled a Yahtzee—"

"What in goodness name is a Yahtzee?" questioned Janet.

"You roll five dice, Mrs. Walker, and—"

"Whatever," responded Janet holding up her hands. "Go on. I'm sorry for interrupting."

"I just rolled five fives and the screen went blank. I thought the batteries died, but then the border–tiny as it is–began to glow . . . "

"Awesome," nodded Roger. "I wish mine would show up that way."

"Yours do seem a little old world, Buddy. You get 'em on stones and bricks," Rusty observed as he finished his wine.

"David sure finds interesting channels for his messages," noted Skip.

"I'm still not convinced it's David, but–"

Skip interrupted Rusty, "I'm not sure you'll ever be persuaded, but let Beverly finish." The group leaned forward.

"The flaming font materialized almost immediately. I was half worried it would be another 9-1-1 call, but it wasn't. Let me write it down."

ENTRPRNR FAM COUNSL

"Mine was abbreviated too."

"He's space-constrained."

"An angel? Constrained? Please. Give me a break." Rusty, emboldened by alcohol, reacted loudly.

"If you need to communicate in a tight space, wouldn't you be creative and cut down?" pondered Carol. "I always use shorthand with Jay and the kids."

Skip studied Beverly's writing. "So if this is abbreviated, you've got: Entrepreneur, Family, and Counsel. Right?"

"Well, that's what I came up with. And to cap it off? I got a call on Thursday from Max Diamond. I don't know if I ever told you his name, but he was the guy who wanted to discuss a job last fall, just as Mother got ill."

The group nodded.

"Well, he called out of the blue. I figured I had burned that bridge. I guess some people are so thick-skinned that rejection rolls off them more easily."

"Amen to that," Carol jumped in. "Have I told you about–" but before she could start, Janet interrupted, "Beverly, please."

"Max said he'd shared my résumé with a headhunter. It was a good thing he gave me a heads up, as within the hour, I received another call. A very interesting conversation."

"Say more," coaxed Janet.

Carol chuckled, "I would tell you about my most recent job inquiry–a real nutcase, but I suspect you'd tell me to stay focused." The group joined her laughter.

"This headhunter said her practice is launching a network of independent contractors who serve families dealing with high-stress situations—could be illness, substance abuse, sexual abuse—you name it. They want people with a background in education and social work. My background was particularly interesting, given my work right after college. When I talked about Mother, the woman got even more enthusiastic.

"In short, I'm going in to learn more. It's rather entrepreneurial—I create my own portfolio and serve with as much time as I can give. It sounds intriguing, though I'm not sure I would've jumped just yet but with the message from David, I thought—"

"What else could you think? You have to go for the discussion even if nothing comes of it." Skip agreed.

"I bet you'll find a match. Look at each of us," Carol winked at Roger. "We've all gotten some job counsel: how to do best with what we've got."

"Even as a retiree, I'm getting counsel on how to use my gifts."

"Me too, actually," added Roger.

"How so?" queried Skip.

"The bricks in my garage lit up again last weekend. I just finished delivering papers on Saturday. I was alone, and I noticed the same circle of fire. 'Course this time, I knew what to look for. The bricks were blinkin' on and off, but pretty soon, words showed up.

LEAD
ROLE MODEL
BBALL +

"That's awesome, buddy," Rusty cried out, giving Roger a friendly back slap.

"You play basketball?" asked Skip.

"Intramurals. I didn't make the school team. But our team is pretty tough. We're eight and one so far, 'bout halfway through the season."

"I can't think of a finer young man to lead the team," Janet uttered.

"Thanks, Mrs. Walker." Roger blushed a deep pink, his dimple popping out around his shy smile. "I'm not the team captain though."

"So, what do you make of it?"

"I don't know, but I'm thinkin' there's something coming where I'll need to do the right thing. Kinda like with the rabbit, I guess . . . " His voice trailed off.

"Perhaps," agreed Beverly. "It's reassuring to know that you're viewed—from afar—as a role model."

"From way afar," added Rusty.

"And you? Our wine connoisseur? What's happening in your world?"

"Well, hey," Rusty refilled his glass. He was the only one still enjoying the cabernet. "I'm not sure what mine are about at this point." He took a large swig and looked around the table. "See, I've gotten a couple more messages echoing the one from just before our last little party."

"Say more, son," encouraged Skip.

"I'm getting to it." He paused for more wine. "I've gotten three more since last time. All at work. All on my desktop." He hesitated once more. "Oh, and one more at home on my TV, one night, along the bottom."

"Still not believing it's David?"

"Whoever it is sure has been persistent."

"So, stop with the suspense, what did the messages say?" urged Carol. "Inquiring minds like ours want to know," she laughed and was joined by Beverly and Skip.

"They were all the same. No difference.

COMMIT STOP CAROUSEL B LOYAL UNC"

"Verrrry interesting," nodded Carol with great exaggeration, as Rusty swirled some red wine in his mouth before swallowing. The wine passed behind his stubbly jawline and down his throat.

"That's nice. Can I pour some?" he purred.

"I'll take a splash," responded Beverly. Skip pushed his glass toward Rusty, who obliged with a generous serving for each.

"Whoa, man. You may drink this like it's water, but I've got work tomorrow."

"Oh, Rusty. That's way more than–" Rusty raised his hand. "I will ensure none remains in your glass when you are sufficiently done. It's against my constitution to allow good wine to be wasted." Roger smirked slyly as Beverly and Skip each took a swig.

"So, Rusty, what do you make of your messages?" inquired Janet.

"I'm not so certain. I told you about the one before, right?"

"You mentioned it briefly, but remind us," suggested Beverly.

"I don't remember this at all," said Carol.

"Well, if I recall–"

"Come on, Rusty. We all know in excruciating detail each of our messages. I suspect you do as well," prodded Skip.

Rusty blushed deeply below the ruddiness resulting from the wine and the windburn. "I suppose so. The day before coming here, that message was, *Join First Circle. Stop One Nights. Commit.*"

"Of course. You weren't going to join us and then you did."

"That's right," Rusty shrugged with a guilty half-laugh. "I figured I was just one more of the nuts in this sack. No disrespect or anything. The message that Saturday morning kinda pushed me."

"So, the first part is pretty clear. But what's the rest?" inquired Janet.

"Well, I . . . " Rusty seemed lost for words. Wordlessly, he considered what to share. He shook his head; these people thought he was some angelic guy.

"I don't know. I have a habit of bouncing around from project to project. Some people think I have ADD . . . Attention Deficit Disorder," Rusty added, seeing Janet's questioning eyes. Rusty's broad smile was not returned from around the table. "Maybe that's the intent. Focus on longer projects."

The group looked at Rusty kindly, but with skepticism.

"Maybe, but one nights? What's that?" Beverly led off.

"Like I said, it doesn't make much sense to me."

"There's gotta be an explanation. Commit is repeated. Stop carousel is new. Could that have anything to do with nights?"

"Been to a circus lately?" Roger suggested.

"Well, I've been to a restaurant called the Carousel. Maybe . . . " Rusty faded.

"No way. You didn't act on the first message. You didn't commit." Others nodded with Roger's assessment.

"David follows up with me. He's doing the same with you," added Skip.

Rusty blushed again, "But how can I act if I don't understand?"

"You have to think harder, man," observed Roger. "You're not giving it enough effort."

"Just cut the shit, buddy." Rusty reacted more harshly than intended. The group let out a collective gasp.

"Watch the language. It may be appropriate at the office. It's not here," Beverly reprimanded.

Rusty looked down. "Sorry, I'm just frustrated. You all seem able to figure out your messages and who's sending them, but I can't."

Skip watched the young man closely and thought, *'Or you don't want to.'* Skip suspected the derivation of one nights and carousel. *'Just what was Rusty into anyway?'* he wondered.

"So, what about you, Carol? You've been so quiet," Rusty redirected. The others laughed.

"Carol? Quiet? You are quite the comedian!"

"I don't know that I've ever been tagged as quiet. I'm going to disappoint you. I've only gotten one message in the last two weeks. Maybe I'm just not loved. I mean, he only was my English teacher. I was beginning to think he had lost interest!" Carol smiled.

"Of course, he delivered his message with a bang–literally. We just got a new microwave, one of those sophisticated models that you need a Ph.D. to operate. There I am trying to make popcorn for the kids after school. I place the bag inside and press the button marked POPCORN. Who would think they wouldn't correctly set the timer for my particular bag?"

"Oh no, I can smell the outcome . . . " Beverly laughed.

"I'm surprised you didn't smell it. We sat waiting while it did its popping thing. Pop, pop, pop." Carol added hand choreography as her volume and expression matched the expanding popcorn.

"Pop, pop, pop. It keeps going. Real nice." Roger winced, anticipating the punchline. "And suddenly there's one heckuva BOOOM. The kids come running to the kitchen, just in time for me to open the door and be met with the worst smell you can imagine. Smoke billows from the bag. Little flames flicker at the sides. The microwave is charred. The smell of burnt popcorn permeates the first floor. Kelly and Kevin both flee the scene, leaving me with the clean-up."

"This could only happen to you," Beverly chuckled.

"You are one-of-a-kind," agreed Skip.

Rusty sat quietly, sipping his rapidly disappearing wine, delighted that the spotlight now rested elsewhere. Roger was all smiles picturing the explosion. Janet looked sorrowful.

"I'm remembering the smell. I thought we'd need fumigation services to clear the house."

"And the message?"

"Yes, I'm coming to that. Well, I pull out the incinerated bag. There is nothing resembling the advertised movie-style buttered popcorn. I figure I'll just take the whole bag out to the garbage. Then I notice some popped kernels are buried under the black on top.

"Well, I am not one to waste food. As you can see, I rarely miss a meal." The group smiled as Carol patted her stomach.

"You're not that big, dear."

"Adjust your glasses, Janet. There's more of me to love each year, I tell Jay. I paw through the bag and dig out the few unblemished pieces of popcorn. I taste one and then another. They're not that great, frankly, but I wonder if there could be something to salvage.

"Well, I end up dumping out the rest of the bag, and then–now don't ask me why–I look inside the bag." Disbelief meets Carol's gaze. "Yes, I know–

hard to believe, but that's what I did. It's then I see, really burnt remnants —charred pieces of popcorn, smoked beyond recognition—sticking to the bag. But here's the catch," she paused expectantly, "they're not just sticking in any ol' random pattern. Nooooo . . . "

"You're pulling my leg, right?" Rusty piped up. "Words out of charred kernels?"

"No way," agreed Roger.

"Words—clear as day. I guess I'm just the food-and-drink maven in this crowd. I get messages in tea leaves, bacon residue, and now popcorn. Wonder what's next? My morning cereal? Little dancing Fruity Pebbles all lined up? Or maybe choreographed Alphabet Soup?"

The group laughed energetically.

"But, what did the popcorn say?"

Carol responded, "Let me write it down."

PERSIST
FAM MINSTR NSG
LAF

"The bag had that odd glow on the inside. Not just butter, either; it was yellow, but burnished with deep gold and orange. It looked like the flames I first thought I sa—" Carol interrupted herself. "Oh, I bet that was it! It wasn't really flames. I hadn't thought of that before."

"It really is confounding, how you get your messages."

"Just be very careful what you eat at my house. When we say, 'Eat your words,' we just may mean it!" The group laughed heartily once more.

Carol quickly outlined her interpretation of the message. Recently, she and Jay had been assessing HomeHealth. The job was incredibly satisfying—thanks in large part to the work she'd been doing with the extended Langdon family—but the hours were long. They debated her returning to her part-time Medical Center role.

"So, I said to Jay, 'I guess I need more time. Persist couldn't be any more clear. I can minister to families through nursing at many places, of course, but persist must mean HomeHealth. And we agreed that 'Laf' meant to have more fun on the job."

"I think it's well beyond that. You're intended to make others laugh: your patients and their families."

"I agree with Beverly. You're called to minister to families with nursing and laughter. What a wonderful gift," enthused Janet.

"The ladies," observed Skip, "—with David's observation from a distance—have nailed it."

"You know, this whole notion of ministry might be why we're together.

To minister to others using our collection of talents."

"That's a pretty broad agenda, don't you think?" noted Rusty, pouring himself more wine.

"I don't know. We've been helping Bernice with our individual gifts. Now, David is sending messages that are more expansive."

"But the messages are about each of us individually," Rusty shot back.

"Except for the ones that keep bringing us together. 'Connect six' seems clear to me." Beverly chimed in.

"To do what?" Rusty anchored the devil's advocacy corner.

Skip plowed forward. "Look at the message we all got this week." He scribbled it on Beverly's notepad:

CONNECT 6 PRAY GROW FAITH

"There's something more to this than just individual talents. I'll bet there's a broader mission to pursue." Skip concluded, followed quickly by Beverly.

"You're absolutely right. We are called to strengthen our faith by coming together."

"The Bible[2] says, 'for where two or three come together in my name, there am I with them,'" Janet noted.

"So, does that mean—"

" . . . that Jesus is the messenger? Or God? Not David O'Neill?" Rusty completed Beverly's question.

"We've been over this ground before. If it was God—or Jesus for that matter—wouldn't He call us by our names? Why so cryptic?"

"David fits better," nodded Carol.

"Except for me," Rusty glumly noted, staring into his glass.

"What if we follow the direction this time and pray?" Janet suggested.

"As a group?" Carol's eyebrows rose archly.

"I'm not much of a prayer person," Rusty looked concerned. Only Roger looked more anxious over the conversation's new direction.

"I imagine there are many ways to pray as a group. Perhaps Janet could lead us again?" suggested Beverly.

"I'm happy to begin, but I don't know that I have the praying gift you suggest. My prayers are usually silent and alone."

"Maybe we could add to what you start."

"Well, I suppose," acknowledged Janet.

"Excellent. I believe collective prayer is a good thing." Beverly was

[2] Matthew 18:20

suddenly convinced this was the right direction.

"I once attended a men's breakfast that discussed prayer," noted Skip. "We all think it needs to be some big formal affair, and many of us get anxious. I liked the way some of the older men suggested you just think of it as a conversation with a friend–casual and informal. God just happens to hear your thoughts as well as your words."

"I like that," smiled Carol.

"So, I can start out, 'Hey dude'?"

"If it works for you, it can work for God," Skip winked at Rusty.

"Even though this is getting outside my zone," noted Rusty, buzzing on his wine, "I'll give it a whirl, if that's what everyone wants to do. I'll tell ya . . . "

"Shall we pray?" Janet intervened quietly, encouraging the group and silencing Rusty. Like the wave in the stands at a football game, one by one, heads bowed around the table.

* * *

"Let us pray," Janet began stiffly. "This evening we come to you, Lord, in gratitude and humility, seeking your blessing and guidance on the road ahead. You are generous, creative, and inspirational, Lord. We praise and worship you, each in our own individual ways and collectively in fellowship. Bless this gathering of your people. Help us to see the right paths, making your ways our ways, your words our words. Thank you for all you have given us.

"Lord, help us understand the purpose behind our group, the mission of this First Circle. We hope to use our gifts in ways that glorify your name and your desires. We are in awe of the communications you have sent to us, your holy and loyal servants."

'What a drone,' Rusty thought, enjoying his mild intoxication. Janet picked up steam; the sing-songy nature of her voice lulled him into a near-hypnotic state. He wondered whether others felt the same. He cautiously opened an eye and peaked around the table. The others appeared to be concentrating, though Roger fidgeted under the table. The teen was trying hard to stay focused and respectful but was losing the battle.

Carol's head bobbed downward and then suddenly jerked up, as if she were nearing sleep. Beverly and Skip seemed the most reverent as Janet moved into worldly issues–the starving, the poverty-stricken, and lands torn by war. Rusty closed his eyes. He felt something slide past his ankle. He opened an eye once more and looked down where a small, gray cat stood. He winked at the cat as it wound its way between his hiking boots.

'Just when will this be done?' he reflected. He tried to concentrate on Janet's words. She had paused. Much like at a concert when the band hits a long rest and the audience starts to clap thinking the piece is over, Rusty began to say, "Amen." He was assertively interrupted as Janet moved into

asking for God's peace to come to Bernice, her extended family, and others who suffered from long, debilitating illness. As the roll call of unknown people extended, Rusty's concentration waned.

He raised an eyelid and looked around. He contemplated taking a sip of wine to maintain the warm euphoria but decided that would be rude–maybe even sacrilegious. His thoughts wandered back to the earlier discussion of his messages and what he had, importantly, not shared.

He covered the same ground trying to find a different interpretation. Relentlessly, his mind returned to one theme, *'It's gotta be the carousel of guys. What a buzzkill, but someone is saying, 'Make a choice. Commit.' Shit.*

'I'm twenty-seven and having the time of my life. I'm careful. How can you think about a long-term relationship if you don't check out different possibilities?' He paused guiltily amidst his rationalization. Janet remained deep in conversation with the Great One Upstairs–and here he was having a profane internal dialogue in the presence of who knows who. *'Good thing they can't hear my thoughts,'* he smiled inwardly.

'Who wants to commit to anything before thirty? End up in some boring relationship that's going nowhere. No can do.' Rusty shook his head more vigorously than intended, resulting in a wave of lightheaded dizziness. Reflexively, he reached out to the table and gripped the sides.

'She was going to give others a chance to jump in,' Rusty thought involuntarily. *'Not that I want to, but still . . . another voice would be good, if this is going to keep rolling.'* The clock chimed once from the front hall. *'What time could it possibly be? The last I noticed, it was just after eight. It must be eight-thirty.'* He lifted an eyelid again to survey his watch. He looked around the table for a third time and noticed Roger also spying surreptitiously. He winked at the teenager, who blushed and quickly closed his eyes as if caught cheating.

As Rusty's eyes moved from person to person, he became aware of a light. It radiated from a space between Janet and Beverly. *'Odd,'* he thought. *'What's that?'* It appeared that a powerful spotlight beamed behind the two women. The bluish-white light began rather dimly but grew more brilliant as Janet spoke. Rusty opened both eyes to be sure squinting didn't create the effect, but the light only intensified.

He watched, increasingly intrigued. *'This is like a fucking séance,'* he thought. *'I wonder if anyone else can see this or if this is some hallucination from the wine. I sure hope I'm not getting sick.'* The light's progression was slow and measured. Rather like the sunrise at dawn, its brilliance blossomed.

The intense illumination provided a bold backlight, which no one else seemed to notice. Even if Rusty shut his eyes, the light remained evident. He experimented a couple of times to be sure. The light stayed and with each passing minute expanded.

Janet finally reached a lengthy silence. She closed with clear direction to the table, "Hear our prayers both silent and aloud as we offer them before you. Be with us Lord, as we share our prayer requests." No one appeared ready to bite. Rusty figured everyone was pretty well prayed-out by Janet's verbosity.

Suddenly, Beverly kicked in, continuing the thoughtful request on the purpose of their group. As she gained confidence, Rusty circumspectly watched the light behind her. The light began taking shape. Rather than just a round glow from a single source–like a spotlight would provide, the light became more animated, with increasingly discernible angles and contours. Rusty's assessment suddenly stopped, as he realized the light emanated from a figure. While not completely clear, the light appeared to be a man, standing behind Janet and Beverly.

Rusty closed his eyes. Oddly, he could see the man more clearly. *'I am fucking dreaming,'* he thought. He quickly blinked his eyes open again, but the man's features were not as clear. Tightly closing them, he could see that the man was clothed in a white turtleneck and tightly tailored white pants. He was older, though the all-encompassing light made precise age determination impossible. Clearly, he had white hair, thinning on top. He smiled warmly as he looked around the group. He exuded a subtle, but clear graciousness and class. Rusty did not recognize him.

Beverly paused, and Carol picked up the baton–praying for those around the table, saying a prayer for her family, and asking for guidance and a sign of what was next for the group. "Come to us and tell us how we can help," she concluded. Prayer leadership passed naturally to Skip who asked for God's grace on the group, on Bernice, his family, his firm, and to grant God's wisdom as he humbly attempted to pick up the reins of leadership for Dane & Caldwell. Silence prevailed.

The man of light nodded directly at Rusty and lifted his hand as if to say, "Go on. You can do this. Add something. Contribute." He smiled across the table.

'And just what should I say?' Rusty thought.

"Say what comes naturally," the illuminated figure surprisingly responded.

"Hey dude," Rusty started out with a mumble. Roger emitted a little chuckle as Janet inhaled loudly. "Hey, I'm not real good at this. Help me–no, help us understand what you want: where you want us to go, what you want us to do. I'm not so sure I can do what you suggest, but–well, I guess I can try. Give us some direction. Light the path. Yeah, provide some light for where we should go. Light is good. I'm ready–at least as much as I'll ever be. Help this group be the best we can be."

Rusty stopped. He felt exhausted and energized simultaneously. While he spoke, he was less aware of the man of light. Now following his brief prayer and with his eyes scrunched shut, the man was once again vivid. He smiled broadly and raised his hand in apparent blessing. He gave a universal sign of peace and good will, raising his right hand and putting up his thumb and first two fingers in greeting and—what turned out to be—farewell. He winked at Rusty and turned. The light faded.

After Roger finished a short contribution, Janet concluded. "Thank you, Lord, for your ongoing care and love. You have been abundant in your blessings to us, the most sacred of which was sending your Son to die for our sins, giving us—through your grace—eternal life. Thank you. And it is in His words, we pray together."

> *Our Father, who art in heaven, Hallowed be Thy name. Thy kingdom come, Thy will be done, on earth as it is in heaven. Give us this day our daily bread. And forgive us our sins, as we forgive those who sin against us. Lead us not into temptation but deliver us from evil. For Thine is the kingdom, the power, and the glory. Forever. Amen.*

"And amen again," Janet added as a soft postscript. Opening his eyes, Rusty reached for the wine bottle.

"That was powerful," sighed Beverly. "I felt close to all of you and to our angel. Perhaps he's our guardian angel."

"I'm not sure that would be David," smiled Skip. "He wasn't always that angelic in life."

"Well, none of us know just how angels work, but somehow God is using David and us to do good. I'm convinced," Janet nodded.

"Well, did anyone else see it?" Carol interjected excitedly.

"See what?" Janet inquired.

"The light."

"You saw it too?" Rusty exclaimed.

"You too! And you said you didn't believe!" Carol's excitement bubbled over.

"Me too. Right there," Roger pointed.

"I thought I was hallucinating," nodded Rusty.

"What precisely did you see?" questioned Skip.

"It was a light—dim at first, but then it grew bigger, brighter, bolder. It was actually pretty cool. Though I didn't know if I was dreaming or what."

"I saw a man," Roger added. "He was all lit up and wearing white."

"Really?" Rusty sounded shocked. "I thought that was in my head. You saw the man?"

As Roger nodded, Carol excitedly jumped in, "Precisely. I saw the guy. Brilliant white light. I never opened my eyes, but he was there. Here, I mean. Right here at the table."

"How would you describe this man?" Skip probed persistently.

"Older. White hair."

"But thin on top, balding."

"Dressed all in white. A turtleneck."

"A turtleneck?" Janet lifted an eyebrow.

"Did you see his pants?" Rusty inquired.

"Looked shrink-wrapped," Carol grinned.

"A little tight for my taste," nodded Rusty.

"He smiled a lot," Roger added.

"Good point. He did smile a lot."

"Interesting," Skip stroked his chin. The group watched him put the pieces together. "Actually, I saw him too."

"You holding out?" Rusty flicked the back of his hand against Skip's shoulder.

"I didn't believe it."

"You're telling me," nodded Rusty.

"What about you?" Carol looked at Beverly and Janet. "Did you see him?"

Both shook their heads. Beverly's face contorted with a slight frown. "You know, I was aware of a presence. I felt like I was sitting with a broader audience, more than just us. The thought passed through my mind, but I let it go."

"The room was somehow warmer. I sensed light, even with my eyes closed. I do know I was feeling warm. It felt like a heater was blowing on me," concluded Janet.

"You're right," nodded Beverly. "A duct was suddenly turned on and blew a warm breeze. It hit my back and side toward you," she gestured at Janet.

"Well, I'll be. I think David–in some form or another–was here," Skip said.

"You recognized him?"

"No, the light was too bright, but the features we all saw were certainly consistent. I'd have to say–with the exception of the tight pants–you could be describing my brother."

"Isn't this intriguing? The first time we pray together and David joins us."

"Prayer is powerful," cited Janet. "I never knew just how much in the moment."

"You sure we're not just making this whole thing up?" Rusty's jaded cynicism reappeared.

"How could we all see—or feel—the same thing?" Beverly questioned.

"And with our eyes closed?" Carol shook her head.

"It's pretty strange," Rusty reluctantly noted. The wine buzz evaporated precipitously, making him clear-headed and focused.

"If we pray together, will he show up consistently?"

"I think not," Janet counseled. "That's like asking for a sideshow act, much like when Jesus was tempted."

"I remember that," Roger jumped in. "From Sunday School. The devil said, 'Come on, show us a miracle if you're the Son of God.' "

"Yes, something like that," agreed Janet. "I believe he came amongst us this evening to reinforce our growing understanding and the power of prayer in a group."

"It could also be the notion that strengthening your faith is not a solo sport," noted Skip. "It's something that grows and is galvanized with other people."

Janet nodded, "My women's group explored that topic. Not just building a relationship up and down with God, but with groups of people side-to-side."

A thought dawned for Rusty. "That's kinda like the cross. A vertical relationship and a horizontal one make the cross . . . "

"Exactly," smiled Janet.

"It's rather mind-boggling," murmured Beverly. "So much to digest."

"My goodness, what an evening!" exclaimed Janet.

"This is so cool," added Roger.

"Well, I'm still not sure we know our full purpose, but I believe we're on the right track," suggested Skip. "Use our unique talents and gifts, help other people—like Bernice—through those talents, and try—it seems—to strengthen our collective and individual relationships with God." He paused. "Well, I'm kinda making up that last part. It sure seems to fit certainly for where I am."

Beverly agreed, "I couldn't say it much better."

"So, who's our next client?" Rusty laughed.

"Always the comedian."

"Maybe we're a new version of the A-Team. None of this First Circle stuff. We're the Angel Team." Others joined his laughter.

"Perhaps, but who says we're finished helping Bernice?"

"Good point." Beverly looked down at her watch. "Look at the time. It's almost nine, and we've not even checked on her!"

"I'll run up. Maybe you, Janet, and the guys can start cleaning up?"

While Carol checked on Bernice—who had watched a movie all evening and was doing just fine ("Thank you," she said), the others made short work of the kitchen. All were gone by half past nine, with the exception of Beverly, who stayed overnight for Monday's chemo. Through the dark night, the warm, inviting hospitality of the little white window candles grew—much like the apparent return to health of the home's owner.

FORTY-FOUR

The sleek red, blue, and silver plane touched down smoothly in Nashville on Friday evening, Valentine's Day. While Rusty always enjoyed returning, he hadn't been back in more than a year. His parents had visited him the prior summer, and Christmas had been spent with his parents at his brother's house, sixty miles north of Bedrock. As a Vanderbilt alum, he had friends in the area. The overly homey familiarity of the small city made him glad he didn't live here.

The warm twang of a southern accent rang out across the cabin, "I want to welcome y'all to Nashville: Home of the Country Music Hall of Fame and the Grand Ole Opry. Local time is eight-oh-five. But we don't worry quite so much about moving fast down here. Welcome home, y'all."

Rusty smiled, *'Sometimes it's hard not to love this place.'* With minimal delay resulting from sitting near the front of economy, he strolled up the jetway and into the concourse. His parents would meet him at baggage claim as they'd agreed on email.

He took his time walking through the airport, stopping at the men's room and noting several new additions to the terminal. Starbucks seemed to be popping up everywhere, but he passed none here. Rather, Whitt's Barbecue and The Coffee Beanery monopolized prime real estate.

Frank and Betty Stillwagon stood at the baggage carousel searching for their son amid the wave of inbound travelers from three flights. Several limo drivers with little placards bearing names lined the area as well. When Frank saw Rusty, he grinned and held up a sign, "Still Waggin'?"

"Ah, Dad. Jeez," Rusty smiled, embarrassed. "Don't ya think that's gettin' a little old?"

"Not at all. I want you to prop it up inside my box, when you've got me laid out."

"Frank, really," a sharp-tongued Betty countered. "Rusty, come here." She reached out and embraced Rusty in a hug as he stepped toward her.

"Hey, I decided not to check any bags. So, this–" Rusty gestured to his black and red duffle bag, "is all I've got."

"I wish you would stay longer. It's such a short visit," Betty picked up where they left off Monday night.

"I know, Mom." Rusty responded with some exaggeration. He felt like a teenager being reprimanded. "But, work . . . you know."

"I know: busy guy. A manager now," Betty said, twinkling with clear pride.

"It's not that big a deal."

"I'll pull the car around."

"You don't need to, Dad. We can walk. It can't be that far. This is Nashville."

"Now don't you be putting down our fine town. You grew up here. These are your roots." Their perennial banter resumed its familiar rhythm.

The white Ford Taurus soon headed north on the Briley Parkway. They passed exits for the Grand Ol' Opry and the adjoining Opry Mills retail center.

"I can't get over how big that place is. It's larger every time I'm home."

"I want us to eat at the Opryland Resort, while you're here. Your father and I ate there a few months ago. It's just lovely inside. At Christmas, it was really nice."

"Whitts' got me thinkin' some barbecue would be excellent."

"Oh this will be so much better. It's a special occasion. We'll walk through the atrium. You can choose which restaurant you prefer."

Rusty shrugged, "I guess. I really had a hankering for some smokey, drippin' ribs. But, if you want some classy event, I–"

"Well, we'll just have to do Bubba's as well. Maybe we can go there tomorrow. And then do Opryland on the way back to the airport on Sunday evening. How would that be?"

"Fine, Mom. Just fine." Rusty settled into the back seat and slid down. Every time he got back home, the cadence of growing up returned. The only thing that had changed was that his dad now enjoyed sharing a drink or two of Kentucky bourbon with him in the study or on the wide porch. Rusty smiled in anticipation of the fiery whiskey he could almost taste sliding down.

His mother filled the remaining car ride to the northern suburbs with a running litany of what was happening with family members–close and far, neighbors, and friends. Rusty sank into the familiar comfort of being enveloped by his past. Successes and issues, illnesses and deaths: all were continuing threads in the rich, colorful tapestry of growing up. It all seemed so familiar, and yet so different from his life today. He periodically provided affirmative, vague grunts to punctuate the running monologue.

As the car pulled into the garage, his mom was finishing on church, " . . . and I told Reverend McConnell that you were coming in. He's looking forward to seeing you on Sunday."

"Awww, Mom. Really?"

"Of course. We always do church. We can do the late service to let you sleep in."

Rusty frowned but said nothing.

"Now don't you worry. The eleven o'clock service has really changed."

"Oh, no doubt," said Rusty sarcastically.

"You talk right to your mother."

"Oh, it really has," Betty went on, ignoring Rusty's tone. "We have a bell choir now."

"Reeeeally?" Rusty tried hard to inject some genuine interest, but failed as Betty continued unfazed. "Can't wait," sighed Rusty. This was already looking like a long weekend, and they weren't even in the house.

He grabbed his bag and headed upstairs to "The Shrine." His parents had not changed his room since he left for college. Still the same dark blue corduroy bedspreads on the two twin beds. Same medium brown 'cardboard' wallpaper on the upper walls, separated by a chair rail from the bottom half covered by dark midnight blue tweed. A few splashes of red provided the only pop. The walls still held the same pictures and posters from the early nineties. *'Some things just don't change,'* he thought, looking in his old mirror.

'. . . though you can't argue with the workouts, now can you?' He lifted his t-shirt to reveal his tight six-pack and ran his hand over the hard muscle. *'Yeah, some things may not change, but others sure can.'* He admired the results of the hard work he put in several days weekly.

Moments later, he hit the top of the stairs, as Betty appeared at the bottom. "I made you your favorites. I've got some Snickerdoodles, peanut butter chocolate chips, and some double fudge brownies. I know–"

"Aww, Mom. It's kinda late for all those carbs." Reaching the bottom of the staircase, Rusty perused the plate.

"You're thin as a rail. You must be starving yourself."

"Lean muscle, Mom, from working out."

"You look emaciated. You need some good Southern cooking."

Rusty shrugged. "Where's Dad?"

"I think he's in his study." She pushed the plate toward him, "Take these with you. You and your dad can start. I want to wrap up the rest in the kitchen, so they don't go stale. I'm sending some back for your roommates."

"You don't have to. It's really okay."

Betty shook her head and left Rusty standing with the plate. Rusty's head mirrored his mom's, recognizing the futility of fighting her iron will. More ab crunches waited over the next couple of weeks. He took the fragrant baked goods and entered the cozy office, as his father poured bourbon over ice.

"I figured you'd be ready for a good stiff one," smiled Frank.

"Excellent," agreed Rusty.

His father handed him a glass, "Bottoms up."

They each took a healthy swig of the Kentucky single malt. "That hits the spot," Rusty grinned appreciatively.

"Warms you up, doesn't it?" Frank sipped some more. "Smooth," he added as the strong liquor's heat descended.

"It's great, Dad. Thanks." The two men sat quietly, enjoying their drinks and looking out over the moonlit dusting of snow on the back lawn. As the bourbon warmed them, conversation flowed easily—college hoops, the upcoming baseball season, and local Nashville politics. Betty joined them as Frank poured another round. Betty chose Southern Comfort and nursed it the remainder of the evening. The flickering flames from the fireplace danced and shimmered across the walls of the book-lined office as the threesome conversed on everything and nothing until nearly eleven, at which point, Rusty proclaimed great fatigue and headed upstairs.

Feeling well-rested and energized, he awoke late Saturday morning. The smell of bacon wafting under his bedroom door didn't hurt, eliciting an easy smile. He cracked open his door and seeing the hallway empty, padded over to the hall bath. He splashed cold water on his face and brushed his teeth. He decided to postpone shaving. Back in his room, he threw on a faded blue sleeveless Ridgewell t-shirt and headed downstairs.

"You are going to catch your death of cold," his mother welcomed him as he entered the kitchen. His dad sat at the table, immersed in the morning newspaper and drinking coffee. Betty poured Rusty a cup and poured half and half in it, turning it light tan. "Just the way you like it," she smiled. Rusty frowned at the now lukewarm mug of coffee.

"Yeah, I guess," he muttered. While he usually drank it black, a little milk—preferably skim—was fine. *'I've got a helluva lot of work cut out for me this week at the gym,'* he thought. Betty placed a plate of four large pancakes and five strips of bacon in front of him.

"Wow," he commented. "I never eat this much for breakfast."

"Well, you should. Just look at you. Nothing but skin and bones. Eat up. There's plenty more."

"Ma, I'm sure not gonna have more than this." Rusty took his first mouthful of syrup covered pancakes. "Hmmm, they sure are good," he acknowledged. "Been a long time." He chewed slowly, savoring the taste. He worked his way through the plate and neither resisted two more pancakes his mother flipped in his direction, nor the three additional slices of bacon.

"More coffee?" his mother was already up.

"I'll get it, Mom. Here, let me." He stood quickly to avoid receiving the half and half pollution. "I think I'll just take this one black." He smiled at his mother, "Gotta watch that figure, you know." His mother laughed.

"What's happening in the news, Pop?"

"The usual. Nothing more, nothing less. You folks up north are sure having a tough winter. Look at this—another foot of snow dumped across the Northeast. Days like this, it makes me glad we live where we do."

"Yeah, it has been snowy. Across the board."

"I can't believe how hot the presidential race is already. It's nearly two years away, and the candidates are already slugging it out. Simply remarkable—the money and time these folks have to snipe at each other rather than doing something productive."

"I guess," Rusty shrugged. They were moving into one of his father's pet subjects: politics. It held little interest for Rusty. His mother joined them with a fresh cup of coffee.

"So, what's happening in the big city?" she queried, sipping her coffee.

"A little of this, a little of that. Not much new."

"That's hard to believe! How's that new manager job going?"

"I like it. Takes more time than I ever would've guessed to manage a few people. But, it's kinda cool being the boss." His mother mirrored his smile.

"Seeing anyone these days?"

"Not really. I go out. Mostly with friends."

"Surely there must be some nice Southern girl up there to charm you?" She was tenacious.

"I've not had too much time for girls," Rusty replied.

"Too busy with Ridgewall?"

"Ridge-well," Rusty emphasized, though kindly. "I guess."

"Too much work, not enough play . . . gives you stress and an early heart attack. Just look at your Uncle Larry. He had his heart attack, and he wasn't even fifty."

"No, Frank. He was fifty-three when he had it," corrected Betty.

"Whatever," Rusty's dad shrugged. "You get the point. Don't go to an early grave working too hard."

"I don't think you need to worry about that," Rusty laughed.

"Hey, I do have a question for you guys." His parents looked over at him more closely as if to say, "yes?"

"Well, it takes a little scene-setting." Rusty wondered where precisely to start. "It all began last fall. I thought my computer was acting kinda screwy."

"How so?" his father asked.

"Well . . . " As Rusty shared his story with his increasingly incredulous parents, he didn't necessarily use the precise language of each communication ("Oh, I don't remember them exactly, but it was something along the lines of . . . " became his refrain).

Rusty grew more excited as he warmed to his tale. "When we all came together–except for Skip, we tried to figure out why we were receiving the messages. Why us? And, of course, who–" the last word received additional emphasis, "–was sending them?"

"It must be to help this professor, Mrs. Bernice–" his mother stopped.

"Langdon," Rusty helped. "Yeah, that's what we thought. Particularly after her suicide attempt–"

"She tried to take her life?" Betty paled.

"Really?" his father, the retired newspaper editor, became more intrigued. "You're sure?"

"Well, yeah. I was there."

"What?!" Both parents exclaimed simultaneously.

"Don't get excited. I'm okay. She's okay. I just happened to be there." His parents were visibly anxious. "I was there because of a message on my computer. Actually, two of them . . . the day she tried to off herself."

"Rusty, don't be so cavalier about an attempted suicide."

"I'm not, Ma. It's the way it happened." Rusty explained how the rest of the group, including Skip, showed up due to individual messages. He recounted the rescue, the ambulance, and the subsequent meetings.

"I thought you said there wasn't much new," commented his mother at one point.

"Well, this is so off-the-wall; I wasn't going to just dump it on you." Rusty laughed. "You at least needed to be sitting down."

"This is all rather unbelievable."

"You may have a freelance story here. It's quite sellable, I'd wager. We could even write it up together. Have you given that some thought?"

"I really haven't. I've been trying to get through the whole thing first."

"So, who's the sender?"

"The group believes–get this–it's a dead guy."

"A little far-fetched, don't you think?"

"A person who has passed on?" added Betty.

"I thought it was impossible too, but there's no other sensible explanation. The thing is: the group–the other five–could all make a connection to the same guy. A man who died about two years ago. All except me."

"Who? Some local celebrity?"

"No, it's Skip's brother. This guy was an English teacher. He taught Carol and one of Beverly's kids. He was on the church board with Janet. And, it turns out he was a second uncle to Roger."

"Quite a coincidence, isn't it?" murmured Betty.

"But what about you? Why you?"

"That's what we can't figure out. We both sang in the Metropolitan, but David left before I joined." Rusty paused. "The only clue: he refers to himself as 'Unc' several times." Rusty stopped to think. "I've been thinking it meant Uncle, like in Roger's case. But I don't know all the possibilities there, of course."

Frank and Betty Stillwagon, Rusty's adoptive parents, gazed back at their son. He'd been with them since he was just several days old. He and his brother, their biological son, were like two peas in a pod. They never thought of them any differently. They were only ten months apart and some thought they were twins–particularly when they were growing up. From early on, Rusty knew he was adopted–but it never fazed him or his brother. He never expressed any great interest in knowing his genetic history.

"It's somewhat of a mystery for all of us," his mother cautioned.

"We don't know much about your biological parents," added his dad.

"That's what I figured."

"You may recall, we talked a little bit about this–probably when you were a teen," continued his father.

"Yeah, I sorta recalled some, but no real particulars. It was over at Nana's house, during a holiday."

"That's right," agreed Betty. "Somehow the subject came up."

"I've never really cared. You're my family. I really don't have any need to know the others." Rusty paused, "Well, until now. It would seem."

"So, what do we know?"

"It was a young unmarried couple. They must've been in their early twenties. For some reason they didn't or couldn't get married and raise a child. I don't recall."

"I'm not sure we ever knew, Betty."

"He was in graduate school, I believe. Business?"

"I thought it was law."

"Maybe. I don't remember."

Frank paused, "No, you're right, it was business. Management comes to mind."

"I do remember their names."

Rusty yelped, “You do? Really?”

“Well, just their first names. Marilyn and Charles.”

“I don’t remember Charles. He must’ve had a nickname.”

“Yes, you’re right, I’d forgotten that. They were from somewhere up north, weren’t they?”

“Well, he was. He attended Vanderbilt. She was local, I believe.”

“What was it?” reflected Betty quietly going back to the names. “Chuck? Buff?”

“Maybe.” Frank thought long and hard. “I don’t think I’ll get it.”

“I’m going to keep thinking about that.”

“Like a dog with a bone?” Rusty laughed at the in-family joke regarding his mother’s tenacity to resolve meaningless trivia.

“You laugh, but an hour or two from now, I’ll have it.”

“We’ll see.” Rusty stood and stretched. “I think I’ll head upstairs for a shower. We doin’ Bubba’s tonight?”

“If that’s where you’d like to go.”

“Sure. That would be fine with me.”

“I’ll do a home cooked meal tomorrow.”

“I thought you wanted to go to Opryland.”

“I’ve got to make you at least one good meal while you’re here.”

“Ma, you treat me too well. You don’t have to work that hard. Let’s just go out. Breakfast was great!”

“We’ll see,” nodded his mother, but Rusty knew that dining at the Opryland Resort was no longer on his itinerary. His mother would not allow the northbound plane’s departure without at least one mom-made supper in his belly. He ascended the staircase and enjoyed a long, hot shower in the old hall bath.

* * *

Rusty saw several friends, ate too much food at Bubba’s and at home, and caught up on his sleep. After attending church with his parents, he watched basketball with his dad for much of Sunday afternoon. His mother was unable to definitively name his biological father. “Maybe it was Chuck,” she finally said.

When his parents thought the student was an aspiring lawyer, Rusty fleetingly considered the possibility that the graduate student was nicknamed Skip. But with the growing sense Charles pursued a business degree, the odds seemed infinitesimal. It would prove easy enough to check when he got home if he wanted.

By Sunday night, his stomach tight against his jeans, he was back on the plane. “Love ya,” he hugged his mom and embraced his father at the jetway door. They’d walked him back.

“Next time, you bring a nice girl with you,” advised his mother.

Rusty smiled broadly. “Maybe I’ll surprise everybody,” he winked. Frank arched an eyebrow but said nothing further.

The ride through the chill February sky proved uneventful, as did the cab ride back to the University Sector. His adrenaline always pumped upon returning to the city, despite how comfortable everything was in Nashville. He’d hit the gym early Monday morning, he decided, and start peeling off the extra calories he’d plastered on over the weekend. *‘A new week, a new resolve,’* he thought, sinking beneath his down comforter.

FORTY-FIVE

On Monday, Bernice woke feeling remarkably refreshed. She lay in bed quietly as the cold February sun vainly attempted to break through her shades. With a relieved sigh, she formed unspoken words of gratitude that this Monday was a respite from chemo. For unfathomable reasons, she felt more at peace with her poison regimen these days.

As Spirit snuggled deep into the rarely used extra blankets, Bernice looked over at the dresser. A crystal vase of two dozen dark red roses, adorned with a wide white ribbon and baby's breath stood at attention, keeping watch. For Valentine's Day, Beverly had stopped with Caitlyn and Brad, bringing the bouquet. Bill was taking time off and the four were heading to the mountains for a long ski weekend, "unless you'd like us to stick around," Beverly had queried.

"Of course not, it's unnecessary. I've got plenty to keep me occupied. I seem to be tolerating chemo better. I'll survive."

"You're sure?"

"Yes, dear," Bernice had tried—unsuccessfully—to hold the icy sarcasm back, but the words slipped out nonetheless. Beverly had grimaced. "I'll be fine."

After more hemming and hawing, Beverly had acquiesced and agreed they'd be on their way. Carol would stop by Saturday; Janet planned to visit on Sunday. Beverly believed that Skip was nearly complete with the estate plan and might drop in.

Brad cajoled BeBe into visiting the computer room, where they found an online gaming site and played several rounds of "Harry Potter's Quidditch." Beverly assessed the visit as above average when she saw Bernice moving her Quidditch seeker up, down, and sideways at blinding speeds keeping up reasonably well with "PotterHead."

At Caitlyn's insistence, Bernice ate a homemade brownie (with little red hearts baked on the top). The visit lasted comfortably long. After they departed, Bernice enjoyed a new video they lent her with just one glass of cabernet over the course of the evening.

Time had passed pleasantly over the weekend with her predicted periodic visitors. Her new cat was settling in. While not feeling fabulous, Bernice didn't sense death's door. She felt serenely comforted by an awareness of a nearby guardian spirit. Periodically, she looked for the brilliant white illumination. While it never materialized, she felt its presence.

'Whatever,' she shrugged inwardly. *'If that's helping me through this, so be it.'*

At long last, she drew upright and headed for the staircase just before ten o'clock. *'Perhaps a bagel would do me good.'* In her light blue housecoat and dirty off-white slippers, she passed the small windowed mirror in the upstairs hall and paused to assess her reflection.

"I look like shit," she muttered. "What a helluva way to live." A pale-faced, smooth-headed elderly lady stared back from the mirror's depths. Dark, hollowed circles neighbored her sunken eyes. Not one tuft of hair adorned her head, nor did any eyebrows break the grayish-yellow flesh. Bernice sneered at the image and shuffled away.

As Bernice sat at the kitchen nook, the remains of a toasted bagel got colder and harder. A cup of decaf tea–her second–warmed her hands as she surveyed the snow-crusted lawn. Three squirrels playfully ran across the hardened ground. Spirit lay entwined at her ankles, providing some warmth. In a reflective mood, Bernice watched the world, sipping her tea periodically.

* * *

On Beverly's return from the family ski trip, she emailed the First Circle. With Bernice handling chemotherapy better, the group's collective purpose waned. Each now pursued new, individualized directions. Was this the optimal outcome? She proposed gathering the group to share perspectives, strengthening them individually and collectively. Once more, Carol and Janet jumped on board readily, provided the discussion fit around their schedules. Roadblocks arose around the guys.

Skip was increasingly busy with his new role. Beyond delivering the estate plan, he was buried in Dane & Caldwell issues. Unless a clear purpose existed, he–regrettably–would decline meeting. Roger's parents were hesitant about further involvement, given his heavy course load in the second semester.

Beverly heard nothing from Rusty. Though Ridgewell was busy, Rusty wrestled his own demons. He refused to embrace the near-certain implication of the messages. Each day, the same message burned from his screen saver.

COMMIT STOP CAROUSEL B LOYAL

The Uncle signature had disappeared. *'He figures I know,'* Rusty thought. He couldn't bring himself to reengage with the group. Participating made him feel guilty and uncomfortable. Beverly's email sat unanswered in his inbox.

As a result, Beverly felt increasingly frustrated as she loaded the dishwasher on Thursday evening. She sensed a need to assemble the First Circle, yet the group was resistant. As she rinsed, an unbidden thought emerged, *'Pray.'* Persistent and throbbing, it rhythmically tapped her brain over and over. *'Pray for the First Circle. Pray hard.'*

She stopped and listened to the silence of the house. The kids were doing homework. Bill attended a dinner meeting. The furnace suddenly ignited, its rumble resonant from the basement as warm air blew against her from the duct under the cooktop, adjacent to the dishwasher. She closed her eyes and slightly bowed her head.

"Lord. I don't know where you're leading me. I sure don't know where you're leading us, but help me understand. Help me move the group in a useful direction. Be our companion as we walk this unknown road. Help each of us see our part, the role we should play." She didn't know where to go next. An unbidden thought blossomed. *'Rusty needs to believe.'*

Contemplating this thought, she tried to progress her prayer aloud. "Help Rusty find you, Lord. He seems to have the biggest struggle of our group. I don't know what his personal battles are, but he seems to need you. To find you. Help him see your light, your love. Be with all of us." Beverly slipped into more generic prayer. "God, I hope I can understand better, and be filled with your grace and peace. Be with my family and my mother-in-law. Support each step in our journey. In your name, Amen."

Beverly opened her eyes. She didn't feel particularly reassured but remained restless. Something eluded her, remaining shrouded in mystery—cloaked in a fog of darkness. *'If only the group would reconvene,'* she ruminated, though she couldn't logically articulate a compelling rationale. On some level, she could appreciate the resistance to meet. She sighed as she finished loading the dishwasher.

As Beverly turned on the dishwasher, Janet sipped tea in her own kitchen. In their basement, Walt worked on a project for one of the grandsons. She reviewed some "homework" from the Stephen Ministry training. She enjoyed the class more than she had anticipated. The fact that Walt had chosen to participate made the class more special. They talked about what they were learning almost every night over dinner, or as they settled into bed.

As she reviewed her notes, she mused on the First Circle and how her time with Bernice, while continuing a long tradition of visiting elderly shut-ins from church, had directed her toward becoming a Stephen minister. *'I wonder where the First Circle will go. It seems like our work with Bernice—while not done—has passed a critical point and helped her embrace her therapy more fully. I hope and pray so.'* Janet closed her eyes.

"Dear and Loving Father, be with us in our continued journey here on Earth. We need you. Allow your wisdom to fill us, inspire us, and move us in directions consistent with your ways. Be with Bernice as she continues her journey through the valley of the shadow of death. Give her peace. Let her not be afraid. Be with her family. Support them. Give them strength. Let them know how to best support her.

"Be with Skip as he leads his firm, exercising grace and humility, being a role model of your ways to those he leads. Give him the courage to make the hard calls, to hold firm to his principles, to enable his organization to do good—making impact in the community and the world more broadly, consistent with your ideals."

As Janet prepared to transition to Carol, Rusty's face popped into her mind and persistently tapped her conscience. Going with the thought, she paused in silence–seeing where the stream of consciousness might lead. She envisioned Rusty on a merry-go-round. Smiling, she quickly realized this was merely a visualization of his messages from David. Rusty rode one horse and then another. He kept moving amongst the gaily painted steeds. He moved at a rapid clip, which accelerated in her mind.

"Good and gracious God, be with him. Help Rusty find you. He seems unable to commit, to focus. He–certainly as much as any of us–needs you. We are all here to support and help him in his journey. Let him know your peace and your love. He's such a fine young man; I hate to see him drink so much. Perhaps you can help him find peace through you–and not through alcohol. If it's Your will, dear Lord."

Janet sank deeply into contemplative reverence as her tea cooled. She moved through the others in the First Circle, Steve and his family, Walt, other relatives and neighbors, and closed with prayers for herself. She concluded with a recitation of the Lord's Prayer and opened her eyes.

Unusual for her, Janet shared Beverly's feeling of restlessness and incompleteness as she finished. Nearly always after prayer, she was centered and at peace. Tonight, however, she couldn't shake the feeling that something was amiss. A puzzle remained unsolved. She kept cycling back to Beverly and the First Circle. She had willingly agreed to join the group again but had heard nothing further from Beverly. She frowned as she lifted the cold cup of tea toward the microwave. *'I'll give Beverly a call in the morning,'* she decided.

* * *

The message changed on Friday. When Rusty arrived at his office and booted up, a flaming font traversed his screen, a now daily event.

GROW STRONG ATTEND CH_ _ CH WHAT'S MISSING?

He couldn't help himself. As he doffed his winter coat and gloves, he smiled. "Just not going to take 'no' for an answer?" he exhaled. "And I suppose you have a church in mind?" The golden-flamed font continued scrolling across his computer with no specific church named. As the morning progressed, Rusty periodically would minimize the windows on the screen to see the same message burning on his blackened monitor. He just shook his head, both amused and irritated by the sender's persistence.

Over lunch, he googled churches in the University Sector; a lengthy list resulted. *'Where do you start?'* he thought. None of his friends attended church. Beyond Janet, he wondered where the First Circle members went. Perhaps tagging along with the Walkers might be best. *'It's so inconvenient to drive out there,'* he grimaced. *'Though it would be nice to know someone.'* An internal debate raged. *'Maybe I should just forget the whole thing. How critical could it be?'* By mid-afternoon, he felt worn down.

"Okay, I get it. I'll find a way to get there this weekend." The message brightened as he voiced his decision. "Sickest ever," he said as he watched.

He visited the Bedrock Hills website to determine the schedule of services. He stuffed the printout in his backpack, along with a listing of other churches in his neighborhood. He circled a few, putting a big exclamation mark next to St. David's Presbyterian, which was about a mile from his apartment. "Maybe that's a sign," he muttered. With the broad decision made though no specific church chosen, he focused intently on work. At least Ridgewell would get his full attention for part of the day.

* * *

Roger sweat profusely late in the last quarter of the intramural game. He had played the majority of a very competitive match-up between the Wildcats and Rolling Thunder. His face was red and his forehead glistened with moisture, as the five guys took a timeout. Roger gulped Gatorade as the team listened to their coach. The team was down by three with 1:25 left.

Putting their hands in a collective pile, the team shouted, "Wildcats!" before retaking the floor. Immediately the ball whipped down the court. As planned, Roger took position on the outside. Receiving a pass, he arced it toward the basket. With a swish–all net–the game was tied with less than one minute to play. The Wildcats grinned as the ball rocketed down the court under the other team's control. Thirty minutes later, Roger and his teammates still celebrated their buzzer-beating two-point victory in the locker room.

Within the hour, Roger was delivering newspapers. Due to the ice, he was forced to walk. When he got to Professor Langdon's house, he walked tentatively up the icy sidewalk. Rather than just drop *The Ledger* on the doorstep, he rang the doorbell, signaling the paper's arrival. Halfway down the walk, the door opened. The gaunt, graying body of Dr. Langdon stood in the doorway. She motioned weakly to come closer. Retracing his steps, he trotted back–taking the three steps to the front stoop in one leap.

"You're gonna kill yourself on the ice," growled the professor.

"I'm okay." Roger paused. "How are you?"

"Well, I'm not dead yet," Bernice cackled, her lips briefly curled upwards. "Not today, anyway."

"That's good, I guess," returned Roger, somewhat nervously.

"Can you step inside?"

"For just a moment. I have more deliveries," the tall teen shrugged the nearly empty bag on his shoulder.

"Won't hurt you to warm up," a grim-faced Bernice responded.

Roger stepped through the doorway.

"You're taller than the last time I saw you."

"My mom says I'm still growing."

"Speak up. You're mumbling. How tall are you?"

"Almost five ten. I'm just about my dad's height."

"I see. Let me get you a hot drink."

"You don't have to. I'm okay."

"No, I think you could use it. I certainly could. Hot chocolate?"

"Are you sure? I don't want you to have to . . . " Roger's voice trailed off.

"Nonsense. I am certainly capable of making hot chocolate. A cup for you and one for me."

"Okay, but I can't stay long."

Bernice shuffled toward the kitchen. Roger dropped his knit cap and gloves on the radiator in the front hallway. He unzipped his parka and followed the professor, after wiping his boots on the doormat.

"Take your coat off. Sit a while."

Reluctantly, Roger finished unzipping his coat and placed it on a kitchen chair.

"So, what's new?"

"Not much, I guess."

"I've been stuck in this house so long. You must have something going on."

"Well, we won our basketball game today: 56–54."

"Good. You play much?"

"Yeah. I played almost the whole game. It was way close."

"I see." Conversation halted as Bernice moved around the kitchen. Spirit mirrored every move.

"Your cat really stays with you."

"Quite different than my last cats. They were independent. This one is more of a companion."

"I see." Quiet returned, save for the soft tick-tock of the entry hall clock.

"Had any messages from the angel lately?"

Taken aback, Roger stuttered, "Well, it's been kinda quiet." He hesitated. "Do you get messages from him?"

Now Bernice paused, as the milk slowly warmed on the cooktop. "No, but I've seen him."

"You have?" Roger professed surprise.

"Can't imagine who else–what else–it could've been."

"Some of us saw him the other night, here in your kitchen."

"Really?" expressed Bernice, jolted. "Right here?"

"Yeah, at the table. When a bunch of us were over." Bernice looked across the top of her large, thick glasses. "You know: Mrs. Langdon, Mrs. Kneffler, Mr. O'Neill–"

"They all saw the angel?" Bernice interrupted.

"Well, not everybody. Just most of us." Roger thought back. "Rusty, Mrs. Kneffler, me, and Mr. O'Neill too."

"Not Beverly?"

"Mrs. Langdon?" Bernice nodded. "No, she sensed a presence, but didn't see him. The man was behind her."

"Really?" Bernice removed the bubbling hot chocolate from the stove and poured two mugs. "Did this angel speak?"

"Not really. He was just kinda here, while we were praying."

"I don't pray much."

"Maybe you should." Bernice glared at Roger suddenly. "Well, maybe not. I don't know." Roger sipped his cocoa too fast, burning his tongue. His eyes watered, but he said nothing.

Bernice finally spoke, "Perhaps I should. Funny, I didn't consider it much before. Now that I'm sick, I wonder if I'm missing something." Roger didn't know what to say and chose to sip his slowly cooling hot chocolate.

"So what has this angel told you to do?" Bernice pushed.

"I don't know. The last message–well, before saying to meet with the others–was to be a role model. He said, 'Lead.' Had something to do with basketball."

Bernice's face softened, "Well, you're certainly a fine young man. I suspect you could be quite a role model. Maybe for more than your team."

"I dunno," Roger blushed and smiled, his deep dimple showing.

"Leading comes in lots of varieties."

"But Brian's the captain."

"No matter. You can lead others: in your classes, through your friends, with people you meet. Hell, you could even be a leader in this angel group."

"Nah, they're all older than me."

"Doesn't matter. Age has nothing to do with it. Be a leader to others. Set an example for them. I bet you can do more than you think."

Roger stammered–his mouth opening and shutting like a beached fish. Reflexively, he drank, yielding a dark chocolately line above his upper lip. He licked it away.

"You might even teach me a thing or two," smiled Bernice.

"No way."

"Now I don't share this frequently, but I always learned from my students. Sometimes more from them, than I think they got from me. It was a good semester if that happened."

Roger stared back at Bernice in disbelief.

"Really." Bernice sipped the end of her chocolate and sighed. "I'm starting to feel a little tired. Chemo really saps your energy."

"Well, I better go."

"Thank you for visiting."

"Thanks for the hot chocolate, ma'am."

"Stop with the elders. Let's just be friends."

"I'll try, Professor."

Roger pulled on his coat and collected his gloves, scarf, and hat. He handed the newspaper to the professor as she reached the bottom of the staircase. "Here's your paper. Maybe you'll feel like reading it later."

"Maybe. Thanks for stopping by."

Roger stepped out into the frigid cold as Bernice ascended the stairs very slowly. As Roger walked away, the little candles in the windows flickered to life in the growing dusk. Unsettled by the newsboy's visit, Bernice climbed into bed and closed her eyes. Memories of the brilliant, illuminated angel flooded her. She couldn't pinpoint what made her restless and alert, despite her deep fatigue.

"I don't pray much."

"Maybe you should."

The two phrases bounced around like two wildly careening ping-pong balls. Even with her eyes closed, the words sparkled in her mind, as if branded on her conscience. She opened her eyes. "Shit," she muttered to Spirit. "Maybe I should." Closing her eyes, darkness enveloped her.

'I don't even know how to start,' she thought. Uninvited, the phrase, "be yourself," entered her brain, rocketing across her synapses with clarity. It joined the drumbeat of her conversation with Roger.

In a raspy voice, Bernice began, "I give up. I'm talking to you. Whoever you are. Hello, God. How are ya? I've been better. Can't say otherwise. And what is this cancer all about? Did you dream this one up? What did I do to deserve this? Shit. This has been horrific. I know I'm not that religious, but is this the consequence? Tell me."

But God and His angels remained silent. For the first time in decades, Bernice stumbled through a conversation with God.

"I don't get this cancer thing. Is it going to kill me? I know I almost did myself in, but it all seemed so hopeless. I was so ill. Now, at least, I feel I can handle it. Seeing that vision was comforting. And now, I feel like it—well, whatever it is—is with me. Is that you? Or some angel? Is this the same angel this group sees? And talks to? Could it be David?

"I'm not too sure; this isn't my field. I'd like to trust in some divine plan, but it's excruciating not knowing and—I hate to think it—I'm cynical. You know, glass half empty?" Bernice smiled midprayer. "God, help me understand. Help me get better. All right, I admit it; I can't do this on my own. I need your help. Please, Lord."

Bernice muttered the same phrases over and over, and she was soon crying a steady stream. Her cheeks moist, she opened her bloodshot eyes nearly an hour later. Unexpectedly, she felt great peace. While certainly not cured, she felt in control of her body, senses, and thoughts. A burden had lifted. As her eyes adjusted to the room's dimness, she became aware of a growing light radiating from the bathroom.

'Did I leave a light on?' she wondered. The illumination grew in brilliance and then began moving. Drifting toward the doorway, the light flickered—moving from brilliant whites to deep golden hues. Bernice watched fascinated as the light filled the transom between bedroom and bath. A man's profile became more evident in the center of the light. The warmth cascading from his presence was overwhelming. She felt excitement, awe, and fear as the light continued its journey. Transfixed, a virtual paralysis pinned her to the headboard as the figure and the surrounding golden white glow moved close.

Attired in white, the man smiled gently and floated to the edge of the bed. Sitting down, he leaned over and stroked her arm. An oddly pleasant burning sensation entered her frail forearm, filling her body. This penetrating warmth traveled through her as the angel continued caressing. The radiation ended just below her breastbone, warming her central cavity. She wanted to look down to see if her chest and torso glowed as they felt so warm. But she could only stare into the startling brown eyes of the angel, seated on her bed.

> *"You are blessed, Bernice. Your journey continues, but God will be with you always. I bring you certain and glad tidings. May the peace and love of God be with you today and forevermore. Go out and share this light with others. You are blessed, Bernice. Deeply and truly blessed."*

Was the angel speaking? Or was she imagining dialogue? She couldn't tell, nor did it matter. The love he shared was abundant and everlasting. The angel's eyes were kind and deeply familiar. Yet, she couldn't identify this man who sat on her bed. This was clearly the same presence which accompanied her as she hovered between life and death in her car and later at the Medical Center during chemo.

"Is that you, David?" she wanted to say, but found she couldn't. "Please, stay. Don't leave again. Your presence is reassuring. I feel secure and strong. Don't leave." Her mouth remained paralyzed. No sounds came forth, but none were needed. The angel nodded.

"God is with you always, Bernice. Be a witness to that. Even when the light is not visible, it is always–eternally–with you. Go in peace. Serve Him well."

Bernice again couldn't tell if the angel spoke. The words melodiously came to her, as if received in a different dimension, using senses unlike the familiar five. As she watched, the angel rose. He touched her forehead with his brilliant hand–making the sign of the cross and murmuring a final blessing. He smiled and walked toward the curtained window. He looked over his shoulder, held up his hand in an apparent benediction, and glided effortlessly through the closed window creating a glittering trail of light behind him, which slowly dissipated like mist in the morning.

With his departure, Bernice felt a deep calm. This all-encompassing inner peace contrasted sharply with the earlier tranquility she felt, which now seemed small and insignificant. Her entire body felt touched and warmed by the presence of this emissary of God; a spirit had sat with her and in her. The aftermath of being touched by an angel caused more tears to flow freely as she lay quietly, enjoying the residual glow from her vision. Bernice fell into a deep, serene slumber–not waking for the phone, which rang periodically through the evening.

Beverly worried about the unanswered phone, but Bill convinced her that his lunchtime visit was good. His mother likely just called it an early evening. As a result, no one else visited the house on Fox Den that evening, after Roger and the angel departed. Behind the windows of little flickering lights, the house and owner were at peace.

FORTY-SIX

The lobby clock showed seven when Rusty left the Ridgewell building Friday evening. Eric had suggested they connect for drinks and chow at the Marina Grill. Rusty found him standing at the bar, talking with friends.

"Hey, good lookin'. Buy you a beer?" Eric smiled in his direction.

"Sounds good, man. What a day."

"You and me both, bro. Glad it's the weekend."

Momentum carried Rusty from cocktails through dinner to a series of bars around Harborside. He and Eric parted shortly after ten, when his roommate hooked up with a twenty-something clone. Drifting down the street to the Railroad, Rusty shifted to Jack & Coke to intensify his buzz. At the busy bar, a thirty-something couple was having a hard time keeping their hands off each other. Surprisingly, they allowed Rusty to squeeze in. While he waited for a drink, he became increasingly aware that the woman kept bumping him. Assuming some level of drunkenness, he ignored her until she ran her hand down his side, giving his tight abs an appreciative squeeze. When he looked directly at her, she winked and laughed. He smiled back, assuming that her growing inebriation caused some overly friendly flirtation.

The crowded bar slowed the bartender. Rusty patiently waited and again, the blonde's hand rippled down his side, ending with a squeeze. Looking over, realization abruptly dawned that this time the hand belonged to the woman's dark-haired boyfriend. He turned abruptly and the couple giggled.

"Hey, what gives?" Rusty demanded.

"You're cute, that's all," responded the blonde. "I'm Ellen . . . and this," she pointed dramatically, "is Mark." The guys shook hands.

"We just wondered if you were up for playing . . . " the guy's voice trailed off.

'You've got to be kidding,' thought Rusty, as unexplored terrain beckoned. Aloud, he stumbled, "I don't know. I've never really . . . you know, it's not been my thing."

"There's always a first time," laughed Ellen. "We like adding a little spice now and then."

"That's right, a little spice," Mark's straight white teeth sparkled. "Maybe we could buy you a drink and just get to know each other?"

"I don't know," stammered Rusty.

"Sure. Look here's your drink." Mark leaned over the bar. "Hey, put this one on our tab. Our treat." He grinned again. "No commitments. Just a friendly drink, okay?"

Rusty shrugged. "Well, okay, I guess." He sipped his Jack & Coke. Mark and Ellen monopolized the conversation initially, after confirming that Rusty was single and alone. Discussing their open relationship, Rusty clearly understood that it was not just Ellen who was interested. Provocatively, Mark's appeal grew. *'A little variety could be good,'* Rusty thought. He nursed his drink and smiled.

Saturday morning, Rusty awoke but kept his eyes closed, enjoying the luxury of no alarm. He burrowed more deeply into the covers, as he reflected on the prior evening. Mark and Ellen plied drinks for another couple of rounds. The physical touch quotient rose sharply as the clock wound toward midnight. He found himself becoming more intrigued with the possible permutations that might emerge.

As the clock hands merged at twelve, he spied an antique tin placard hanging over the bar. The aging, yet still bold red letters promoted *Carousel Beer.* An Old World merry-go-round with several horses stood guard on one side. The horses' hooves shot off little flames, as if moving so fast they created combustion. Never before noticing the *Carousel* ad, his inner core shook even through his pleasant buzz.

Suddenly, Rusty pled the need for the restroom. Mark chose to stay with Ellen though his eyes suggested broader interests. Within moments, Rusty was several blocks away hoofing it toward home.

Lying in bed, he remained surprised with the outcome. *'I'll bet they were pissed,'* he thought. *'But it actually feels okay. Maybe–just maybe–I am changing . . . at least for one night.'* He smiled, *'Though hard to believe.'*

He spent Saturday doing laundry and paying bills. While using e-banking, he received another message–no longer any surprise. He had taken a phone call and gotten a soda; when he returned, the screen saver blinked.

GOOD PROGRESS   NIX 1 NTS   CH_ _CH   GROW FAITH

"I know: I'll be there. I've got the info right here." He pulled out his notes as if to substantiate his plans. "The one nighters? Shit, I don't know. I wasn't even trying to hook up last night. Things happen. Can I help it if I'm such a good looking stud?" He laughed. The burning letters silently marched across the screen with their shimmering flames.

Deciding that attending with someone he knew would be preferable, Rusty called the Walkers. Janet was delighted ("Your coming to our church is like an answer to my prayers," she gushed.) Rusty stayed home that evening with a rented movie both to ensure he was up early and to try to bravely follow his messenger's counsel.

*   *   *

Rusty arrived at the Presbyterian church midway through the prelude. As Janet saw him start down the center aisle, she stood to flag him. He nodded in acknowledgement and joined the Walkers in a pew near the front.

Janet gave him a hug, "I'm delighted you're here. I hope you enjoy the service. Dr. Andrews is preaching. I know you'll find him inspirational."

Walt reached over to shake hands. Rusty smiled in return and looked around the sanctuary. He saw the O'Neills and gave a friendly little wave to Skip, who smiled and nodded. As the choir entered, Rusty perused the bulletin. Janet reached over and pointed out the "Young Adults" outing, scheduled for Wednesday evening.

"A very fine group, I hear. You might enjoy getting to know them. I can find one of the leaders so you might even connect today." Rusty smiled but said nothing, as—fortunately—the senior pastor strode to the pulpit and began his welcome.

The packed congregation sang hymns robustly, proving energetic and lively throughout the hour. While not a charismatic group ("We Presbyterians are the frozen chosen, you know," Walt chuckled over brunch), the group was enthusiastic and engaged. They laughed appreciatively and applauded when the "Cherubs Choir"—a group of fifteen pre-schoolers—worked through two songs with an abundance of seemingly unchoreographed hand motions.

The sermon moved Rusty far more than he expected. Reverend Andrews was blessed with a gift for bringing scriptures to life. In his message, "Opportunities in Disguise," he used scripture to articulate God's plan and design for Christians. Challenges people face are truly just opportunities waiting for discovery and action, he preached. Rusty felt drawn increasingly into the sermon. The pastor referenced 2 Corinthians 4:17:

> *For our light and momentary troubles are achieving for us an eternal glory that far outweighs them all.*

Dr. Andrews proclaimed purpose exists in suffering. Problems present all people with opportunities. They remind all of Christ's suffering. They help Christians avoid becoming full of pride and arrogance, resulting in faith-filled humility. Problems serve as reminders that eternal life is far more important than this brief life on earth. Earthly challenges also provide God with opportunities to demonstrate His awesome power.

Rusty thought of Bernice. Her troubles set up her eternal life. They forced her to focus on broader issues than her mortal life. Through her pain and suffering, she also reminded all those around her that God was using this opportunity to draw people closer to Him.

Rusty's eyes welled up several times, as he considered his own life and challenges. His focus strengthened further when the pastor referenced Hebrews 13:7:

Remember your leaders, who spoke the word of God to you. Consider the outcome of their way of life and imitate their faith.

'Who are the leaders in my life?' mused Rusty. *'My parents? Sue?'* He reflected on who influenced him most. His daydreams drifted toward the First Circle and the omnipresent messenger.

Pastor Andrews clipped along rapidly, his passion building. "You must keep your eyes on the prize; we all must. Christ is our ultimate leader–not the humans around us, regardless of how much they might offer. Christ will never change and always will be the same forever. Friends, each of us," and here Rusty swore the pastor stared directly at him. "Each of us can trust our unchanging Lord. So, when troubles present themselves, first we must trust in our ever present, ever capable, awesome Lord. Further, we should look at those problems as opportunities to grow faith." Again, the pastor looked deeply into Rusty's eyes.

Dr. Andrews transitioned to a final story, sharing how being present in the final days of his father's life had been excruciating, yet made him stronger. He was convinced that in his father's last breaths, the angels of God were present to embrace him and take him to a better place. Emotionally moving and physically draining, he was convinced that this pain–this problem–was a means of strengthening his own faith and, in some humble way, that of those around him. A problem was an opportunity to listen to the ways and means of God.

Rusty felt drained by the end of the sermon. Janet reached out as the pastor concluded and gave his hand a gentle squeeze. She seemed to sense the pastor's impact. *'Wow,'* he thought. *'The messages–regardless of who is sending them and what my connection is–they have clear intent.'*

"Now, I know this is unusual for us Presbyterians, but I invite you forward, if you are so moved, for a traditional altar call. Bring your troubles, your problems, your opportunities to Jesus. Trust in Him to help you along your path in life. With other elders of the church, I will meet you at the front of the sanctuary, during the singing of the last hymn." Pastor Andrews found Rusty again. "Come, join us. Grow your faith."

Rusty's eyes filled once more. The pastor kept echoing the messenger. Maybe stepping forward would bring clarity. Without much thought, Rusty nudged past Janet and Walt and headed toward the front of the church.

Moments later, Pastor Andrews grasped Rusty's hands tightly and stared deeply into his soul, welcoming him as a growing believer. "We're all learning. We're all striving to understand and grow faith. Good progress–day by day–that's how Christ strengthens you and reinforces your beliefs. Confess your sins, repent, and through His grace, you are granted forgiveness and eternal life." He paused and surveyed Rusty's countenance.

"Are you ready to bring your sins to God and repent of them?"

Rusty nodded.

"Do you accept Jesus as your Lord and Savior?"

Rusty thought back to that long ago time when he sat in Sunday School at his parents' Nashville church. The image of Jesus standing at a door waiting to be invited in entered his mind. He mumbled, "Yes," and again felt his eyes tear.

Pastor Andrews placed his hands on Rusty's bowed head. "Gracious Father. Be with our brother as he continues his journey of faith. Strengthen him, abide with him, help him to choose the path that serves you best. Help him grow his faith. Amen." The minister paused as he and Rusty stared deeply into each other's eyes.

"Go in peace, son. Serve the Lord. Take each day step by step. Make good progress. Grow your faith."

Rusty straightened up as the pastor made the sign of the cross and stepped back to the pulpit to give the closing benediction.

After church, the Walkers and Rusty stood in line to shake hands with Reverend Andrews. The O'Neills stood behind them.

"Some sermon," Skip summarized.

"I'll say," nodded Rusty, his eyes puffy.

"I have to agree. You know, I was thinking about Bernice as . . . " Janet injected.

"You too?"

"So was I," agreed Skip. "Her illness has been such a galvanizing event for all of us. The sermon makes me see it as a huge opportunity to grow our faith."

"Like the story of his dad," added Rusty seriously. "I hadn't thought about all of this as an opportunity."

"I should say so. My, he is such a good speaker. He always makes me think."

The threesome approached the double doors and shook the pastor's hand. Janet introduced Rusty as a surrogate son (of sorts) who had been helping with Bernice Langdon.

Dr. Andrews beamed warmly as he took Rusty's hand, "Sounds like you were sent by God. Right time, right place. I could've used you as an example this morning. Making problems into opportunities?"

"I don't know about that," Rusty reddened and shrugged. "I was just there and knew enough to help out." He paused, "Thank you for your personal words. They were more meaningful than you might imagine. I sure hope I can live up to them."

"You've done the important thing–you've stepped forward and accepted your Lord and Savior. Our faith journey is lifelong. Step by step, day by day." The Pastor now spoke more fully to the group surrounding the door.

"Wherever your life adventure takes you—the highs, the lows, the beginnings, the endings—God is with you, helping and supporting. Listen to Him. Abide his counsel. Grow your faith."

'There he goes again,' thought Rusty. *'It must be more than coincidental.'*

"Now you come back and be with us again, okay?" twinkled the senior pastor. Reverend Andrews turned to Walt, as Janet and Rusty followed the O'Neills to the crowded narthex.

"Now, Rusty, you'll join us for brunch? I won't take no for an answer. You've driven all the way out here and must be famished."

"I don't know. I've got a lot—"

"Like I said, I won't accept no." Rusty acquiesced and followed the Walkers to one of their favorite after-church haunts, where the three caught up, starting with Bernice, her health, and the First Circle members. They moved to Walt's latest woodworking projects, Rusty's upcoming choir concerts, and Janet's new leadership role in shepherding several emerging Stephen ministers.

"I can't say that I'm necessarily the best at this. There was a need for someone to help and I agreed. It's more like being—oh, what do they call it—a player-coach?" Rusty and Walt nodded. "Though I'm learning as much (if not more) than all the others in the class."

They ended their brunch on the topic of technology. The Walkers were contemplating getting new internet service. Using layman's terms, Rusty tried to resolve their confusion between a 'digital subscriber line' provided by the telephone company and cable service offerings. Sharing his own experiences with DSL, he explained the benefits and downsides and outlined the questions they should ask the two vendors as they made their decision.

"So, we end our brunch where we first started?" Walt chuckled. "You talking about technology and us Neanderthals trying desperately to understand and not ask too many dumb questions!" The trio laughed. The Walkers treated him to brunch, despite Rusty's protests. Moments later, the two cars departed in opposite directions.

On the drive back to the city, Rusty thought through the church service and his takeaways. How could his problems be made into opportunities? Could he really trust the inputs he was receiving through the First Circle and, allegedly, David O'Neill to steer him in the right direction? This acknowledgement of faith and its implications seemed clearly less exciting in the near-term, but might be more fulfilling in the long haul. Admittedly, those who appeared closer to God seemed more at peace. While exemplars included Reverend Andrews and both Walkers, even Skip seemed more balanced. Maybe he could achieve a better equilibrium as he committed his life to God. Was this the commitment David suggested?

Driving fast, he remained confused and torn. Was enjoying his current 'carefree life' too shallow? Were the messages on target? Returning to the central question: Should he commit? And commit to what? A person or his faith? Had he already done so at the altar? He smiled, *'This may be a problem, but it's really a disguised opportunity.'* He turned up the volume as the oldies radio station cut to, "*Dust in the Wind,*" by Kansas. *'How apropos . . . '* he thought.

"All we are is dust in the wind . . . "

FORTY-SEVEN

By mid-March, life resumed normal rhythms for the First Circle. While spring was still several weeks away, a growing brightness filled the air. The experiences of the winter were woven inextricably into their life tapestries. David's messages were no longer a dynamic intrusion in their days.

Leading Dane & Caldwell proved all-consuming. The possibility of scandal mushrooming still hung over the firm, but with his partners' support, Skip navigated the fine line of moving the firm back toward its core, principled business of serving clients. His warm, accessible engagement–putting the interests of others in the practice first and leading with grace and humility–set a new tone for the firm.

Beverly's lunch with the executive director of the loose-knit federation of social workers resulted in an offer to join the network, which Beverly accepted–after discussions at the family table. She served two different families who were in crisis, while continuing to accompany Bernice to chemo. Busier than ever, Beverly felt energized and fulfilled.

Carol spent two full days at the Langdons' after each chemo, but was needed less and less as Bernice radiated a new peace. While the initial days following treatment remained brutal, she handled recovery better. In apparent remission, Dr. Esch thought treatment might end by early April. Carol began work with three new clients. She continued logging extensive hours ministering to these families, leveraging her keen sense of humor and good-natured commonsense. Her gift–helping others through painful, stress-filled times–grew in distinctiveness.

The Stephen Ministry engaged Janet and Walt. Janet led weekly seminars, based on her personal experiences. She and Pastor Bob got along surprisingly well, given that he still "really wasn't one of her favorites." She complemented his unique attributes with her talents, achieving powerful impact across the congregation.

Though unlikely to make either the JV or varsity teams, Roger tried out for the Whittaker baseball team. When Roger learned that the Whittaker administration was contemplating starting a ninth grade team, he initiated a campaign to find sufficient guys. He quietly but effectively canvassed the halls throughout Whittaker High. By mid-month, he accumulated the requisite headcount and was named team captain. At one point, he realized "Uncle David" might not have meant basketball after all.

Rusty's journey proved arduous. Even after the altar call, he remained in turmoil over his faith and his life. He partied on the weekends, and on one occasion hooked up, though guilt racked him afterward, leaving him more conflicted and confused than ever. Celebrating his twenty-eighth birthday with friends also fell flat. Fortunately, Ridgewell completely consumed him. He received rave reviews for the impact of two major systems efforts he led. If only he could get his personal life running smoothly.

Janet invited him to church, but he always found reasons to decline until mid-March. With no plans, he acquiesced on a Saturday afternoon. *'It can't hurt,'* he reflected. *'Maybe it will address this unsettled feeling. Things can't go downhill.'*

One month after attending his first church service in Bedrock, Rusty's Miata was once more parked in the large church lot. He joined the Walkers just as Reverend Andrews began sharing notable events in the church calendar, chock full due to the nearing Easter holiday.

His Lenten sermon spotlighted the Gospel of John. John, a fisherman and a disciple, tended to be selfish and have outbursts of anger. Yet, Jesus considered him one of his three most intimate disciples.

"So what can we as Christians learn from John?" The Pastor moved toward his conclusion. "John sets an example. He came to realize just how much he was loved. By recognizing that pure, abundant love, he was able to replicate and grow his love for others. We also learn something vital to each of us." Dr. Andrews looked around the congregation and found Rusty; his eyes burned into him as he spoke.

"When God changes a life–as He did with John, He does not take away individual personality. Not at all." Rusty felt the pastor's penetrating focus. "Rather, He puts those eccentricities, those elements of who we are, to abundant and wonderfully unique use–serving His needs, His desires, and His master plan. Have you–each of you," he finally looked away, "put your gifts, your talents, your personality quirks, and traits and eccentricities to use for Him? Or, are you fearing that in turning over your life to Him, you'll need to give up some part of who you are?

"Certainly, He asks for sacrifice. You can't keep the bad habits, the ungodly aspects of your life. You give that away for something far better. It's a small price, and yet–He asks–in fact, He demands–that you use your individual strengths, profiles, and talents in ways unique to you to serve Him."

Rusty was shaken. This was precisely his fear. He didn't want to give up his personality, nor his idiosyncrasies. Could he maintain them and still be faithful? Could his life still be fun? Subconsciously, he shook his head. *'I know I have to make changes–sacrifices, but maybe I can still be who I am . . . '* Janet watched Rusty process the preacher's words.

As the minister closed with a brief prayer, Rusty bowed his head and closed his eyes. Though listening to Dr. Andrews, he drifted to his own tangential conversation with God.

'God, I am so confused. This is just messed up. I thought everything was

going along just fine . . . but now, I'm just not so sure. What's happening? It seems like I'm being called to something different . . . to change. But I'm not sure I want to. Shit, what's the matter with me?' Rusty blushed spontaneously with the expletive.

'Sorry, God. I just don't know. I'm just not sure what to do, or how to be. Everyone else seems to know so clearly.' A thought unbidden entered his head. *'What? Just say yes? Yes to what? You? Just be with me? Be a part of my life?'* Rusty's eyes moistened.

'I don't know exactly what you mean, but I need help. I guess I need you. Will you really join me? Enter my life more fully? Help me be stronger? Understand better what this is really all about? I'll try, Man. Really. It's gotta be better than this . . . '

Rusty continued his prayer as the congregation rose to sing, "Number 525: *Here I Am.*" The lump in his throat grew unusually large making singing episodic as he opened his eyes. The Walkers' voices mixed beautifully as he listened to how the Lord moved them and the other congregants belting out the chorus,

"Here I am Lord. It is I Lord. Help me find the way . . . "

Following the service, Rusty needed solitude. He bid goodbye to the Walkers and soon buzzed back toward the city. Despite the gorgeous blue sky and bright sunshine, he looked through a wet windshield as he navigated the highway.

* * *

Returning home after church, the Walkers, the O'Neills, and Rusty found identical voicemail messages from Beverly. She and Bernice extended an impromptu dinner invitation for that evening. They hoped the First Circle and their respective "better halves" would gather for a cookout at six. If each would bring a side dish or dessert, Bill would man the grill. Given the still present chill, they would eat inside.

Though not at church, the Knefflers and Roger received the same message. Remarkably, all were available except Rusty. He begged off; he'd been to the suburbs that morning and wasn't up for another trip. Despite Beverly's enthusiastic efforts, she hung up with his regrets resolute.

After the call, Rusty lay on his bed, his eyes closed. *'Why not go?'* he questioned. *'Why am I not joining them? What is the matter with me? I'm trying to embrace this faith thing, but then I don't want to. I just feel this emptiness. Sheee-it, I'm psychotic or something.'*

Restless, he sat up and strode to the computer. "Where did I leave off?" he muttered. He scrolled down the Word document, skimming his prose. His stream-of-consciousness journaling had taken a twist in recent weeks as he attempted to analyze his innermost feelings.

He reread earlier excerpts:

Went to altar. Don't quite know why. Felt drawn to do so. The Pastor was talking to me. I just knew it. I accepted Christ, but I'm not sure what that means. Shouldn't it be more clear?

Don't know if I can make this journey. Not remotely clear on where it all goes. Am I giving up too much? But what if I don't? Maybe I'm giving up more. Shit.

He scrolled down. In one entry, he labored over the pros and cons of deepening his faith and connecting more fully and intimately with Christ. As he read his confusion, he felt tears build again.

"This sucks," he said aloud. "Why is this so hard?" His cheeks glistened, as the last communiqué seared his mind,

GOOD PROGRESS NIX 1 NTS CH_ _ CH GROW FAITH

Feeling unexpectedly driven, Rusty sank to his knees and held onto his desk chair. "Please God, help me. This sucks as it is and I don't understand. I thought I'd feel different right away. I really want to get my shit together . . . and maybe, just maybe, I need to trust you. I'm giving it to you, Big Guy. I can't seem to do this myself. I want more fulfillment. I want something more. Please–please–enter my life. I'm yours. I'll try hard. I can't promise perfection, but I'll give it a whirl. Help me learn from others and learn from You. Lead me to use my gifts, and keep me unique."

Rusty's tears fell ceaselessly as his conversation with God continued unabated, as the sun crossed the afternoon sky. Nearing three o'clock, he opened his eyes as if waking from a long sleep. For the next hour, he poured himself out in his journal. With a growing smile, an unexplained serenity filled him as he wrote. He couldn't understand why such angst and uncertainty consumed him a few hours prior.

This is awesome. I feel more energized and focused than I have in - well - forever. Wow. I hope this doesn't end. I don't know that I'll be the best Christian out there, but I'm gonna die trying! :)

With that, Rusty saved the document one last time. As he prepared to close the window, his monitor blackened; the omnipresent screen saver stayed absent. As he watched, the border–unsurprisingly–began glowing, ember-like. The perimeter expanded in width and quickly assumed its familiar burning appearance.

"I just knew it would be here." Rusty patiently waited.

BE WHO YOU ARE
CONTRIB 2 CIRCLE
BE LIGHT 4 OTHERS

Rusty shook his head. "Well, I'll be. I'm not surprised." He pointed at the screen, "It's like you're watching, and now you want me to attend this party. Whoever you are, you sure can get inside my head. I'm not sure what all this means," he smiled, "but it fits with what I heard and what I'm feeling.

I guess I can't just closet myself away and expect that to be sufficient. I need to use whatever modest talents I've got." He laughed again. "Glenwood: I'm on my way."

As he stepped away, Rusty didn't notice the message fade. Nor did he note ten minutes later when the border began to glow again.

* * *

Bernice's house was hopping by shortly after six o'clock. Kelly and Kevin joined Roger, Brad, and Caitlyn in a spirited croquet match in the side yard despite the cool temperatures. In the kitchen nook, Bernice maintained a wonderful vantage point to watch dinner preparations inside, the smoky grill outside, as well as certain key wickets.

Amy accompanied Skip, though the three boys stayed home with Domino's. Janet and Walt were the last arrivals, as the butter-cream frosted chocolate cake ("Made with a cup of hot coffee–that's the secret," Janet whispered conspiratorially to Beverly) took longer to cool than predicted. Bernice greeted visitors regally from her perch. She hoped Monday's chemo was potentially the last round, based on continuing good indications from her lab work. Only Rusty was missing at six thirty.

"We shouldn't hold the burgers and dogs on the grill; they'll be charred beyond recognition," pronounced Bill.

"I don't know where he is. He left a message just after four saying his plans had changed. He said he would be here," noted Beverly to no one in particular.

"Not to worry," interrupted Carol. "He can grab something when he gets here. Looks like we've got plenty."

"Of course," nodded Beverly. "Shall we get everyone around the island for grace?"

Janet offered grace in a more informal, casual manner than in the past–practicing what she was learning in her Stephen classes. "Engage with our God as you would a friend. Don't feel compelled to be stiff and formal," counseled Pastor Bob. Soon after, all the fixings of a summer picnic created mountains on the festive dinnerware. The smell of grilled hot dogs and cheeseburgers filled the air. Clusters of people filled the kitchen, dining room, and office. The clink of silverware and glasses punctuated the laughter and conversation.

The clock chimed seven and several people–mostly the men and Roger–continued visiting the buffet line.

"I'm worried about Rusty. Do you think everything's okay?"

"Oh, Janet, I'm sure it is," soothed Walt. "He was just fine this morning."

"Is that why he was already out here?" nodded Beverly. "He mentioned being in the suburbs."

Janet smiled, "He joined us at church. Such a good service today."

"That was a strong message," agreed Skip as he rinsed his plate. "I know I was moved."

"I believe Rusty was as well. I think he's wrestling with some personal demons. I hope today's message spoke to him."

"I would agree. He's got much to offer. I hope he finds some peace."

Skip listened to the two women, "I may be out in left field on this, but I think–like you–he's been fighting some personal battle. We all worry about his drinking, but I think there's something more."

Janet nodded sympathetically. "I'm sure the good Lord will help him. Going to church is a good start."

"Shall we get out dessert? I've got a hankering for some of that famous chocolate cake I've heard so much about," laughed Carol.

"I'll make coffee," noted Beverly. She set up the coffeemaker and plugged it in. She gasped, as the Mr. Coffee clock blinked to life. The flame-colored gold numbers were distinctly not the norm.

9:11 alternated with *AS:AP*

"Oh my," gulped Beverly, "Guys, we have a problem." Automatically, she turned toward where Bernice sat, sipping tea. "I'm not sure what . . . but there's a new message."

Skip strode purposefully into the room. "Hey, I just got a message," he announced. "On my Blackberry, while I was in the bathroom:

9 – 1 – 1 ASAP "

"You too?" Beverly's color paled. "Look. On the coffeemaker."

Carol burst into the kitchen. "I was upstairs, getting the kids–they're in the computer room–and I got a text message on my cell phone. These things are like a ball and chain. It's that glowing border and–"

Beverly interrupted, "9-1-1. ASAP?"

"How'd you know?"

"Skip and I each received the same," she pointed toward the coffeemaker.

"Now, wait a minute. I'm the one who gets food and drink messages. Not you," Carol tried to lighten the escalating anxiety. "Bad attempt. Sorry."

"So, what's the emergency?" Skip asserted quickly.

"It's got to be Rusty. Don't you think?"

"Mother's accounted for. Where's Roger?"

"Fine. He's upstairs."

"Rusty's not here. Something's happened. I sense it." Beverly's color continued draining.

"Beverly, sit down. I don't want you passing out," Carol advised, as Janet stepped into the kitchen. She immediately sensed the mood.

"What's wrong?" she asked quizzically, though before anyone could answer, Roger came downstairs to investigate dessert.

"Doesn't look like you're cutting the cake yet, huh?" When they all turned to stare, Roger responded, "Hey, what's the matter?"

Beverly pointed at the flashing coffeemaker. Skip seized the moment, "So what are we going to do?"

Beverly lifted the phone, "I'm calling his home. Let's see if we can reach him." Moments later, they heard his voicemail greeting on the speakerphone. She hung up after leaving a curt, "Rusty, it's Beverly. Call me ASAP. Thanks." The group stood quietly.

The other kids entered the kitchen. "Let's cut the cake for them, while we try to figure out our options." The kids soon inhaled generous slices of the chocolate cake. Brad, Caitlyn, and Kevin all helped themselves to chocolate chip cookies as well. Roger surreptitiously snuck several to hold him over while the adults quietly discussed possible actions.

"Let's try his home phone again," suggested Carol.

"If he's not there, I have his cell phone number," noted Janet.

Minutes later, neither phone was answered beyond respective voicemail greetings. His office extension also yielded another dead-end, after Janet dialed.

Carol raised a new idea, "What if I try the Med Center? I know a bunch of folks there; it's close to where he lives."

"Sure," Skip nodded. "I could try the local police as well. While I don't do much local practice, I can work some connections."

"Sounds like a long shot," suggested Amy who listened from the side, "but couldn't hurt."

"You know, if he's been in an accident, it might be on a police scanner–"

"Jay, isn't our scanner at home?"

"Yeah. I can run over and get it, if you want . . . " he trailed off.

"Let's see what we learn first with a couple more calls," asserted Beverly.

Carol came back shaking her head, "Nothing downtown. I checked with my former supervisor who checked the ER. All's quiet."

Skip came back shaking his head. "No-go on the local police. I couldn't find anyone willing to talk or that I knew."

Roger reentered the kitchen. "Hey, I was upstairs online. We went looking for traffic reports–just in case. There's an accident reported on I-82, about halfway between here and the city. He's probably tied up in traffic."

"Wouldn't he answer his cell phone or call?" raised Skip.

"Not if he doesn't have it on. If I were him, I'd turn it off on the weekends!" smiled Carol.

"Shoot, I hope that's it," smiled Beverly weakly.

Roger nodded enthusiastically, "They say it's a huge back up. Multi-car collision. Not many details yet."

"I don't know what else we can do."

"Wait I suppose," nodded Beverly reluctantly.

The group's energy and mood declined in lockstep. While each chose something for dessert, very little consumption occurred–except for Roger, who ate as if this cake might be his last.

Shortly before eight o'clock, Bernice finished her second cup of tea. "Beverly," she quietly but insistently commanded across the kitchen. "Could you look at this?" She tilted the cup toward her daughter-in-law. There, prophetically spelled out in tiny tea leaf residue were letters.

911
CAR
ER

Beverly gasped and her color dropped precipitously once more. "It's the accident. I knew it." Her mind raced like lightning. "Carol, can you call downtown again?"

"What? The Med Center?"

"Yes, look." Beverly tilted the cup for all to see as they tightly clustered around.

"Unbelievable," yelped Skip.

Carol leaped to her cellphone. She nodded with her mouth open a couple of times. "Yes, yes. Thanks." She clicked off and turned, "Several people from the accident have been brought in. No names. Mix of men and women. She said four or five victims. She's not certain if others went elsewhere. I think we should go."

"Is there anywhere else you'd go for the ER?" Janet questioned.

"That's really the only one. There's Glenwood for less serious issues, but the one downtown is the big trauma unit," confirmed Carol.

"We could be doing this for nothing. His plans could've changed . . . " Skip's voice faded. No one acknowledged his suggestion, their faces grim with growing certainty.

"Bernice was taken to Glenwood," Janet stated the obvious.

"True. Should we check there first?" Beverly nodded.

"How close was the accident?" Carol asked.

"No clue. The website gave an exit number, but I don't know where . . . "

"Well, let's swing by Glenwood on the way to the city," said Beverly heading for the hall closet to collect her coat.

"Let's get going," Skip finally agreed. "Though I hope we're wasting our time."

"I'll drive. I've got the van." Beverly trampled Skip's thought.

"I'll take Bill and the kids home," Amy injected across the departing group.

The group of five piled into Beverly's minivan and bolted from Fox Den. In the rush to leave, no one asked if Bernice wanted to join the expedition and, as a result, she sat in the kitchen nook, contemplating the tea leaves in her cup. The other guests left shortly thereafter as the air in the party balloon had abruptly popped.

The First Circle rode quietly but quickly. After a brief, unsatisfying stop at the Glenwood satellite, they rocketed toward the city, with increasingly gloomy expectations.

FORTY-EIGHT

Shortly before seven o'clock, the overhead public address crackled into life.

"Incoming. Multiple vehicle accident. Three units. Extent of injuries undetermined."

The ER staff barely noted the interruption in the ongoing flow of humanity populating the overcrowded waiting room. The frenetic rush of care moved forward unabated. One more patient needed what the trauma center did best.

"Fourth unit dispatched to I-82. Severe burns on two. More in transit. Stand by."

Dan finished work on the kindergartner's knee after an intern's three stitches had closed the gaping cut the boy received during a tussle. "There you go, bud. You're all set."

The little guy sniffled back tears and tried to smile. His mother looked gratefully at Dan. "Thank you. You've really been great with him."

"Just doing my job," smiled the young nurse. His gold cross glinted from the rope necklace. "Another satisfied customer on a Sunday night." He turned to the five-year-old, "And you, fine sir. Be more careful when you're chasing your big sister. You hear?"

The boy nodded.

"Would you like a sticker? I've got Scooby, Thing One and–"

The little lad snagged Scooby Doo. "I thought you might like that one." Dan winked at the mom. "Let me stick it on your shirt." Wiping his remaining tears on his sleeve, the boy gave Dan a big smile. He then slipped off the examining table and ran over to his mom who gave him a hug.

As the pair headed toward the discharge desk, Dan prepped the space for the next patient. He heard his name as he sprayed antiseptic. "Yeah, man?"

"Gettin' a new wave. Accident," his ER nursing supervisor said.

"I heard. Burns?"

"Some. Don't know if it's the whole gang. Should be here soon."

Stepping from the exam area, Dan looked at his boss, "Anything 'til then?"

"We're covered. Make sure we've got burn set-ups."

"Will do."

"Six minutes out. Three burn vics. Two severe trauma." The radio sputtered ongoing updates.

Within moments, the throbbing sirens of ambulances approached the ER. Less critical waiting patients once more remained unattended as nurses and physicians rushed toward the automatic doors. Flashing red-and-white lights beat a rapid staccato from the outside bay where five stretchers were extended, wheels down for the rapid roll into the ER.

Burn victims lay on the first three gurneys. Two were deathly quiet, while the last screamed in agony from burns covering her body. Fortunately, the worst of the fire that swept her vehicle missed her face.

The attending yelped instructions like an air traffic controller at rush hour. "Burn vics–one, two and three. Trauma female: bay six. Last one into number seven. Let's move 'em, guys.

The nursing supervisor directed RNs. "Dan, seven." Dan frowned, as he wanted burns experience. This was no time to debate; patients needed help fast. From extensive burns to overwhelming blood, the injuries were massive.

Dan hustled to Bay Seven. The young man on the stretcher inhaled and exhaled in light, shallow breaths. He looked up as Dan arrived.

"Hey, man. Ran into some dashboard." His coloring pale, the twenty-something attempted a smile. "I think I'm okay . . . just banged up some." He let out a soft little moan.

Dan joined the ER physician, an intern, and two nurses around the gurney, as the paramedics called out stats much like reading a stock market ticker: "Blood pressure, 140 over 80. Breathing shallow. Oxygen 93. Pulse 100. Has a pretty nasty cut on the forehead–he hit something hard. Numerous lacerations. Complaining of ab pain."

"One, two, three." The group transferred the patient's body from the gurney to the examining table in one rapid, frequently practiced move. They reconnected the intravenous bag from the gurney hook to the tall pole next to the ER table. "We got him. Thanks." The doctor nodded toward the medics, who were already hustling out the door. "Okay, what do we have?"

The intern's voice was equally clipped. "I'm seeing significant hemorrhaging on the torso as well. Let's see what we've got." Dan moved in with scissors and slit the shirt from bottom to top, cutting down the sleeves and stripping it from the man.

"Hey man, watch the threads. They're a favorite." The patient closed his eyes again, scrunching up his brow.

A long ragged slice cut across the torso from the midpoint of the man's abs up toward his right armpit. "God, what the hell happened?"

"Must've run into one nasty piece of body frame."

"Should make cars out of plastic. Maybe people'd be less traumatized."

"The cut's long, but doesn't appear deep. Get compresses. What else?"

"His breathing's shallow. Listen."

"No shit." The intern had a stethoscope up to the patient's chest. "Might be collapsed. Can't tell. Heartbeat's strong."

"What's the head source?"

"Deep forehead laceration. Down to skull," a nurse commented factually.

"Can you wipe the blood off his face? See if there's another bleed."

"Could be internal." Just then another blood geyser erupted from the nostrils. "Shee-it."

"Compress. Stet."

Dan reached in with sterile pads and pressed hard on the forehead cut. Another nurse tilted the head up and back, attempting to stave off the nosebleed. As it slowed, the physician shouted, "Watch your angle. He'll asphyxiate."

The young man's eyes widened with fear, his breathing accelerating.

The nursing team worked out a better rhythm. Dan held the compress on the forehead; the second nurse got a better angle on the nose and the bleed slowed. The third sponged the face. As she did, Dan was suddenly riveted by the emerging profile. He slipped his eyes down the well-chiseled chest and abs. Suddenly, with searing recollection, he remembered New Year's Eve.

Rusty moaned softly again, his eyes screwed shut. "Hey, I've got a little belly pain. Is that gonna be okay?"

"Hold on, just a sec. We gotta get this hemorrhaging stopped first."

The bleeding slowed, the doctor moved to Rusty's stomach and palpated across his abs and down toward the groin. "Modest pulsing. Doesn't seem to be in severe pain. Let's keep a watch. Get some of these worst lacerations resolved."

A sudden yell from Bay Six pulled the ER physician who provided final direction on his way out, "Get him cleaned up, stabilize his vitals. Tag him serious, but not critical."

The doctor stuck his head back through the curtains. "One last thought: before you close that forehead . . . Who's on in Plastics?"

Dan slightly relaxed his pressure on the forehead, "I'll check. I didn't see anyone listed."

"Get Plastics on the head. We could do it, but it's nasty and the scar's gonna show."

"So, am I gonna live?" Rusty tried to smile again as Dan reentered Bay Seven having checked a plastic surgeon's availability.

"I'm guessing you're gonna make it to another day," Dan reassured. "You got one heckuva lot of cuts that need some attention, including this one we keep referencing on your forehead. But we'll make sure we keep you whole." Rusty closed his eyes again, wincing a little.

"Something hurt?"

"Just my stomach. No big deal. Probably rammed into the steering wheel."

"Scale of one to ten: how bad?"

"Three? Four, maybe?"

"Yeah, you're gonna be bruised up. You'll be hurting for a while–no doubt. Let's see what we can wrap up while we wait for Plastics to show." Dan paused. "Keep me posted on the stomach, 'kay?"

The medical team tightened their circle around Rusty once more to suture the less visible and seemingly less critical wounds. As they worked, an ER clerk replaced "John Doe 3" with "R. Stillwagon" on the whiteboard in the ER as a wallet had been located.

* * *

The van ride into the city was tense. Tuning to the traffic channel, they learned more about the accident. While not the absolute standstill that westbound I-82 presented, rubbernecking slowed their eastbound progress to a near standstill.

Approaching the accident scene, the staccato lights of various emergency rescue vehicles punctuated the early evening darkness. As they passed the accident, a long line of headlights waited to move on the other side. Two vehicles smoked; two more cars showed substantial damage, and a motorcycle lay on its side, demolished nearly beyond recognition. Just as they accelerated, Roger cried out.

"Hey, is that Rusty's car?"

"Oh, my. I think it could be," gasped Janet.

"I believe it is," observed Skip. Beverly forced her eyes to the road as traffic picked up speed.

"Do you think so?" queried Carol.

"Hurry. Please hurry," Janet pleaded. Silently, she lifted a prayer on Rusty's behalf. In the tense silence, four others did the same.

At the Medical Center, Carol led the group to the ER admitting desk.

"We're checking on a possible admission this evening," Carol inquired sweetly, yet assertively.

"And who is inquiring?"

"We're very close friends with someone we believe may have been in the accident on I-82. Rusty Stillwagon. Is he here?"

"I'm afraid I'm not at liberty to disclose patient information. I'm sorry," the desk receptionist was pleasant, but equally firm.

"If he's here, he has no family nearby. We just want to know if he's been brought in."

"I'll need some identification."

"I don't think that will do much good, as we're not related. I used to work here. Five West. Annette Billings was my supervisor."

"And so?" The receptionist arched her eyebrows and looked across her half moon reading glasses.

"And so, I just thought you might be able to share–"

"You thought wrong. I'd like to be helpful," she said, all efforts at civility fading, "but I can't do much for you, if you're unrelated."

Carol let out a huff but then smiled as she looked past the admitting desk to the trauma unit behind. "Hey, BoyToy," she called out, as her former colleague hustled past with a chart. He paused, looked over, and grinned.

"What are you doing here?"

"Just checking on you. How goes the battle? What are you doing down here in ER?"

"Transferred here a couple months ago. Five West wasn't the same after you left," he smiled. "Wanted to see some real action." He paused. "Guess I got a little more than I anticipated. This is a war zone!" He frowned, "But what are you doing here?" He looked from Carol to the group surrounding her.

Carol's smile faded. "A friend of ours: we expected him for a party . . . We think he may have been in the accident on 82. He may be here." Dan frowned.

"That group just came in. Pretty bad shape. What's his name?"

"Stillwagon. Rusty Stillwagon."

"Really? You know him?" Dan responded. "I actually worked on him an hour or so ago. He's pretty banged up."

"How's he doing now? Where is he?" Carol questioned.

"They were gonna transfer him to a room. Doc thinks he's serious but not critical. He may already be moved."

Dan went over to the admitting desk and typed the name. The stern-faced receptionist looked even grimmer as the Stillwagon record opened. "Yup, he's moved."

"What's the prognosis?" Skip queried.

"Not sure. A bunch of external bleeds and gashes. He has one major laceration that Plastics put back together. I'm guessing he's gonna be bruised and sore, but do okay."

Carol turned to the group, "As you heard, doesn't sound too bad, all told."

"No, I'd say not. He was talking a little, but he did look pretty beat up," Dan smiled.

"Though sometimes you can't tell," Carol shook her head.

"That's for sure. Couple other people–they're a mess. Two others went up to IC Burns. Don't know how they're doing. Must've been one heckuv' an accident."

"Looked like a doozy . . . We just drove past it. Traffic jammed up for miles," Carol agreed as the others stood expectantly.

"Listen, I gotta scoot. We're swamped. Good seeing you, Carol. Hope your buddy comes through okay."

Carol turned to the others as Dan hustled back into the flurry of activity.

* * *

After his forehead was sutured by the plastics specialist, Rusty was wheeled to STTC–the Short-Term Trauma Care unit. In STTC, he would receive more active nursing support in the initial, critical period after severe trauma. Other I-82 accident victims filled adjoining cubes.

Hooked to two different IV lines, Rusty rested with his eyes closed. The five First Circle members gathered outside the glass windows of the cube, watching the rhythmic up and down movement of his chest. The bandage across his forehead seeped blood. Similarly, blood saturated the surgical dressings wrapping his torso.

"Wow, he's in more serious condition than I expected," observed Carol.

"I can't believe it," added Beverly.

"And no family here," murmured Janet. "I know he's from Nashville, but I don't know how to contact his mom and dad."

All nodded their heads. "Maybe his roommate?" suggested Skip. "Do we have that number?"

Beverly pawed through her purse, "It's right here." Skip retreated to call.

Minutes later, Skip was back. "I talked with his roommate who was shocked. He'd heard about the accident–apparently, it's all over the news. He gave me the Stillwagons' number. I'll call, but perhaps you could tell them more about his condition?" Skip looked at Carol.

"We don't know a whole lot. He's serious. Do you think we should wait until morning?"

Janet pursed her lips, "I'd want to know, but then again, there's nothing they can do. They'll get no sleep and can't very well come tonight."

Skip shook his head, "No question: I'd want to know if it was my son."

Janet's shoulders sagged, "Oh my, if this were Steve . . . "

"You'd want to know sooner rather than later?" encouraged Skip. Janet nodded, her eyes welling up.

"Who's going to call?" Beverly interrupted.

"Carol should. She can handle their questions best—even with limited information," Skip suggested.

The decision made, Carol and Skip walked to a quiet corner. Using Skip's cell phone on speaker mode, they spoke gravely with Frank Stillwagon.

Returning, Carol posted the group on the conversation. As she did so, Rusty opened his eyes and looked in their direction. He gave a tightlipped smile. Roger noticed first.

"Hey, Rusty's awake."

The group neglected STTC protocols and entered the cube, clustering tightly around the bed.

"Hey, I didn't realize we were gonna party here. I've got wine in my car." Rusty tried to smile but winced again.

"Don't push yourself. You need rest."

"You okay?" asked Carol.

"Not quite ready to dance, but I'm okay . . . Guess I got dealt the Advance to Hospital card, huh?"

"You never saw it coming?" Skip gently asked.

"No way, man."

"You made the news, Rusty."

"Not really what I was shootin' for . . . " Rusty grimaced again. "My stomach is all bruised up."

Skip explained what he'd heard from Rusty's roommate. "A motorcyclist was hot rodding through heavy citybound traffic and lost control, starting a chain reaction. The motorcyclist was killed instantly. Two cars caught fire. Another car crossed the median strip, dealt a glancing blow to an overpass concrete support and then plowed into two other vehicles in the westbound lanes. One of them was you."

"Hmmm, I never saw it, that's for sure. Bummer." Rusty closed his eyes. The cube became quiet, save the sounds of medical equipment adding rhythmic percussion to the evening stillness.

"We'll be right here, Rusty. We called your parents. They're on their way."

Rusty opened his eyes once more. "Ahhh, they don't need to do that. I'll be okay. Just a couple of bruises. Good as new in a day or two . . . " He exhaled sharply. "Shoot, this is really hurtin'. . . " He moved a hand to his stomach.

"Let me get a nurse for you," noted Carol, stepping from the crowded cube. Rusty nodded and closed his eyes.

A nurse, clearly irritated by the group of people clustered around Rusty's cube, checked Rusty's monitors and asked him how he was feeling. Not opening his eyes, he responded, "Not so great, actually. Can you give me something for my stomach?"

"Let's try some Tylenol and see if that will take the edge off," responded the harried nurse striking a more sympathetic tone. "I don't have directions for anything more. I can ask a doctor to stop by if it keeps feeling worse."

"Please," gritted Rusty through tight jawed lips.

More to herself than Carol and the group, the nurse noted Rusty's blood pressure, which had subtly dropped to 120 over 70. "Not a concern, but mindful of watching," she concluded as she left.

Rusty became quite still, as the remainder of the First Circle sat quietly.

"I suppose there's not a whole lot else we can do this evening," noted Beverly somberly.

"He's in good hands," Carol noted. "This unit does a good job."

"I still can't believe it," Janet murmured. "I'll come back in the morning."

"Why don't I get us all home? Carol, perhaps you can keep us apprised of his status? You have connections."

Carol smiled, "Sure. I'll check in the morning and call around to let you all know."

Just as the group got up to leave, Janet suggested, "Perhaps we should have a word of prayer before departing?"

"Yes," "Excellent idea," and other murmurs of assent rose from the group. The five offered a group prayer for Rusty's speedy recovery with each contributing an appreciation for his gifts. Whispering good night to Rusty who appeared to doze, they walked down the hallway.

As they passed the nurses' station, two nurses nearly bowled them over as they rushed back down the corridor. Simultaneously, the PA burst into life. "Code Blue. Cube Eight. Code Blue."

More medical staff materialized–from break rooms and other cubicles, running toward Number Eight.

"What number was Rus –?" began Skip, but Janet cut him off.

"He's in Eight."

"Oh Lord, what happened?"

The First Circle reversed course and ran after the medical staff, which already crowded Rusty's cube. They could only watch helplessly from outside the windows.

"Can't get a blood pressure," yelled one tech.

"Pulsing in his belly is strong . . . shit, what gives?"

"Check the monitor. His BP's dropped like a rock."

"Ah, shee-it," yelled an attending. "Don't lose this guy. What the hell . . . "

"He must be bleeding out."

"He is not gonna bleed out on my watch. Goddamn it."

Rusty writhed in pain on the bed, his face contorted by the escalation of agony in his belly.

"What do ya think? Ruptured spleen?"

"We are not losing him. Get him to OR. Stet. We're gonna have to open him up."

Rusty was quickly transferred to a gurney and rushed from the cube. The First Circle stood in stunned silence outside the empty cube.

Janet wept quietly. Beverly also had tears.

"Will he be okay?" asked Roger, pale-faced and leaning against the wall.

"This is much more serious. They missed whatever is going on internally. Easy enough to happen, but you knew something was going on when he kept saying his stomach hurt," advised Carol. "I hope they can get him back together."

"You think they might not?" Beverly choked the words out.

"He's young; he's fit . . . he stands a good chance of pulling through."

"Oh Lord, I hope so." Skip appeared equally shellshocked.

The group walked slowly to the little waiting area outside STTC, after asking whether Rusty would return there. "Unclear, ma'am," responded the same nurse as earlier. "Depends on what they find when they go in."

"I can't go home when he's got no one here," said Carol.

"Me neither," added Beverly. All agreed to wait out Rusty's surgery. No one would be able to get sleep if they departed. With a call home, Roger's parents agreed that he might stay as well. The First Circle continued their vigil.

* * *

Near midnight, the nurse from earlier came out to the group.

"It's not protocol, but I wanted to let you know that Mr. Stillwagon has gotten out of surgery. He's in recovery as we speak. I anticipate he'll be moved to ICU at some point during the night provided he remains stable."

"How's he doing?" inquired Carol.

"Well, he made it through surgery. In all honesty from what I heard, it was touch and go. He had a ruptured spleen and nearly bled out. He's lost a lot of blood and needed transfusions. The first forty-eight hours are always touch and go. Say a prayer 'cause he's sure not out of the woods."

Rusty was wheeled into ICU just before eight o'clock on Monday morning. His monitors stable, his body attempted to deal with the trauma of the accident and the subsequent surgery. The First Circle moved to the ICU waiting room. Rusty remained asleep and unchanged throughout the day. "In part, this is medically induced sedation. We hope this gives his body time to recover more fully," an ICU nurse counseled.

Periodically, each of the First Circle players went and sat with Rusty. They held his hand or stroked his forearm, with no reaction. Hourly, someone different bowed and prayed for a smooth and rapid recovery.

"They say that even in a coma, the body can process other stimuli. Like sound, or touch. Maybe smell." Carol searched for ways they might be helpful.

"You could blow up some popcorn," smiled Roger, resulting in quiet chuckles.

"Perhaps we should talk to him," suggested Beverly.

"Or sing. He loves to sing," added Janet.

"I really can't sing very well," blushed Roger.

"It's not how well you sing, it's that we do it together."

"We're here to help him. Much as we helped Bernice."

"With my voice, we just might wake him," smiled Skip.

"No matter. Let's try," nudged Janet. With the agreement of the nurses, the group circled Rusty's bed. They warmed up by singing *Do-Re-Mi* and *Happy Birthday*. Carol suggested *Deck the Halls.*

"He'll think he's been asleep for months!" giggled Beverly nervously.

"Well, it might wake him," Carol responded. After a rousing rendition, the group moved to *Jingle Bells*.

"This is nuts," frowned Roger. "Christmas carols in March?"

"Then make a suggestion," Carol encouraged.

"*Jesus Loves Me*?"

"Why that's an excellent thought," agreed Janet. The group moved through a series of children's Sunday School songs and hymns. Thirty minutes later, they were sung out. Rusty showed no responsiveness, but the group felt better.

"You know what I like most about Rusty?" Roger initiated. "I like how cool he is. And his car's cool too."

"He is such a thoughtful guy. He spent so much time with Walt and me helping us figure out our computer. And then with Bernice . . . "

"My, yes. He really jumped in. Getting her set up with that cable connection. He's so talented."

"Not to mention knowing CPR."

The group quietly nodded.

"But let's not get down. He's on the mend, right?" Skip sought to buoy the group's spirits. Twenty-four hours after the accident, Rusty showed no signs of waking. The group offered an additional prayer and then exited the room, giving the nurses space to change dressings and check his vitals.

"Wasn't Bernice scheduled for chemo?" inquired Carol as they waited.

"We postponed until tomorrow. She wanted Rusty to have someone here, once she knew his family situation."

"When will the Stillwagons arrive?"

"I spoke with them again this morning. Rusty's dad searched most of the night for flights," Skip explained.

"Flights from Nashville are that popular?" queried Carol incredulous.

"It's a combination. First, not many flights. Second, the two early flights were sold out. And the last–which they're on–gets in around nine."

"Really? Nothing sooner?" questioned Beverly.

"Oh my goodness, how disappointing," added Janet.

"Frank didn't think he could concentrate to drive. He said Betty is beside herself."

"I can only imagine; she–" but Janet got cut off.

"Code Blue. 333. Stet."

Nurses flew down the corridor as the intercom crackled to silence.

Carol's face went white. "Rusty's in trouble. Quick."

On the heels of the medical team, the five hustled down the hallway. The attending doctor and four nurses surrounded Rusty's bed. The First Circle stood outside the room, gazing once more through the windows. Another nurse raced down the hall pushing a crash cart. Banging through the door into Room 333, the care team parted.

"Clear." The doctor placed the defibrillator paddles on Rusty's chest. The current entered his body with no reaction. "Up." The machine was adjusted. "Clear," the doctor ordered once more. The current zapped Rusty's inert body. The monitor showed a momentary blip, but then collapsed in silence again. "Shit. Up again. Stet." The physician yelled the order to the nurse who already spun the dial. "Clear." The body jerked and the monitor portrayed a heartbeat again.

Ten minutes never felt longer to the First Circle members. They stood motionless–fear and anxiety crossing their faces as the medical team stepped back and Rusty returned to a quiet peace, his monitors returning to a more familiar cadence. As suddenly as the crisis materialized, it evaporated.

The nurses and the doctor stepped out. Conversation among them suggested things were stable following his cardiac arrest, but when Carol inquired, a former colleague's answer was measured, but concerning, "We believe he's struggling. He's not responding to surgery as expected. He may still have a bleed. The doc is considering going back in."

Carol reported back to the group; while Rusty appeared stable, the prognosis was uncertain. "We should have another word of prayer," Janet suggested.

"Let's be with Rusty," suggested Beverly.

The nurses watched the group enter Room 333 and stand around his bed, but chose to ignore another break in protocol. The fivesome reached impulsively for each other's hands and formed a circle around Rusty's bed. Beverly took Rusty's one hand and Skip took his other. Janet started,

"Dear Lord, we cannot know Your ways and Your will. If there's any way in which we can help Rusty in his journey toward recovery and health, please show us how. We want what's best for him. If it's Your will to allow his rapid and full recovery, we pray most fervently for it . . . "

As Janet continued praying–articulating gratitude for all the gifts the Lord bestowed on those present, as well as continued supplication for Rusty's return to health, the room seemed to fill with an additional presence. Afterward, each of the five acknowledged feeling the presence of something big, bold, and all-encompassing. While the feeling stayed ambiguous and shapeless, they all were aware of a Godly presence. As this sense of light filled the room and their very souls, Rusty's hands jerked away.

While still apparently deeply sedated, Rusty's hands formed a circle with his thumbs and index fingers . . . and then a one. A circle and then a one, in smooth succession and repetition. As the group finished their prayers with a unison "Amen," they stared as Rusty's hands formed the circle and the one slowly but surely. As they did, the monitors raised their siren cry again; his body once more reached the precipice of life.

As feet pounded in the corridor and the intercom crackled, Rusty's eyes opened. He gazed toward the corner of the room, past the First Circle. He stared so intently that all five were drawn to look briefly where he focused, but they saw only a shimmering white glow–unexplained and unprompted. The aura steadied and held. Rusty's hand reached toward the light, his eyes looking beyond the earthly confines of Room 333. His sparkling blue eyes gradually dulled to a vacant stare and his hand slowly fell to his chest, joining the other hand in a final circle of fingers. A small, slight smile turned his lip and his eyes closed–just as the medical team entered the room.

The First Circle pushed to the perimeter of the room and watched as the crash team worked on Rusty's second cardiac arrest within the hour. A well-choreographed ballet, they maneuvered in measured chaos again and again. At one point, Rusty gave a start and the bed shook. He appeared to breathe and then stop. The team tried desperately to bring him back, to will back the spirit and life in his body. Another sharp intake of breath preceded stillness. More than thirty minutes passed as the stunned, teary-eyed First Circle watched. Finally, the lead doctor straightened up.

"Shit. Call it. He's gone." The medical team reluctantly pulled back from the twenty-something patient, a patient whose vibrancy and life had vanished due to the split-second carelessness and irresponsibility of another youth.

The glow in the corner hung like sparkling mist throughout the heroic efforts of the team, but as they pulled back, it vanished. The monitors went quiet. Tears fell from all who had held hands around the bed. Rusty was gone.

FORTY-NINE

After the decimating shock, the Stillwagons welcomed Janet's suggestion to have an initial memorial service at Bedrock Hills. On Thursday evening, a long line wound from the church lounge through the narthex. Frank and Betty stood near the casket, propped up physically and emotionally by Janet and Walt. The people paying their respects included colleagues from Ridgewell, a vast network of friends and acquaintances, members of the Metropolitan Men's Choir (who later sang during the service), and the First Circle and their families.

The Stillwagons planned for Rusty's internment in Nashville following a second service on Sunday afternoon back home with the extended family and friends. Now, they greeted the line of people somberly. Puffy eyes abounded. As the First Circle members reached the front of the line, they stepped out and stayed with the Walkers and Stillwagons, standing quietly.

Just before the seven o'clock service commenced, the pastors closed the doors to the lounge and left the Stillwagons, Janet, Carol, Beverly, Skip, and Roger standing, contemplating Rusty's peaceful countenance.

"He looks at rest."

"Indeed, he does."

The body–cold and lifeless–was clearly dead. This mere vessel for Rusty's earthly journey was of no further use. Asked to select the music, Skip had burned a CD. Michael W. Smith's "*This is Your Time,*" inspired by the tragedy at Columbine High School years earlier, played softly. The group gathered around the body to say goodbye one last time.

"I still can't believe it."

"He's just so young."

"How could it happen? I don't understand," quavered Beverly, staring down at the casket.

"We can only hope it's for a greater purpose, a bigger plan we don't understand . . . " Skip trailed off speechless.

"We should look for the good in this," suggested Janet thoughtfully.

"He had such an impact in his short time," Carol joined the sad voices.

"He certainly spoke highly of you. I can't imagine going through this without you being here," Betty's voice broke. "You shared a special bond."

"He saved my mother-in-law, you know."

"Yes, we heard," nodded the newspaper editor. "He told us. We sensed you were helping him find his way."

Skip shook his head slowly, "I don't know. I hope so. We certainly shared a strange and unexpected bond."

"That you did."

Roger stood very quietly, tears occasionally rolled down his cheeks. "He was so cool. How can he be dead?"

Beverly reached over and gave him a hug, drawing him nearer. "We should head into the sanctuary," she said as the lounge doors opened and Dr. Andrews motioned. Men from the funeral home materialized silently to roll the casket behind the sad processional led by the grieving parents.

* * *

"Please join me in saying the Twenty Third Psalm," invited Dr. Andrews. The deep, somber intonations of the congregation ebbed and flowed as they recited the well-known poetry from David:

The Lord is my shepherd, I shall not want
He makes me lie down in green pastures
He leads me beside still waters
He restores my soul
He guides me in paths of righteousness, for his name's sake
Even though I walk through the valley of the shadow of death
I will fear no evil, for you are with me
Your rod and your staff, they comfort me
You prepare a table before me, in the presence of my enemies
You anoint my head with oil; my cup overflows
Surely goodness and mercy will follow me all the days of my life,
And I will dwell in the house of the Lord forever.
Amen.

Integrating hymns and gospel readings, Dr. Andrews led the attendees in attempting to find hope in Rusty's death and see how it could be part of God's bigger plan. "I now invite you to share your reflections on Rusty's life, his personality, and his impact. Please, come forward if you are so moved by the Spirit."

The congregation sat reverently, most of the young people looking straight forward–not daring to twitch, thinking they might get cold-called by the silver-haired preacher. Janet, seated next to Betty, slowly stood and walked to the front. Pastor Andrews smiled warmly and invited her with a hand gesture to climb the pulpit.

Once standing at the high lectern, Janet perused the throng and cast her eyes down on Rusty's closed casket, resting below. "I came to know Rusty Stillwagon over the last six months of his life. What a fine young man he proved to be." Her voice wavered, but visibly, she steeled herself.

"It's hard to believe he's gone–and such an abrupt and sudden end to his young life." She paused and looked down at her scribbled notes on the back of an index card. She smiled. "Rusty was certainly full of spirit. In the short time I knew him, he had a real impact. He helped my husband and me unravel the complexities and confusion of technology. He was willing to get on his hands and knees and reconfigure wiring and cables and teach us how to use our own computer! And all of it on his own time.

"Rusty was generous in sharing his time and talent. He had a gift for making the difficult seem straightforward. He had a way to make people laugh and enjoy life. With very little prompting, he became part of a unique group of friends, here in Bedrock and Glenwood." With that she paused, moving her glance from person to person in the pew seated next to the Stillwagons. "He stepped in and helped one who was quite ill, providing her with a pleasant diversion–the computer and the internet–to speed along her convalescence.

"Young people today are often unforgiving and impatient with the confusions of those of us who have walked the road before them. Rusty was none of this. He patiently and warmly engaged with others–regardless of age or experience. While I can't say what he was like in the workplace, I can only imagine him as a forthright and caring employee."

Continuing her circuitous remarks, Janet imagined Rusty's impact on others and drew to a close. "I sense Rusty was still searching. He often seemed–in some way–unsettled and looking for closure. I pray that in his premature passing, he has found the peace that he seemed so desperately to want and yet not quite sure how to find in life."

Two Ridgewell colleagues, including the CIO, next spoke glowingly of Rusty's contributions to the firm and their technology. Chip and Eric followed and stood together. Between them, they got the room to laugh, recalling Rusty's antics and unconventional sense of humor. They recounted evenings at the Harborside, his tendency for practical jokes, and his interest in all things outdoors.

When the two guys returned to their pews, the sanctuary fell silent once more. Just as Dr. Andrews stood, anticipating no further speakers, a head rose at the back of the church. Slowly, haltingly, a gaunt elderly woman made her way down the center aisle. The black and white scarf on her head provided stark contrast to her pale skin and charcoal gray pants and tunic top.

Carol nudged Beverly and raised her brow quizzically. "She insisted on being here," whispered Beverly.

Finally reaching the pulpit, the woman stood, unsteadily, behind the lectern and looked out–peering through her big, oversized spectacles. She grasped both sides of the podium with her gnarly gray hands. Her voice, thin and reedy initially, grew in volume and steadiness. The room became deathly quiet.

"My name is Bernice Langdon. I nearly died earlier this year, and it could happen yet. Cancer is a nasty business. The fight is a brutal one. I can certainly attest to that—and more. I've not been to church in a while. I should've. But, I didn't. No real explanation. Just didn't make it."

The congregation strained to hear the clearly ill lady's words. They leaned toward her. She took a deep breath.

"Rusty saved my life." There was a collective intake of breath across the church. "He really did. I wouldn't be here—at least not standing in front of you talking, if it weren't for what Rusty Stillwagon did." Several people let out nervous giggles. "And for that, I'm grateful. I wasn't at the time, but I am now. He saved my life, but gave his. It doesn't seem quite fair, I suppose, but I am coming to believe it's part of a much greater plan than any of us can know or understand.

"Rusty is part of a group of people—they sit here in front—who have taught me. Taught me to pray, and to accept the challenging road on which I've been placed. It's this, even more than the technology that Rusty set up, that empowers me. I've come to believe that Rusty's gift to me and to all of us is profound. He gave me life, and through that second chance, I must believe that I'm here for some additional purpose. He also teaches us to use our talents, even when we don't realize they are being directed by a greater being.

"I'm continuing to learn, even through the pain and the difficult path I'm traveling. I can only hope that through the pain and the grief that each of you feel in Rusty's passing, that you can find a glimmer of hope, a new piece of wisdom by which you can grow. You know," Bernice looked at Janet and gave a brief, grim smile, "I'm not as sure that Rusty remained unsettled in life. I sense he found that peace, that commitment and that focus before his life met its end. I am blessed to have met Rusty. I wish I had shown him that gratitude more fully in his lifetime."

Bernice swallowed hard, choking down the lump that had grown in her throat. Her eyes welled up as she stepped down, slowly, from the pulpit. Beverly stood up to help her down the center aisle to her seat. Beverly's eyes also glistened as tears anointed her cheeks. Many reached for tissues as the ailing professor finally sat.

Dr. Andrews returned to the pulpit. "This is clearly a distinctive young man, whose life we celebrate this evening. I appreciate his unique gifts even more as I listen to the wonderful ways in which he's had impact. Thank you for your reflections. What a miracle life is indeed. Praise the Lord."

After the congregation sang "*How Great Thou Art*," Dr. Andrews based a brief meditation on two scripture passages, the first from Philippians 1: 20-21.

> *I eagerly expect and hope that I will in no way be ashamed, but will have sufficient courage so that now as always Christ will be exalted in my body, whether by life or by death. For to me, to live is Christ and to die is gain.*

"This is a young man who lived life to its fullest. Based on talking with Rusty's friends and family in the last few days as well as my own brief words with Rusty several weeks ago, I believe Rusty was learning about Christ and coming to accept Him more and more each day. In Paul's letter, he suggests that dying is even better than living because in death, our worldly troubles are removed. We come face to face with Christ. In fact, if we're all not ready to die, then we are truly not ready to live. If you are ready to die, you can devote your lives to what really counts. Rusty Stillwagon was doing just that.

"In Rusty's final hours on earth, he chose to drive out to join the group that had supported Bernice Langdon through her long (and continuing) bout with cancer. He chose to forego whatever personal priorities he might have had at the moment, and chose to be a part of something bigger than himself. Even his screen saver suggested, much as Bernice alluded, that he was pursuing a broader, more important path for his life. His screen saver, you ask?

Be who you are. Contribute to circle. Be light for others.

"His parents found this rolling across the monitor when they visited his apartment." Each of the First Circle members gave a surprised gasp, as they learned of Rusty's final message. "Rusty contributed his gifts and talents to this circle of friends. Through his life and now his death, he is a light for all of us.

"I close with a second scriptural reference. This comes from the parable of the wealthy landowner who entrusted his fortune with his servants. While one can interpret this as solely about money and material possessions, it is truly much broader. It is the tale of the talents: each servant receives a different measure of talents to invest and deploy as he sees fit. In the case of the first and second employees, they invested and grew their talents. How does the master assess these investments? As stated in Matthew 25:23:

"Well done, good and faithful servant."

"I say the same to Rusty as he leaves this life. Rusty used his talents well, leaving an indelible impression on those around him and the lives they lead. Be it Bernice Langdon, the members of this circle of friends, the colleagues at Ridgewell, and beyond. Rusty, well done! Yes, well done, good and faithful servant. You have reached your reward.

"As we sing our closing hymn, let us light the sanctuary with candlelight. Let's allow Rusty's light to shine across our midst." As the organist opened with the first bars of music, Dr. Andrews lifted a candle toward heaven and then stepped down to the ushers to light their candles who slowly moved the flame to candles throughout the congregation. As the candlelight grew, the overhead lights were dimmed and then extinguished. Rusty's light was the light in the church.

The congregation continued standing as they sang the closing hymn, *Amazing Grace*. As the music grew in volume, Roger looked at the stained glass window. His eyes were full and–at first–he thought it was just the blurriness of his tears, but with each passing phrase in the hymn, he became increasingly convinced that the stained glass was beginning to glow–in the panel that depicted Peter's feet walking on water, following Jesus' command to come. Roger watched as the intensity of the panel grew. He finally nudged Skip, standing next to him. Roger pointed and Skip quizzically followed the line of his pointing hand.

Skip stopped singing as he stared. Roger's hand movement attracted Carol's attention as well and she too looked at the stained glass, her focus drawn immediately to the same colorful panel. As the trio looked, a warm breeze kicked up from the front of the church–originating near the glowing window.

Roger, Skip, and Carol all noted that each was feeling the apparent trade wind wafting toward them. They watched it ruffling Janet's and Beverly's hair as well. The air's movement finally captured the final pair's attention. The Stillwagons remained silent as well, due to their teary gaze being affixed on the closed casket. They paid no attention to the breeze, which they didn't feel.

As the five stood transfixed, a sudden starburst of color–much like the burst of fireworks in a darkened summer sky–exploded from the miracle panel of stained glass. The burst of sparkling light was comprised of warm, flame-like glowing embers interspersed with a second color–sparkling blue sapphires danced in the air. The glittering particles blew on the wind, a stream of two-toned color swirling across the front of the sanctuary.

The dazzling blue and silvery-golden particles swooshed across Rusty's casket, creating a colorful swath of energy. Roger glanced around to see if anyone else reacted to the light show, but no one showed any indication of seeing. The shimmering gemstones in the air created a conduit from the casket to the high ceiling of the sanctuary as if creating a bridge from earth to heaven. The channel of color glittered in the evening light, contrasting sharply with the candlelit sanctuary.

As the hymn drew to a close, the bridge of glittering color burst once more and danced from the vertical column to individual swirls of color floating above each member of the First Circle. Much like the early disciples at Pentecost, the glittering fire from Rusty's bridge to heaven baptized the five. Tears streamed down their faces as the blues and golds sparkled in the soft candlelight. As they stood, the light transformed, becoming two bands of color–one, a flickering flame-colored gold, the other a translucent neon circle of startling blue glitter. At the back of the sanctuary, Bernice watched, transfixed by the miraculous highway of color and stood below a similar dual halo.

The sanctuary quiet once more, Dr. Andrews stood to give the benediction:

> *Go out into the world in peace; have courage. Pursue and embrace the light of God– allowing His light to shine through and permeate the very being of all whom you touch . . . making them part of an ever growing circle of light from our Lord Savior. May the grace of our Lord Jesus Christ, the love of God, and the peace of the Holy Spirit permeate, sustain, and enrich us all. Amen.*

With the pastor's final Amen, the glittering light above each of the six faded.

* * *

"Wow!" Excitedly, Roger initiated dialogue as the congregation began departing.

"That was remarkable," observed Skip.

"It was like Rusty was here," nodded Carol. "Just like him to use a techno-light show."

"Did anyone else besides us see?"

"It didn't look like it."

Sitting once more, the Stillwagons appeared too drained to begin the walk from the sanctuary. They held hands tightly and clung to one another, occasionally whispering.

Carol chimed in, "So what do y'all make of it?"

"It had to be Rusty and David. Did you see the difference in colors?" The pieces fell in place for Beverly, who verbalized others' thinking.

"Had to be," agreed Skip.

"It's all so intriguing," Janet nodded.

"That's really cool. Did you see how it made a bridge toward the sky?" Roger remained amazed.

"A staircase to heaven. Why are we so blessed?" Janet pondered.

As the group talked, Bernice moved against the departing flow of people. "May I join you?" she inquired.

"Of course, Mother. By all means."

"Your remarks were so thoughtful," noted Janet.

"That took real strength, Bernice."

She waved her hand dismissively. "I take it you were discussing the light show?"

"You saw it?" Beverly looked stunned.

"Yes, I had a good view from the back."

"We thought it was just us."

"As best I could tell, it was just you, and, for some reason, myself. Frankly, I didn't look around much. It is rather captivating when a display like that suddenly erupts."

"Others would be talking about it, if they'd seen," agreed Beverly.

"No doubt," commented Skip.

"So what's it mean?" Roger eagerly added.

Carol interrupted, "Did you hear what was on Rusty's screen saver?"

"Rather remarkable," Skip lifted his eyebrows.

"His parents didn't mention it," Janet shook her head. The Stillwagons remained deep in their grief as they spoke quietly.

"'Be who you are. Contribute to circle. Be light for others'. . . and that's just what he's continuing to do." Beverly surveyed the scribbles on her bulletin.

"Awesome," commented Roger.

"I'm still confused. Other people die and this doesn't happen. Why?" Carol frowned.

"I don't know that we'll ever understand," Beverly answered.

"You know, as I said up there," Bernice pointed toward the pulpit, "I'm not a deeply religious sort, but listening to all of you over the past few weeks has forced me to think; I've had time on my hands." She smirked wickedly. "Now just among you," Bernice whispered conspiratorially, "I've started praying—not something I've done much in the past." She paused. "I also got to thinking about this David O'Neill notion."

The group looked at her expectantly.

"I had to sort a few things out." Bernice inserted a rather dramatic pause, and then drew herself up—as she once did when she delivered the key teaching point during a lecture. "I knew David."

"No!"

"No way."

"You did?"

"I can't believe it, Mother. Really? Why didn't you say?"

Bernice ignored the specific queries, "I was getting my Ph.D. He was in one of my TA sections."

"What's a TA?" asked Roger.

"Teaching Assistant. They're grad students who help professors in labs and grading papers," Skip responded. He turned to Bernice, "But David wasn't the biology type . . . "

"No, clearly. He was an English major. He stunk at biology. Probably was bad at any science." She smiled. "I don't remember, but I suppose he needed to take a science course for some requirement. He ended up in my lab."

"He must've been younger than you."

"Yes, of course." Bernice curled her lip slightly. "He was quite a bit younger—maybe ten years." She stood up a little straighter. "I was a late bloomer when it came to doing grad work." She sighed. "Well, I helped him through the course. He was dreadful–did I mention that?"

"Yes, Mother, you did."

The group hung on each word. "Well, I suppose I helped him a lot. He came to depend on me to make it through the course." Bernice looked down.

"Mother, you're flushed. Are you okay?"

"Yes, just fine. But, well–" Bernice paused and the group stood silently. She haltingly stumbled, "David developed something of a crush on me . . . "

"No," gasped Beverly.

"I can't believe it," smiled Carol.

"But you were so much older," noted Janet.

"I never heard about this," reflected Skip.

"He did. I know: scandalous. But it happened. And well, we uh–," Bernice let out a little cough, "we, uh, went out."

"You dated?"

Bernice paused a long time. "I'm not sure you'd call it dating. We spent time together."

"Dr. Langdon. You? And one of your students?" Carol laughed. "I am just so put off by the immoral behavior of your youth!" She shook her head in mock disapproval.

"How long did you see my brother?"

"Oh, I don't recall. It was on and off . . . maybe a year or two."

"A year? Or two? Mother, why didn't we know?"

"He wanted it to be more." The pale professor hesitated in a shower of pleasant memories. "I figured it couldn't, and by then, I'd met Bill–already a rising leader on campus."

"You two-timin' hussy, Professor," Carol chided.

A dagger of fire flashed across Bernice's face chilling Carol and the rest. "It wasn't like that at all. He was a young man with raging hormones. I was the first woman who paused and took interest in him, I imagine." Bernice coughed and looked down.

"You cared for him!" Skip determined, as Bernice's color darkened more. She nodded slowly but with certainty–a tear running down her face.

"But Bill made more sense. He was more my age. He was going places in the university. David was a pleasant dalliance, I rationalized. I didn't lead him on, even when he insisted. I told him it wouldn't–no, it couldn't work.

"He took another class with me in his junior year. By then, Bill and I were planning to marry. David wanted more than I could give–or at least thought, at the time." Another tear dribbled down her cheek. "He and I did spend a little more time together," her voice choked, "–uh, tutoring." She straightened up, "He needed more help to make it through." Quietly she added, "and so did I."

Bernice paused once more, looking at the group. "Before I knew it, I was married and Bill Junior was on the way. Even with that, David kept in touch. He sent flowers periodically while he and I were still on campus . . . and then we lost touch."

"He clearly carried a torch for you," nodded Janet. "He had feelings for you."

"But you didn't respond after the class ended?" Beverly asked.

"No, how could I? The flowers eventually stopped."

"But he must've still felt something," insisted Skip.

"I never knew he continued to feel that way," said Bernice with regret. "I never imagined it."

"You know, if he didn't think you paid attention to him then–even with sending flowers, when he saw you in need later in life–" Skip began.

Beverly continued, "Then he may have felt a need to influence you through others."

"He couldn't come to you directly. You might not have listened," continued Skip with growing insight.

"Or paid attention," added Roger with an adolescent perspective.

"Which brings us full circle to our group," smiled Janet warmly.

"I wonder why he was able to come back," thought Carol aloud.

"We'll never know that," speculated Skip.

"And work through a group of people he knew," noted Beverly.

"Except for Rusty. And now Rusty's gone," concluded Janet.

"Maybe there really wasn't a connection to Rusty? Maybe that's why he . . . " Carol stopped in mid-sentence.

"He must have been related in some way. We just never figured it out," Beverly shook her head vigorously.

"Yes, it's too coincidental that he would receive the messages he did and connect with us, without a relationship. I wonder what it was," Skip shook his head sadly.

"We need to get them moving," suggested Janet quietly nodding toward the silent Stillwagons. "Betty? Frank? Are you ready to go?"

They nodded and then slowly stood. The casket still stood at the base of the pulpit. The funeral home attendants awaited the departure of the final group from the sanctuary, before rolling the coffin out to the chill night air and preparing for its final journey.

The group of eight made their way down the long center aisle, pausing to thank Dr. Andrews for the service and his support.

"It was so nice how you wove the final screen saver into your message," commented Janet.

The reverend's eyes twinkled as he looked at the Stillwagons just behind Janet. "Well, I did use a little artistic license—with Rusty's parents' okay."

"How so?" Janet arched her brow.

"Okay to share?"

Frank and Betty nodded simultaneously.

"Well, when they reached his apartment, his computer was in fact on, but it had a stationary message on it,

SKIP 82   CHOOSE DIFFERENT

It was written in the oddest red letters, almost looked like they were on fire." The Stillwagons nodded vigorously. Janet gasped.

"But as they watched, the screen saver began scrolling across, so the message I shared wasn't precisely the first thing they saw. Rusty's last action item or reminder, I'm guessing, seemed inconsequential. The scrolling ticker tape,

Be who you are. Contribute to circle. Be light for others.

In honesty, that fit so well . . . and really summed up his life. What a fine epitaph for anyone leaving this life. Almost like he wrote his own, unknowingly."

Betty piped up, interrupting Janet who was about to speak, "When we moved the mouse, the screen saver disappeared, but 'Skip 82. Choose Different' never returned. His personal journal did, however." She paused and swallowed hard. She tried to speak, but words would not form.

"He must've been writing in it just before he left to drive out," noted Frank. "I don't think he was as confused or unsettled as what you thought."

Betty, recomposed, continued, "Absolutely. He had made a choice and was committing his life to Christ."

As the story unfolded, the First Circle members leaned in. Warm smiles blossomed across their faces.

"He seemed to feel really good about his decision, and just hours, it appears, before his accident—he wrote a line that will surely stay with me,

I don't know that I'll be the best Christian out there, but I'm gonna die trying!

"No!" echoed around the First Circle.

"I knew it," sagely Bernice nodded.

Each First Circle member reflected further on this odd twist in events as they made their way into the narthex, where the group disbanded, walking out into the cold March evening under a ceiling of sparkling stars.

"Sure are a lot of stars out tonight," commented Frank as they opened the doors to the Walkers' car.

"Some of them seem to have a blue sparkle to them, don't you think?" smiled Betty.

Janet twisted her head quickly and looked at Betty quizzically. "Did you say bl–?"

Betty had already shut the door and didn't hear. By the time Janet slipped into her seat, conversation was well underway between Walt and Frank. Hence, the gray-haired elder of the church dropped her question, but she puzzled over Betty's reference all the way home.

FIFTY

On the Monday after Rusty's funeral service, Skip stood in his office with Penny recapping the past week as they sipped coffee from Java Jane's.

"Before I start on these briefs," Skip shifted gears, "could you get Support Ops to hang some pictures? Now that it's painted, the office could use some personality . . . give it a little warmth."

"Sure can. Do you know where you want things?"

"I believe so. Maybe they could do it this afternoon, while I'm in meetings."

"Your boxes from the old office are over there." Penny pointed below the windows.

Skip walked over and thumbed through the contents. Penny stood ready with a yellow legal pad. He selected prints and lithographs, eying up their potential placement. Near the back of the last box, Skip retrieved an elegant black-framed diploma. "Hey, would you look at this? I'm surprised it's in here. Where was this?"

Penny looked at Skip's business school diploma. "I kept some things tucked away as you didn't have room in your old digs. That whole box was unused. I thought you might be interested."

"We should hang this one, near the law diploma. Show people I actually have both," Skip's blue eyes twinkled. The overhead lights reflected dully off the dusty glass.

"Here, let me wipe it off, so we can actually see it once it's up," suggested Penny. With her dusting, the full details emerged of the Master of Business Administration from Vanderbilt, *with highest distinction* that Charles O'Neill had earned. "You know, Boss, you just don't strike me as a Charles."

"Haven't used that in years," chuckled Skip. "Just didn't seem to fit."

Penny's laugh reciprocated, "Well, I can handle things from here."

"Oh, you usually do," laughed Skip. "I should start getting productive. Hold my calls, would you?"

Penny slipped from the room and quietly closed the door. Skip took one last look at his old b-school diploma and reflected–ever so briefly–on that long-ago time in Nashville. He hadn't thought of those years or all that happened down South in ages. Funny that Rusty came from there.

* * *

The Stillwagons held a moving and emotionally draining service in their jam-packed Nashville church that weekend. Their pastor's message focused on using times of pain—of trial and difficulty—to grow closer to God and to strengthen one's faith. While no sparkling blue halos exploded above their heads or anywhere else in the small brick church, they felt closely connected with their late son.

* * *

Bernice endured one more round of chemo in early April and was declared "in remission, if not wholly cured," according to Dr. Esch. During the last round of poison—as she still called it, she got the distinct impression that a brown-eyed man in glowing white garments once more sat beside her. She almost regretted the end of her treatment, as it might be the last time she was in the presence of angels.

She shared her vision with Beverly on the ride home. Her daughter-in-law drove in silence, marveling at the professor's unusual burst of energy and propensity for conversation after chemo. Her reactions to chemo were no less draining, but Bernice sustained a deeper peace than in the early months.

Late in the second week, Bernice sat sipping tea in the office, offhandedly browsing through a magazine her son had left behind. *'Bill Jr's aging well,'* she thought. *'A little premature gray at the temples lends a growing gravitas to his bearing and complements his sparkling brown eyes. So unlike my husband's placid sapphires,'* she reflected.

She contentedly let her mind wander back to his birth. *'What a hard labor,'* she sighed. *'Seemed like the toughest pain I'd ever endure, and yet . . .* . Her thoughts bounced to the present and then back some thirty odd years. *'Where is his baby book?'* she wondered.

Bernice looked along the bookshelves and spied it. Selecting *The First Years*, she flipped through birth statistics and early developmental milestones. As she did, a little faded blue card fell out. She opened it and reread it for the infinite time.

Can't wait to visit
and see
your baby
With love,
D

Even after all these years, the note previewing a visit that never happened elicited a tear. She looked at the handwritten note—no one had ever detected the different ink that created the smudged 'y' in 'your' which she had hastily added the day the card arrived. "You cared until the end and then some," she smiled through moist eyes.

Based on her experiences—battling cancer, enduring chemotherapy, falling down the deep hole of depression, and achieving a rebirth through growing faith, Bernice began writing a book entitled, *Rusty, but Undiminished–A Life Renewed.* As she wrote–over the spring and summer, periodically, her desktop monitor developed a sparkling blue glow around the edge. While no words materialized, the sapphire luminescence always inspired her musings and never failed to elicit a smile. It came as a great surprise two years later to see this little book climb high on a host of booksellers' lists as a thoughtful, inspirational treatise.

* * *

The remainder of the First Circle returned to life's normal rigors and rhythms. Skip's law firm grew and thrived as did Beverly's practice of family counsel in periods of crisis. Carol served family after family through her affiliation with HomeHealth, while always looking for messages in her tea leaves, burnt popcorn, and bacon residue. Even without, she maintained a clear sense of direction for life and career. Within six months, Walt and Janet became the spiritual leaders for the Stephen Ministry at Bedrock Hills, when Pastor Bob answered a ministerial call for a Nashville church. Roger was elected president of his class in Uptown House and distinguished himself as a role model across his high school years.

Periodically, the First Circle held reunions, typically at Bernice's insistence. She became a deep believer in the support and comfort one receives from a place far beyond, yet closer than one understands. While the messages had ceased, all felt a kinship and an inner peace that gave them purpose. Explicit messages proved no longer necessary to provide direction and inspiration. Life was enriched by the experience they shared and the strength they knew radiated from a powerful, shimmering, glittery light within them.

EPILOGUE

It was a hot summer day and Chip sweat profusely. Having returned from his run along the Harbor, he entered the little courtyard beyond his sliding glass doors. He peeled off his wet tank top and let the sun work on drying the rivulets of moisture running down his chest as he sat, eyes closed, resting. He sipped slowly from his bottle of iced tea. Looking down, his Blackberry's flickering red light signaled an arriving email.

Looking more closely, he noticed that the screen was dark, and yet at the edge, an odd, sparkling bluish border formed. As he watched–intrigued–letters in the same glittery sapphire blue scrolled across from right to left,

DUDE WE'VE GOT A MISSION

ACKNOWLEDGMENTS

Any creative effort represents a culmination of inputs and support. One name may grace the book cover as author, but many provide the space, the motivation, the content, and the experiences to bring the effort to life.

First Circle would not be possible without the unlimited support of my wife, Beth. Her willingness to allow me space and time to write it, to put up with hearing unending dialog about characters and plot twists, and her limitless love allowed the idea of First Circle to grow into a novel. Additionally, the early readers of the manuscript who provided inputs and suggestions – motivated me to keep pushing the initiative. Hence, many Fentons (Beth, Julie, Peter, and Doris), Cheryl Hollinger – a pastor at our church, Jane Bernard, and Kevin Nofziger all contributed.

Other key players: Leanne Beidler, M.D., gave medical input early on. (Though if the way events unfold is unrealistic, that's on me!) Our son, Peter, introduced me to City Limits Publishing and helped shepherd me through the publishing process (though as he said, "Usually nepotism goes the other way, doesn't it?"). And, of course, the City Limits team – who advocated for First Circle and had the confidence to bring it to life.

Finally, I acknowledge you – the readers. You took the time to purchase or borrow a copy and navigate through the challenges Bernice Langdon faced and the First Circle who surrounded her. You took a chance on a new author. For that, I am endlessly grateful.

ABOUT THE AUTHOR

JIM FENTON is an executive coach, leadership development consultant, and talent management executive. He currently leads an entrepreneurial consulting practice.

With more than thirty-five years of experience in premier professional services firms, Jim brings significant perspective to his consulting engagements and writing. Prior to launching his independent practice, Jim was a partner with McKinsey & Company, was Managing Partner and Director of Global Resources for AT&T Solutions, and served as Chief Administrative Officer with CEB (subsequently acquired by Gartner, Inc.).

Jim holds an MBA from The Wharton School, University of Pennsylvania and a BS, Mathematics, from Albright College.

Complementing his business career, Jim is a freelance writer and creative. He and his wife, Beth, have three adult children and split their time between Lancaster, PA and Asbury Park, NJ.

CPSIA information can be obtained
at www.ICGtesting.com
Printed in the USA
BVHW071029200521
607794BV00002B/100

9 781955 631037